Serpent in Paradise

JULIAN WEST is a distinguished war reporter.
She has reported from Iran, Afghanistan, Sri Lanka,
Nepal and India for the *Daily Telegraph* and divides
her time between London and New Delhi, where she
was the *Sunday Telegraph*'s correspondent. *Serpent
in Paradise* is her first novel.

Julian West
Serpent in Paradise

Atlantic Books
London

First published in trade paperback in 2007 in Great Britain
by Atlantic Books,an imprint of Grove Atlantic Ltd.

This B-format paperback edition published in Great Britain
by Atlantic Books in 2007.

9 8 7 6 5 4 3 2 1

A CIP catalogue record for this book is
available from the British Library.

ISBN   978 1 84354 448 7

Designed by Lindsay Nash
Printed in Great Britain by
Clays Ltd, St Ives plc

Atlantic Books
An imprint of Grove Atlantic Ltd
Ormond House
26–27 Boswell Street
London WC1N 3JZ

To M for the gifts of courage, freedom & love
and in memory of my mother, Carmen.

'What is true today, may not be true tomorrow. Everything has its roots in the river of time.'

Prologue

Everything she would ever learn about love and destiny and betrayal began in that moment when the cards of her life were laid out: the hand she was dealt and the one she could choose. For it was in that moment, when she knelt in the road beside her father's car, that the seeds of heartbreak and loss were sown. And a lifetime of running away would begin.

It had happened two years after her last childhood trip to the island. It was a visit in which she discovered roads lined by jungle as thick as a wall, wild flowers heady enough to scent a room, men so brave they could lure cobras from baskets, elephants who asked at the kitchen door for bananas (in their own language), turtles in temple moats who were really monks – according to her grandfather, and a man who could rub holy ash from his fingers and produce for her a stale sweet.

Soon after, she and her mother returned to London, her head full of jungle noises and a much-envied model fishing canoe, and her parents shut themselves up in her father Armand's study. She could hear his raised voice through the wall behind her mother's bed. And when her mother cuddled her in bed later, she could feel the sadness on her breath. Then he was gone. She didn't really notice. She had hardly known him. He was the person who sent messages down the corridor, telling them not to make so much noise.

Things might have been fine if death had not entered their fragile world, shattering her mother. The first to go, confounding everyone's expectations, was her uncle, a crack shot who could swim across the island's largest harbour before breakfast. He was thirty-seven. Eva's mother said he had died from coronary thrombosis, which meant his heart 'had stopped'. Like a watch.

Then, her grandfather died. Her mother said 'his heart was broken'. Cartoon images of two heart-shaped lobes, red-wrapped like chocolates, throbbed in her head. Each time, her mother flew to the island, returning with snapshots of yellow- and rust-robed monks and a big black tombstone with a white marble swastika on it. Her mother explained that the swastika was 'the right way round'. Unlike Hitler's, which was reversed. Eva couldn't understand death's finality: a future without an uncle or a grandfather. But she could feel her mother's grief. It was as if black ink had seeped into the pictures of their life, turning the colours grey. Her mother's sadness crushed Eva, like a serpent coiled around her heart.

One day, while her mother was abroad, her father came and took her away in his silver sports car. With no room in it for luggage or picnic baskets, or anyone else but him. Just like that.

For one school term, she lived with two old sisters and their six cats in a bewildering limbo. One had dyed blonde cherub's curls, a cupid's bow of lipstick and smelt of powder. She was fat and had wanted to be an opera singer. Sometimes she sang out-of-tune snatches of arias to prove the point. The other was thin with long dark hair and a kind face. She was bedridden and so unable to escape her sister's small cruelties, which Eva noticed. Their house stank of boiling fish bones and mysterious entrails called 'lights'.

Every week, Armand came in the inconvenient car for tea and crumpets. She remembered very little about these visits, except asking to see her mother. Her mother's absence bewildered her, leaving an icy void in the place where a warm glow had been. As if the sun in her sky had been eclipsed and never reappeared. One wintry English afternoon she told her father how much she missed her mother. He flew into a rage and stormed out.

She ran after him. Knelt in the road beside his growling car, the frozen tarmac biting her knees. Pleading with him not to leave her. But his face was cold and hard. 'I never want to see you again,' he said, before driving off in a roar.

And though she waited in the road until the sky turned dark and the corner where he disappeared had faded into dusk, he never came back. Not that day. Nor for a long time to come.

Her world collapsed again, with her underneath it. And she had no idea what to do but get up and learn her first adult lesson: that life doesn't end with heartbreak. It goes on. And on.

For years, Eva and her mother were not allowed to see each other. She never knew why. Her mother sent her letters and presents that she never received. Later she found out that her father had given her school instructions not to pass them on. But she soon learned from her father's rages not to mention her mother. It was as if she were dead.

Eva learned to keep quiet, to ask for very little. Never to tell anyone her real feelings. And, above all, never to voice the only thing she really wanted. She locked up her heart. And eventually, like a broken horse or a caged beast, her heart grew used to its prison. Deep down though, two intense passions burned in her, like fire in a coal mine. She never forgave her father. And until the end of her mother's life, she felt she could never make up for the love that had been taken from them both.

'I never want to see you again.'

Those words had slipped into her blood like venom, poisoning her loves, corroding her heart. Until they drove her back to the island. She didn't know yet what she was seeking there, nor where she might find it. But something in her sensed that here, lay the key.

Part One

One

No one was sure when they dropped off or collected the bodies. Only that they would be there at the crossroads in the early mornings, haloed by the steel skeletons of burned tyres, and then gone before anyone had gathered the courage to look again. Sometimes, in the soft night, when the jasmine-heavy air pressed the city to its bosom like a heavily made-up courtesan, a lonely drunk or a huddled pavement family would hear the sounds of a diesel engine, the dull thuds on tarmac, the curses and then the whoosh of petrol-fuelled flames. They would smell kerosene and burning rubber, the sickly-sweet scent of human flesh, mixed with their own sweaty fear. But mostly, too many other terrible things were happening to wonder about the corpses: the poison-pen letters, the death threats typed on manual typewriters; the menacing graffiti; and, more distantly, the other war in the north. And so the bodies came and went, like pavement nightmares, leaving only their spirits howling through the city like lonely winds.

Eva stood up in the *betel*-stained colonnade where she had been crouching and stretched, her limbs tense with damp and concentration, her nostrils clamped shut. The sour reek of body fluids reminded her of rot and death. It was just after dawn but already the sea air was heavy. It groped at Eva with thick damp fingers, smearing her skin with salt and starching her hair. She blew away a damp tendril from her forehead and shrugged loose the linen shirt from her body, bumping the Nikon against her chest. Glancing around, she quickly snapped out the film, hid it down her bra, and clicked in a new roll.

December and January should have been the best months. But that year, something, a slough of low pressure to the north-east or the gloved punch of a distant cyclone, had broken the pledge of crisp nights and balmy days and, instead, driven black clouds over the island like a bad omen, trapping sweat, banishing sunshine and promising, but not bringing rain.

A tan bitch with a white muzzle, who had been worrying at the corpse until Eva shooed her away, looked up at her with liquid eyes, expectant and a little crazy, like all pi bitches who've lived too long on the streets. Ahead, the wide avenues of the old city centre, built to make some forgotten statement about Empire, flowed silent and empty towards the beaver dam of stalls around the train station: the former native quarter in the days when such things were legally categorized, like ingredients and E numbers in food.

She switched lenses to get a wide shot, but it was too early and the picture was fuggy. So she began walking towards the cross-roads. The other dumping ground.

'Hey, listen.' She heard it before they saw it: the hob-nailed prowl of a diesel engine powering through the fog.

Eva and the boys pricked up their ears like dogs. It was coming from the narrow lanes of the old town.

'It's the cops.'

They had been cataloguing corpses in these streets since the terror began, a month ago: Eva, Navahiru, the law student who had first brought her here, and two of his classmates. At first, they went out at night. But that was worse, because the dogs were out in packs and there was too much risk of being exposed by Eva's flash, or the streetlights that lit them like ghouls. So they worked at dawn, when the dogs were mostly sleeping and the squads had gone home. And the boys, especially, who knew that the soul of a body burned at a crossroads would never rest, tried not to be spooked or to let superstition crawl through their skins into the bone. But they still said silent prayers. Secretly, each to himself.

'How do you know?' It was still too dim to see anything at a distance.

'Because that's where the central police station is.' Navahiru always knew these things. 'We should go.'

But Eva wanted pictures. She had never seen the squads in action. Reaching into her bag, she fitted the long lens and slid back into the smelly embrace of the colonnade.

She had come here before with her mother, who had been born on the island, when it was still innocent and her family was whole. Two adults and a seven-year-old squeezed into a Singapore rickshaw pulled by a man with skin burned black, his muscles hard and polished like billiard balls in a sack. She had hated that noonday ride, hot with injustice, and had tried to clamber out to help the man pull. But like all such memories it had healed. Turned into a black-and-white snapshot with serrated edges: 'Traditional Rickshaw Puller with His Rickshaw'. A postcard in one of the dusty shops that once sold pictures of ebony-skinned pearl divers, bare-breasted gypsy girls and up-country chieftains dressed like meringues in tri-cornered hats.

Six months ago, soon after her return, she had returned here, drawn by the old postcard shop and its twin that sold 1940s Shanghai lingerie, folded in tissue like butterflies. But the postcards had been replaced by tourist tat: ebony elephants, red and yellow lacquered boxes, factory-stamped brass trays. And the silk petticoats in the Chinese shop had been husked by moths, although the Chinaman, older but no less bad-tempered, still refused to reduce their price.

The place had charmed her then, with its shabby arches, its memories of lace parasols and ladies with cooled coffee skins. Now it looked like another political tragedy: dead bodies, death squads, corrupt cops; the killed and the killers.

'Watch out,' Navahiru called to her.

A scavenging dog had overturned a nearby dustbin, releasing a potpourri of perspiring fruit, rotten vegetables and fish guts. All cities are built on corpses, she thought. Ancestors of the living, bones of humans and hairy mammoths. Dust to dust. Or, in the tropics, dust to grime. She swallowed a retch.

The bodies didn't disturb her. For all the fanfare and bother, she thought, humans die quietly, taking up no more room, in the end, than a suit of their own clothes. It was the living that moved her: the mothers and sisters of these boys who had 'disappeared'. Thirty thousand, some said fifty, torn from their beds in the dark of night, shot against walls or into pits, or left half-burned in the road.

She wondered what unnatural compulsion, disguised as professional detachment, enabled her to photograph these bodies. Different faces, different ages, some messy, some clean, but all wearing death's uniform. Why she wasn't more repelled?

'We shouldn't be here, Eva.' Navahiru was behind her, tugging at her arm.

There was some graffiti on the *betel*-stained wall. JNP, PLFP, SOP, VMP, SHUP, IMMP, the acronyms of the island's main political parties: a string of nonsense, playground jokes, except, like children with guns, they weren't jokes.

'It's OK. You go on,' she said. 'I need to get pictures.'

But she didn't, really.

She had spent too many years in the time-capsules of airports and hotels, photographing the same disasters. What she wanted was change. So when she and her mother received word that their ancestral home, Tara, was being requisitioned by the government, she had bought a ticket without thinking. Sensing, perhaps, that the island held the missing piece of a puzzle; the answer to something, unnamed, that had been troubling her all her life.

The diesel engine had become a roar. It was a jeep, an old green Willis, not a lorry. And it stopped near the place where she had been shooting. She crept back into the arches, snapping as she went – hoping whoever was in the vehicle would get out – changing and hiding film as she shot. She was ready to risk calling to them if they didn't emerge on their own. But she didn't need to. The policeman in the passenger seat had already seen her and was yelling something. She shot on.

The pictures were OK: the angry face, the bottle-green jeep, the heap of embers – but what she really wanted was the whole person, not just a head.

'Say, you! Miss! MADAM!'

His eyes were black-ringed and bloodshot. He looked like a drunken panda. Or perhaps he'd been up all night.

'MISS! STOP! *Mala huthak!* STOP, WILL YOU? No pictures! Not…'

She continued clicking. Lozenges of vest, stretched grey by a rice belly, burst from the buttons of his khaki jacket, like fat thighs through fishnets. He had a Bakelite nametag pinned over his breast pocket: 'Piyadasa' in yellow letters on black. His hands were like giant paws. He was yelling something.

'*KARI HUTHI!* STOP! I ARREST YOU!' That was in English.

He was clambering from the jeep like an old bear lumbering from its cage. She snapped on. Not thinking. Wanting him in the frame with the body. But still she kept her eyes on the gun at his hip. And his hairy paws.

'For Christ's sake!'

He had lunged for her camera, missed, but caught the thick black logo neck-strap, which he was tugging, pulling her off balance. They tussled but he was too strong for her. Kneecaps cracked on pavement.

'Just wait!' She wanted to give him the film before he broke the camera and her neck. Where were the others?

She hadn't seen Navahiru running towards them through the colonnade.

'Leave her alone!'

The policeman had the camera now and was fumbling with the opening.

'Stop it! She's a journalist! A foreigner!' Anger was making him reckless. Too reckless for a young male student in those days.

But to their amazement, the cop backed off. For a second, he stood still with his mouth open, the Nikon swinging limply. Then he started yelling.

They were both screaming. She didn't understand anything. She didn't need to. What she *saw*, but didn't grasp until much later, was something that shocked her. A spark, a moment of mutual recognition, between these two men who had never met each other. The intimacy between a torturer and his victim.

It was just a moment. And then it was gone, back to the clearing house of old moments. A snapshot that would reveal its secrets only later. A forgotten image on an old roll of film.

All she knew, when at last the cop threw the camera back at her, was that she felt empty. As though she had won the battle but would lose the war. But then she just felt dense and ignorant, as if she had failed to solve a simple puzzle. She watched the jeep roar off in a pall of diesel-fuelled oaths.

'You're so stupid, sometimes, Eva.'

His voice echoed her thoughts, shocking her back to the moment. The pi bitch, taking advantage of the diversion, had crept back up to the corpse, hoping to grab a leg.

'OFF!' Eva clapped her hands. The animal cowered but stood her ground. She bent to pick up a stone and the dog ran off.

She turned back to him. 'And you're not?'

For a moment they stared at each other, the climbing sun burning off the mist. And then she laughed: an odd laugh, like water running over stones.

'See you later.'

'Tonight?'

'OK, tonight.'

When she turned the corner he was still there, smiling. A flash of white teeth in a dark jungle pool.

She drove along the coast road to a beach on the city's southern boundary, wanting to wash away the dirt of that morning. A serpent kite played on the air currents over the shoreline, its long tail dipping and streaming, soaring smaller and smaller. She wondered who pulled the invisible strings. Who was absorbed, triangle of face tilted skywards, in the highs and lows of getting airborne. Who dared to dream in these times. Was it a small boy in navy shorts and a white shirt? Or a grubby village kid? Or a slab-muscled youth with an open face and a younger brother, clear as a sunbeam or a pane of glass?

She had always been bad at kite-flying, remembering too much string and glider-like frames, as hard to get airborne as a Sopwith Camel. For her, kites had represented only another frustration. But today, they seemed like miracles. Life and joy in the face of death.

There was a second one now, playing with the first. A red, white and blue sea anenome, floating on the breast of the wind. And then a third. How rarely people look up. Kites were part of the skyline, as common as crows and seagulls, or the white cattle egrets, that inland coasted on the wind like paper birds. She supposed people flew them to escape; to feel a freedom denied to them on earth. Had he flown them in the years before he began counting bodies? She felt a flicker of envy and then a sudden pain, which she attributed to the events of that morning.

It lingered with her until she ran into the ocean. It was warm as blood and soft as a baby's skin; a living creature enveloping her in liquid light. As she rolled on its breast, washing death from her body, she felt a tremor of joy and laughed out loud. Her mind was empty. She was alone in the ocean under the great blue sky.

Two

Carl put his notebook back into his shirt pocket and looked at his watch. It was seven and the party had barely begun, but already the salons of the ambassador's villa were hot and uncomfortable. The strain of forced conversation and unspoken needs tugged at the evening like seams on a too-tight dress.

In the marble-floored reception hall, men in batik shirts guffawed over tumblers of Black Label, rice bellies bulging, artificial hairlines dribbling in the heat; while their wives sat bored on rigid gilt chairs, silently sipping passion fruit juices; eyes alert as carnival crows for a useful minister or the ambassador from whom to extract a study permit, or a visa. Between them, slid barefoot servants bearing silver trays of drinks and 'shorteats', occasionally bending to murmur '*passiona*?' into the ear of a matron with an empty glass.

Carl spotted the ambassador before the wives did, pinned down in the corner of the drawing room by a posse of businessmen. He looked harried: his eyes darted around the room as he listened. The room stank of sweat, cheap scent and sycophancy. Carl wished he'd stayed home with a beer and a joint.

He dutifully worked the room, making notes, exchanging visiting cards, arguing with an economist about the IMF. He eyed the women. A few Westerners in pallid cotton frocks – embassy wives, a couple of aid workers – perched among the silk-clad locals, like sparrows strayed into a flock of birds of paradise. There was a pale blonde, who sounded Dutch, and a plump woman with light-brown hair. He cast around for a boyfriend or husband but the Dutch woman seemed to be alone. He thought of hitting on her but decided it wasn't worth the effort: she looked like a Birkenstock type. So he ambled into the side room, looking for a way out to the garden for a smoke.

The room he had entered was dimly lit and sparse, with a plain white sofa and a single, high Gothic window, its thick walls and high ceiling muffling the party chatter to a distant hum. It seemed to be empty, but as he peered into the shadows he saw someone. She was standing alone in a far corner, her back turned to him; a woman in scarlet against a stark white wall, a wound on white skin. She was startling but his first thought shocked him. It was of murder in a chapel, blood on the walls of a crypt.

Carl leaned against the doorway watching her. She was quite tall, and her low-backed Spanish dancer's dress followed the line of her waist and hips before swirling to the floor. Her bare shoulders and back were the colour of bronze, and a rope of damp, black hair hung between her shoulder blades. One hand was raised to her throat, pinching the fine hollow of skin at the base of it. The other was on a gently bracketed hip. His mind stepped across the shallow trench separating drugs from sex.

The woman still hadn't noticed him. And, for a moment, he turned his attention to whatever she was looking at so intently. There were two paintings: a pair of oils in elaborate, matching gilt frames. The pictures were small enough almost to be miniatures. In one, a clutch of saffron-robed monks under orange parasols wandered along a paved avenue bordered by palm trees; in the other, a small white Buddhist *stupa* perched on a rocky outcrop in a landscape of wooded hills. The style was that of a watercolourist: impressionistic and delicate, with a misty palette. Although he knew little about art, he appreciated it. To his untrained eye, they seemed charming and probably good.

'They're by Edward Lear,' she said without looking around. Her voice was deep and soft. 'Did you know he'd been here?'

She half turned towards him. She wasn't beautiful. Not in the classical sense. Her features were too uneven. In some lights and to some eyes, he thought, she could even be ugly. But her eyes were as unexpected as a splash of cold water: green, intelligent and luminous, with a hint of sadness that snagged him like a fish-hook. He half mumbled a reply. He had no idea what they were talking about.

'I love these paintings,' she whispered, as if to herself. 'They're like a dream; of something lost.' She raised an eyebrow at the wall and laughed. 'They're also the only things in this house that I'd like to pinch.'

She sank down into a chair and extended her arm. 'I'm Eva. And you?'

'I'm Carl. Carl Brautigan. I've heard a lot about you,' he lied.

'Only half of it's true.' She laughed again. To his relief, she seemed to take it for granted that he would know who she was. She reached for a plate of reef oysters on a table next to her, offering them. Ten rock-rimmed genitalia at the end of a long, bronze arm. 'Are you hungry?'

'No thanks, I'll pass.'

He watched her brainlessly, as she squeezed a lime over an open shell, concentrating as intently as she had done on the paintings. She threw her head back, letting the transparent flesh slide down her throat, like a swan swallowing a fish. Boy, you're in trouble, he thought. He wondered if he could get her into bed.

One by one, she threw back the oysters, her eyes half closed, tipping the tart juices into her mouth until the shells were bare. She gave a satisfied sigh, licking the last shell. 'I hate these parties.' She was like a naughty schoolgirl sharing a secret. 'I only come here for the wine and food.'

'Me too,' he said quickly. 'They're a drag, but they're useful,

16

aren't they?' He was looking for a connection. To his relief, she caught it.

'Why?'

'Well, I'm a journalist...' He let the information hang in the air for a second, but she said nothing. She seemed preoccupied. Or uninterested. He couldn't tell. 'And what do you do?'

She gave him an odd look and reached for a finger bowl. Long brown fingers with short unvarnished fingernails dipped into the water, like a bird taking a bath. 'I try to take pictures of beautiful things—'

'Hey, that's great. Do you ever do press stuff?' He couldn't believe his luck.

'—but horrible things seem to have much louder voices. Why is that?'

'What do you mean?'

'I mean that darkness often seems easier to portray than light. It's easier to grasp, creatively; it has more immediate impact. Look at the work of so many famous photographers: Salgado, Capa – his most famous picture in the Spanish civil war – Mary Ellen Mark. Look at the best press stuff, the strongest newspaper stories. It's a cliché, but bad news is popular.'

'That's certainly true.' He laughed. 'I guess it depends what you're photographing, though.' He was still trying to get a purchase. Christ, he sounded stupid.

'It's a conundrum,' she went on, ignoring him. 'Not just so far as subject matter goes, but in terms of creativity itself. I mean, does one have to be tormented to create great work? Is happiness antithetical to art?' She pulled a packet of untipped Camels from the front of her dress and shook one out at him.

'Well I guess...' he began, reaching for the cigarette.

'I've been puzzling over it for years,' she said, interrupting him. He realized she hadn't really been talking to him. 'And I still haven't found the answer.' She smiled and reached for the glass beside her. 'Perhaps I'll find it here.'

She had been speaking softly, but the silence in the room when she stopped was almost audible. The low hum of all old houses, their song.

'It's a pretty house, isn't it?' she said, abruptly changing the subject. 'My mother used to own it. She designed it herself.' A shadow crossed her face. 'And then she lost it.' She tucked a pair of narrow, bare feet under her and shot him another sad half-smile. 'It seems to be the story of our lives.'

She was strange, exotic and, he guessed, complicated; fascinating and repelling in equal measure. Why did he go for women like this?

'You don't seem very upset,' he said out loud.

She shrugged and lit her cigarette. 'Inheritances are very fragile. Most people have nothing. There are far more precious things in life.'

'Like?' Where he came from, inheritances were pretty damn important, if you could get them.

A beautiful smile lit up her face, turning her momentarily into a happy child. 'Let's talk about that some other time.' She stood up, plucking an open bottle of champagne from a side table. 'This party's so boring. Let me show you something else we've lost.'

He followed her out of the room on to the pillared verandah, skirting the raised voices and brilliant lights of the reception, and into the dark well of the garden beyond. The grass was sodden and the thick foliage around the lawn's borders perspired with the heavy odour of jasmine and queen of the night. He trailed behind her, half doubtful, half expectant, as she slipped through an unseen gap in the hedge. Beyond, hidden away like a mad relative from the ordered garden, was an acre or more of jungle, from which rose a great old battered house, a galleon riding a green sea.

'Tara. My grandfather's house. It belongs to the government now.'

Through a gap in the trees, a cup-shaped moon hung in the sky, bathing the immense house in cold white light. It was more of a palace, with its heavy *porte-cochère* and great stone walls, its almost audible presence seeping out towards them, whispering its secrets.

'The house seems sad.' He realized he was whispering.

She didn't answer but passed him the champagne bottle instead. For a while they sat on the overgrown lawn. He debated whether to roll a joint in front of her, not wanting to disturb her reverie.

'I suppose it's sad to say goodbye to us and we to it,' she said eventually. 'We've been through a lot together. Marriages, births, deaths, family quarrels, tragedies, broken hearts. A lot of love. The usual stuff.'

'It's a big thing to lose.'

'Yes.' For a while Eva was quiet. She had flown inside a small upstairs window, where a child built a mosaic on her bedroom wall with a very tall man whom her mother had once loved.

'Why did you bring me here?' he asked softly after a while.

'I'm not sure. I wanted to get away from that party. I like being here. I guess I wanted to see it one more time.' She looked up at the house. 'It's my only real home, even though I've never lived here. All that I think of as good in the island comes from here.' She shrugged. 'I suppose my mother and I will have to get used to losing it. As we always do.'

'You don't come from here?' He looked at her again, reappraising. 'Do you mind if I roll a joint?'

She laughed. 'Of course not.'

'You still haven't told me where you *do* come from and what brought you here. Apart from the hunt for beautiful images, that is.' He passed her the joint. Thank God she was opening up.

'I came to close up the house.' She paused. 'And to look for paradise.'

'You're joking.'

'I wasn't. At one time.'

She got up quickly, surprising him again, leaving him no time to make a move.

Before he could think of something to retrieve her, she had slipped back through the hedge towards the lights of the embassy party. He tossed away his joint and stumbled after her.

Most of the guests had left. The few that remained were seated on chintz-covered sofas in the ambassador's private drawing room, talking intently. In the driveway, she turned to him, smiling and held out her hand.

'Goodnight. And thank you.'

'Look, where do you live? I mean, can I give you a lift?' He couldn't stop himself, his words were tumbling out like an adolescent on his first date. At least she was smiling, he thought.

'Thanks, but I've got my car here.'

He fumbled around in his pocket and found a visiting card. 'Please. Give me a ring. You know, we could meet for dinner or something.'

'Or something?' She raised an eyebrow.

Was she flirting? 'Well, a drink or something.' There he went again. What a hash he was making of it.

'Perhaps,' she said.

He watched as she walked over to a battered old car, got in and drove off with a wave.

Three

It was quiet but for the whisper of thoughts flying out of the mara trees to nest in her hair, as she drove. Thoughts stirred by the old house, afloat on its green sea. It had been empty since the death of her mother's cousin, who had looked after it after her grandfather died. Its smaller treasures were missing: a sad-faced Modigliani, which people said looked like her mother, Vivien; two Dali statuettes; a Watteau painted on glass. The spoils of heartbreak. Of what was left, she had retrieved some old photographs and Vivien's papers and books: volumes by René Guénon, Marco Pallis and Titus Burckhardt, Gurdjieff and Ouspensky, Arthur Avalon, messengers from the twilight world in which she had shut herself; a few paintings and pieces of sculpture; and a Safavi tree of life carpet. The boxes and books had taken over Eva's bungalow, the old house squeezing itself into her smaller one, a little grumpy at its reduced circumstances, but determined to be there all the same.

The rest of the furniture – a grand piano, a billiard table, beds like frigates – had mostly been carted off by antique dealers. Eva hadn't attended the auction, although she had supervised the packing. It was too sad. All that remained now were ghosts and memories, scurrying between the floorboards, and Vivien's huge ebony bed, carved like lace, which had intimidated her as a child.

It was too big for any normal house and no one had wanted it, except for a man who told Eva he intended to cut it up into miniature elephants. Hundreds of elephants for the price of one.

She had spent that morning going through the photographs. They were so evocative she could almost smell the air in them. Old air, from a long time ago. She riffled through until she found faces she knew: her grandfather with his half-moon glasses and beak nose, broken while boxing for Magdalene, a Monte Cristo clamped between his teeth; Eugenia, her half-French grandmother, regal as an ocean liner, who had died when she was a baby, leaving her enough scratchy hand-embroidered underwear to last until the age of twelve; Mickey, her handsome, sharp-witted uncle, leaning on a polo stick, who had blazed across their skies like a comet, whom age never dimmed; and, finally, Vivien: a photo-record of her life from childhood until she flew away to England, when, so far as the family photograph album was concerned, she stopped living. Perhaps there was some truth in that.

Eva wasn't sure what she was looking for or why. But she knew that it was something other than curiosity or nostalgia, or her interest in early photographic techniques. Somewhere, she believed, she might find the key to the sense of loss that infected her like a virus, dormant, waiting to come to life.

The various faces of her mother, which stared out from the first album, were serious. A barefoot mer-child with long ragged hair, in white cotton, solemnly pushing her baby brother along a studio beach. A convent schoolgirl staring fiercely out at the camera, girl-guide badge pinned to her chest. A teenage rider in jodhpurs and a hard hat, crossly perched on a supermodel racehorse. A young woman, on the cusp of adulthood, standing outside a plantation house. That was the age her father had begun receiving marriage proposals for her: '*Sir, our son is honours matric with first-class job prospect.*' She had turned them all down, refusing even to look at the photographs of young men with liquid eyes and domesticated hair, preferring her books.

Only two of Vivien's pictures resembled the mother she knew. One was of her and Caspar, the man she had been engaged to before she married Armand. They were leaning against their Silver Clouds (had they really meant to drive the same car?) against a background of palm trees, a picnic spread in front of them, with hovering bearers. He tall and languid in white ducks, smoking. She impossibly fragile in a picture hat and a chiffon dress. Two Hollywood stars, whom Eva vaguely recognized, were seated on the picnic cloth. Everyone but Vivien was smiling. She seemed to be frowning against the glare.

The other was a black-and-white studio portrait, taken not long after her wedding. She had lost her childish roundness and grown into an ethereal beauty with a long, slender neck and transparent skin, marked with a single beauty spot on the chin. But her eyes ambushed Eva, making her turn over the image, quickly. They were large and hunted like a fleeing doe's. It was as if the sadness that had crept into them later, like a cuckoo in the nest of their happiness, had been there already, lying in wait.

She had tried to find Vivien's wedding picture, something of her and Armand together. There wasn't one. Only a black-and-white shot of her and Caspar at the engagement party. He large-chested in his white dress uniform; she in a strapless black evening dress, smiling that sad half-smile. Then, a month later, it was over. There was no pictorial record of that.

Her mother hadn't told anyone why she broke off her engagement to the handsome ADC. All Vivien had ever said to Eva was: 'Darling, I couldn't have.' Nor did she say why she had married Armand so suddenly afterwards. 'I married him for his brains' was the only reason she ever gave. A family friend had once told Eva that she did it 'to get away from her domineering mother', who had cooked up the engagement, and to escape the gossip after she abandoned the island's prize catch. Eva had assumed she had married on the rebound. Or that it was a shot-gun wedding.

As for the divorce, she had once heard Vivien tell a friend that it was for mental cruelty, 'the hardest grounds'. As if that proved a point. But Eva herself had been too young to know anything more than the sounds of her parents' rowing and her mother's grief.

Her grandfather had hated her father. For what was never quite clear. Of course he wasn't good enough. '*Parvenu*' was a word that floated through Eva's memory. There were vague stories later, about Armand's extravagance and a string of nannies, who, one after the other, were swiftly sacked. Probably he hated him for taking away his only daughter. Perhaps he had destroyed their wedding pictures after the divorce. Perhaps, after all, he had been right.

Eva was disappointed. She wanted to see them together, as they were when they were young and, she supposed, happy. She had no image of them. No idea of what they looked like as a couple. Separately, yes: her father in his study at the desk with the quill pens; a distant figure who sent messages to the nursery to stop making so much noise; her mother dressing to go out, always alone or accompanied by the glittering friends who seemed to admire her so much, letting Eva choose her jewels from the old iron safe, turning the dials until they matched up and there was a satisfying click.

'Where are you going, Mummy?' She hated her mother leaving.

'To Timbuctoo, darling.'

And Eva, whose knowledge of geography was as limited as her world, but who knew when she was being duped, would get cross. 'You can't be! There's no such place as Timbuctoo!'

And her mother would flutter a kiss on her cheek and vanish on a cloud of scent. But there was nothing, other than Eva herself, she supposed, to suggest that they had ever even known each other, those two very different people from different ends of the globe and different inner worlds.

Eva thought of the mother of her childhood. Something had happened to her in England. Something more complex than a tropical flower failing to take root. Bit by bit, the princess had lost her glamorous friends and her money. Alone, moving from hotels to borrowed rooms, she took to the only place she felt safe: her bed. She supposed her mother's courage had failed her, after the men in her life left. First Mickey, then her father and finally Armand. But the biggest loss of all had been Eva, her only child. She had never really recovered after that. Eva thought of her now, living in the rented flat where she visited her, though less and less often. The place depressed her and she found Vivien's bouts of insanity confusing and frightening. She hated herself for neglecting her mother, for failing her, and often wondered what it was she held against her. And so she had come to pack up the house for Vivien, to atone for her inattention, to do something for the mother she couldn't love enough.

Vivien herself had never returned to the island after the last funeral. She had begged Eva not to go either, not grasping her explanations that Tara, too, had finally gone. It was as if the island held some secret she wanted to keep hidden. Or that she believed it was unlucky, cursed. Eva had attributed her mother's fears to a distrust of the society that had rejected her. But Vivien had offered no explanation. All she said was: 'Darling, I wish you weren't going there' when Eva told her. That was all.

Eva thought of the strong old house that held in it all that was good, her happiest childhood memories. She wondered what would happen to it now the government were taking it over. Who would love it and whom would it love back? She had been too busy with packing and crating, of furrowing through the dust of family history. But now, for the first time in a month, she realized what the loss of the old house meant. And suddenly she felt like an orphan, the small girl abandoned in the road.

Four

The house was in darkness but for a dim light in the sitting room and an upstairs bedroom. He went through to the kitchen, opened the fridge, grabbed a beer and a dish of tuna salad. He carried it all into his office, slumped into a chair, his feet on the desk, and rolled a joint. He looked at the snapshot of Nancy, windswept in a white halter-neck sundress, a flat grey-green sea behind her. She looked like a coffee vanilla sundae. It had been taken when he'd been working on the rigs, making the money to continue studying, while she went shopping with her girlfriends.

Nancy. He thought back to the moment he had first seen her getting out of a beat-up old Chevy that hot night outside a club in LA. How later, after he'd spent the evening buying her tequila slammers, her car wouldn't start and she'd frowned at him from beneath a curtain of short black hair and said: 'Jew gonna jus standere, or elp me?' (She never did learn to pronounce her 'Y's.) Their out-dated courtship, her reeling him in, fending him off, making him wait until they were married, by which time lust had become indistinguishable from love. The bad feeling in his gut on the day of their wedding at her family's house in Santiago, when he had been surrounded by what seemed like five hundred of her relatives, all drinking Sangria and jabbering in a language he had never understood. For the thousandth time he wondered if it had been doomed from the start. His friends had warned him: 'Watch out for those Latina *chiquas*. They got one aim in mind: a *gringo* and a wad of cash.' Or had love simply been ground down inexorably by the millstone of his student penury, her deadbeat jobs, his failure ever to make enough money to satisfy her. Until the end, he had loved looking at her, she was like a ripe peach. He asked himself if he was still in love with her. For the first time in years, he didn't know.

He turned the photograph face down. He didn't want to think about her tonight. He finished the joint and ate in front of his computer. His last story was on the screen: he had sweated over it all day, far too long. He looked at it, unable to see it. He switched the computer off.

He couldn't get rid of her, she was still with him, like a drug slipped into his bloodstream. The shock of that first sight of her: a blood-red gash on a white wall. The lamplight in her hair, making a halo of chestnut highlights. Her gold skin with the green eyes like a splash of cold water. Her odd laugh. Her abrupt way of changing the subject. Her sadness and then that wholly unexpected smile. She was trouble, a challenge, no doubt about that. A strange feeling of inevitability washed over him, like drowning in a warm blue sea.

He switched off the downstairs light and went up to his bedroom. Mary had turned down the single sheet. He threw himself on to the bed and wondered how he was going to find her. She had obviously been alone at the party. Not just alone, he thought. Solitary. The ambassador's secretary must know her, if he could think of an excuse for getting her number. Then he remembered: he didn't even have her last name. He wondered if she'd call. He picked out a video and slotted it in, flipping through until he reached the bit he wanted. There were two women; one of them was oriental. She had pale-gold skin the colour of Eva's. For a moment, he wondered idly what secrets lay under that red dress. Then he gave in to the surge pulsing through his veins.

He walked back into the kitchen with the tray and yelled for Mary. He could hear the television on in her room at the back.

She came out, dressed in the frilly housecoat she wore on her nights off, with a quizzical expression. 'Yes, sir?'

Could she tell he'd been jerking off? She seemed to know a great deal more than she revealed.

'Have we got any chocolate?'

She bustled in the fridge, emerging with a bar of Lindt. Mary. She thought of everything. What would he do without her? He climbed up the stairs to bed.

Navahiru was standing in the doorway of her room. He had waited for her in the dark outside, then slipped in after her when she returned from the embassy party. Navahiru, whose name meant 'early-morning sun'. It was a rare name, even there.

He didn't say anything. He never did when they met like this. He just smiled, when she turned, half surprised to see him, put his arms around her and sniffed her neck, like a dog looking for clues. It tickled. She supposed it was his way of kissing because they never kissed properly. But when she asked, curious and amused, 'What are you doing?' he didn't reply. His velvet skin smelled of musk.

She had been introduced to him as a contact and at first had mistaken him for a soldier. He was open-featured, with strong, smooth muscles like the young officers at the checkpoints. His skin was the texture of melted chocolate, his smile like clear water. Although he was younger than her, he lacked the shyness of most island boys. They had become lovers quickly and easily with no snags or hidden snares.

She thought of him as a dark-skinned angel: as comforting as opium, offering forgetfulness in place of turmoil. He was like the island. The one she loved. That night, they fucked in the shower, their bodies rippling together like seals, and then again in bed.

The first time, he had surprised her with his skill. But what pleased her was how they fitted together seamlessly. Like a fine piece of joinery, or a violin in a perfectly made case. The sun and the moon. Two bodies from the same soil, singing the same tune.

It was easy being with him. He rested on her mind as lightly as a sunbeam. It was all she wanted, during that time, when the paradise she had dreamed of was crumbling and doubts troubled her sleep.

That night they wrapped their smooth-skinned arms around each other and she lay on his shoulder, murmuring nonsense. Then they slept: a dark-brown body and a bronze one. One simple, one intense. He crept out of her room at dawn, before her maid came.

Carl was woken the next morning by Mary with a pot of coffee and a slap on the butt, her usual morning greeting. He opened his eyes blearily, half expecting to see the woman in red. He had been dreaming of her and now, he noticed, his pillow was slightly damp. Had he been crying? Mary left to make breakfast, leaving the door ajar, and soon he could smell bacon, wafting up the stairs. He had never been surprised by her early-morning familiarity, and although he had nothing against sleeping with servants, it had never occurred to him to read anything into it; probably because he never thought of her as a woman. She was just his pin-sharp housekeeper: a thirty-nine-year-old virgin (he was pretty sure about that), who, in island terms was on the shelf. Besides, he had known her so long he barely thought about her. She was just a fact of his life here, like bad driving or leaking roofs in the monsoon. All he really knew was that she was unmarried, she came from a village somewhere in the hinterland, her name wasn't really Mary – that was just an anglicization of a local name, which he couldn't remember – she spoke excellent English, cooked Western food, washed and ironed his button-down shirts, and ran the house, with only a minimal servants' cut (which he overlooked) on the shopping.

Mary had been his wife's maid more than his. She had worked for them when he first came to the island and when he'd returned, after the divorce, he'd sent for her. Nancy had chosen her – probably because Mary spoke better English than she did – they still corresponded and his ex-wife sent her money and souvenirs from the States. In return, the woman had yoked herself to Nancy's memory with the fervour of a votary; a passion he, as an ex-husband, found hard to understand. He had once glimpsed a photograph of Nancy on a small shrine to the Buddha in her bed-room, along with a collection of indecipherable little packages, roots and other paraphernalia, which he imagined were some sort of native jujus. There was a man who telephoned sometimes, who may have been a relative or a suitor. Everyone in the island, what-ever their religion, seemed to be entangled in magic; it was the bass beat throbbing beneath the surface of island life like jungle drums in the night. They were probably love charms.

Carl tried to remember his dream of the woman. It was fading in the daylight, but snatches remained. They were lying together naked in a dimly-lit sea-green room, deep in a fortress at the bottom of the ocean. Her thoughts were veiled; she seemed as mysterious as in real life. But he felt alive with joy. Then some-thing happened and a great sadness enveloped him, as total as his happiness of a moment before. He sensed that he had failed her in some irrevocable way. That a test had been set and he had failed.

He sat up in bed and reached out to pour a cup of coffee, brush-ing away the dream's last traces. As he inhaled his first cigarette of the day, letting his thoughts wander, an old memory came back to him. It was one of his secrets: another time when he had dropped the ball life threw him. And, as often happens, the morals of it were complicated.

He was on the *Santa Maria*, the crab boat he crewed on in the wild arctic seas off Alaska. King crab fishing in the boom decades of the 1970s and 1980s, before they fished the sea-beds bare, was notorious for being America's most dangerous profession: there were a hundred ways to die. Crab boats were small, no more than a hundred to a hundred and fifty feet, and hung low in the water. Seas reached forty-five feet; winds, a hundred knots or more. Storms were common, and the grey-green waters of the Bering Strait and the Gulf of Alaska could chill a man to death in minutes. But it paid big bucks, which is why he and the rest of the crew were doing it: five thousand dollars a week for the deckhands, twenty-five for the skipper, on most trips. As a result, a whole cast of weirdos had rocked up to Alaska: desperadoes, drunks, adventurers, blue-water bikers, flipped-out vets, kids paying off college loans, all drawn by the cash and the frontier's town atmosphere. Alaska in the 1980s was a wild, wild place. And not just because of the weather.

It was around midnight near the end of one of their week-long, 24-hour-a-day trips. The big search lights were on, illuminating a heavy grey sea, and the thousand-amp speakers were blasting out rock. That late in the trip, most of the five guys crewing the boat – himself included – were strung to the gills on coke and lack of sleep (coke and rock being the only ways to stay awake working those hours and deal with the fear). One guy Carlos, a Greek who bugged the hell out of him, had been playing the same song over and over. He forgot what it was, Dire Straits or something. He went up to the wheel house, took the tape out of the deck and, in front of Carlos, stamped it to pieces. The guy went mad, screaming and yelling like a New York taxi driver on crack. 'Whadya do that for? That's my favourite toon. You watch, I'm gonna get you.'

They made it into port and for the next few days he stayed clear of Carlos. But a week later, they went out again and again the Greek was on the boat with him. The first day out, they were laying pots – immense steel cages, the size of a small room, that weighed almost a ton – out along the sea bed. He was on deck coiling rope and Carlos was up in the house, manning the hydraulic winch. Suddenly he looked up and saw a crab pot swinging straight for him. There was no room to duck and he saw in a flash that if he stayed put, a ton of steel would either crush him to death against the boat or send him flying overboard. As the thing swung towards him, he judged his moment and jumped. The pot, with him on it, arced out over the ocean. For what seemed like for ever, he hung there over the freezing water, looking up at Carlos's laughing face. The guy was insane. Then, very slowly, he winched him in. In the Greek's eyes they were even.

That would have been it, if something else had not happened that would alter the way he would think about himself for ever. It was on the same trip and they were on the return run. Full pots of furious, burgundy-shelled crab were mounting up on deck, weighing the boat down to inches above the water. The sea was a slumbering god: grey-green rollers no bigger than six feet, carrying them shoreward before a fifteen-knot wind. Only a day remained before they'd sight the dealers and hookers waiting on dock, and they could get laid and stoned without watching their asses. Then, without warning, as often happened off Anchorage, a freak wave caught them. He was working, clipped on, in the lee of the house when it came, almost capsizing them. Without thinking, he balled up. When the foaming monster withdrew, he saw that Carlos had gone over. No one else on board had seen the accident. It was him and the Greek. And this time, he held the scales. He grabbed a snake of rope by his feet without thinking, and then stood motionless, holding it. Carlos was in a life-jacket but he wouldn't last long in those icy seas. He was yelling, pleading for him to save his life. For what must have seemed like an eternity to the man in the water, he did nothing. He just watched. The man had tried to kill him. It wasn't something you forgave or forgot that easily.

There were two endings to this story: the one he told other people and the one he learned to hide, even from himself. Carlos was saved in the end; and he left Alaska soon after. But a question remained trailing, like dirt on the end of a broom. As he thought about it that morning, he let his mind waver over the story's ending. He was young and angry. It was one of those things he'd rather forget. Long ago, he had persuaded himself that the man's life wasn't really in danger. It was just a moment's hesitation. The case was closed. But the void it left, the gaping hole between his ideal self and his real one, remained. That single failure had yoked him to a lifetime of proving himself; of worthy causes, good deeds and acts of courage. But the incident still festered in him, an unresolved problem he hadn't had time to deal with yet.

He shook himself and leaped out of bed. What was going on? The last fifteen hours had been weird. He switched on the short-wave radio and stepped into the shower, letting the news and cold water clear his head.

The local news was full of the forthcoming elections, more police raids on the rebels and an attack on a ship off the north-east coast. He got dressed quickly, went downstairs to his office and started making calls.

She looked at her alarm clock: it was seven. She had slept straight through Navahiru's dawn departure, but his smell had imprinted itself on her pillow as strongly as if he had been in there. She lay thinking about the night before. Something he had said returned to her. As usual it was cryptic, but innocuous. He had simply said: 'I might be away for a while.' But a trace of urgency in his tone had made her wonder if there was anything more to it. She hadn't asked him where he was going or why. They were just lovers. But something in her felt alarmed, now, for no reason. Not for herself but for him.

She ran through everything she knew about him. The fragments of each other's lives that lovers trade. He had almost finished his first year at law college and was hoping to specialize in human rights. She had run into him once while on an errand, outside the High Court in the old Dutch part of the city. He was with a haggle of black-gowned lawyers rushing between courtrooms, briefs tied in pink tape under their arms, like crows escaping with titbits. Law hadn't been Navahiru's real love. Like many islanders he had an innate ability to conjure beauty from everyday things – leaves, shells or sand – and he had spent three years at the country's leading art school. Eva had seen some of his work: bold, semi-abstract studies of village women in thick oils, raw and urgent. Like most island artists, he lacked external references (years of import restrictions had deprived them of art books), but some were good. She loved his sand paintings most: castaway's dreams between glass. He had given her one. Shy and apprehensive, until she hung it on her bedroom wall. It reminded her of him and the island: mysterious and clear, solid and impermanent, other than it seemed.

A year earlier, though, something had happened that caused Navahiru to switch from art to law. His older brother, a lieutenant in the army, was killed by a landmine or a home-made bomb, no one was sure by which set of rebels, leaving him as the only child. The tragedy had ripped through the family like a second blast. They had been notified, like most relatives, in a terse letter composed on a manual typewriter on Ministry of Defence writing paper:

> 'We regret to annonce that your son Lieutenant de Soysa died in the service of his country on 19th May. Pleese accept our condolances and those of his fellow officers...'

it said, in letters that bounced up and down. They gave the communiqué an air of misplaced jollity, like an invitation to a children's tea party. The slovenly spelling and the cheap paper only made the news worse. Because he was an officer, the letter had been delivered by hand rather than by post. A stiff-lipped official from the Ministry had arrived at their house in a staff car with a flag snapping to attention. A few weeks later, they got the coffin: a plywood box containing his brother's remains. Or so the family presumed. Perhaps there was nothing in it. Perhaps it was just a coffin full of earth. But nobody wanted to think about that. Or open it up.

The death of their eldest son had grieved his father and shattered his mother. For months, the couple sat silently holding hands on twin planter's chairs, like newly-weds or old *arrack* drunks, his mother constantly dabbing her eyes. Each item of clothing, each sock, each memento she found in the weeks of clearing out his things, provoked a fresh shower of uncontrolled sobs.

Navahiru, who, as the younger child, had always been close to his mother, cared for her as if she were the child and he the parent. He took her shopping, ran errands for her and tried to find ways to distract her; taking her to the cinema or to ladies' bridge afternoons. It had brought him closer to his father, too, and had contributed partly to his decision to abandon art and study law. His father was a lawyer and, like most fathers in the island, wanted one son to follow in his footsteps. Navahiru was trying to please him, to be a good son, to stay out of trouble. But some things about his brother's death still haunted him. He had been his hero. Quietly, secretly, a worm had begun eating away at him.

Eva knew no more of this than that she loved him. For caring for his parents, and for her. She wasn't in love, but she loved him: for his big heart and truthful spirit. Love is not a bad interpreter: of the little she knew of him, she was certain that, unlike so many islanders, he concealed no areas of darkness, no demons lurking in his soul. He was as clear as a pane of glass, a burst of early-morning sunlight. A flash of white teeth in a dark jungle pool.

Satisfied to some degree with these thoughts, she slid out of bed and went into the bathroom, eyeing herself critically in the mirror as she brushed her teeth. Mostly, she didn't like what she saw: her chin too small, her nose too straight, her eyebrows too unruly – not seeing the odd beauty of the whole. This morning her eyes had shadows under them. But even she could see that above the dark half-moons, they sparkled with happiness. She laughed. Early-morning sunshine. She stretched, remembering momentarily the man who fancied her the night before. She had registered no more than that about him. He was just one of those people you meet at parties: pleasant, nondescript, American. His card was lying on the floor by her bag, crumpled into a little wad. She picked it up and, without thinking, threw it into the wastepaper basket.

Five

It was midday, the colours and forms baked flat by the glare, when she turned off the coast road, across the bleached green paddy fields, up the red-rutted track, with its tricky turn by a banyan tree, and into the tall iron gates. She entered the sudden cool of the drive, expecting at every turn of the avenue of royal palms to see a house. Instead, the mossy driveway gave on to a gravel circle, flanked on one side by a doorway and on the other by an iron gate set into a bay hedge. Lorne, which never seemed like a house from the entrance, but the setting for a mystery, looked deserted.

She had come unannounced, wanting to see Caspar again after so many years, to photograph him and his garden. They had last met when she was a teenager, but her fondest memories of him were from childhood. Painting a fresco together on her bedroom wall; teaching her how to creep towards a kingfisher in a tree, so that she could photograph it before it flew off; poring over art books to learn how the great masters understood light, composition and form. Like all children, she had loved him for paying her attention and had thought of him as her special friend. She hadn't told Vivien about this visit, although she planned to later. Something had warned her not to, as if somehow, her mother might not approve.

She paused, uncertain, wondering which way led to the house. Or if this even *was* the house. A verdigris'd bronze bell hung by the doorway. She rang it and waited. Silence. Several more clangs. Nothing stirred the midday soup. At last, she heard a soft padding of bare feet on stone, the muffled snapping of a cotton sarong. A smooth-skinned boy appeared at the entrance, one foot on the step behind him as if ready to shy away. He stared at her, his face empty of the usual welcome. For a moment, she wondered if she should have come. She didn't know that Caspar had opened his gardens to the public and the houseboys were tired of tourists.

'My name's Eva, I've come to see Caspar,' she said, answering his unspoken question. She hunted for the key to unlock a welcome. 'Tell him it's Vivien's daughter. Please.'

The boy vanished. The house shut its face. Heat hung heavy over the driveway. From a tree, a red-breasted trogon called, 'Shoo, shoo, shoo.' A langur eyed her curiously and then swung off through the palms. After a long time, the boy reappeared, smiling. He led her up the flight of steps, past a bronze nude and into a hallway which gave on to a half-lit drawing room. Through the french windows, a long, thin form, clad in a greyish white sarong and vest, lay on a planter's chair under a pergola.

She stopped, glad that he could not see her. The massive shoulders and broad chest of the giant she remembered as a child had shrunk to a skin-draped skeleton. Atop it was a massive cranium that, like his hands and feet, seemed out of proportion to his body. It was as if the memory of the man he once was remained only in his extremities.

She approached him smiling, her hand outstretched, though she knew he couldn't see it. 'It's Eva, Vivien's daughter,' she said too loudly, confusing blindness with deafness. 'I don't know if you remember me?'

A smile washed over the shock of his appearance. His eyes found her and seemed to focus.

'Of course I remember you,' he said. His voice was still deep though the bass boom had weakened. 'You're Vivien's chubby, intelligent little girl.' He stretched out his hand, motioning to the chair beside him and laughed. An infectious laugh like her mother's, which rippled the air like a *punkah*, born at a time when life weighed less. 'I'm so glad you've come, Eva.' He spoke without surprise, as if he had been expecting her. 'Now, tell me about yourself and your mother. Are you still as chubby as you were?'

She remembered the last time she had seen him. They had spent a wonderful afternoon in a darkroom developing the pictures she had taken with his Nikkormat, the first grown-up camera she had been allowed to use. She had watched entranced, as images emerged like phantoms. That moment had sealed her desire to be a photographer; she hadn't forgotten.

She told him she looked like her mother, although less beautiful. Vivien, she said, was fine. She didn't know what else to say about her. They talked and she ran his fingers along the braille of her face, wanting to let him see her. But even as she did, she knew it wasn't important. He had accepted her instantly, without judgement, in a way no one else had. It was as if his spirit had grown as his body shrank, lifting him into a world where paralysis and pain, guilt and regret, blindness and impending death no longer mattered. He reminded her of Vivien. They both came from the same vintage, one from which only a few bottles remained.

They drank tea and talked, then Caspar called for the boy. He led her across the sunbaked lawn to a small white house on stilts, overlooking the sea. 'Here,' he said, fumbling for a long-barrelled key in the folds of his sarong. 'We hope you'll be comfortable here.'

Inside the room it was cool, the heat filtered through the palm fronds. Pale-green light flickered across the bleached walls, whitewashed floor and white bed, making it seem as if the room were deep beneath the sea. Apart from the built-in bed, a carved jak wood cupboard, a round wooden table and a cane-bottomed chair, there was no furniture and no colour. On one wall hung a full-length mirror, which would later capture passion, indolence and dreams.

The room smelled musty, as though it hadn't been used for some time. She went to the windows, looking out on to a balcony, and threw them open, loosening a small spider that scuttled up her arm. The distant rhythm of surf broke into the room and with it a sticky breeze. There was a brass key in the cupboard and for a minute she struggled with it, forgetting that locks on the island turned the wrong way around. The doors creaked open, releasing a gust of old jak wood and dust. She hung up the two shirts she had brought, stashed her cameras on a shelf and flopped on to the low-white bed, letting the hypnosis of the ceiling fan lull her into what she knew of Caspar and his life.

Caspar had been born into an age of innocent vanities and simple affections. A barrel chest, manly shoulders, epaulettes and a fountain of white ostrich feathers spouting from a hat. It was the time when men like him had little but the left-over clichés of colonialism: a dawn canter on the dewy turf; polo chukkas on the maidan; snipe shooting over the tank; drinks at the club. But then something – perhaps several things – happened to eject him from that world. It wasn't just the passing of an era and the dwindling power of the local currency that shrank colonial pastimes to snapshots in an album. It was more personal. His mother died. The stern old lady with impeccable manners, who knew the right thing to do, the right thing to wear, the right card to send, on each occasion, left him (in a funeral arranged by herself in every detail). Taking with her the rule book, the moral compass.

His mother had been the real love of his life, but with her gone his spirit was free to roam. He moved out of his bachelor flat to Lorne, the estate she had left him. From it he created a playground for his friends. Vivien had sailed away by then, although she had visited it once in its heyday. 'Phallo-centric' was how she described the prevailing atmosphere of the place. When Eva, who was seven at the time, had asked her what that meant, she was told: 'Some things are not for children's ears.'

For a time, the goings-on at Lorne were the subject of scandal. But because it was an island, because Caspar was who he was and because Lorne was a place that had hosted the internationally rich and famous, the gossip was whispered and the criticism muted, and soon everyone found other things to talk about. So Caspar and his friends continued their hedonistic lifestyle, with picnics, house-parties and midnight romps. He wasn't wholly gay. He loved women, too. He had loved Vivien in his own way. But he loved men more.

Then he crashed one of the cars he loved, careening off the road into a mara tree, to avoid killing a pi dog. They had cut him out of the bucket seat. But the accident triggered the ailments that stole upon him in later years, like enemy soldiers in the night. Paralysis was the first. Creeping up his legs until it had ambushed his entire lower body, freezing him like a centaur, leaving him helpless to perform even basic bodily functions unaided.

Bit by bit the parties stopped. For a while he wheeled himself around the garden in a motorized chair, supervising his creation. Fewer and fewer people came to Lorne, leaving him alone to tend his garden. But then, in a cruel irony for an artist, his eyes began clouding over, leaving him blind. Vivien told Eva that it was 'a simple case' of glaucoma, that he could have been saved with proper treatment. The islanders, who, like all life-term prisoners, envied the free, whispered that he was being punished 'for his life'. By which they meant one that didn't conform to their own.

Dawn woke her, seeping grey between the cracks of the shutters. She fumbled for her alarm clock on the bedside table and her hand fell away into space. Outside, the birds had begun an aria, piercing the muffled gale of the ceiling fan. She felt a tangle of unfamiliar sheets, opened her eyes, saw the diaries and papers on the round table, and remembered where she was.

The house was silent when she walked through it, napping beneath its smells of cobwebs and must. Outside, in the open-air bathroom, ferns covered the walls like a dead man's beard and when she turned on the tap, chilly brown water dribbled from the rusty shower head. She tried the tap, nestling in a fern beside a satyr's head, not expecting anything. Caspar had intended it to spurt hot water into a scallop shell. But, like most of the house and garden, it had been left to decay. It was dry.

She remembered how Caspar had fretted the previous evening, when she had told him about some small depredations – a crack in a fountain, a broken step – wondering how he would pay to get them repaired. She had been shocked. Unprepared for his poverty.

It shouldn't have been like this, he should have been well off. But he had suffered from his own generosity, giving away most of the land to the young men who looked after him. Then, from the hilltop he had created a garden: a maze of pathways and secret bowers and sculptures, punctuating a sudden vista. It was a riddle designed to seem much bigger than it was. He called it 'a garden to make love in'. And it was.

On the way back, she stopped. There was a view, from the crest of the garden to the sea, still as steel in the dawn. She raised the Olympus Trip she always carried with her. But it was just another picture of a flat ocean and a pink sky. So she watched, breathing in the fresh wet green of early morning. The day, freshly showered before the heat.

Six

She had found some diaries among Vivien's papers the day before coming to Lorne and had brought them with her. Old memories, notes in a bottle set adrift for someone to find, all these years later. The soft leather notebooks that Vivien had kept periodically, throughout her life, until depression stopped the entries, were worn and some of the pages were eaten to lace. Eva sifted carefully through the fragments of Vivien's life before she married, searching for clues.

January 1957

River has tick fever and is terribly anaemic. We may have to put her on a drip. Apparently Margosa oil mixed in the wash will protect the coat against ticks and fleas. I am nursing her and fretting. A terribly anxious mother...

Went to a Theosophical Society lecture with Mama and Papa. High hopes, but the speaker droned on about the theory of root races, sounding like a Nazi, and the room was fusty and hot with no fans. Mama complaining loudly about why we had to pretend we were in Madras in the 1800s, embarrassing Papa and me. Finally, relief: rode on the green with Mickey and Bea at sunset, my favourite time. The colours so vivid, the sea like liquid glass.

Pericles stumbled in a hidden hole and went a little
lame, cutting the ride short...

Motored up to the estate in the early morning. Caspar,
Mickey, Harry, Bea and me. A beautiful drive through
jungle part of the way, and then from there to the falls
to bathe in the afternoon. The water cold and clear.
A dip in liquid light...

September 1957
Papa has shown me another hilarious proposal from his
daily pile: 'Sir, I am very desirous that your famous
beauty daughter will make strong and fertile union with
my son (photo enclosed) between our families. I am giving
bungalow, hot and cold running, one phase connect and
fifteen hectares coconut...' Should write back and say I
want 150 cows as well. (To aid fertility.)

Some of these letters must be jokes... I have told Papa
to get out a form letter thanking them but saying I wish
to continue with my studies. Or some such excuse. I don't
really want to get married at all, although Mama says I
have to, like it or lump it. (Mickey overheard and said,
'Like it or hump it,' which made her very cross, though I
don't think she knew what he meant.) But I'm certainly
not marrying any of these people.

1st March 1958
Incredible news. Caspar has proposed and I have accepted.
I am so happy. I realize now that I have loved him and
him only, all these years. And that a childish crush was
the real thing after all. Now I understand why I was so
averse to all Papa's proposals...

14th March 1958
Our engagement party on the lawn. The syces strung lights
in all the trees so that Tara looked like fairyland. The

girls lovely in silk and georgette, the men very smart
and formal in white dinner attire. C looking handsome as
always. Mama made us pose for a picture, showing off my
ring, which I hated. She is so bossy. Such a fuss earlier
about my dress which she said was 'too *décolleté* . Later,
slipped off quietly to my drawing room. C and I shared
many secrets. I wonder if I am in love. C goes away
tomorrow for a month on some ADC's work. I shall miss him
more than before...

They had lived in the same careless, privileged world with the
island as their playground. So to most people it seemed natural
and right that they become engaged: the handsome officer and the
beautiful young woman, who looked so good together. Which is
exactly what their mothers, who had arranged things, said. The
party was held before the crushing heat. Everybody came, because
Eugenia's hospitality was a legend, because the families were who
they were and because there was nothing else to do and nowhere
else to go, other than the club, in a city where everybody knew each
other.

Neither was really in love. Although Vivien told herself that she
was. No one expected them to be. But Caspar had been a friend of
Mickey's since school and Vivien had idolized him as a teenager.
He was thirteen years older than her and she saw him as a man of
the world. A dashing officer in uniform, a Tolstoyian hero transported to a tropical island. Eugenia knew all this and saw it as the
perfect solution to marrying off a daughter who was becoming
unmarriageable with her obstinacy. Vivien had been thrilled
although she tried not to show her mother. And Caspar had quietly acquiesced. The girl was charming, he liked her and he had
accepted the fact that, at thirty-seven, he was expected to stop
being a carefree bachelor and settle down.

In the month he spent away, they wrote to each other twice a
week. And when he thought about her – her mischievous laugh, her

graceful, glancing movements, the mole on her chin – it was with growing affection. They spent every day together after his return. She watched him play polo. They were invited out to cocktail parties, dinners and picnics. She gave him presents of shirts, cuff-links, a pair of hand-tooled riding boots from England. They rode together and went for late afternoon swims. They were a couple.

But then something happened, to wake them from this happy dream.

What a mistake it is to read another's letters. And yet, it is probably as well that I did. For although I know him to be a man of honour, C still might not have been prompted to tell me everything and then, painful as it is, a mistake might have happened; a marriage, in name only, might have gone ahead...

She had found a note. A gift tag, really. Lying on a table in Caspar's flat. They had gone there that evening after polo, a few weeks after his return from outstation. It was her first visit. He had left her in the high-ceilinged drawing room with its smoky leather smells, and gone to shower after the match. In the gloom of dusk, browsing through a book on a lamp table, a card had slipped out: '*Sumantha. In honour of our first anniversary together. Love C.*' On another table was a framed photograph of a boy, handsome, inso-lent. One of Harry's tight-arsed, cocoa-skinned nudes. She had glanced at it, wondering, and then covered the thought with top-soil. Harry's homo-erotic portraits were all the rage.

She had stepped out of the french windows on to the balcony to watch the last act of the sunset. High cirrus clouds tinted livid rose and then purple. A sudden, tart breeze off the sea. When she turned back in, blinded by the light, he was behind her, wearing only a bath towel. She could smell him more than see him. A soldier met in a forest at twilight. Pine needles, dampness and sea-salt musk.

46

His body was cool and wet, soaking her dress. She melted into him, lost from thought.

It was dark in the room when he rolled away from her. The black velvet night covering the tracks they had made. He fumbled for the lamp, lit a cigarette and handed it to her. For a while she lay smoking, silent, her mind empty as a bell.

The fan clacked above them, drying their sweat. She reached for a carafe and poured a glass of water. Thoughts came running back in to greet her like a month of unpaid bills.

'Who's Sumantha, darling?' she had asked.

For some time he was silent. Smoking. She reached out a hand to touch him but withdrew it quickly, scared by his mood. When at last he spoke he told her cleanly, gently, 'I promise I'll try to change after we're married.' He leaned over to caress her, to still her panic, but it was too late.

She was incredulous. Uncomprehending. Dazed by the static of confusion sizzling around her head. The room shifted, reality rearranged itself. But when at last it settled, the punch of realization knocked her flat, winding her of questions.

That night, they went to the cocktail party in silence, a stiff little smile stuck bravely to her face.

But when the next morning, eyes red with tears and no sleep, she told her mother, Eugenia had refused to believe her. And so she had been blamed for breaking off the engagement. In many ways, Eva thought, the island was still like that.

Seven

Eva wanted to ask him so many things, the man she supposed her mother had really loved. Had he loved her? He spoke of her so fondly. Had he ever regretted their lost marriage? She wondered whether he had meant to betray her, or if, like so many things in life, it had happened by chance. But she knew, as she looked at him, that these questions no longer had meaning. It was so long ago. They were both different people. Vivien, the bright beauty, had gone somewhere no one could reach. And Caspar, the virile man in his prime, had shrunk to little more than his breath.

The light beyond the verandah had long since faded. She could barely make out his face, only the pale outline of his form stretched motionless on the chair beside her. Shanta, the smooth-skinned boy, came with an oil lamp and a mosquito coil. Caspar gave some instruction and turned to Eva.

'You will stay for dinner?'

She hesitated. It was obvious the household ran on very little money and she had already been there for twenty-four hours. She made an excuse about driving back to the city before it got too late.

'Please. Stay longer. Spend the weekend. One of the boys can give you another sarong if you haven't brought enough clothes.'

They ate dinner early and then she left, wanting to spare him the indignity of watching while they moved him from the verandah. It was too dark to take pictures but she wanted to explore.

At the foot of the lawn, a formal Mughal horse he had carved from stone pranced stiffly, silhouetted against the dim light from a kerosene lamp in the house. Caspar could see something once and then sculpt a perfect replica from memory: there were examples of his talent all over the grounds. It wasn't true art, it was imitation: in this case, of a horse he had seen somewhere. But the way in which Caspar used his statues – as resting places for the eye, as punctuation marks in his garden – transformed it back into art. It was an ability George, his own brother, had envied, stealing it from him and claiming it for his own.

Perhaps nature too had coveted Caspar's eye, which is why, in a fit of pique, she robbed him of it. She already knew that of his 'pharmacopia' of illnesses, it was his blindness that pained him the most, robbing him of his ability to create and to enjoy the things he had created.

That afternoon they had gone through an old photo album, Eva talking him through each picture. When she came to a small black-and-white snapshot of a sacred bull taken in the 1950s outside a temple in Mysore, he had stopped her.

'Describe it for me,' he implored.

She tried, lacking a sculptor's eye or the skill he needed.

'If only I had my sight,' he said, impatient, his long fingers moulding the air, willing a form from the shadows.

She watched a flame of hope flicker across his face.

'Perhaps I could still make it?'

'Perhaps you could,' she offered traitorously.

His hands fell to his lap. It was too late and they both knew it. For some time they sat quiet, swallowed up by his despair.

After sunset. The colours had bled from the day, leaving dusk to hang like a piece of dirty washing over the garden. A sooty cloud of moths and other insects were blackening the lamps. From the sea room, where she was readying to leave, she could see Caspar stretched out motionless, his white sarong grey in the faded light, a corpse beneath a shroud. Around him were the works of art that he had collected; gifts from the artists; layers of his various loves. There was a poor, cubist-era Picasso imitation, a spectral oil, a few sculptures, a fresco of cavorting villagers, like an exuberant tropical Brueghel, a stone Ganesh, trunk curled over a protruding tummy, a *coco de mer*, carved and polished to resemble a woman's vulva and buttocks. The lamplight threw the objects and the shabby furnishings into shadowy relief, revealing how time and the weather had worn them. The fresco was peeling and its riotous colours were faded and damp. Only the Ganesh and the fecund, tantric coconut had survived undamaged. The house was dying along with its owner.

She was walking across the lawn, to say goodbye, when she saw that several figures had entered the room, slipping into it unseen like garden spirits. Shanta was with them and there was a murmur of talk, like moths against lamps. She knew too little of the local language to understand, but she saw that they were carrying guns.

They were just old Lee Enfield rifles, but guns all the same. She paused, wanting to turn back for her camera, but instead hurried on. Shanta spotted her as she reached the verandah, signalling with his eyes to come no further. But the boys had seen her. '*Kauda?*' Who is it? one of them asked sharply of Caspar. She supposed he was the leader. The clouded eyes turned. He extended an arm.

'Eva my dear, come in.' He indicated the group. 'This is Commander Perera and Commander Pieris and some of their men. They're all very high-ranking. Much more senior than I was.' He smiled.

The youths looked uncomfortable; a whisper rippled over them like a light breeze.

Was he making a joke at their expense?

They were the second generation to mount a revolution with old-fashioned guns. Twenty years earlier, their uncles had staged a failed *coup d'état*, which was swiftly and bloodily put down within days. There was an island-wide curfew, but people who lived near the river had reported a log-jam of corpses and waters red with blood. There were still scars from that brief volcanic eruption in the island's tranquil landscape: former revolutionaires in their forties, doing respectable jobs, who had a thumb missing, or an ear torn off. And the embers still smouldered, dormant but there all the same.

Then, two or three years ago, they sparked to life. A new generation emerged from training camps in the jungles, led by the same Marxist firebrand who had urged them to overthrow the government the first time. He had collected some half-baked theories at a university in Moscow, with a reputation for 'turning people's brains into cubist paintings', as Caspar later joked. And once again he turned to unemployed rural youths, from the poorest parts of the island's south, to foment revolution. This time, though, the red-hot flows of rebellion were devastating far greater swathes of island life. The rebels had a better strategy: attack police stations and raid private homes for weapons; there were more of them spread over a wider area; and time, or perhaps the erosion of older, gentler village values, had made them, and the police and soldiers who hunted them down, more brutal.

Caspar turned to them and said something, introducing her. She felt the tension leak from the room like air from a balloon. 'They've asked me to give them my guns,' he explained. 'I've told them the only thing I have is my grandfather's snipe shooting rifle. It'd probably kill them first, but they seem quite insistent.'

He gave an instruction to Shanta who disappeared. Then he invited the boys to sit. The two commanders perched on the edge of a chair while the rest squatted on the polished cement floor, nervous as schoolboys. Shabby as the room was, they seemed overawed by their surroundings. Caspar began questioning them gently, and as they talked, she watched them. They were probably in their twenties, although one of the commanders looked older.

Village boys from poor families. The two leaders wore trousers, shirts and rubber flip-flops, but the rest were clad in cheap striped sarongs and one boy was barefoot. They didn't look like much of a fighting unit.

Under Caspar's prodding they opened up a little, the commanders doing the talking. They came from a village nearby and had been hiding in the jungle for some months, ever since the police and army began searching villages. They needed more guns, ammunition and food. Now that the army had become involved it seemed it was harder for them to capture weapons from police posts.

She let them talk for a while and then said to Caspar: 'Can you ask them why they're doing this, why they joined and what they want?'

A rapid dialogue ensued. The one who called himself Commander Perera and had a small beard, seemed humourless, an ideologue. She recognized the words 'Marx' and 'Lenin'. The other commander was less didactic: a country boy, easy-going with an attractive, open face. He seemed to be providing the personal details: they all smiled when he spoke. There was a pad of bare feet. Shanta entered, bearing a tin tray with eight cups of milky tea and biscuits. Behind him, Tissa, the chubby-cheeked cook, carried another tray on which lay an ancient blunderbuss.

The boys fastened on this contraption, curious and disappointed. With a little bow, the cook presented it to their leader, who lifted it off the tray and turned it over gingerly, before passing it on. The younger man held it to his shoulder, pointed into the garden and squeezed the trigger. Nothing happened. Just a small puff of dust. They all laughed.

While they slurped tea and munched biscuits, the gun was passed around. They played with it like little boys, flipping the flintlock, admiring the engraved chasings. She was amused. So these were the feared southern rebels. Caspar had warmed them like pebbles in the sunshine.

He ordered a bag of rice and some other dried foods, which the two youngest boys shouldered. One by one, despite his protests, all but the older commander touched his feet. Then they slipped into the dark pool of the garden, as silent as they came.

'What did they say?' She was curious.

He sighed. 'It's sad. Such a depressingly common story.'

The two eldest had come into contact with the movement at university. One was a political science student and had picked up fragments of Marxist–Leninist rhetoric. They came from neighbouring villages and their fathers were poor, high-caste farmers who had sold land and saved to send their eldest sons to university. Like so many newly-educated village boys they found on graduating that their families had neither the political clout nor the cash to pay the necessary bribes for jobs. Neither father wanted them back on the land: what was the point of spending all that money only to make their sons farmers? So, for a time, they had idled aimlessly around the local town, applying for jobs they had no hope of getting. One day, they ran into a friend who had become a local rebel leader. It took little persuasion for them to enlist. The younger boys were from their villages and because they too were unemployed and had little else to do, they tagged along. None had seen his family for over a year.

'Their parents must be witless with worry,' said Caspar, at last.

Eva nodded. She knew, as well as he, how their story would end: six blackened corpses, haloed by the steel inner rings of tyres in an unholy canonization. The grim image swirled in her head.

'Caspar, why do they so often burn them at crossroads?'

For a long time he said nothing, as if considering the question. Then he sighed. 'I'm not the best person for this, but so far as I know, it's a superstition. There is a belief here that the spirit of a person who dies at a crossroads will never rest. I don't believe it but they all do. It terrifies them.'

So it was magic. Fed by belief and fear. A diabolical double blow. The families would not only lose their sons in a hideous death, they would be haunted by the knowledge of their wandering spirits. The hungry ghosts of those boys, not yet dead, floated in from the garden, circling the room.

Caspar's voice broke in. 'I don't want to hurry you, but it's getting late. Perhaps you should be leaving?'

She had forgotten. There were checkpoints into the city at night.

'Yes.' She hesitated. There were so many things she wanted to ask him about. Himself, her mother and father, the paradise they had lived in. How he had felt about Vivien's sudden marriage to Armand. What, above all, was Vivien like as a young woman before she learned that there are other finalities than death? But it was too late and, perhaps, too soon.

'May I come back and see you?'

'My darling girl. You must come and stay for as long as you like.'

She kissed his forehead. He clasped her arm. Shanta accompanied her down the steps. He would take nothing from her, however much she insisted. So she turned back down the drive, her heart as light as air and heavy as lead.

Eight

30th April 1958

How strange life is. Armand came to the house today,
looking for Mickey. What a nice man he is and how good at
listening. Within minutes he had a chair drawn up and I
told him everything. Making me cry again. He was looking
awfully serious, so I made some silly joke about trying
to play Schubert underwater. Then, suddenly, he asked for
my hand. I thought he was joking but I could tell from
his face he wasn't. He looked so serious and anxious. And
then, before I really had time to think what I was doing
or saying, I said yes.

Armand is very understanding and clearly loves women
and he seems to be very enamoured of me. I admire his
brains and he shares my interest in philosophy, even if
he does seem a bit impractical. I'm sure I will grow to
love him, too.

Talked to Mickey who smiled but didn't say anything.
I haven't told him about Caspar but I'm sure he knows.

Armand says we can honeymoon in Egypt en route to
England. So exciting to see the pyramids and explore
those secrets, first-hand at last. I must read Paul
Brunton again.

Secret thought: I'll be thousands of miles away from Mama.

Armand had found her in tears, the morning of her broken engagement to Caspar. She was seated, still in a pale-green chiffon peignoir, at the glossy black Bechstein, upstairs at Tara, trying to play a Schubert impromptu. Her tears wetting the keys. Between sobs and chords he had extracted the story, or part of it. He had been sympathetic, attentive, the perfect knight in armour, offering his hanky to a damsel in distress. He was good at charming women and masking his coldness. Besides, he had wanted her from the moment he saw her, this exquisite creature from another world. And she had been flattered.

Before she knew what was happening, he was down on his knees proposing. She had accepted, as dizzily as changing dance partners at a dance, hardly realizing what she was doing. As if she were a parcel, delivered to the wrong address and re-routed. It was what islanders would have called 'a love match', ordered like an arranged marriage and without love.

Eugenia was pleased and said she thought he was 'a nice young man'. Although Vivien always believed that it was to save herself the embarrassment of cancelling the earlier wedding. All that needed changing was the name of the groom. It was a convenient arrangement for something that should have been taken far more seriously. 'A marriage of inconvenience' was how she referred to it, later. Armand had loved her deeply, judging from the depths of his subsequent hatred. But for the odd, biting comment, he had refused to speak about her after the divorce. But like all far-too-neat arrangements, it was probably doomed from the start.

A few days before the wedding, while discussing which things to ship and which to leave behind, Vivien had mentioned getting quarantine papers for River, her beloved Dalmatian, daughter of Beauty and Bounder, her father's pair. Armand, who had kept his loathing of pets carefully hidden from her family of horse- and dog-lovers, flew into a rage. 'Your bloody dog is staying here,' he had yelled, shocking her into silence. The syce told her, later, that he had suggested the animal 'be put down'.

But when she confided in her cousin, Dorothy had told her that she was too attached to her dog and Armand was 'probably jealous'. She added that, anyway, most men were domineering or tried to be after marriage. 'It's your last chance, Vivvy, you've got a "reputation",' she had said. 'You should count yourself lucky.' She declared herself 'pro' Armand, as did her best friend Bea. Only later did Vivien realize that he had charmed both of them, seducing them into believing he loved women, whereas the truth was that he feared and hated them.

Still the sense of unease didn't leave her. It hung over those days in which guest lists were disputed, flowers ordered, menus debated, marquees struggled over, quarrels endured, tears mopped and reconciliations effected, like the ghost of an unwanted guest.

Why do I feel so apprehensive? As if I'm trying to force a key into the wrong lock. Is it just pre-wedding nerves or fear at flying to a strange country? He is attentive and charming and seems to love me. But I hardly want to eat anything and my body seems to have gone haywire, probably from nerves. How much I would like advice. I feel so confused and uncertain about myself, my own feelings, even my own opinions. I seem to have lost all sense of what's right and what's wrong.

Much later she would wonder why she hadn't followed her intuition and cancelled the wedding. It was as if something had made her former courage fail her, so that suddenly, the daredevil rider and the fearless swimmer, the young woman who had planned lone treks across the Himalayas was enfeebled. She had taken what she sometimes called 'the path of least resistance'. The easy option that so often turns out to be the hardest, in the end.

Her father had seen through Armand. He worried about his lack of money. But he had refused to discuss him, once he saw that Eugenia and Vivien were set on the marriage, and didn't attend the wedding. Consoling himself by going abroad to buy horses instead.

They married at sunset, on the great lawn at Tara. The gardener had constructed a small arbour made of palm fronds, beneath the bodhi tree, where they both stood. The legal ceremony had taken place earlier in the day in the fusty formal drawing room downstairs, which smelled of ancient relatives and which the family rarely used. In spite of all Eugenia's threats and entreaties, Vivien had refused to wear a wedding dress, insisting that it was 'inappropriate' so soon after breaking up with Caspar. Instead she wore an ivory jacquard Balmain coat and dress and a string of pearls. As if to emphasize the pared-down nature of the whole arrangement.

Mickey was best man, because Armand knew no one in the island. Dorothy and Bea were witnesses. Armand had had a ring made at a local jeweller's. A thin band in cheap gold that Eugenia whispered later 'looked like a curtain ring'. Vivien had given it to a beggar after the divorce. The engagement ring, a beautiful pigeon-blood ruby, in a byzantine gold setting, was her own.

Almost a thousand people turned up for the wedding party that evening. '*Le tout*' that Eugenia had wanted. The women, decked in diamonds, rubies, sapphires and silks, the men sweating in tropical evening dress. The wedding presents, a room full of crystal, china, silver and gold – 'People sucking up to Papa, not us,' Vivien had noted tersely in her diary – were on display in the billiard room, a large salon off the nave of the hall. Her grandfather's present, a maroon Rolls, had already been shipped.

Caspar had arrived late, looking sad and a little drunk. He kissed Vivien, who had changed into grey lace for the evening, and congratulated Armand. 'May I borrow your wife for a minute?' he had asked. Then he took her to a quiet part of the garden near her father's orchidarium, where he presented her with a slim velvet case. In it was a two-hundred-year-old diamond and gold filigree necklace: a family heirloom that had belonged to the island's last queen. He clasped it around her neck and then kissed her. When she took it off that night, she saw 'Forever C' engraved on the back. He had slipped out soon afterwards and when Vivien tried to find him later, wanting to share a joke, he had gone.

Armand had spent the evening looking out of place and uncomfortable. Like a dull-feathered London pigeon at a gathering of humming birds and macaws. The local women were either unimpressed or nonplussed by his charm; and he had nothing to talk about to the men, who were more successful than him and whose interests were politics and sport. For a while he shadowed Vivien, or followed Mickey around like a lost dog. Finally he retreated to a sullen corner behind the bar and got drunk.

When they left to spend the wedding night in a grand hotel by the ocean, the servants had to spatula him into the car. Vivien had drunk little, but she spent the night alone in the bathroom, vomiting. By morning she had a temperature of 103°. Armand, who had woken up with his eyeballs punched against the back of his brain, bleared at his wife of less than twenty-four hours and turned over. A car came to fetch her from Tara. Where she lay sick for the next five days.

'That should have been an omen,' she confided to friends, later. The rows started after the honeymoon.

Eva was born in the icy pre-dawn of that December, three weeks before Christmas. She was premature, an eighth-month baby, and weighed only four pounds. The doctors said it was 'because of all the travelling and stress': Vivien had spent the months of her pregnancy squeezing all the furniture they had brought from Tara, the sixty-two-piece dinner service, the ormolu sconces and the crystal glasses, into a rented flat. Armand's last business scheme had failed but he refused to let her look for something larger. It was all he could afford. The baby girl was long-limbed with fine black hair and milky blue eyes, which would later turn green. Vivien thought she was the loveliest thing she had ever seen.

Armand's sense of failure seemed to grow worse, not better, after the birth of his daughter. He moved a bed into his study and almost stopped speaking to Vivien, except for fights over money. He had found himself in the unhappy trap of a penniless dreamer married to a wealthy woman. He accused her of making him feel inadequate and Vivien, preoccupied with a new and fretful baby, found that nothing she said could reassure him. Anger turned to spite and then slow-burning hatred. His baby daughter aroused such a range of emotions in him that he scared himself. Adoration, bewilderment, jealousy and terror. He would creep into her nursery at night or in the afternoons and spend an hour or so gazing at her, frightened to touch the tiny dozing creature, with her perfect lotus-bud features. He wondered what she dreamed of when she wrinkled up her face, and he blew gently on her tummy. But then, he began flirting with the nannies. And soon he was spending whole nights out.

Eva grew up hardly knowing her father. Occasionally, he would call her into his study, which smelled of tobacco and old books. She would ask to play with the quill pens on his desk, he would lift her up to a painting, above the fireplace, to tickle the cherubs' rosy bottoms with a quill and they would both giggle. But for most of the time he was a distant figure, or not there at all; leaving only his name, 'Daddy' – the faint, tobacco-scented idea of a father – to hang in the air.

Then Vivien took her daughter on holiday and when they returned, the study was bare. Armand had taken his clothes and most of Vivien's books. In place of his smells and grumps and fust, there was the stale void left behind by someone who has packed up and gone.

Vivien began smoking again and drinking too much. There was a picture of her in the newspapers going to court for the divorce, a fragile figure in enormous fly's-eye dark glasses and a grey bouclé

Saint Laurent suit. Underneath was a caption: 'Heiress divorces'.

Armand had told the court she was heir to a large fortune, which wasn't true, and pleaded poverty in order to avoid paying maintenance. 'Two pounds a week,' Vivien would jeer, when she had had a few drinks. 'Two pounds a week!' It became an uncomprehended refrain of Eva's childhood, the password to a confusing adult world.

With Armand gone, Vivien poured all her love into her little girl. For Eva, her mother was like the sun in her sky, and for Vivien, her child with intelligent laughing eyes that made her look older than she was, was like a lark's song in a battlefield. Vivien dismissed the nanny to devote herself to looking after her daughter and for a year, they lived in a hermetic world. An egg of mutual love, protected by their fragile shell from the storm clouds gathering outside.

But then Armand began fighting for custody of his daughter. Appealing each time he lost. He didn't really want her, he had already told her. And he had nowhere to bring up a young girl. But something in him, a vein of venomous blood, made him want to take away Vivien's only child, to destroy her. 'I'll drive you insane,' he would yell over the telephone. The second refrain of Eva's childhood. It wasn't a very good recipe for life.

Finally, after two or three years in court, Armand succeeded. The girl moved from the house where she had been boarded, with the two old women. She went to live with her father in his impractical, dusty flat, haunted by the grieving ghost of her mother, whom she was forbidden to mention. Armand didn't know how to bring up a growing girl. She had few clothes and none of the trinkets teenage girls collect, and was too afraid of her father to ask for them. Periods were explained to her by the cleaner. Ashamed of her shabby appearance, she grew up crippled by self-consciousness, scared to walk along the city's pavements. She and Vivien separated by a sea of sadness.

Without her child and with her father and brother gone, too,

Vivien retreated to bed and to her books, getting up only to visit the astrologers and mediums in whom she had sought refuge. These were spongy-faced women, with names like Sybil or Phyllis, who held court at round tables in heavily-curtained rooms. There Vivien continued her desperate quest to find anyone who loved her. It was sad and the sessions always left her feeling bleaker and more alone than ever.

She gathered around her a brittle circle of new friends, who drank too much and talked too loudly, attracted by her money and free-flowing hospitality like insects to a sputtering flame. When her money ran out, they disappeared. The shallow young men, the rake-thin women, the fake Eastern European counts and princes. Even her best friend, a dark-skinned Russian who claimed to be a gypsy princess, stopped calling.

That was the beginning of her decline into the dark folds of chronic depression. On rare occasions – a visit from Eva, some chemical shift in the soil that entombed her – a hand would flutter out from her shroud. A glimmer of the bright, witty young woman with the sun in her soul and the warm blue sea in her eyes. But mostly, she barely lived. As if the chill, northern air had crept into her blood and frozen it.

Nine

It was raining. A heavy, tropical rain, as if the ocean had been
gathered into the sky and then returned, all at once, to earth.
Damn, Eva thought, as she opened the door, letting in a sheet of
water. She had left the hood of the car down, it was an ancient
Morris Minor, and wrestling it up was like cramming an errant
child into its clothes. Now the seats were soaked. She slammed the
door shut and a small pool of water welled under it, trickling
across the red waxed floor of the room in a necklace of moon-
stones. A gecko on the wall croaked.

Minutes later the rain stopped abruptly, like an orchestra obey-
ing a conductor's cue. She got a towel and went out, skirting the
bush by the gate with the fire ants on it. It needs cutting, she
thought, noticing, for the first time, how it had swelled in the monsoon.

It was dark with just a single street light in the lane beside the
empty blackness of the golf course. Beside the verge, her old green
Minor, with the front passenger seat missing, gleamed as if it had
been re-painted. She opened the car door and a torrent poured
out. Placing the towel on the sodden driver's seat, she got in and
turned the engine. It was a small source of pride to her that, ram-
shackle as it looked, her car started every time. She glided on to the
glistening tarmac feeling the cool air, fresh with promise after the

rain, as if it had woken up. It cleared her head a little and her mood lifted.

She hadn't really thought about going anywhere in particular. She had been cramped over a light table all day and wanted to get out of the house. It was seven, too early to see people. She headed for the petrol station on the corner near the park.

As she drove into the brightly-lit forecourt, something, or rather someone, caught her eye. She noticed him simply because he was a white skin among the brown ones. He bounced around next to a station wagon, a ripple on the periphery of her vision. An aid worker, she thought. Or, vaguely taking in his khaki trousers and close-cut beard, an environmentalist. He looked a little like the actor in the old shark film: she couldn't remember his name.

In the background, mahogany-skinned petrol pump attendants in brown shorts grinned inanely, scratching their balls and picking their noses. She wondered how long it would take them to amble over and serve.

As she pulled into the pumps she saw that, without her noticing, the station wagon that had been in the forecourt a moment before had cut in front of her. Blast! she thought. As she waited, mentally drumming a beat on the steering wheel, she noticed a sticker on the back window. It read 'Press'. Her thoughts drifted towards the north.

A week earlier, war had erupted again in the northern tip of the island; a dry, languid place of fan-shaped palmyrahs, difficult love poetry, dark oil-stained temples and different gods. The north was only 250 miles away, but it could have been another country, another century. Nothing had changed there, except the war. It had been one of her favourite places. With the purity of bleached bones and sunswept desert. At night, a million stars shone in the arid air. Now it was in the hands of the rebels, with their Disneyland iconography and pastry-cutter ideology. They were childish, but like any child with power (and many *were* children), they were deadly. She had friends and contacts there, but telephone lines had been cut after the bombing. She had no idea where or how they were. The news was threadbare and came in blips, like morse code.

The man was signalling to her. Did she know him? She glanced behind her. They were the only people there. When she turned back, he was ambling towards her, a smile on his face. It was the man from the embassy party.

'Hi,' he said.

She scrabbled around for his name and failed to find it. Conrad? Chuck? 'Have you just come from somewhere?' she asked pointlessly: the station wagon was covered in dust. He looked excited, like a puppy.

'I've just driven down from Ponaya. I was wondering if I'd run into you.' His excitement drooped. 'I was hoping you'd call.'

Ponaya was the shabby town on the road north. It served as an unofficial border on the changing line that truncated the island around its middle, leaving either half dangling. Two halves that might one day spring together, like the sawn-in-half circus lady springing out of her box. Ponaya wasn't really a town or even a border. Just an untidy crossing point for refugees and returning visitors, laden with plastic bags of possessions and cans of kerosene used to light houses and jump-start engines, which otherwise ran on vegetable oil and water. On most days, Ponaya looked more like a brown river, filled with plastic bags and cans, flotsam and jetsam, flowing this way and that.

'What's happening there?' she asked, ignoring his hint.

'The fighting's started, the government's going at it. A helicopter gunship got us in its sights, aiming straight for us. We almost got killed. It's a mess.'

His words tumbled out and over each other like unruly children, as they had when he had said goodbye at the party. Perhaps he's shaken. Or nervous, although he didn't look young or shy enough. He probably spends too much time alone, she thought. His voice struck her, though. She wondered how she had missed it earlier. It was soft and deep with only the after-note of a twang.

He was by her car now, leaning on the window frame. 'I've gotta go shower and change, but would you like to have dinner later?' he asked, looking down at her.

She followed his eyes and noticed for the first time, what she was wearing. It was an old red and white flowered dress with two buttons missing and no shoes.

He misinterpreted her hesitation. 'Or we could meet for a drink?'

She smiled directly at him. 'Yes, I'd love to. Let's meet at my club.' There were always enough people there for her to slide away. She rummaged in her bag for a pen and scribbled down an address. He seemed relieved.

She watched him drive off with a wave. He was staring at her in his rear-view mirror. She filled her car up and drove back home down the wide avenue, glistening like a wet seal after the rain

The Theatre Club wasn't really a club. It was where the island's collective amnesia concentrated, like spores under a microscope; a party on the deck of the *Titanic*, the place where everyone went to forget about it all. Like all such places in wartime it was surreal, with the feverish glitter of those who had escaped death, the desperate need to party. So the talk was more shrill, the consumption heavier, the romances stranger and the love deeper for being shorter. It was the place to fall in love in an evening and fall out again the following week. But because it was the place where people who weren't involved in the war came, the desperation was layered with cynicism. It was a place that could corrode the soul without really meaning to. In a jovial, well-meaning, boozy kind of way.

That night, Eva could tell, from the raucous brays and brassy squeals clattering down the stairs, that the club's upstairs verandah was bursting. As she stepped on to the long, whitewashed-concrete terrace, the full blast of the din hit her. Four wooden ceiling fans stirred lazily overhead, swirling the smells of stale beer, cigarette smoke and the occasional whiff of grass around the heavy columns of the open room and out into the cool, jasmine-scented night air.

She peered through the heads and smoke. Most of the regulars were there. Locals. In a corner, Aru, a small rotund figure in a white shirt and sarong, was holding forth in a Donald Duck voice, about the war in the north. 'What we need is more SAX,' he screamed, meaning sex. His companion looked weary. He had heard this line of argument before – a reference to the virginal lifestyles of the rebel fighters – even though it might be valid. He pulled on a joint.

'Hey, Ravi, how's your cousin Kara? I hear she's found God,' halloed an unidentifiable woman's voice.

'Correction: she's married God. Started her own church,' a masculine voice drawled back. 'She always was a social climber.'

'You know Ajith's had a death threat?' asked another voice.

'What for?' asked a woman.

'Keeping his factory open during a *hartal*,' explained the first voice.

'How fashionable,' Ravi interrupted. 'I wish someone'd send *me* a death threat. I feel quite left out.'

In her usual corner by the teak-topped bar, Niru, the resident lesbian and manic-depressive, sat nursing a scotch, her arm around a slim, unusually pretty girl. Niru was wearing three sweaters, in spite of the heat, making her look even plumper than usual, and a cap with a pheasant feather pulled down over her granny spectacles. Her thin brown legs protruded from a tucked-up mini sarong like knitting needles from a ball of wool.

'You shouldn't be drinking, Niru,' said Eva, who had come up to say hello.

It was clear, from the peculiar assortment of clothes Niru was wearing, that she had descended into one of her manic spells of creative activity, where she forgot to take her Lithium. It was always the same: Niru would write a play in a fortnight, get a new girlfriend and then be carried off to the mental hospital. Then she'd return to her usual, old-colonial cycle: a visit to the club, then home for dinner. Just like the old men.

'You know I'm madly in love with you,' said Niru, ignoring Eva's remark.

Some of the men shot a glance towards the bar. Niru's prowess with women was a mystery to everyone but her girlfriends and Eva, who had once extracted the secret of Niru's success. An excruciatingly long process of flattery and cajoling, which depended on the sexual inexperience of the island's women and the clumsiness of its men. As Niru explained: 'I give them the first orgasm they've ever had.'

'How come Niru always gets the best girls?' one asked.

The same man turned to Eva. She recognized him vaguely. He was good-looking, a playboy from a strict Muslim family, who was busy spending his father's money on imported sports cars and designer drugs. 'So, who are you waiting for this evening?' he asked, flirting.

'Oh just some guy I met earlier. Another journalist...' Eva was distracted. In a corner, chatting to the friend who had first introduced them, was Navahiru. She was surprised. She thought he had left town for a while and, besides, he never came here. She guessed that Mohan, her rubbery-featured gay friend, had invited him up: they were chatting intently with four or five grave-faced men of Navahiru's age who looked like university students. Navahiru spotted her at the same moment and smiled, broadly, a clear white smile that shone across the room. Mohan followed his eyes and saw her. He gave Eva a slightly discouraging smile.

For a moment she thought of rescuing Navahiru, he would be a perfect get-out, if she needed one, although she was pleased to see him. She was on the point of deciding that he could look after himself, when she saw that he had disengaged himself and was now excusing his way through the crush of bodies. When he finally reached her he put an arm around her and, for the first time since she'd known him, gave her a long, passionate French kiss. She was amused.

'Are you trying to impress Mohan?' she laughed.

He squeezed her even tighter. 'Let's go to bed, darling.'

'Navahiru, you're drunk.'

She turned her head and, at that moment, saw Carl, looking flustered and out of place in his neat journalist's khakis, trying to fight his way through the room.

'Let's talk later,' she said. 'I have to meet someone.'

She saw his eyes light on the reddish-white face moving towards her and, for a split second, flash anger.

'Please, Navahiru. It's just someone I have to talk to. I don't really know him. I'll see you later, I promise.'

He released his hold on her, but the two men had seen each other. There was a look in both their eyes now like prize bulls facing each other off in a ring.

'Hi,' said Carl. He introduced himself to Navahiru (so *that's* his name, thought Eva), who muttered his name and a sullen 'hi' back. Eva searched the room for an empty place to sit. There was a momentary pause in the hubbub. Overhead, the ceiling fans clacked loudly and, from the blackness beyond the verandah, a chorus of crickets burst into the silence, like gatecrashers clamouring to be let in.

'Hey, this is a great place. How come I never knew about it?' Carl's American twang, now too bouncy, too New World, echoed too loudly. 'How do you get to be a member?' Several heads turned towards them. He was the only white man in the room.

'Let's go somewhere else,' she whispered. 'It's too crowded here to talk.'

As they squeezed towards the staircase, the din rose up again behind them like a flock of angry starlings disturbed from their perch.

Ten

Toots was napping on his black plastic chair, in the circular drive, when the bass burp of a car horn shot him awake. He leaped up and fumbled at the heavy catch. The black iron gates swung open.

Toots wasn't his real name. It was what Carl, who found Tirunanachelvam as unpronounceable as Mary's name, had thought up one night when he was tooting outside the gate. In the days when island life seemed fun. The joke – half pun, half jazz trumpeter's moniker – had stuck. Toots had been bemused and a bit offended at first. But he was an easy-going man. So, he had shrugged off the slight, accepting his transformation into a Jamaican Soca player-cum-child's car horn, affectionately. He even thought it might bring him luck. His dream was a doorman's job at one of the large hotels: the perks and back-handers. He imagined himself in a gold braided cap and a white uniform with epaulettes. Toots had the right ring.

Tonight he noted that his master was with a woman, even if she was following behind him in a battered old car. (The *mahataya* had been very generous, sending Toots's handicapped son to school to learn English, and he had often felt a proprietorial concern for Carl's solitary status. Although he was a grass-widower himself – his wife and three smaller children were back in the village – he still felt that it was one thing to have a wife a day's bus journey away, and another not to have a wife or a woman of any kind at all.) He gave a small bow of the head as the two cars drove in. Poor fellow, he thought. I hope she makes him happy. When he trotted over to open her car door, which almost fell off in his hands in the process, he made sure to smile.

'Toot-sweet, Toots,' Carl laughed.

Yes, he was in a good mood, thought Toots, missing the pun.

From her bedroom window, Mary had also seen the two cars arrive. She examined Eva critically from behind the curtains, noting with disapproval that she was not, apparently, a *suda nona*, but an islander, like her. She took in Eva's untidy black hair, ripped jeans, creased man's linen shirt and heavy silver jewellery, compared them with her own smoothly-oiled bun, crisp starched dress and delicate sparkly earrings, and tossed them into a mental dustbin. If she had been in company, she might have sniffed. As it was, she thought, Hippy. And then, semi-consciously, since she was too prudish to use the word: Whore.

If Eva had noticed Toots's smile, she would not have known how to interpret it. Nor the sudden pang of jealousy that Mary had diagnosed incorrectly as indigestion. She was irritated. Using various invented excuses, he had lured her back to his house – he was expecting an overseas telephone call, he had a story to send – he had brushed aside her suggestion that they go to one of the hotel bars or coffee shops. So she had followed him back through the city's wide avenues, slicked black with recent rain.

'Come in, chill out, make yourself at home. What'll you have? There's gin, vodka, scotch, beer.' He squatted on the floor with his back to her, rummaging in a cupboard.

'I'd like a soda.'

'Ri-ight. Hang on.' He darted out of the room. She could hear clattering and then a yell. 'Goddammit!'

She got up, following the shout into the kitchen. The cupboard doors were open and he was throwing things out. 'What's the matter?' she asked.

71

'That goddamn woman!' He turned to her, his face red and angry. The vein on his left temple throbbed. 'We're out of soda.'

'Don't worry. I'll have anything. A beer. A glass of iced water.' His face stopped the laugh in her throat. 'Look, it's OK. Really.'

He fussed about, fetching drinks and glasses, dimming lights, putting on some old jazz, apologizing too much. She had glimpsed the emotional chaos of his back bedroom and he was embarrassed.

She looked around. Pink terrazzo, Scandinavian furniture that had come in a kit, plastic gilt wall sconces, a tutu-pink glass chandelier in the hallway, no pictures. The house revealed nothing. She assumed it had been rented furnished. It had the kitsch taste of the island's new rich who were hiding black money, from kickbacks and arms deals, in property to let to foreigners. Bland yet sickly. Like Hallmark cards. Or cheap scent.

Apart from two ugly, African-style wood figurines that could have been his landlord's, there were no signs of life, no clutter, no details, no hints of who lived here. Even for a man's house, it was as anonymous as a hotel room. Something more basic was missing, too, though. Something she had expected to find. She worried at it for a moment, like a pip lodged between two teeth, and then it was out: there were no books. Not even an atlas. Or a dictionary.

'How long have you lived here?' she asked.

'Yeah, I know. I guess it's kinda spartan.'

'You don't have a girlfriend?' She already knew the answer.

He shrugged. 'Nope. Or not yet. But I'm always hopeful.' He looked at her and his eyes were suddenly large and brown and liquid. She wished she hadn't asked.

They sat uncomfortably in silence. Two strangers trapped in the lift of the moment. She tried to make conversation but it was heavy-going. He seemed uncurious. As if having brought her here, he had lost interest. He seemed to lack something essential. Like a man in a film. A cowboy in blue denim against a cinematic blue sky.

Suddenly, as if triggered by a memory or a train of thought, he began talking about his ex-wife. The vein on his temple wriggled like a worm. He had a list of grievances. An inventory of the private possessions that to other people always seems like junk. Her thoughts wandered. To Armand, his rages and grudges. To other men. She wondered why so many believed a woman could be seduced by grievances. And why this man was so angry. He had divorced his wife five years ago. Perhaps anger was a substitute for depth. Or perhaps he was just a journalist of the old school who drank too much.

She wondered how this man would react to danger. Would he be a good companion or a coward? And then she wondered why she was thinking like that.

'...and another thing.' His voice had risen, shocking her out of her daydream. 'She tried to put a curse on me.'

'How do you know?' Eva was alert now.

'I just do,' he said grumpily. 'She was sleeping with the servants. They were in it together.'

'An *American* woman? Sleeping with *servants* and trying to put *a curse* on you? I don't believe it.' She tried not to laugh.

'Well, believe me or not. It's true.' He was grumpy as a schoolboy caught lying. 'Anyway, she's not American. She's Latin American and her mother's Brazilian. That's what they're into down there.'

'So what did you do?'

'What did I do?' Anger flamed in his eyes for a moment and died, like an empty cigarette lighter. 'We divorced. That's what.' He slumped back and shrugged. He seemed suddenly very tired.

'Look, Eva I'm sorry. I shouldn't have said all that. It's just... You're the first woman I've seen here I can relate to. That night at the party—'

'I think I should go now.' She got up and held out her hand, forestalling the kiss. 'It's late and I've a lot to do tomorrow.'

He looked like a kicked mongrel.

'I'll call you,' she said, relenting. 'Maybe we can go on a story together. As friends. I could shoot pictures for you?'

He tried to smile. 'I don't know if I could handle that. Let's see.'

A maid servant hovered in the shadows beyond the dim hallway, as she walked through. Eva murmured a greeting but the woman stared back, sullen. In the second their eyes met, she saw something startling. It wasn't dislike. It was more visceral. If it wasn't so improbable she would have said it was hatred.

What a strange pair, the man and his servant. Perhaps he was fucking her. Islanders were so jealous.

She thought of Navahiru. As she drove home through the empty streets, she wondered if he'd be there. A dark body waiting in the shadows. No past, no future. Clear as a pool and a flash of white teeth.

Eleven

Strangers may have wondered idly why Mary was still unmarried, long past an age where even the island's least marriage-
able girls – those with buck teeth, say, or a squint – had acquired a
drunken husband and a brood of knobbly-knee'd kids. But no one
in her village, grown into a small town, was in any doubt. Back
there, among the mud huts and concrete houses built on Gulf
earnings, everyone knew what had happened to Mary. For a while,
it was the talk of the village pump. The silly girl had fallen in love
with a *sudu*. A foreigner trying to teach the village children
English, who, as anyone could have told her, had fucked her (he
hadn't, but everyone assumed he had, which was the same thing)
and fucked off. So much for her 'poren farssfort' and *poren* this and
poren that, sniffed the village gossips, muddling up their fs and ps,
their fucks and pucks, as usual, delighted with their *schadenfreude*.
Now she was ruined. Unmarriageable. On the shelf. Serve her
right.

For Mary, though, her unmarried status was not a consequence
of anything she'd done – her virginity could always be proven if
necessary, with the morning-after-wedding-night sheet – but a
choice. She had wed herself to hope. Her passion for Burt, her
former employer, with his beautiful white skin, freckles and ginger
hair, had been replaced, but not dimmed, by her crush on Carl. It

remained burning in her breast all those years later, like the eternal flame at the grave of the unnamed soldier. In her case though, the flame was secret, buried by a thick layer of social convention that served only to increase its brightness.

She kept his letters with a Wisconsin postmark (the two he had written after leaving the village), filled with platitudes and phrases – 'Darned if your curry wasn't as good as Mom's apple pie' or 'It's the Superbowl and I'll be rooting for the Broncos' – she barely understood.

A dog-eared photograph of them both outside his house – he smiling broadly under a floppy khaki hat, she standing stiffly to attention – lay hidden in a book of sutras on her altar. Unbeknownst to Burt, she had also kept back a pair of his socks from the laundry, which she now slept on, tucked into her pillow case. One had a hole in its toe.

Mary Piyadasa had been one of a pair of difficult siblings. Her younger brother Sarath had bullied her as soon as he could walk, cutting off her plaits, giving her Chinese burns and punching her, whenever their mother wasn't looking. She, in turn, had reacted to these acts of brotherly thuggery by telling tales to their mother, forging tears with an onion when there were no real ones, and writing poison-pen letters to her brother's teachers.

The other village children had hated her, for refusing to play mud pies or catch minnows in the dirty pond, for her too-neat plaits, which the boys pulled when she wasn't looking, and for her know-all attitude. At school, she was always the first to raise her hand (even when she didn't know the answers) and she sucked up to the teachers.

By the time she was a teenager, most people in the village disliked Mary. So when she landed a job with the only white man to visit the village in living memory, it was viewed as a wholly predictable extension of her self-importance. If she had been popular, her innocent-enough crush on Burt might have been overlooked.

'*Kauda, rajini vaga?*' was how the village summed up its feelings on the matter. Which translated more or less as: 'Who does she think she is, Lady Muck?'

The result was that Mary, who indeed thought rather a lot of herself, became a snob. No matter how presentable the boys her parents arranged for her to marry were, she invariably turned up her nose at them. *She* wasn't marrying a carpenter or a farmer, or a village boy, she told her farmer father. She wanted a 'big man', with a big house and a big government job. Her father, who had squirreled his life's savings on a respectable but small dowry, despaired of ever marrying off his daughter. When she began talking of a '*poren farssfort*' and a life in America, the old man no longer knew what to think.

The story of how Mary had fallen in love with a Peace Corps worker was prosaic enough. She had worked for him as she did for Carl, though on a simpler level (Peace Corps workers were supposed to live like the villagers): washing and ironing his clothes, cleaning his small concrete house and making him basic vegetarian meals. Like many Westerners unused to servants, Burt treated her like an equal. Which was where the trouble began.

Burt's easy familiarity, so natural in his country, so alien in her's, was misconstrued by Mary as encouragement. Every morning, she channelled her passion into his laundry, scrubbing and thumping his shirts and underpants until they were worn as thin as fine muslin. Every night, she reviewed the day's quota of friendly thumps on the back and cheery 'hi's', assigning values and adding up totals until they reached a sum far greater than that intended. With little experience of human relationships beyond her own family, and none whatsoever of sex, Mary convinced herself that they were both equally in love.

On the day Burt left, Mary was certain, as she helped him pack his neatly ironed shirts and underpants, that at any moment he would take her in his arms and sweep her off her feet to America. Instead, he shyly pressed an envelope into her hand – 'It ain't much, but you know how it is with us Peace Corps guys' – hugged her for the first and last time in an embrace she would remember for ever, picked up his rucksack and left. She watched as the three-wheeler, with a freckled arm waving back at her, belched and burped down the rutted track until it was out of sight. Leaving her in a pall of diesel smoke.

For a while, Mary held out hope that he would write asking her to join him wherever he was. But as one and then two letters arrived, with no mention of passports, airplane tickets or any of the other things she had listed as necessary for travel, her hopes began to waver. For two or three years, she carried on writing letters, painstakingly rendered into 'English proper' by the court clerk, who squatted under a tamarind tree outside the courthouse pounding an ancient Olympia typewriter. He never replied and her letters began coming back, stamped 'Return to Sender – Address Unknown' in blue type.

In the years since, Mary had not eased gracefully into spinsterhood, developing an obsession with small children, religion and cats. Instead, beneath the starched cotton dresses, her heart had soured. With the intensity of steamy little islands, the passion so long buried inside her had found vent in envy and an obsession with good and bad luck. Like many islanders, she consulted astrologers, light-readers and magicians. Unlike most, she took to learning the charms and spells herself.

Carl opened the drawer in his bedside cabinet. Inside was an evangelical anthology, put together by his mother's church, containing local newspaper clippings about the deaths of people he couldn't remember: Tom Harman, the Rotary Club chairman, Laverne Cooper, who had helped his mom with the flowers on Sundays, Jack Coon, the head of a small construction firm. Beside it was a collection of old school report cards and family photos, the earliest ones in black and white; a bottle of beets in vinegar; a quasi-biblical homily from his dad called 'Arriving' on the perils of being an achievement junkie ('Swim in Lakes More Often! Eat More Strawberries! Dance in the Moonlight! Remember, Getting There is the Fun!'); a pocket address book of personal numbers; a pile of old *New Yorkers*; and the keys to an ex-girlfriend's apartment in New York.

There wasn't really any reason why he kept the keys. But he liked to think of the apartment as there. Like the magazines, the fine print of whose 'Goings-on About Town' columns he had once memorized to impress suburban friends. It was his link to a city he would have liked to claim as his own.

When non-Americans asked Carl where he was from, he generally fudged. 'All over,' he'd say vaguely, referring to his family's occasional moves around the Midwest. He and a college friend had a joke about the Midwest. 'I hear that to graduate, college girls in Oklahoma gotta give a horse a blow job,' he'd say. 'Yeah. But to graduate with *honours*, they gotta swallow.' It was the kind of joke you had to come from Oklahoma – or some other bumfuck place – to *really* get.

Among the snapshots was one of him and Nancy and his parents taken outside their retirement home in Boca Raton. His mom looked slim and pert in a floral frock, her grey hair tinted light-brown and gently waved. She was a second-generation German immigrant, like his father. He, by contrast, was overweight and balding. His scalp beneath the strands of white hair was pink, with potato-skin blotches. All of them were smiling but Nancy's smirk looked forced. His parents had disappointed her by not being rich and she had never let him forget it. It must have been taken sometime before they'd sent shockwaves through their families by telling them they wanted a divorce.

Carl flipped through the address book. There were one or two acquaintances from the places he'd visited: Canada, Central America, South America. A few college friends from the States. Most of the pages were empty. That just about sums up my life, he thought. He tossed it back in the drawer and slammed it.

He flopped back on the bed in his large bare room, his arms behind his head. He was thirty-six, he'd fucked up his marriage, he was single and lonely. What was he doing here? Building a career, right? How was it going? Slow. Carl thought about the last conversation he'd had with his father: 'When am I going to be a success, Dad?' he'd pleaded. That was when his father had sent him that little text telling him to relax, to enjoy life. Yeah, that's all right for him, he thought. He's near the end of his. It was the old cliché: 'Life's a bitch and then you die.'

He thought about his family. By coincidence both his grandparents had come from small towns in the Rhine valley, hardly fifty kilometres apart, and had kept their staunch burgher traditions and German work ethic. His father had come from generations of sod-turners, men whose thoughts turned as slowly as cows chewing cud. He'd been the smart one, the odd one out of the litter, and, like his son, he'd worked to put himself through school. He had now retired as head teacher at the junior school he taught at, but the pension was small, so his mom had kept on her job as a midwife. Carl's elder sister was a psychiatric nurse. The other was a housewife with two kids. Both of them had his mother's good looks. He, he noticed wryly, feeling his gradually lengthening forehead, was taking after his father. His difficult, demanding father who had a temper scary enough to send him and his mother out on month-long cross-country Greyhound bus rides. 'Your dadbreaks,' she called them. He could still remember the sour smells of American poverty – rolling tobacco, homeless people, winos – in those bus stations. But the trips had thrilled him. Like every kid, he'd read Kerouac. He was drunk on the romance of the road.

The family had grown up near Madison, with nothing but a thousand miles of prairie and the great blue sky between them and civilization. He couldn't wait to leave. His father had alternately cajoled and bullied into him the belief that you can get anything if you work hard enough. So Carl had started learning tennis. He figured it was his only way in to the local country club, where the rich girls hung out. He got so good he won a junior championship. That day he lost all interest. He'd achieved what he wanted. There was a picture of him in the local paper, throwing his racket and balls into the town reservoir.

When he was ten or so, his father got a job in St Louis and moved the family with him. He was a strong believer in civil rights and, as part of practising what he preached, he sent Carl to an inner city school. As the only son, he was the semi-conscious focus of his father's own unfulfilled ambition. But on his first day at school he saw another kid fixing up in the urinals. Two days later, the head teacher was stabbed. He was pretty much the only white kid and, until his friend Luther taught him how to fight dirty, he spent most of his time trying not to get killed. His father wondered why he was getting such bad grades. Eventually, the family moved back West, where he finally got into college. But three things stayed with him from grade school: his walk, the pimp roll (which Eva, who had no idea where it came from and wouldn't have cared, had noticed and thought cool); a slyly crippling inferiority complex; and a matching case of paranoia. There was one other thing that had remained from those years. His father's unswerving belief that hard work and determination could get you anything. That determination had won him two master's degrees and a well-paid job in an environmental aid agency. But what he lacked was staying power. Like his tennis, once gained, the job seemed less appealing and he had left to pursue a new career in journalism. It was the pursuit that counted, the challenge and, for a time, the acquisition. He was a hunter and then a collector. Right now, he had determined to pursue Eva. As much for the challenge as for her beauty or sex-appeal. She was like a rare, elusive butterfly. He would play her in gradually, he thought. Gradually but surely. Until she lay pinioned on his pillow.

He looked at his bedside clock. It was 10 pm. He wondered whether to call his dad and tell him about her. He usually had good advice. Nah. It was too soon. He thought about the other evening.

Boy, had he blown it. Why couldn't he have kept his mouth shut? It was this goddamn island. It was getting to him. He was losing it all the time. With Mary, with Leo, with the guy who drove him, with the girls at the business centre. He needed a holiday. No, that wasn't what he needed. He needed to get laid. He wondered if it was too late to catch the girls at the Grand Plaza. Maybe not.

He dialled the hotel and asked for the Health Club; they were still open. He flipped out of bed, splashed water on his face, ran a hand through his hair, grabbed his wallet and car keys, and bounded down the stairs. He'd taught two of the girls there how to give proper blow jobs. They were useless before. What were their names? Lalitha and Rohini, that was it. They almost certainly weren't their real names: they'd giggled and looked at each other when he first asked them. He called them Babs and Tricks. He hoped they were there.

Twelve

The full moon hung high in a clear cold sky, silver-plating the narrow streets of the old quarter, the rotting rubbish, peeling paintwork, tattered curtains and fetid, daytime smells; bestowing magic on poverty.

Mary, black handbag clutched tight under an arm, had no illusions about where she was. She picked her way past barking dogs, shuttered shops that sold sweets in jars and warm sticky drinks, darkened tea *cadays*, the illicit 'Adults Only' movie shop (*Private Lessons*, *Special Nurse*, *Bed Timing* in plain white covers), with nostrils clamped and eyes averted. *Tchik!* She had stepped in an oily black puddle, which seeped through a hole in her pumps and squelched around her toes. Why did the *penakaraya* live in such a slum?

Next to a barber's shop with a cracked mirror and ripped vinyl chair, disgorging grey rubber intestines, was a battered wooden door hung with snakes of blue paint. On the whitewashed wall was a red pentagram in a square with squiggly characters in each quarter. She knocked. After some time she heard shuffling. The door cracked opened. '*Kauda*?' asked a rasping, *bedi*-smoked voice. She announced herself. A few inches more of feeble light seeped out and was immediately swallowed by the dazzling moonlight. Mary stepped into the single room.

The *penakaraya* nodded peremptorily, ignoring the customary greeting. Mary bent to touch his feet. He motioned to the grubby straw floor mat while he settled back on his cot, folding his stick-like legs neatly under himself like a collapsible chair. The old man looked quite unlike anyone else on the island and even to Mary, who was used to him, he came as a shock. Six long dreadlocks hung from his polished ebony forehead to the floor, a blood-red sash, indicating his devotion to the god Skanda, circled his waist and a collection of evil-looking gris-gris hung from his belt. Most striking of all though, were his hot, black eyes and the discordant atmosphere surrounding him, as if the molecules in the room had been displaced.

For a long time they sat in silence as Mary took in her sur-roundings. On one wall were shelves of bottles containing roots, herbs, pickled reptiles or their skins; a few dried insects, chickens claws and other unidentifiable shrivelled objects; as well as some brown and amber liquids. Above his cot were more shelves crammed with books, *ola* leaf texts, cracked, leather-bound vol-umes and files of yellowing paper. In an alcove, a cluttered altar was strewn with wilted flowers, on which sat various gods, smeared with red and yellow paste. While in the far corner was a jumble of soot-bottomed pots and a kerosene stove, with a line of clothing slung above: sarongs, dingy vests, a greyish shirt. There was another alcove, hung with a curtain. Mary had never seen it opened. She thought there was probably something unnerving behind it. As if anything could be more unnerving than what was already on view.

The old man gave a prolonged, phlegmy cough and hawked into the brass spittoon next to his cot. '*Mokkhada?*' he rasped, display-ing a graveyard of *betel*-bloodied teeth. Mary shifted on the mat, fiddling with her handbag. Now she was here, she wasn't sure her-self why she'd come. She felt uncomfortable in the hot little room with its dead body parts and clutter. The *penakaraya*'s eyes drilled through her for a few seconds. Then, in a flash, he was at the stove where a pot was boiling. Taking a cup from the shelf above and wiping it with the end of his sarong, he poured some brown liquid into it and handed it to Mary. She drank the bitter tea, grimaced and returned the cup. Mary knew enough to realize that this was simply a ritual intended to give the *penakaraya*'s clients something to focus on, to reassure themselves. He had other means of divining what was going on. He stared at the remains in the cup, turning it this way and that, mumbling. Then threw the leaves on the floor. His head shot back, his vulture's neck arched, his dreadlocks swung behind him. And in a high, fibrous chant, quite different to his own voice, he sang out a few phrases: 'There is a woman. And two men. Two of these people are known to you. You are troubled but you should not be. Many things are going on. They will take care of themselves.'

It wasn't very clear. It never was, Mary thought.

'Who is the woman? Is she local or a *sudu*?' she demanded.

The *penakaraya* either didn't notice or ignored her sharp tone. 'Yes, she's a foreigner,' he sang back. 'And so is one of the men. But you need not be concerned about her. I see death. Death resolves everything.'

'Who? Who is going to die?' She was alarmed. *Penakarayas* never mentioned death as a rule, even if they saw it.

'I cannot tell you any more now. It is not the right time. You must return later.' His voice was fading and his head swung forward on to his chest.

Mary waited, hoping for something more. But the session was over. She fumbled in her purse, extracted a hundred-rupee note and, with a small bow, put it on the altar. Then she slid out into the street.

As she picked her way back through the grimy maze of streets, she thought over what she had heard, trying to unravel the riddle. Was the foreign woman Nancy *nona*? Was she ill? Who was death hanging over? Her, or the *mahataya*, or the other man, whoever he was? Or even Mary herself? Why had he not seen the woman who had come the other night? *Tchik!* she said to herself finally. It was too confusing. She shouldn't have wasted a hundred rupees coming to this slum. She would plot her own method.

It was past eleven when she returned home. Toots let her in. 'Out late?' he asked, smirking. She snapped her face shut. What business was it of his? It was her evening off. The house echoed and there was no car in the driveway. The *mahataya* was out. She went into the living room and closed the outside door, ensuring that Toots, whose quarters were outside near the gate, couldn't see her. Then she picked up the telephone and dialled.

Officer-in-Charge Piyadasa glanced at the clock in a tarnished brass case on the green wall opposite his desk. It was eleven-fifteen and he had almost finished the evening's paperwork. He opened his eyes wide, stretching them, exposing a ring of yellow eyeball veined with red. Then he blinked slowly, squeezing his lids tight several times, like a sleepy lizard.

He had spent the last half-hour crossing out names in the police station's second ledger, the one used for 'unofficial' arrests: prisoners who had never 'officially' been detained or, for that matter, entered the police station. The White Books, as some of his men jokingly called it, referring both to the white worn at funerals or 'whitewash', depending which way you looked at it. If the prisoners had never been there, they couldn't have gone missing, he thought with a chuckle. You could call it a kind of double-entry book-keeping. Or perhaps, he thought, correcting himself, 'shadow' accounting. At any rate, all the police stations were practising it these days: orders from some bigwigs higher up, probably. As he was running a red pen through the last name on the list (Somana, son of Galugama, eighteen years; he had clung to the constable's feet, he remembered now; whiney little bastard), his concentration was shattered by two sounds: an earpiercing scream from one of the cells down the corridor and the jangling of the old-fashioned black Bakelite telephone on his desk.

'Shut that bastard up, will you!' he yelled down the corridor, while simultaneously picking up the receiver and putting his hand over the mouthpiece. 'If you don't shut that frigging *vesige putta* up, I'll cut off his balls myself. Then he'll have something to scream about!' he yelled, elaborating. There was a dull crack of something hard landing on flesh and bone. A moan. And then silence.

'*Kauda?*' he barked into the telephone. The line was crackly but he could make out the thin tones of his sister. What was she doing calling him at this time of night? '*Akkhi*, how often have I told you not to call me at the station?' he asked, his earlier good mood thoroughly shattered. 'It's almost midnight. What's the matter?'

He winced, trying to interpret between the static. His sweaty features massed into a dark cloud. She was babbling on about a woman and death. What was she talking about? Sure there was death. It was here in the police station. ('Unofficially', of course.) It was everywhere these days.

'Malwathi, please calm down,' he said, using her given name to show he was serious. He took out a large white handkerchief and mopped his forehead. It was bad enough having the prisoners yelling blue murder when they roughed them up. Not to mention his wife nagging him about getting home late. 'Look, I'm sure it'll be all right in the morning. Yes. Yes, of course. Yes!' (*Annay*, was she annoying.) 'I've already told you a dozen time. Yes! Yes, of course I'll help you if you need me.'

To his relief, the line went dead. There was something to be said for a lousy telephone system, he thought. He snapped the ledger shut, opened the bottom drawer of his desk, threw it in, locked the drawer and pocketed the key. A small *pilum* poster of a bosomy starlet in a white boob tube and tight white pants, straddling a motorbike, smiled up at him suggestively from under the desk glass where the ledger had been. He leered back.

He was just tossing up whether to go down to the cells and give that bastard one himself, when the phone started jangling again.

Akkhi! That decides it, he thought, letting it ring. He unhooked his long steel truncheon and automatic rifle from the pegs on the wall, locked his office door behind him and strode out to his motorbike. Beside the police station the row of tyre shops that had recently opened (in what Sergeant Piyadasa thought a commendable spirit of enterprise) were shuttered. In their forecourts, tall stands of tyres rose up like obelisks, a deeper black against the night.

Thirteen

Sometime before midnight, Carl ambled back through the brightly-lit hotel lobby, swinging his car keys. The doorman, who sometimes found hookers for him, observed the bounce in his step and gave him a knowing leer. Carl handed him a note and waited for his car. At that moment three men and a girl walked past.

'Hi,' said Carl, recognizing one of the men, a local photographer. He knew Eva. Carl had seen her nod to him as they left the club.

The men greeted him. Two of them knew him vaguely. He was that hyperactive American journalist. A bit too eager, full of inane questions.

'Why don't you join us for a drink?' suggested the photographer, sensing the loneliness that seeped from him like tea from a used teabag, and in it a chance to tout for some work, to make a contact.

'Sure,' said Carl. He'd been too obsessed with work to make friends in the city. And he had reasons of his own.

They chatted for half an hour or so in the bar. Carl, trying and failing yet again to bridge the gap, to penetrate the veil of thinly-disguised contempt that curdled all his meetings with the country's English-speaking classes. The small deracinated layer that sat on the island's simple, tropical exuberance like a bowler hat on a calypso shirt. Not for the first time, he wondered why, beneath the smiles and seeming hospitality, they were so xenophobic. If he had been British, perhaps. But with an American? Finally, Carl turned the conversation to the subject that had lodged in his brain like a piece of toffee stuck between two molars.

'What do you know about Eva?' he asked, as casually as possible.

'What do you want to know?' asked the photographer, a little guardedly, Carl thought.

'You know. Who she is, what she's like?'

They exchanged glances, and the couple sniggered.

Carl laughed uncomfortably. 'Well? Come on, guys, it can't be that terrible.'

One of the men – tall, long-haired with a neatly-trimmed beard and a jaded, cutting wit, whom Carl had made a mental note to treat with caution – turned to him. 'Perhaps you should ask her…?' he said wearily.

The others nodded in agreement. The subject was closed. Carl finished his beer and left.

It was high tide as he drove along the esplanade. Surf pounded the rocks beneath him. He turned inland, and the melody changed. Wind rushing through empty tree-lined streets. He thought over what they had said – or rather, not said – about Eva. Was it her, or him? he wondered, misinterpreting their reticence. Or was it a warning not to cross into forbidden territory? They were just like the blacks he had grown up with, he thought. *They* could fuck your girls. But heaven help you if you fucked one of theirs. Motherfuckers. He smiled unpleasantly. Eva had become a more interesting challenge than he'd thought.

It was raining and the house was in darkness when he returned. Steel nails of rain, glinting under the streetlight, hammered into the circular driveway, spinning off gravel, splashing his shoes. He let himself in through the glass doors, switched on the downstairs lights, walked into the kitchen and got himself a beer. It was almost one, but he wasn't tired. He slotted in a jazz tape, rolled himself a joint and let his thoughts slip back over her.

Eva. Nice name. It suited her. Eve, the first woman. He wondered what his friends would think of her. What, come to that, *he* thought of her. A nice body. Great moves. Very sexy. But there was more. A sexual tension, strung beneath the surface like a threat. He thought back to that first night. A hollow of liquid honey at her throat, brown fingers plucking at it like a bee. A wound on white skin. She'd been hurt. That much was obvious. He took another toke on his joint. It'd be a crash-and-burn relationship, if he ever got her into bed. But he knew he was hooked. He just needed to fix that young black guy, the one at the club who seemed to be sniffing round her. Good-looking. Another motherfucker, like the rest of them.

The same nasty half-smile came and went. Vanishing like a stain on a piece of washing.

The telephone rang in his office. He looked at his watch. The desk. He wondered why they were calling: he hadn't filed that day. He lifted the receiver cautiously, listening for the minty-fresh tones of the desk secretary, trying to compose his voice to sound straight.

'Hell*oo*?'

'Hi man, you awake?' It was the fruity lilt of the Captain. Carl relaxed.

'Sure. What's up?' His friend often called at odd hours. Carl guessed it was his work schedule. He'd probably been on the late-evening shift.

'I'm close by...' There was a burst of static on the line. '...of putting in a visit.'

Military telephones, thought Carl. Like the soldiers, they didn't work in the rain. 'Sure. Come on round. But make it quick, eh?' He put down the phone. Shame he hadn't called earlier, he thought. The young Special Forces officer was a good source of girls.

Fifteen minutes later, the Captain strode into the room. He had the straight shoulders and rolling walk of a man used to wearing uniform. A uniform that could barrel straight through the middle of life. But his smile was disarming. Simple, clear, gleaming white. A smile with no secrets.

Carl's relationship with the Captain had begun opportunistically: he was a good source of stories and information. A useful man to have on your side. But Carl was also curious to understand what motivated someone to join a force ready to murder and torture its own citizens. What made him tick. The answer, he discovered, was simple. Like any young man in a place with too many people and too little work, the Captain wanted a job. He followed orders, tried to avoid 'the dirty business' as he called it, spent his days off drinking and *pucking* his pretty, large-bottomed wife, and no time at all asking himself tricky questions about the conduct of the authorities or his life.

'*Annay*, I can't be doing with all that stuff, man,' he finally said one evening, pushed by Carl's questioning. 'Eat, drink and be merry, no?' He paused. 'And of course, a bit of...' He poked his forefinger through a circle described by his other thumb and forefinger and winked. 'That's my philosophy, if you want one.' So, having summed up the matter in one crude cliché, he returned to the topics that interested him most: women, cricket (of which Carl knew little, but he was learning) and booze.

Perhaps Carl had picked the wrong man. But, as time progressed, he realized that he was typical of an island where no one thought very much about anything. It was just too much trouble. Things happened and then they were over. It was as simple as that.

He remembered a village he had stopped at once. The local headman had flashed his teeth, in answer to Carl's enquiry, waggled his head like a marionette and declared firmly: 'No, no problem here at all.' It was then that Carl had spotted the pyramid of skulls, neatly arranged behind the man's shoulder. Thus, he thought, was terror, its fangs and claws dripping blood, despatched to the same murky depths of the psyche as murder, incest, domestic violence, penury and all the other ailments of life in a tropical paradise. That it festered there like a cancer was of course no one's problem.

Carl was never certain whether to attribute this attitude to denial, pragmatism, or an extreme case of tropical lassitude, aided by fatalism and the promise of a better deal next time. Whether it was healthy or unhealthy, in other words. In the long term. But of one thing he was now certain: the Captain was not the man to provide deeper insights. In that sense, he was a very good case study, after all.

Over the months, though, the two men had become drinking buddies and then friends. Between them was a bond of mutual respect, understanding and, in the Captain's case, affection. He looked on his American friend as an older brother, wiser in the ways of the world. This suited Carl: as the youngest with an older sister who had teased him, he had acquired the habit of adopting younger brothers. He gave the Captain advice and tips on bedtechnique. In return, the young officer called him his 'sex guru' and offered him village girls or prostitutes. It was an easy-going, buddy kind of friendship. By the third whisky the conversation had turned to the topic that had cemented their friendship.

'So man, you're having a new girlfriend, then?' The Captain leaned forward. 'Like?' His hands described the ample, pot-shaped curves of his ideal woman.

Carl interrupted him. 'Well, I've only just met her. And she's not my girlfriend. Not yet.'

'So? What's the problem, man? Married?'

Carl smiled and shook his head. He hesitated, wondering how to describe Eva. How to explain something less simple than a mistress or a one-night stand. He decided it wasn't worth trying. It was too complex. And perhaps too important, for a man like the Captain.

'W-ell. I think she might have a boyfriend,' he said, for want of a better explanation.

The Captain roared with laughter and slapped his thigh. When he'd recovered, he leaned forward, a twinkle in his eye. 'That's a problem? For *you*? My sex guru?' He slapped his thigh and laughed again. '*Porener?*'

'No, local. Good-looking. Like a soldier. Or one of your guys, I guess.' He smiled. 'He looks a bit like you.'

'*Imposseebul!*' The Captain smiled, raising his glass to himself. 'What's his name? Can check him out, no?'

Carl hesitated. Something was sounding a warning in the fog of his memory. But he was too befuddled to hear it. 'Nav-nu, Na-nu?' It was an unusual name, he remembered that. 'Something like that, de Soysa. Sound right to you?'

'Navahiru, you mean,' said the Captain, correcting him. 'Easy. Not so many of them.' He grinned. 'No problem. I'll put in a word. Ask him to steer clear, like.' He paused, spotting Carl's look of alarm. 'No heavy stuff, man. Not if he's one of our boys. Just a word. For a friend. Right?'

'But how will you find him?' Opportunism and anxiety mixed like equal parts of whisky and water in Carl's voice.

The Captain tapped his finger to his nose and grinned. 'No problem, OK? Now, how's about one for the road?'

If it had been earlier, or he had not been so stoned, Carl might have recognized that fate had just blinked. But as it was, it was late and his brain was reeling. Minutes after the Captain finally left, he was asleep. By the following morning, the conversation, and even the circumstances of the Captain's visit, had faded. Like a dream. A moment time forgot. A flicker of fate's eyelid.

Fourteen

There was very little left now. Just faint changes in the temperature and the air, still or moving, on his skin; the calloused, gentle touch of the boys as they lifted him from his bedroom to the verandah and back; the smells of day – heat, grass, water, a faint whiff of araliya blossoms; and then night-flowering jasmine and mosquito coils, the cooler scents of night.

Time shrank and stretched without reason, keeping beat only with the pain that travelled his body, varying in its intensity, but always there.

The twittering of birds told him dawn had broken; the chatter of the boys and the smells of cooking marked the formalities of breakfast, lunch and dinner, although he ate like a yogi. The infernal buzzing of mosquitoes signalled the dusk. Once a day, there was the painful visit to the bathroom where the boys prised the stools out of his drug- and paralysis-constipated body.

He thought back to the time when he had first taken over a bare hillside. The rubber trees, each with its tribal cicatrice, beneath which hung half a coconut shell of white blood. It had begun as an escape from a world that might judge him too harshly. But then, like all endeavours that take time and attention, it had become a passion and, finally, a labour of love.

Love: that was all that remained and all that had ever really mattered. He thought suddenly of his brother and his petty thefts and meannesses. He had once told someone: 'You know the difference between George and me is that he has always fallen in love with things but I've only ever been able to fall in love with people.'

Was that true or had he been fooling himself, as he had fooled himself about so many things?

He heard a movement.

The electricity had failed and Eva had finally been forced to stop her portrait session. She had spent the early part of the day shooting in the garden, using the light filtering through the green shadows, trying to capture its alien presence, its mystery. But in the late afternoon she had turned to the garden's creator. She had been using a portrait lens, enabling her to shoot in the fading day and on into the evening, a time that lent itself to the twilight world in which Caspar lived. She wanted his spirit, the beauty in that cavernous head, the love that moved him.

There was the sound of things being rearranged. A chair, some contraption. And then, silence.

'Caspar, what's it like to be blind?' The voice, so much like her mother's but deeper, interrupting his thoughts.

He returned to that last sight of her, her face shaded as always by a hat, standing with Armand in the shadows behind her, waving a white gloved hand from the steps of the DC4 taking them to Bahrain and then England. She had written to him. Blue airmail letters about the cold, their cramped flat in Ebury Street and later, pictures of Eva. At first the letters came regularly, then less and less often. He had seen her only a few times since.

He felt a hand on his wrist tugging him back to the present.

'Caspar?'

'Yes?' He looked towards her, hearing the direction of her voice.

'What's it like to be blind, Caspar?'

'What do you mean, child?' He wasn't surprised or offended by her question. He'd become used to her blunt way of talking.

'I mean, is it always dark for you, or do you see something, like light?'

'No, it's not completely dark. I see pictures. A bit like films, although they're not wholly distinct.'

'Are they in colour or black and white?'

'They're black and white.'

'And are they memories from the past or like dreams?'

'I'm not sure. Perhaps a little of each. I rather enjoy them. They entertain me while I'm lying here with nothing to do.'

His smile flickered in the faint moonlight filtering through the windows. He reached out, until he felt her hand. 'You know, having you here makes me wish that Vivien and I had married after all: then you'd belong to both of us.'

Eva squeezed his hand, feeling its thin dry skin and bony fingers in hers. 'Yes. But I suppose, in a way, I do.'

For a while they were silent; she listening to the night sounds outside – a distant barking dog, the faint screech of a bat, the silence displaced by a night flying bird; he lost in old memories.

The pictures were still quite clear. Both of them on the upstairs verandah at Tara. Vivien smoking, rapidly but never inhaling, the way she did when she was nervous. 'What is it, darling?' he had asked. But he already knew. And then, it had come out in a rush.

He had said the things one says. The meaningless platitudes: 'Very well, darling, if that's what you want'; and 'No, it's fine'. And that was the end of it. He had felt sad. But only fleetingly. He felt sadder now, with Eva bringing back memories of what could have been but was not.

'Caspar, why did Mama marry Armand?' The ghost of Vivien's voice again. As if she had read his thoughts.

What could he tell her? He barely knew himself.

He thought back to the sudden wedding on the lawn at Tara. The old lady, who had liked Armand, looking stately as always, seated like a queen on a throne, receiving guests. Vivien herself, flushed and shy for once and more fragile than ever, with Armand, who seemed overwhelmed by it all, holding her arm as if she might collapse.

Why *had* she married him? He supposed it was to escape the island, the gossip.

'Caspar?'

He sighed. 'I don't know, my dear. How does one know these things? I'm just so sorry your mother had such a terrible time. She didn't deserve that. And nor do you.'

He'd cabled Viv, when her father had his stroke and seemed on his last legs. He'd lived alone in that great house after the old lady had died of cancer and Mickey had gone. Rattling around its rooms with nothing but two Dalmatians and the servants to keep him company, a shadow of the acid-tongued courtroom scourge. She'd come eventually, her marriage in tatters, but by then it was too late. All that was left was to bury the dead. That was the last time he saw her. She seemed on the verge of a breakdown and thinner than ever; chain-smoking through a cigarette-holder; pacing through the house; living on alcohol and nicotine and her nerves. No wonder she had collapsed.

From a distance of half a century, it was easier to see what a tragedy it had all been. He had the wisdom now to read Vivien and her life more clearly than he ever had at the time. It seemed now as if they had hardly known each other. It was a different era: people locked up feelings. He was half-baked by the brusque camaraderie of the officers' mess, for whom women were a mysterious alien species. And she was young and ignorant of real life when their mothers threw them together in that ill-suited engagement.

He smiled to himself. They knew as little about sex as their daughters, with their plans to find brides for him and Mickey. Still, he had loved her and it might have worked. But would it have changed her life for the better? Perhaps it might have been less hard. But less tragic? Perhaps not.

'Caspar, tell me more, please. You're the only one who was there. There's no one else I can ask.'

She was stirring the soup of his memory now with her questions. What had the island been like then? Had Vivien and Armand been in love? And once more, why him?

'I don't know, child. The island was a wonderful place then. There was less of everything bad – people, cars, bustle – and more of everything good. More of nature. We had so much fun then.' He sighed.

'And my mother? How was she?'

'Your mother was beautiful. But you know that. Exquisite. But she had something more. The heroine quality that few people have, of making men and women – animals, too – fall in love with her. Without ever intending to.'

'I was in love with her.'

'Of course you were.'

'And Armand. Was he in love with her?'

'Oh yes. Very much so.' He turned to Eva, as if looking at her intently. 'But you know that's the suffering these adored creatures face. Those who love them, especially those who love them the most, end up hating them, wanting to punish them and then to flee them.'

'And you?' She spoke softly and for a long time he was silent, as if he might not have heard.

At last he turned to her smiling, but he looked sad. 'You know, my dear, I loved your mother in a different way. Not less. But differently and for different reasons.'

He took her hand, wondering as he did how much she already knew and how much should stay locked within his own memory.

She lay in the sea-room, looking up at the gently clacking ceiling fan, and saw a pattern of a kind she hadn't noticed since childhood. The three small screws that attached each blade and the attaching shaft, had formed themselves into the faces of three kittens. Her eyes moved along the ceiling and down the wall. Patches of damp, peeling paint, shadows, doorlocks, had turned into animals, birds and beings. The room was peopled with mythological creatures, some realistic, others dreamlike; as symbolic as the cave paintings of Lascaux or the great southern deserts. She was re-entering the world she'd left behind in childhood. The world of our ancestors, of so-called primitive people, who saw in the landscape not rocks and hills, but creatures, and in the night sky, an ever-changing story of light.

She was a child in bed. Awake. Frozen by a sense of impending doom, as if this were a nightmare or a terrible, repeating reality. The door opened and two ghostly giants, tall as the ceiling, entered. The figures, a man and a woman, were backlit by the bright light of the hallway beyond, making them seem like phantoms. Her heart was beating and she was very afraid. And then the terrifying vision slid into darkness. She realized then that this image was the only time she could remember seeing her parents together.

Fifteen

It was late when Eva returned from the airport through fine rain. She had spent most of the night looking for a passenger or a crew member to take film to her agency in Paris. At last a Frenchman, whom she had spotted making eyes at her in the airport lobby, had agreed to take her package. She had driven home, exhausted, but relieved to have done the job and to have the road empty: a rain-slicked conveyor belt that she had rolled along in auto-pilot, like a car on a production line, or a tram on an electric rail.

As she turned into her road, she thought of flat white sheets, her bed, sleep. But as she neared the house, something snapped her out of her dream. A figure was slumped in her doorway, shadowed by the streetlight, half crumpled like an undelivered parcel. It was half past four in the morning. She could hear the doorbell ringing through the watery night. She parked her car beneath the streetlight and got out.

Navahiru leaned against the doorframe, his finger on the bell, bare-chested in a worn sleeping sarong. There were half-moon shadows under his eyes and a crescent of stubble around his chin, But beyond all that, she smelt his fear and his exhaustion. Instantly, her annoyance vanished.

'I'm so sorry to come at this time,' he murmured. The ghost of his smile flickered, like a firefly. She saw then that one lip was bruised and swollen.

'What's happened? Are you OK?'

He nodded but said nothing.

'Come in.' She took his arm, unlocked the door, switched on the lights and led him to a sofa. 'I'll get you some tea.'

When she returned with two cups of sweet, black tea he was asleep. Sprawled open-limbed like a child on the cushions. She watched him for a while, but he had gone to a place beyond dreams.

'Goodnight, Navahiru,' she whispered, running her fingertips along his cheek and down his shoulder. She saw him wince in his sleep and removed her hand. Then she tiptoed out into her bedroom.

She drew the muslin curtains and looked out. It was still inky-black outside, starless and windless, but she was too awake now for sleep. She drank the tea, waiting for daybreak, running through the many alternatives of what might have happened. She supposed he must have been injured in a brawl or a street robbery. It was unlike him, but not impossible, she thought.

On a sudden impulse, she leaped up, picked up a camera, a long lens, some film and her car keys, and, moving softly through the sitting room, let herself back out.

Outside, pre-dawn clouds quilted the city, hiding the stars and softening the breeze. She drove through empty streets still wet from the rain, fingers of air trailing through her hair, to the main cemetery. The tall iron gates were locked but the parapet was small and there was no one around. She climbed over.

In the east the sky was lightening, silhouetting the maras, flamboyans and ficuses in the graveyard like sentinels, guardians of the nether worlds.

The grand old families were buried here. And as in life, there were classifications, distinctions. Catholics to the right, Protestants to the left, Methodists in the middle, and, in the larger rear half, Buddhists. As if each might be offended at sharing ground space with the other, or their souls might be delivered to the wrong part of heaven. There were no Hindus. Or Muslims. They or their ashes lay elsewhere.

Long avenues, lit occasionally by lamps, bisected the various religions, punctuated by small placards with uplifting exhortations: 'Do Not Put Off for Tomorrow What You Can Do Today'; 'Laughter is the Key to Long Life'; 'More Haste Less Speed'. And so on. Eva wondered if they were intended to cheer up mourners or make them feel worse.

She walked quickly down the main avenue, peering beyond the dim pools of light into the thickets of stone. She liked cemeteries and would often spend afternoons in them, reading the tombstones, noting how the flourishing, germ-rich air of the tropics killed so many so young: 'Mary, beloved wife of Arthur George Fernando, died in childbirth aged twenty'; 'Lt Nicholas Petrie, aged nineteen, felled by typhoid fever'; 'Our beloved daughter Isobel, three months old – an angel with us too briefly'; 'Evelyne de Groot, aged twelve, sadly taken from us by dengue fever'…

She left the main avenue to cut across a section of graves, peering through the greying gloom.

Stone angels rose out of the undergrowth of granite, stone, and black-and-white marble. But for the dark grey-green trees, it was monochrome here. She shot in black and white, intending later maybe to wash the pictures with green. There was something fantastical about this place at dawn. The creepers and monstera leaves, the dripping foliage, the fields of stone sculpture floating disembodied on the pre-dawn mist.

She had been wanting to take pictures here for some time, though she had no idea why she had come this morning. It was just an impulse. Something to do when sleep wouldn't return. But she was glad now. It was fresh here, even amid the stone and marble. Perhaps because of the sheer exuberance of nature: proof of life amid death. Perhaps because here, at last, there was an end to worldly cares and struggle. A stillness of sorts.

Her family grave was here, beneath an enormous old ficus tree, and she wanted to photograph it. She had come here once before and it had seemed then oddly like a sanctuary. The one place left to them on the island that, in a strange sort of irony, was theirs.

She took a few shots, mainly for Vivien, and then went closer to read the roll of names. Her beloved grandfather was here, the grandmother she never knew and her uncle. Ancestors going back two hundred years to the time when the cemetery was made. Graveyards were a relatively new thing, dating from colonial days. Before that, she supposed, Buddhist families scattered their ashes to the wind.

The black marble looked cold, smooth, inviting. She laid her cheek against it, letting her worry about Navahiru fall away. She should have brought flowers, an offering of some kind. She cast around until she found a frangipani tree and laid three of the heavy scented blossoms, one for each of her nearest relatives, in the elbows of the swastika, the revolving wheel of life that topped the gravestone.

She was about to walk back when she saw a white van parked at the end of the avenue near the cremation ground. She turned towards it, curious to know what was happening at this hour, supposing it to be the grave cleaners, or the caretakers.

As she got closer, she heard yelping. The sounds of wounded dogs. Quickly she clicked on the long lens and ran forward. Four men, two of them with nooses, had lassoed a couple of strays prowling around the cremation ground and the animals were screaming to be freed.

She sank down behind a tombstone buried in the undergrowth. The men were busy with the dogs but still, she didn't want to risk being seen.

She had heard about the dog catchers. Their work was illegal. Animal rights groups and vets had protested, and a law had been passed. But she knew that some municipalities still rounded up strays and killed them, if no one claimed them from the pound. They worked late at night and at dawn, when the city was empty. She remembered now that they went into the cemetery, too.

As she shot, she watched the two men with free hands pull long rods from the back of the van and fit something to the end of them. She kicked herself for leaving behind the motor drive. Before she could grasp what was happening they had jabbed each dog in the chest, aiming, she supposed, for the heart. The animals jerked and leaped hideously for some minutes, in a gruesome dance. And then it was over. She continued snapping as the men picked up the bodies and threw them into the van.

She had it all on film. And she was angry. The barbarity had shattered her calm and she was shaking. She walked back out of the cemetery, determined to get out the pictures as widely as possible. To do something.

She calmed down on the drive home, her anger blown away by the wind and other thoughts. It seemed ironic that at the moment she had found tranquillity, something had happened to destroy it. As if something in the island, or perhaps in her, were determined to reveal the horror within its beauty. Or perhaps it was just the times, the face it was showing now.

She remembered Navahiru then, wondering if he had woken. And what story he would have to tell.

It was eight-thirty by the time she returned. He was still slumped on the sofa, his sarong loose and twisted around his legs. She sat down beside him and gently shook his shoulder. He stirred in his sleep, groaning. It was then that she saw the burn mark just above the paler skin of his groin, where the cloth had slipped.

'Navahiru. Wake up.'

She shook him again. This time he opened his eyes. Staring at her in uncomprehending terror.

'It's OK. You're safe. It's me, Eva.'

She called to her maid to bring tea. Not caring what she thought of the strange man asleep in the house.

'Can I have a shower?' He had sat up and was smiling faintly. 'And a shirt, or anything that might fit me?' He sounded small, like a child. Eva went to rummage in her cupboard until she found an old man's bush shirt, a sarong and a clean towel, which she laid out. Then she went to order breakfast.

When he emerged, clean-shaven, with his hair wet and glistening, there were soft white rice pancakes, fiery coconut sambol, fruit juice and coffee on the table.

'So?' She raised an eyebrow. 'What happened?'

'It's a long story.'

'I'm patient. And I want to hear it.'

It *was* a long story. Or a disjointed one. And getting Navahiru to talk was like leeching a wound. But by insistent questioning, Eva pieced it together. Three days ago, a friend had driven him down to a small town in the south where somehow, through friends – a group of human rights lawyers – he had made contact with the southern rebel leaders. He knew the names only of two and, because they had blindfolded him for part of the way, he wasn't sure where he had been. Just somewhere in a remote hamlet in the interior jungles.

'It seemed to be an abandoned village. There was a small cluster of mud huts, nothing else. Very primitive. Not even any mats to sit on and hardly any food. Just red rice and *parippu*, no vegetables. I only saw three guns: two old Lee Enfields and a country-made mortar. They were crazy, all of them.'

'But why? Why did you go?'

Perhaps it was exhaustion and what he had been through, perhaps he was embarrassed or just confused, but he seemed hardly to know himself. He muttered something about trying to find out who had killed his brother. About using his status as a human rights student to win their sympathy, to let them know he was on their side.

Eva was astonished. Navahiru was sensible, practical. Young, but wiser than his years. Wiser than her, sometimes: he cared for his mother as if she were a younger sister. She had sensed the passion beneath his smile, but no trace of accompanying wildness. Nothing to match the wild streak that led her to the brink of life. He seemed too level-headed, too rooted for hare-brained adventures. She reflected again on how little she understood the islanders. How beneath the surface, the race to which she only half belonged was as mysterious and strange as the jungle. How little one understands another human heart.

'But surely, even if they did kill Nanda, you didn't expect them to tell you?'

Navahiru got up, walked to the window and stared out, silent. When he turned, his eyes were liquid. 'Eva,' he made a gesture of helplessness, 'our hearts make us do strange things. Mad things.' His voice was soft. 'I loved my brother.'

She walked to embrace him. He wrapped his arms around her, squeezing out her breath, burying his head in her neck like a child.

But there was more. She pulled away from him and ran a finger over his lip. 'What about this?' She glanced down at his belly. 'And that?'

He sighed. 'The cops. They must've been tailing me or were tipped off. They picked me up in Maluwela, roughed me up a bit, accused me of being one of the boys, told me I'd be dead on a tyre in the morning.'

'How did you get out?'

'There was one cop there. He knew my father. They'd met on a case. He persuaded them I was OK. But I had to stop him from calling *Tata*. That's why I came here. *Amma* would go crazy.'

'What will you do now?'

'I guess I'll stay over at a friend's until this has gone down.' He fingered his lip. 'I'd already told them I was going down south to the beach with some of the guys. They won't be expecting me till Saturday. But first...' He grabbed her waist.

She wriggled away to examine him. The story hadn't shocked her as much as he had. She wanted time to adjust, to re-arrange him in her brain.

'Please.' He seemed near tears.

The sun was sinking behind the mara tree outside the house, filtering gold through its filigree, when they awoke and untangled their sweaty limbs. They had made love with a fierceness and intensity that left her wounded and empty.

'Are you all right, darling?' he murmured. 'I was too rough, I'm sorry.' He was stroking her breasts gently, pressing into her.

'I'm all right. But we can't fuck again.' She bent down and kissed him. 'Haven't you had enough?'

He shook his head, laughing.

'Well.' She jumped out of bed, laughing, too. 'You'll just have to do it yourself.'

He leaped up, caught her and pulled her into the bathroom, and turned on the shower. He pushed her head down on him under the spray, turned her over and grabbed a jar of cream from a shelf. She felt herself falling into a deep, dark well. Immersed by a dark, possessive wave. When it was over, she lay curled on the tiles, water streaming. Head empty. A circle of blue sky high above.

It was dark when they dressed; night had dropped as fast as an opera house curtain. A light rain fell, cooling the air. She smelled its freshness.

'I love you,' he said, as he held her goodbye in the doorway.

She said nothing. She knew he didn't mean it any more than she would have. She felt overcome by the sadness of small love. There was something else, though. But what it was, she couldn't tell yet.

That night she heard the cry of a strange creature outside her window. Not a cat or a bird but something else, beyond recognition. It was like the cry of a familiar, a beast sprung from a medieval peasant's ergotomine dream. It troubled her then and afterwards.

Sixteen

It's odd how siblings can be so unalike. As if God, or perhaps nature, had muddled up the genes, resulting in an unkind trick being played on the recipients. Even before time had turned the tubby little bruiser in navy shorts – who terrorized the schoolyard, stole *bidis* from the janitor and made lewd comments at girls – into Sergeant Piyadasa, giant panda and professional thug, and the girl in neat plaits and spotless dresses into Mary, domestic servant and amateur black magician, it was hard to believe they came from the same family as the other Piyadasas. They even *looked* different. From each other, from their parents and from the other members of their extended clan: the uncles and aunties and cousin-brothers, the *nandas* and *mamas*, *massinas* and *nanas*; the father's-mother's-sister and sister's-daughter's-son. As for any psychological resemblance – well, they were like *chunam* and *pol sambol*.

For while after first Mary and then Piyadasa stopped looking like blobs of Play-Doh and became recognizable human beings, people in the village-not-yet-grown-into-a-small-town whispered that at least one child must be the product of a paddy-field romance. A malicious neighbour, with a long-standing grudge over a boundary wall, even gossiped that *Amma*, as Mrs Piyadasa was widely known, wasn't really an *amma* at all, but barren.

Her pregnancies were pillows that she stuffed into her cloth every morning (he claimed to have seen her washing at the tap, with a flat tummy) and the babies, when they arrived, had been procured from the Little Sisters of Mercy orphanage. When the other women, who liked *Amma* as much as they later disliked her daughter, asked why, in that case, had she gone to the local Base Hospital with labour pains, he retreated to the dark looks and knowing nods of people who don't really know anything at all.

In time, though, everyone got bored with the gossip and accepted that some families had been thrown together by biological confusion, or planetary malevolence, or both. When *Amma*'s son landed a job as a policeman and was then promoted to sergeant, even the village's most serpentine tongues stopped. No one wanted to offend a police officer.

As adults, Mary and Piyadasa saw much less of each other, but they still got on each other's nerves, while remaining perversely interdependent. In good moods they bickered and in bad ones they had full-fledged rows, poisoned by childhood hatreds. It was like a life-long bad marriage.

Thus it was that on that particular February New Year's Day when, five minutes after arriving at his father's house, Sergeant Piyadasa discovered that Mary had invited her *sudu* boss, his festive spirit instantly fermented.

'So?' he demanded, glaring over the remains of his second Old Faithful and water. 'What's he coming for? An anthology lesson?'

He guffawed loudly at his own joke and then glared around the hot concrete room at the front of the house where the men of the extended Piyadasa clan had gathered on green and white plastic-wicker chairs, as if daring someone to contradict him. A neon tube light sizzled in the silence like an unacknowledged fart. The Piyadasa siblings were famous for their fights and no one wanted to miss a good quarrel.

'You mean anthroffology lesson,' corrected Mary, as if on cue, muddling up her fs and ps as usual. She had been bringing in an aluminium tray of *kokis*, *konda kaum* and *kiri baath* from the back verandah kitchen, when her brother launched his jibe, and turned to give him a cross look over her shoulder.

A small bat hung upside-down from the rafters under the corrugated asbestos roof, like a folded cocktail umbrella.

'That's what I said!' He glared at her again and took another gulp of the muddy gold liquid. 'Anyway, why's he coming? Looking at the natives in their natural habitats? Showing off his white skin? Teaching us missionary positions?'

He hiked up his vest to give the fur on his tummy an airing, guffawed again and, as if to make the point, heaved a pair of meaty legs on to the extended arms of the planter's chair like a giant panda in a gynaecologist's surgery. Or a self-satisfied police sergeant off-duty.

A smaller, secondary wavelet of polite laughter lapped over the male relatives seated in various states of dress and repose. Those closest to the main trunk of the Piyadasa family tree lounged around, like Sergeant Piyadasa, in vests and sarongs. The more distant – the third cousins once removed, the brothers-in-law, or the poorer relatives – perched as rigidly as government job applicants, in nylon shirts and tight polyester trousers. The room was filled with clutter – flying geese, laughing Buddhas, a porcelain boy in lederhosen, plastic flowers, a ballerina under a perspex dome – and musky with sweat, stale grudges and sycophancy. From the smoky back verandah came the high hum of women gossiping, baby-minding, cleaning jak fruit and sorting *parippu*, pierced now and then by a child's thrilled scream.

'No need por pilth, child,' piped up a broken, flute-like voice. Everyone stopped chattering and looked towards the doorway, where a tiny bundle of twigs in a traditional white lace jacket and flowered cloth squatted. Great-aunt Nilmini, whose skin rustled like rice-paper. There was another silence as everyone wondered where on earth an upright old lady had learned of such concepts. 'No need,' she repeated, nodding. Sparse white hairs stretched across her polished skull like violin strings. 'No need, no need at all.'

In a corner, old Mr Piyadasa's brother's son's wife, Shanti, whose family were Catholic converts, looked up from the infant sucking noisily at her breast and whispered to her husband: 'Vot's the missionary fosition?'

'Missionary, nothing doing,' snapped Mary, reclaiming her status in the conversation and the house as the Hostess of a Foreigner. She had no idea what her brother was talking about either, except that it was probably something rude. 'He is coming because I am inviting.'

She gave Lalitha a pitying look, intended to convey her opinion on the stupidity of all local men, whom she regarded as inferior to foreigners. But her sister-in-law, who had been straightening her son's red-and-white spotted, clip-on bow-tie, was laughing. Her belly fat sent ripples of merriment across the front of her dress.

Shanti, whose husband's whispered answer had made her blush, fussed and bothered over her baby, who was vomiting thin lumps of milk down his bib.

From the rafters, the bat let drop a jet of greenish-white guano, which narrowly missed a piece of *wattalapam* on Mary's tray. Two of the teenage boys nudged each other and giggled when she didn't notice.

'Well, whatever, it's a damn fool idea,' said Piyadasa, reverting to his initial bad temper. He regarded white men with a muddle of fright, loathing and servility, and was alarmed one was arriving at his ancestral home. What did the fellow eat and drink? Worse – he suddenly remembered the white porcelain footholds flanking the unspeakable black hole – where would he shit? '*Damn* fool!' he said again, and polished off the last of his drink.

'Now, *putta*, enough,' said their father softly. He had been a widower for almost twenty years but his wife's early death of tuberculosis had snuffed out his youth. He gazed at Mary fondly. 'It's an honour, daughter, a blessing from the gods. We're all honoured.'

A murmur of assent leapfrogged Piyadasa and rippled around the room.

Mary rose to go to the kitchen. 'Come, sister,' she commanded her sister-in-law. But Lalitha was still vibrating with mirth, like a trampoline someone had just bounced on, and Mary's patronizing tone rolled right off her.

Sergeant Piyadasa glared at his sister's back, relieved. He hoped she wouldn't remember whatever it was that had been bugging her the other night. The last thing he wanted was her nagging. He re-tucked his sarong under his balls and stretched out a paw for the *arrack* bottle. 'Father?' He indicated the old man's glass.

'Enough, son, bad for the heart.' He gave a rasping cough to underline the point and reached out for his grandson, who rarely saw the old man and was staring at him wide-eyed, as if he were a possibly dangerous zoo animal. 'Come to *Aachi*,' he said as the child took a hesitant step. 'Come on. No need to be scared now.'

The small boy – whom Lalitha, in a moment of reckless taste, had dressed in baggy jeans and shades, with his head shaved into concentric furrows like crop circles – tottered forward, stopped, put a tiny finger up a gram-sized nostril and, with the other hand, grabbed his crotch. The room beamed with love, watching to see what this miniature gangsta rapper and first grandchild, who had unconsciously mimicked the gesture of every beat policeman, would do next.

'Chip off the old block!' guffawed Sergeant Piyadasa, unconscious of the irony.

'My, so like his *tata*, isn't it?' exclaimed clever cousin Dilrukshi, who was.

'Come baba,' beseeched the old man, stretching out his arms (like Christ, in the 'All Things Bright and Beautiful' poster at Sunday school, thought Shanti, trying to purify her thoughts).

The little boy tottered for a few seconds on his baby high-tops and then did what every small child, weighed down by a roomful's concentrated attention, does: he burst into tears.

'*Amma!*' he wailed. Lalitha lunged forward to scoop him up and carried him to the back verandah.

Mr Piyadasa shrugged. 'I think I'll have that drink.'

'Sure, *Tata*,' said Sergeant Piyadasa, pleased the old man was joining him at last.

'How's work?' his father asked, when his glass had been topped up. The question burped out into the room before he could stop it. He cursed himself. Everyone knew what the cops were up to, although he tried to fool himself about his son. Why, even in their own village, how many boys were going missing? No one wanted to talk about what was going on. Talk could get you killed. He hoped his son wouldn't answer.

Sergeant Piyadasa's eyes, suddenly sharp, dulled again, like a monitor lizard whose prey has fled. His father watched him warily, but in fact, he was thinking about his long overdue promotion: the leg-up he needed, status-wise and bucks-wise, that would settle all his problems in life. He blinked sleepily at his father, wishing for once he could talk to the old man, that he wasn't so... well, so passive, so weak. Mr Piyadasa shrank slightly. He felt like a squirrel trapped in a lizard's gaze.

'*Hondai*. OK,' Sergeant Piyadasa said, finally. He shrugged. 'Same lazy buggers at the station. Same trouble getting a promo. But mostly peaceful, like. Not much going on where we are. You know how it is, *Tata*.' He shrugged again.

Mr Piyadasa nodded, as if indeed he did know. As if the unplumbable depths of his son's job were merely fleeting shadows against the sun. He took a gulp of *arrack* as if to celebrate a tricky pass negotiated, and smiled, pleased and relieved. Beside them, a new table fan, gifted by Sergeant Piyadasa, cut a swathe through the pre-dusk mosquitoes that hovered before their faces like black tulle veils.

Seventeen

The westwardly dipping sun had followed him all the way, drilling through his side-window, mocking the puny air-conditioning, like a heavy-weight champ taunting his opponent before a fight. Finally – hot, bothered and lost – he had stopped the car, gulped from a bottle of over-heated water, wiped his forehead with a shirtsleeve and looked at the map. It confirmed what he already knew: both the village and the small town near it were hidden somewhere in its splodges of tan and green. Unmarked and as lost as he was. There wasn't even a squiggle or an irregular circle of blue he could identify. He cursed himself again for accepting Mary's invitation, for not insisting she accompany him, for forgetting to ask for landmarks. Perhaps he should have asked the woman, she seemed to speak a bit of the language. Yeah, he thought, and ruin a second date.

He looked around. Electric green paddies bordered by the darker green of a palm and fruit tree grove that must hide a farmhouse. Hills strung like a hazy line of blue-green washing on the horizon. Sunlight glittering on a lotus pond. The creased leather horns and glossy patent leather back of a buffalo, motionless as a boulder in the water. The landscape had locked away its secrets. He could have been anywhere in the island: two minutes away or two hours.

The late-afternoon air hung ragged and heavy as a *dhobi*'s washload. He could hear the emptiness, the silence.

He recited again his reasons for driving all this way. To get to know a cop, in the same way he'd wanted to know a soldier. To see one off-duty, maybe ask him a few questions, find out what made a man like that tick. He believed as ardently as a convert in the revelatory powers of journalism. That once under the journalist's microscope, questions and magnification of detail would, ipso facto, produce answers. And that those answers could be fitted, like pieces of a jigsaw puzzle into a coherent whole. That it might be impossible to find out very much about someone by such peremptory means hadn't occurred to him. At those times, it was as if the subtleties of the human condition had passed over him like birds in the night.

Answers or not, the adventure was looking more and more like one of fate's booby-traps; a bad idea that should have been abandoned at birth. Besides, this was his day off. He slammed into gear and shot forward in an angry screech of hot rubber and spinning gravel. The mud-cooling buffalo, sole living occupant of the landscape, didn't even look up.

This part of the island was heavily built up. Soon the houses punctuating the landscape became a straggly line and then the outskirts of a town. He passed ancestral homes, iced with wooden lace; solid Eastbourne villas, with embossed construction dates; crinoline churches fit for an *infanta*'s wedding; a Catholic Home for the Elders with a sari-clad madonna out front; a colonnaded courthouse. The island's colonial past had been layered like a trifle here, squashing the country's traditions into a sludge of bottom-dwelling fruit. But for the barefoot children, the men in sarongs, the bullock carts, the stink of fish and rotting vegetables, he could have been in a historical theme park. It had that sort of unreal, filmic quality about it.

As he passed the court, he thought of the only case he'd ever attended: a criminal trial implicating one of the island's politicians in a series of multiple murders. The politician hadn't been in the dock himself, of course. That burden fell to one of his henchmen: a trunk of meat in a suit, with an IQ of eighty-five. Normally, the man would spend two weeks in jail and then be released on a technicality. But this time the matter had been dealt with more dramatically: the prosecution's star witness had been shot dead on the stand. Carl hadn't been there that day, but he remembered the trial. Witnesses were led into court wearing pillow-cases; the accused stood in a cage with iron spikes and every word of evidence was relayed through three people: the court clerk, the magistrate and the stenographer, who transcribed it before anyone could reply. No wonder cases took years to hear.

The courtroom. Mary had mentioned an old colonial courthouse with a bodhi tree in front. He worried that he'd passed the turn-off.

Traffic in the town centre had expanded and thickened, like boiling rice. Painted lorries snarled at speeding mini-bus drivers; snake-hipped men with coathanger shoulders jostled hairy-legged working girls. A higgledy row of shabby shops and cavernous tea *cadays* with grey plastic tablecloths and stale *vadais* in greasy glass cases bit into the road. The shops were closed for New Year, but the *cadays* were bustling. He passed a school wall, covered with political graffiti: hammers and sickles, confusing acronyms and slogans in elephant-bottom script.

He felt uncomfortable and panicked in these small towns, hemmed in by brown skin, alien smells and jibes in a language he couldn't understand, where beneath the surface lurked the sour-sweet smell of fear. This was rebel territory. Whole provinces had been shut down by *hartals*; traitors were being hung from trees by their intestines; and the wife of a disobedient civil servant had received her husband's head wrapped in newspaper on a New Year's sweet platter, a year ago today. His last conversation with the Captain slid into mind. He frowned, trying to erase the thought, and clicked down the door locks.

'Hey, man,' he yelled at a fat *mudalali* in a white shirt and sarong who was standing in the doorway of a hollow-fronted tea shop, like a single white incisor in a mouth of missing teeth. The man saw Carl and, in a single deft motion, fanned out his sarong from its nesting place under his balls, flipped it up into a mini-skirt, knotted it and stepped out into the road.

'Where's—?

'*Vare prom?*' interrupted the *mudalali*. 'German? Franch?' His grin was bloodied with *betel*. He looked as if he ate raw bodies for lunch. '*SprechenSieDeutsch?*' His accent was surprisingly good.

'No tourist! OK! Understand?' yelled Carl, far more angrily than was necessary. He shoved the map out of the window at the man's face and jabbed at it. 'Where's—??' (he mispronounced the name of Mary's village.) 'Here? Here?'

The *mudalali*, who being a minor big-shot, was used to doing all the shouting, gave him a disgusted look. With the practised aim of a life-time *betel*-chewer, he shot a jet of blood-red juice plumb through Carl's window.

'*Puck opp! Pucking porener!*' he added, unneccessarily.

'FUCK! FUCK!' yelled Carl, frantically dabbing at the sticky juice and *betel* nut crumbs on his face and shirt. 'FUCK YOU! BASTARD!'

But the *mudalali* had already rumbled back into his shop without a backwards glance, like a rhino ambling down a path after a satisfying crap.

Every surface in the back verandah kitchen was encrusted with soot. The mud walls and ceiling, the shelves, the clay cooking pots and *vallangs*. Only the mud hearth, where the soot had burned hard; the cement washing-up area; and the granite grinding stone, ingrained with pulverised coriander, ginger and other spices, had escaped. It was as if four generations of Piyadasa tears, laughter, anger and joy had accumulated in this kitchen. The history of a family contained in a layer of soot. Depending on how squeamish you were, the Piyadasa family kitchen either looked like a corner of hell or a sanctuary, where sadness could be consoled and joy celebrated with hot, tasty snacks.

Lalitha leaned against the door jamb with baby Piyadasa nestled in the folds of her skirt. She was watching her sister-in-law chopping vegetables.

'What cooking?' she indicated with a nod. '*Alewulu* curry?'

'*Neh*, soup.'

'Soup?' asked Lalitha, astonished. The closest thing to soup that anyone in a village ever consumed was *rasam*, for colds. And that wasn't like soup at all.

'He is not eating spices,' explained Mary.

'He?'

'The *mahataya*.'

Lalitha smiled to herself and lifted up her toddler. 'You hear that, *putta*?' she asked. 'A *mahataya* who can't eat spices is coming.' The child's eyes widened. 'A real big man like you'll be when you're grown up.' She tickled the little boy until he squirmed and wriggled in her arms like a small wet fish.

Mary, who didn't know whether her sister-in-law was joking or not, smiled to herself and took down the family's special stainless-steel cooking pot, bought by her late mother after a pilgrimage to *poren*.

'You still believing in all that *katadiya* what-not stuff?' Lalitha asked a few minutes later. She had spread a cloth on the floor, plonked herself and the baby on it, and was offering him a choice of vegetables to play with.

'What what-not?' snapped Mary, who was now furiously wrestling with an unplucked chicken. 'Is all a-one, advanced stuff.'

'So, you can be doing something for me?'

Mary, who had no idea why her sister-in-law had suddenly become interested in the supernatural, said nothing.

'Well?' Lalitha asked. 'You are knowing this stuff or not?' She

119

only half believed in spells but was irritated by her sister-in-law's patronizing tone.

'Of course I'm knowing,' retorted Mary, from inside a cloud of chicken feathers. 'You're wanting a love thing?' she added. 'Or something to make you bewtiful?'

Lalitha burst out laughing. Her son, who had been prodding his mother with a bitter gourd – and believed with the self-centredness of all children that she was laughing because of him – giggled happily and prodded her harder, until she snatched the vegetable away. 'No, no. I want something for to stop him snoring.' And ignoring her sister-in-law's disgusted look, she burst into fresh peals of laughter.

Mary had never yet successfully made a spell, although she had experimented once or twice. (Toots had received a migraine and the *dhobi* had lost all the left socks in his washing.) But Lalitha's challenge had reminded her to try something. As she wrestled bones and entrails out of the chicken, she ran through the possibilities.

When Carl's cooking was finished, she unlocked a small cupboard and took out an ornate brass box and a small book, covered in brown paper. Unlocking the box with a key from her waist, she removed glass vials and newspaper shakings of roots, twigs and herbs. Then, with book open and brow smocked, she began the ritual.

Following the old spell, she sprinkled pinches of gris-gris into a small, long-handled copper pan, kept for the purpose, added drops from three of the vials and muttered words in the older, forgotten tongue as the liquid bubbled on a single flame.

At last, when the muddy liquid had cooled and been decanted, she brought from her pocket a folded paper square, extracted from it a short brown hair, slipped it into the glass vial and corked it.

In the corner, baby Piyadasa sucked noisily at his somnolent mother's breast. But his eyes, which had never left his aunt, were wide as saucers.

Eighteen

There was no moon and, beneath the cloud-cover, no stars. The countryside and its unlit villages slept beneath the quilt of night. Carl stopped the car, clicked on the overhead light, pulled out the map and squinted at it. Inside the bubble of light, he felt protected from the brooding blackness. But it was almost ten, he was tired and lost, trapped in the web of fine lines of minor roads. He rubbed his eyes and stared again at the chart as if it was an oracle. Then he clicked off the light and looked out. Beyond the headlights, darkness waited like a bad omen. The only sign of human habitation, a provision store made of old packing crates, was padlocked, its face tight shut.

He didn't want to go on or turn back. There was no telephone at Mary's family house. But even if there had been, there was nowhere to call from. He scanned the lit pool of landscape ahead, searching for a sign, sure now that he was driving in circles. He felt tired and confused, as if the top of his head had been opened and its contents stirred. If only he could find a main road instead of these endless country lanes with the same stealthy, abandoned air. A secret plague had come and gone, leaving behind only corpses.

He wound up the window, as though afraid of the night outside, the insistent, dripping jungle. He heard a scream like a child's and started. It was a peacock. The trees creaked and moaned like moored boats in a storm. He shivered but wasn't cold. The view outside seemed to have changed. Perhaps it was his field of vision. Something had subtly altered the texture of the darkness beyond. He squinted through the windscreen ahead and saw nothing. Then, as he put the car into gear and looked up at his rear-view mirror, he saw it.

He felt a shock, as if a blow had been struck to the car. Panic sliced through him, the engine stalled and in his confusion, he killed the headlights, plunging himself into chaos.

He was back at sea. A warm, liquid blanket, offering oblivion. It was a starless night with no moon, but he heard the waters moan, the boat creak and mutter. Moments back, he had reached to extinguish a light and there was only the dim glow of his instruments. He was safe. Safe in the warm cockpit of the house, the inky sea rolling beneath him.

Suddenly something shifted in the movement of the boat. He looked back, a sailor's salt-eyed glance, and saw it right behind him: a bad omen, a death foretold, a monster dredged from the island's deep. He ducked instinctively, his hands clutched hard at the wheel.

For a second, maybe two, maybe for ever, he watched. And then it came. He shut his eyes and all turned black.

Carl blinked and rubbed his face. What had happened? How long had he been sitting at the wheel? He looked at his watch. The minute hand had hardly moved. He adjusted his rear-view mirror, looking at it as if it were a Pandora's box that might produce yet more unpleasant surprises. Then he put the car into gear, flicked the headlights and moved forward. Ahead, a lumbering black shape was lit; a stately galleon, its stern trailing a swaying rope of anchor. He slowed to a crawl. It was the last of a string of wild elephants that must have passed him when he'd zoned out just then. Elephants had overturned cars on jungle roads. He cut his lights again and inched forward, hoping the creatures would turn off into the jungle.

*

Sergeant Piyadasa started, opened two blue-black eyelids and blinked at his wife and sister as if seeing them for the first time. He looked at the fake gold Timex nestled in the fur of his wrist. 'Say, isn't it time your boss was here?' he asked, startled to find he had napped for two hours. 'Hell of a time to be visiting, *nehde*? What's he going to do? Stay the night?' And with that he let out a thunderous guffaw that shook awake his father who had also slipped into sleep.

'Wha, wha…whatsamatter?' The old man looked around at his various relatives with a bewildered, milky gaze.

'He can stay at the local resthouse, ip needs be,' retorted Mary, who had reasons of her own for feeling cross.

'What, that bug-pit? Fit for only politicians and off-duty cops!' he roared, forgetting he himself was one. 'Blood's too bitter for biting! Isn't it, *Tata*?' And he sat up, pleased with his new joke. 'Cummon, *Akkhi*, what for such a long face, eh? Let's forget about him and eat, no?' He reached out to give her a friendly slap.

But Mary, who was put out by Carl's failure to show up and her consequent loss of face, as well as the apparent failure of her spell, refused to be humoured.

On the kitchen verandah, the Piyadasa women pickled their thoughts. The general consensus, reached by looks, not voices, was that Mary needed taking down a peg or two. So when Lalitha good-humouredly asked her, as they were piling rice on to a platter, if she had been brewing a love charm, she snapped. For if her spell had worked after all, it was not in the way she had intended.

In the chilly dawn, Carl, more asleep than awake, turned into the wide avenue lined with tyre shops that marked the entrance to the city. Outside one, he saw a battered old green car. It wasn't hers. But he smiled when he realized he had noticed. For the first time in that long night, he thought of her. And wondered when and if he would ever see her again.

Nineteen

For days, she had woken beneath a stone of dread. A cold hardness in the pit of her stomach that weighed down each moment, leadening her spirit, until she half believed she might give birth to that which she feared. When the telephone jangled through the house in the middle of the night, she knew, with the sixth sense of lovers, that something terrible had happened. So she let it ring, afraid to answer.

'Eva, what took you so long?' It was Mohan. 'Navahiru's been taken.' He sounded as if a dead man had walked on his grave.

She looked at her watch. It was two in the morning. 'What do you mean?' she asked. Her somnolent brain refused to grasp the words her heart had already understood. She slid to the floor. Wanting to scream.

'He's been taken. They came to his parents' house tonight. His mother called me.'

'Who's "they"?' She was trying to pull herself together. To think.

Mohan wasn't in a state to be sure. Four men in camouflage uniforms without insignia and with AK47s had arrived in an unmarked jeep. They could have been the army or the police or Special Forces. They could even have been thugs from one of the many private political militias. Navahiru's father was away at a meeting of retired lawyers, so his mother had answered the door in her dressing-gown. Mohan had been unable to get much from her. She was near hysteria.

'She just kept saying: "I don't know why, I don't know why."'

There had been no arrest warrant, nor any stated reason. There never was. Navahiru's last words to his mother as he was pulled from his bed were: 'Don't worry about me, *Amma*.' That, she thought, was typical.

'I'm getting out of town, myself. Those guys spook me,' said Mohan.

She knew he was afraid of being involved. She couldn't blame him but she was angry. Navahiru was his friend.

She thought over his last visit, trying to rein in the rearing horse of her panic with logic. She hadn't heard from him since then; over three weeks ago. That wasn't unusual: often she didn't see him for weeks at a time and then suddenly he would call or arrive on her doorstep. But after the last time she had expected a call, if only to tell her he was all right. She had supposed he was embarrassed. Again, she ran through all he had told her. It seemed tonight's arrest was linked to his earlier trip. But she also knew nothing was that obvious in the island. There were always other motives, other truths.

Heavy rain drummed on the bonnet of her car, beating its fingertips in time to her impatience. She wondered why it was raining now. It wasn't the monsoon. The island's rainfall was a riddle. 'Inter-monsoonal showers,' they said. But tonight it was as if nature, fate, were conspiring against her. She tapped the distributor with the handle of her screwdriver. Nothing happened. No answering click-click-click that usually followed a thwack from under the glove compartment with a hammer, or a few light taps on the little drum itself; the morse that would tell her that the simple mechanism of her car had sprung to life.

'Fuck it!' But the rain drummed out her words. She slammed the bonnet and ran indoors. She felt like crying but anxiety and tension had dammed her tears. She paced the room, smoking and thinking: a streak of nerve endings, adrenalin and rushing blood.

No one would fix the engine at this hour. She thought of Mohan and her other friends but knew immediately there was no point; they avoided trouble, often after having caused it. The diplomats she knew were useless. They wouldn't get involved, either. Navahiru's friends at law school were too young. Caspar would have helped, but he was old and blind and paralysed. She needed clout. Or a white skin: a foreigner, a man. She ran into her bed-room and riffled through the visiting cards on her desk. He had given her another card the last time they met. There was little time, but still she fingered it, hesitating like a rookie punter at roulette. Should she call him? Would he come? She hardly knew him. She picked up the receiver and dialled his number. He answered almost immediately with the name of his paper; he was working.

'Hello, it's Eva. I'm sorry, is this a bad moment?'

'Oh hi.' The voice softened. 'It's great to hear from you, but yeah, I am under the gun right now. Is it urgent? I could call you tomorrow.'

'Yes.' She tried to keep the panic out of her voice.

'I'll call you back in a coupla hours.'

She put the telephone down and leaned on the small shelf, chin in hand. Who else could she ask? She went through her address book. There was no one of any real use. It was as friendless as a telephone directory for a strange town. 'Damn!' She hurled the book across the room. She'd have to wait.

She went into the bedroom and flung herself down, but sleep had eloped with calm. Lighting a cigarette, she lay back and reviewed the options. It was no use. She sprang up, returned to the sitting room, retrieved her address book from under a chair and went into the kitchen to make coffee. She grabbed a pencil and a piece of paper and began listing names, organizations, places they could look and people who might help. She ruled out the politicians, the dealers in slime. She had a few army contacts who might have grudges to settle; Carl might have some, too. There was a good human rights lawyer, maybe a couple of activists. She added and subtracted, doing the arithmetic of hope. Everything depended on who had taken Navahiru and why; how high up the arrest order had gone; whether it was intentional and long planned, or spontaneous and perhaps mistaken.

She stubbed out a second cigarette and lit a third, weaving a febrile chain of hope.

Eva was drifting when the telephone's ring ricocheted through the house like a fire alarm, jarring her upright. It was the graveyard hour between night and daybreak. Fatigue clouded her brain like valley fog. And then remembrance dropped like a sinker.

'I'm sorry,' said a low American voice. 'Have I woken you?'

'No, it's fine. Thank you for calling back.' She felt confused. Unsure what to say next. She hadn't thought this part over. 'I need your help. Something's happened. Something serious. I can't explain over the phone. I could come over. My car's broken down but maybe I can find a—'

'I'll come to you.'

As she made more coffee she tried to think. Wondering if he would help. He had been here longer and would know the workings of the island's terror machine better than her.

The *cafetière* had just finished hissing when he arrived. He hadn't slept and night had left its fingerprints beneath his eyes.

'Great,' he said. 'Coffee.' She carried out the pot and cups. 'So, what's up?'

Perhaps it was because he was tired, but she was glad of his American directness. His clean aim, straight as a Bowie knife. A local would have meandered around to the point on a river of tea and chatter.

She was wrung out by tension and lack of sleep. But she told him what she'd heard. And a bit about Navahiru. 'There is one more thing, though.' She ran over the brief outline of his earlier arrest. 'Do you think it's connected?'

'Yes. It sounds pretty likely.' He paused. 'It doesn't mean it is, though.' He had been in the island long enough to know that nothing was what it seemed.

He shot her a bullet-eyed look. He *was* tired. The whites of his eyes were pink.

'Was Navahiru your lover?'

The question startled her. 'Yes. Is. Not was. He isn't dead yet. Why? Does it matter?'

He stared at her, running his middle finger over his lip. 'To me? What do you think, Eva?' He seemed angry. Angrier than he had a right to be. But she needed help too badly to say so. 'But as to whether I'll help you find him or not? No, it doesn't matter.' He sighed. 'The only thing is, I've gotta get some sleep first.'

'When do you think you'll be ready?' She tried not to sound impatient, but anxiety was leaking from her pores. 'We don't have much time. We still don't know really where he is.'

'I know. I'll pick you up in three hours. Meantime, you'd better start working your contacts.'

It took a long time for the sun to sink on that day. Rain that might have cooled them had stopped just after dawn. For hours, as they waited outside police stations and military camps, they baked in the sun's glare. To Eva it seemed like a relentless eye, frying her nerves and roasting her despair until only a dull cinder remained.

They had spent hours calling army and Special Forces officers and trawling every likely police station in the city. They were much like each other: ochre buildings, yellow with graft, piss and fear. And in each, the answer was the same. At the paramilitary headquarters, hidden behind sandbags and razor wire, insolent sentries carrying Uzis, with the safety catches off, first barred them entry, then directed them to the press officer – a rat-faced colonel with red eyes, who offered them tea and lies.

Yes, of course he understood their concern. These were difficult times. Of course. He'd let them know if he heard anything. There was just one small thing (he looked suddenly coy): his son wanted to study in the US of A but there was the problem of sponsorship. Perhaps they could help?

As the sun climbed down the sky, Eva and Carl drove to the 'unofficial' army camp on a rocky promontory between the railway tracks and the sea, where they took prisoners blindfolded. Where the pounding surf and rattling trains drowned out the screams. Empty-eyed women huddled outside the gate, clutching black-and-white snapshots of their sons, missing or dead. They were villagers, but they knew about the camp hidden from the city. They came there every day carrying their small beads of hope, until time and official contempt and the mocking sea wore them away. All they wanted now was the body. Or something. A medallion, a scrap of sarong, some proof.

The photographs had an old-fashioned look, as if they had been taken just after the camera was invented, when a photograph was a formal occasion for which one dressed-up and posed. She supposed they had been taken by one of those antique cameras, with heavy glass plates and a black hood, that still plodded on like old warhorses in some villages. The boys in the pictures stared intently at the lens, like rabbits caught in headlights. Their shirts were crisp and white and their hair neatly oiled and combed. Eva knew they wouldn't look like that now.

The women had no words to give voice to their hearts, but the facts were heartrending and hideous enough. A son electrocuted by a transformer cable on election day, two years ago; a fourteen-year-old schoolboy taken from his bed at night; a boy last heard screaming in a police station. How to calculate pain and sorrow? In the unforgiving arithmetic of loss, her grief shrank. She was just a lover. They were the mothers of sons. She thought of Navahiru's mother. She hadn't wanted to call her for fear of embarrassing them both. Perhaps, like these women, she had put on white when he was taken. White, the colour of surrender and death.

Navahiru could have been there for all they knew. They couldn't even get past the gate.

'Come on, Eva, let's go.' He was angry and impatient with the women's stories. And a worm of uneasiness had entered his body. He thought for a moment of calling the Captain and then wished he hadn't. 'I think we both need a drink,' he said, instead.

She nodded. She felt limp, as if all that mattered had been taken away from her, leaving her empty even of thought.

They drove to the old hotel by the ocean and drank cold beer in silence, as a blood-red sun slipped from the sky. In the sea lanes, the lights of the container ships came on. An empty vessel with two yellow cranes, hovering like Big Birds above the deck's open mouth, steamed fast away from port. A frill of surf breaking on its bows glowed faintly in the dark.

'I don't want to go home tonight, Carl,' she said suddenly, no longer minding how he took it. She didn't want to be alone in the empty house.

'I've an idea: let's drive out of town. There's a small place on the beach there. It's only got one room, but it's clean and there are two beds.' He turned to her, his eyes suddenly soft. For the first time she noticed that they were as beautiful as his hands. 'I promise I won't do anything you don't want, Eva. We'll go as friends.'

'I'd like that,' she said. She owed him a lot. She could never have got through the last twelve hours without him. She took his hand. 'Thanks.'

Twenty

It must have been two in the morning when they reached the bridge across an estuary on the old coast road. The roads out of the city had been as empty as waiting coffins and Eva had dozed off, cramped against the window. The sudden braking woke her. A white mini-van, like those used by the coastal bus drivers, was parked diagonally across the bridge, blocking the way. Four young men, wearing shorts, T-shirts and rubber flip-flops, stood around the van smoking. One of them windmilled his arms at their car. They seemed to have broken down. Then she saw the AK47s slung casually across their shoulders in the manner of men used to wearing guns. They weren't the army, or the police or the rebels. She shook her head, wishing she were more awake.

One of the youths sauntered up to the car, registered Carl's white face and stopped. He stared at Eva intently, his gaze dropping down to her breasts. Then he thrust his head into the car. His features were contorted and his eyes were bloodshot. He was drunk. Ahead and behind them the road was empty and silent, hemmed in by jungle: a dark-green presence dripping malevolently into the night. Beneath the bridge, the brackish water sucked and gurgled: the tides would take whatever was offered them out to sea.

The youth hesitated, swaying slightly, his eyes still giving her the once-over. Behind him his companions were laughing and fingering their guns. After a long moment in which he seemed to be weighing something up, he waved them on. As they edged past, Eva shivered violently. Although it wasn't cold.

'What was that?' she asked, still fuzzy-headed.

'It was a death squad.'

Carl's face was set and taut. They sped on in silence. A few miles past the bridge he lit a cigarette. His hand was shaking.

'That van was unmarked. If we'd turned off the road there, you would have seen the skulls. Not all the bodies get washed out to sea.' He was angry again. She didn't know him well enough to know that he was not angry but afraid.

By the time they reached the one-room beach hut, the moon was high and the sky cold and clear. Fumbling for the long brass key in a hole in the wall, they forced open the damp-swollen door and flopped on to the hard coir mattresses. He lit two untipped Camels, handing her one. Then he told her about the bridge.

It had been operating for the last three months. Unofficially and only at night. The boys belonged to a local politician, one of several private militias helping the government to clean up the south. No one knew yet how many people had disappeared there. Maybe hundreds, maybe more. But it seemed the bridge was already notorious. Village boys had been taken from there and never seen again. There were stories of them being thrown alive from the cliff above.

'That's not the worst stuff, though,' Carl said finally.

'What is?'

'You don't want to know.'

'Tell me.'

He turned to her. In his eyes she saw something she knew well: an exhausted desperation that was like the pain of war. He stretched his hand out, stroking her cheek with long fingers. This time, she didn't stop him.

'Please. Tell me. I want to know.'

He turned on to his back and drew hard on his cigarette, staring at the ceiling. Beyond the slow clack of the ceiling fan, she could hear the sea dancing its quadrille with the shore. He raised himself on an elbow but wouldn't look at her.

'I interviewed the family of a boy, I think he was thirteen, from that village. They'd caught him putting up a poster. He didn't belong to the rebels. He'd just been buffaloed into helping them.'

He stubbed out the frayed end of his Camel and lay back, still not meeting her gaze.

'Then what?'

He lit another cigarette and, for a long while, he lay staring ahead of him, smoking. Beyond the shutters, a pre-dawn wind had come up from the ocean. Eva could hear it rustling the skirts of the palms. When he spoke again, his voice was hard.

'They took him to the centre of the village – this was in broad daylight – shoved a spike up his ass and out through his stomach. Then they stuck the poster on it and left him out there in the sun.' He paused. 'It took him maybe two days to die.'

'Jesus Christ.' Her thoughts flew to Navahiru and fled away again, not daring even to think.

Then she whispered, 'Oh God. That poor kid.'

For a while they lay on the twin beds in silence, not looking at each other. The image of the impaled boy slid off her brain, no matter how much she wrestled with it. She felt a tangle of emotions: guilt, horror and a helpless despair.

'Why didn't anyone save him?' she asked, finally. Suddenly she felt terribly tired.

'They were too frightened. Those goons run the south.' He lit another cigarette. 'Goddammit, Eva.'

Abruptly he got up, leaving her curled on her bed, and went to the door, wrenching it open. The ocean was still dark, lit only by its frill of phosphorescent surf. But to the east the sky was lightening. He looked at his watch. It was almost dawn. He stood for a moment breathing in the sticky salt breeze, then shut the door against the wind and grabbed a towel.

She listened to the water in the rusty little shower. She had been awake for more than twenty-four hours. She was exhausted and numb. Too much had happened since last night. She needed time alone to think about it. She had a presentiment of terrible sadness, more painful because she knew, in that pre-dawn moment of exhausted clarity, that she would lose not just someone but something she loved.

Carl came out of the shower, his hair slicked back, the towel round his waist. He slid down on the narrow bed beside her, wrapped his arms around her and softly kissed her neck. This time she didn't stop him. Then he swung away from her to his bed and pulled up the coarse white sheet. Beneath her sheet, she pulled off her trousers and shirt.

'Goodnight, Carl. And thank you.'

'Goodnight Eva,' he said.

It was almost noon when they woke and ran across the burning sand to the sun-bleached sea.

He could never remember whether it was then or later, but the image stayed with him for years, appearing when least expected, shattering his concentration. She was standing almost naked in the doorway of the hut, a thin cloth around her hips. Her body, silhouetted black against the harsh white glare. The curves and hollows of her face and figure had vanished. She looked like a faceless Nubian queen in the noon desert.

'Will you help me put the beds together?'

He could tell from her voice she had been crying, although he couldn't see her face.

A sky full of rain was falling down when they drove back the next evening, blurring the oncoming headlights and fogging the indistinct shapes ahead. They could have been lorries or bullock carts or even elephants, Eva couldn't tell. She turned the windscreen wipers on but it was like trying to wipe away a river with a metronome. She could have been driving underwater, without goggles, at night.

'Stop!' he screamed.

'What is it?' But she had seen the blurry shapes at the same moment he did. She feathered the brakes, trying not to skid.

'I wish you hadn't done that,' she said, as the car spun sideways to a halt. Blocking the road in front was a crowd of villagers, their sodden sarongs revealing stick-thin legs, soaked shirts held over their heads like white flags.

'It must be a wreck,' said Carl. 'Look at them. Even in the rain, they're out rubber-necking. Let's just get past. It's getting late.'

It was an accident. But whatever had caused it – a lorry, a car or, more likely, a speeding minibus – had driven straight on, probably afraid of being attacked by angry villagers. There were no vehicles and, it seemed, no bodies. Perhaps they had already been moved. A man was struggling towards them, rain pouring down his face and body, one arm waving. A crumpled nest of limbs lay in the crook of his other elbow. As he neared the car, she saw it was a sodden, bloody little girl, her arms and legs poking out at strange angles, like a smashed toy.

Eva rolled down the window.

'*Nona, apiwa ispiritalite arang yande pulwande?*' He wanted her to take them to hospital.

He was an old man. Probably the child's grandfather. The skin on his bony chest was like polished old leather. Despite the child, he had managed to place his palms together to his forehead, in the gesture of supplication.

'For Chrissakes, close the window,' yelled Carl. 'The rain's getting in.'

The old man stood with his palms pressed together. In his eyes was not just the tragedy of that moment, but of his whole life. It was a look that had crept into even young people's eyes, aging them before their time. She reached back to open the rear door.

'What are you doing?' Carl yelled. He slammed the door in the old man's face. 'We don't have time to take these people. I've got to get back and file.'

'File what?' said Eva. She reached back to re-open the door and gestured to the old man to get in. 'Nothing's happened since we've been away.'

'It's my car, for fuck's sake, and if I say we don't take them, they don't come.' He closed the door again.

Eva stared at him.

'In that case, I don't come, either.' She opened her door to get out.

'Oh for God's sake, Eva. It's raining. We'll take them, but it'd better not take long.'

Eva waited until the stink of sweat, sodden clothes and the child's blood filled the car. Then she turned the engine and slowly manoeuvred through the crowd. It parted gently, like a small wave. A few villagers placed their palms together in a gesture of thanks as she passed.

They drove in silence to the next town. When they reached the hospital, she rummaged in her bag and pressed a note into his hand. It wasn't much. Enough to treat the child. Before she could stop him, the old man had laid the bloody bundle on the car seat and bent to touch her feet.

'Please.' She grasped his shoulder. 'It's nothing. You'd better go, the child is losing blood.'

When they reached the straggle of shops, which trailed from the city suburbs like dirt from a broom, she glanced at Carl. He was still sulking, his face set away.

'So,' she said lightly, to break the ice, 'what's the story you want to write?'

For a moment he said nothing. He stretched his limbs and yawned, like a cat. 'Just a small piece about your lover's disappearance.'

She was stunned. The traffic had become heavier, the jumble of poor country traffic muscling for space. When the tight knot of metal and diesel fumes eased, she turned around. 'You must be joking.'

'Why not? It's a good story: "Tropical Island Society Boy Missing, Feared Dead".'

'He's not a "society boy", he's a law student from a not very well-off family. But even if he was, you can't write about it. Not now. There's nothing to write and it'd be a death sentence, a story in the international papers. They'd kill him immediately to cover it up. You know that.'

She drew into the kerb. He looked sheepish, like a child caught stealing chocolate, but she knew him too little to know whether this was cunning or remorse.

'You can't do it, Carl. Not now. It's too delicate. Even the wires haven't touched it. Later, maybe.'

'But there's no story later, if they release him.'

She was silent. Not wanting to tempt fate. But she thought: you know as well as I do, you'll get your story.

'OK, Eva. I'll drop it.' Words spat out like rivets, nailing the space between them. 'But I wouldn't do it for anyone else.'

'Thank you,' she said. But she didn't mean it. It was a hollow victory even if he wasn't lying. She thought back to the night before: the hard, red-brown body of the stranger beside her. It had been then, at the moment of betrayal, that she realized how much she missed him. A young sun with skin like velvet and an unfathomable smell. A violin and its case. Two bodies singing the same tune.

Part Two

Twenty-one

It was the season when hundreds of fruit bats screeched out of the great ficuses, in the brief moment before nightfall, throwing a black cloak over the dying day. Across the ocean, the wind was gathering speed, driving towering, moisture-laden clouds eastward. But the island lay brooding under a sodden blanket of heat, waiting for the rains. To Eva, the bat-blackened skies and oppressive, pre-monsoon weather seemed ill-omened. There was an uneasiness in the city, felt in the pit of the stomach. As if it lay over a noxious swamp. In the afternoons she sat under the fast-whirring fan, chilling the sweat on her body, trying to ignore the presentiment that terrible things were going to happen, things that couldn't be washed away by the rains.

It had been almost a month and still there was no news. A few days earlier Mohan had telephoned from out of town to say Navahiru's father had tapped all his earlier contacts, pleading for news of his son. But since his retirement the old lawyer was no longer as well connected: people had forgotten him. Only his former colleagues had rallied around. A demonstration of the capital's lawyers against the midnight killings – a thousand people a week were 'disappearing'; and two government ministers were known to have their own death squads – was planned for the weekend. Then the old man had a heart attack, leaving Navahiru's mother to nurse perhaps the only man left to her.

Eva had spent the last few weeks telephoning everyone she knew: her contacts in the government, at foreign embassies and, through journalist friends, two rebel leaders. For the last ten days or so she had stayed at home, not daring to go out in case a call came. But she felt trapped in the house, pacing from room to room like a rat in a wheel; watching the light move across the room, until it left the windows, bringing night and another bout of wrestling with insomnia that would exhaust her enough to fall into a short, frayed sleep by dawn.

Carl was out of town on a story, but when he telephoned her from somewhere in the interior, he had no news, either. Then the other telephone calls began.

They came around midnight. Shattering the sleeping air. She would run to the hallway, heart beating. Silence. Or heavy breathing. That first night, the telephone rang six times, every half hour. But always there was silence. Then the second night a voice spoke in English. The accent was heavy, thickened by alcohol. But it wasn't hard to understand what it said.

'Vonna puck, *poren* bitch?' the voice asked. 'Ve know vare you liw and we're gonna puck you.'

The slurred voice reached down her throat and coiled around her heart, crushing any laughter at his accent. Before Eva could speak, the caller hung up. She bolted the safety locks on the front door and the french windows to the small paved garden before going back to bed.

Half an hour later the telephone jangled again. She let it ring for ten minutes until it stopped. Then it rang again. This time she answered, praying it was not bad news.

'Who is it?' she asked immediately.

'You luw black cock, don't you, vhite bitch?' the voice said. There was a second of drunken laughter.

'Who is it?' Eva asked again, but she already guessed. Islanders were shocked enough by westerners' casual use of swear words. Even a nuisance caller wouldn't have used the words 'fuck' or 'bitch'.

'Vonna suck our cocks, vhite cunt? Vonna real good puck? Shure you do...'

She heard laughter in the background as the receiver went down.

The third night there were no calls. Just the restless silence of something expected that doesn't come. Then, just before dawn, she was woken by ringing. Half-groggy with sleep, thinking it might be Navahiru, she stumbled to the hallway. The voice this time spoke less heavily accented English and sounded sober.

'Stop looking for your bastard boyfriend, OK?' the caller said.

'Who are you? Where is he?' She was tense and scared. Even half-asleep, she could hear the menace in the voice. It rippled down the wires like a jolt of electricity.

'Don't make trouble,' the voice continued. 'We know who you are, we know where you live, we know you're alone. Next time we won't warn you.' The line went dead.

She stood by the telephone, fingers running through her hair. Carl was still out of town. It was too early to call anyone else. She went into the bedroom, grabbed a few clothes and her cameras, and threw them in an overnight bag.

The streetlight outside her house was still on, its yellow light dimmed dirty orange in the cold pre-dawn. She unlocked her front door soundlessly and tiptoed to the gate. The grey ribbon of road by the fairways was clear. She slipped out, praying her car would start. Thank God: the engine turned over on the second try.

By the end of the road she was in third gear. She could hear the motor straining, the old car clattering like rocks in a box. Pushing it as fast as it would go, she drove through the silent city, one eye on her rear-view mirror. An early-morning rubbish truck rattled down an avenue and an empty red-and-yellow three-wheeler. But the road behind flapped empty in the wind. When she reached the seashore, she turned south.

There were three checkpoints out of the city. At each, she held her breath. But the soldiers on duty were half-asleep and she drove through. When she reached the gaudy Buddha at the city's edge, she relaxed, feeling the sea's salty fingers in her hair.

Driving, she let herself be distracted by small things: the varying shades of green in the foliage, the light through the palms striping the road, an old woman with a young girl's body, washing at a well. On any other day she would have stopped to take pictures. But this morning she was running and, as she ran, she searched only for life.

As if on cue, a mongoose trotted across the road, its pointed snout, round brown eyes and twitching whiskers scenting out something in the undergrowth. The inquisitive creature was supposed to be a sign of luck. She couldn't remember where. Perhaps in the mountain country to the north where she had seen a fight between a mongoose and a cobra. It was true what they said: the mammal and the reptile were almost evenly matched. Everyone wanted the mongoose to win and it did, after a virtuoso display of agility and cunning, with a deadly snap from its sharp little teeth. Perhaps the animal carried its own luck. People here seemed to have lost whatever made luck. It was as if the whole island, good and bad alike, had been caught in a net of apathy and despair.

The road turned inland and, as she crossed an invisible line in the paddy fields, she once again experienced the sensation of magic, a barely perceptible change in the molecules of the air. Entering the boundaries of Lorne was like taking a hallucinogenic drug, stepping through the doors of perception into another world.

There were a small number of places on earth like this, she thought. Perhaps, as the villagers believed, they were the abode of benign spirits. Perhaps the thirty billion deities believed to inhabit every rock, tree and river had been so pleased with Caspar's care that they had blessed him and his kingdom for ever. Whatever it was, she felt grateful for its protection. Here, she believed nothing could touch her.

She turned down the driveway of royal palms and into the gravel circle. It was just after seven and the blue-and-white front door was locked. She walked through the gate in the hedge into the garden. Thin mist hung like muslin over the lower terraces and the lawn. The air smelled of dew and fresh flowers. She walked across to the pergola, leaving a line of footprints in the grass, and perched on the low wall, waiting for someone to appear.

The formality of the garden was comforting, as if a Prospero had tamed the wilder spirits and demons, bestowing order on nature's chaos. Caspar's chair, with its rumpled white cushion waited, arms outstretched to greet him. Empty, the simplicity of the verandah revealed itself. The juxtaposition of closed and open space, the few beautiful objects the blind artist had chosen: a headless, Gandhara torso mounted on a wall; a bronze Don Quixote; a Chinese urn. On impulse she moved to the side verandah, where a bench hid against the wall of the house and where she could think about the last twenty-four hours undisturbed.

The telephone men tramped into her brain. Bloated with booze, rubbery lips stretched over *betel*-stained teeth, crushing the morning under steel-capped boots. She was sure now that they were policemen or death squad thugs, punch-drunk on murder. The army still had too much ramrod in its backbone, too much Sandhurst and West Point pressed into its officers' uniforms to make calls like that.

The sour smell of stale alcohol and fear barged into the garden, bullying aside the timorous scent of dew. They would think as little of raping or injuring her as of stubbing out a cigarette on the groin of a prisoner. There would be consequences to harming a foreign photographer. But too late. Still, the calls could mean Navahiru was alive: a coarse attempt to stop enquiries.

A flame of hope flickered. And died. She knew just as well that they could mean the opposite. That he could be dead. Or worse. The thought fell into her stomach like a stone and stayed there. She dared not lift it, fearing what lay beneath. She knew some of the means they had devised to penetrate not just a man's flesh, but his spirit and soul. That was why she had stopped thinking about Navahiru the day Mohan called her. Her imagination had simply reared, flailing its hooves at the edge of the abyss.

And then there was Carl. She felt guilty, so she blamed him. But still she knew that she would continue their affair. That she wanted him far more than she ever had Navahiru. She felt ashamed. And hated him for that, too. She took a few deep breaths, as if to blow away the emotional dust-storm in her head.

She ticked off Carl's faults. He was angry, insecure and paranoid. He cared too much about things that meant little to her: money, materialism, status. He wasn't her type. Most of all, beneath the surface she had seen the wasteland of the American soul: a windswept highway of neon motels, mail-order guns, popcorn hopes and broken dollar dreams. Its desolation scared her. But it was hopeless: she knew already that she was being carried out to sea on a current. That the very things that repelled her about him attracted her helplessly. She felt as immobilized by her own perversity as a fledgling frozen in a cobra's stare.

'Shanta!' The familiar boom from the recesses of the house broke into her thoughts. She rose and walked around to the hallway to catch the boy, so he could tell Caspar she had come.

They drank tea beneath the pergola – his in a plastic toddler-feeder with a spout, hers in a porcelain cup – and she told him everything: Navahiru's disappearance, the barren weeks of searching, the telephone calls.

'So that's really why I came,' she said. 'I'm sorry. I should have rung, but it was so early when I left the city.'

'Please. There's no question. Of course you should have come.'

He walked his fingers over his scalp, frowning.

'Damn these ailments of mine. If only I was well, I'd take care

146

of the lot of them for you. Still, there must be something we can do about that boy...'

He fell silent, in thought.

'Shanta! Call Mahinda, please.'

The slap of bare feet. Mahinda appeared from the passage, his hair wet from a bath. He listened as Caspar spoke, repeating what she had told him, concern rumpling his features. In that tongue the story had a cadence, a lilt it lacked in English. Perhaps this language, which could turn murder into music, was the secret of the island's perplexing amnesia. Its impermeable denial of the horrors unfolding before its eyes.

'Yes.' He was responding to Caspar's last words, an instruction.

'What did you ask him?' she enquired, after he had melted into the house.

'I have an idea. It's a long shot, but worth trying. You remember those boys who came here once? Mahinda knows their leaders. I've asked him to make enquiries. I have my own contacts too in the police and army. I'll see what I can find out for you. Perhaps we can still...' He took her hand, sensing her distress. 'I'm sorry. You must be distraught.'

Eva's face twisted, wrestling emotions. The sudden rush of love from this old man, whom she loved more freely than her own father, released a pressure guage shut all week. She burst into tears.

'I'm sorry,' she mumbled, dabbing her eyes with her shirt.

'Please. Cry. I quite often cry myself.' He laughed and his feeble admission made her smile.

'It's been a tense few weeks.'

'Yes, I know. But now you're here. And as soon as it starts raining, feel free to take a rain bath. That's my remedy.'

'Will you take one with me?' They shared a passion for bathing in the monsoon rain, for the sensuality of being immersed in an element. It was why Lorne had so many open-air bathrooms: for the feel of water and air on naked skin.

'I wish I could. But I'm stuck in this chair. It's one of the pleasures no longer available to me, I'm sad to say.'

His casual reference to his condition shook her. She felt helpless to help Navahiru, but Caspar she could care for. He was here, beside her, alive. 'I'm so sorry. I haven't asked you anything about yourself. How have you been?'

He smiled. '"*Quand le corps est triste, le coeur languit.*" Stop worrying about me. Go unpack and take that shower.'

As he watched her walk across the grass, a shadow crossed his face.

Twenty-two

A chameleon sat on the window-sill of her room, blinking. She turned on the fan, pulled out a book and tried to read but her mind was still racing. 'Thought is the enemy of perfection.' She read the line three times, unable to concentrate. The lizard flicked out its pink tongue, caught an invisible insect and gulped. Under the slow flop-flop of the ceiling fan her thoughts settled. Tears rose in her chest like waves, crested in her throat and leaked from her eyes, quenching the fire in her brain. She thought idly of the rain and her eyelids closed: swollen, heavy, like an afternoon lizard's.

She was lying on the bottom of the ocean in a glass-walled room watching tropical fish swim past. It was strange to be in an aquarium with the fish outside. Dreamer's logic told her it was to stop them getting wet. The fish looked happy, as if painted by talented children. Her attention had fastened on a pair of blue and yellow angelfish nibbling at a sponge, when six moray eels, with thick serpentine bodies, swam towards her glass. As they closed on the window she saw that they had men's faces: blubbery, brown, with bloodshot eyes, thick lips and *betel*-stained teeth.

The eel-men pushed against the wall, licking it with fat, slug tongues. Smears of grey saliva dribbled down the glass. The sea around them turned black and turbulent and began heaving against her tank. The luminous fish had gone. There were dozens of eel-men now, crowding the tank like an angry mob, banging against the glass with their bulbous heads, tongues wagging hideously. She looked up. In the corner, where one glass plate joined another, a thread of water was leaking in. She hoped the eel-men wouldn't see it and re-double their attack; she could already feel the fragile structure rocking. At any moment she believed the glass would break and they would overwhelm her, if she didn't drown first. It had become very cold. Panic rose to her throat.

The scene changed once more. The eel-men vanished. She no longer felt afraid. She was floating through the glass ceiling. Up, up, up. Into a blue sea lit by sunlight. A weight, not heavy not light, lay across her breast. She felt the tickle of bristle against her cheek, and fingers running through her hair, spreading it like seaweed. She smelled skin warmed by the sun, comforting her like hot toast. When she opened her eyes, she was smiling.

It was late afternoon. Gold light streamed in through open shutters. The chameleon had left.

He was lying beside her, one finger tracing a line down her cheek.

'How did you find me?'

They were driving to a bay south of Caspar's house.

'Easy,' he said. He was grinning. 'I called your house and your maid told me. You'd left her a note. I was close by so I came.' He glanced at her. 'You don't mind do you?'

She touched his neck. 'No, I don't. I'm glad. I was having a day-mare.' She *was* glad to see him.

'Is that what they call them? It looked pretty good to me.'

She told him about the calls. She was laughing. Driving to the beach on a sunny afternoon, the wind ruffling her hair, the thick English, sounded funny. She was still young and lucky enough to think death and disaster happened only to other people. Not her.

Not after she had escaped so much else. But he looked worried. 'Eva, this is heavy shit. Those guys aren't joking. You'd better come stay at my place for a while.'

'And what about when you're away?' She was stalling.

'Come with me, we can work together. Or stay. I've got a watcher. You don't have anyone at your place.'

'Toots?' She giggled. He was half the size of Carl.

He smiled. 'He's better than nothing. Look, Eva, it's just an idea.'

She was quiet. She thought of his house: masculine, empty, no books. And she thought of what he would want in return. Not just sex, but her. What perhaps she wanted – and feared to want – too. Lorne was lovely, a secret garden, an enchantment. It was everything his house was not. But it was impractical. Another person would strain the household and Caspar would never allow her to pay for herself. It was isolated and it would be difficult to work from there, even without inconveniencing everybody. She needed time to think.

'Look at the colour of the water.' The sea never lost its power to amaze her. Through the fringe of palms, it was a deep madonna blue, sprinkled with diamonds of late-afternoon sun. The beach, the ocean, the mangroves, the palms all glowing in the unearthly colours of the dying day.

'Do you think it's OK to swim?' With the eye of a practised swimmer, she had detected from the headland that the sea, so beautiful, so innocent from afar, was torn by cross-currents: the threat hidden in the island's waters, the venom in its lovely veins.

'Sure,' he said. He was still driving and hadn't really looked.

The sun was dipping towards the horizon, blinding them as they ran into water soft as a salty lullaby. They rolled and played, dipping beneath the surf like seals, mesmerized by the great ball of the sinking sun and its fiery runner laid across the ocean, calling

151

them to the edge of the world. For a long time they played and chatted, treading water, careful not to go beyond the farthest line of surf.

The air was becoming chilly, and she was tired, when they decided to swim in.

She swam strong and hard for some minutes, before she saw that she was getting nowhere. The shore was still as far away as it had been. She was exhausted and a current was tugging at her legs. On the beach two German tourists on lilos were watching the sunset. They saw the swimmers and waved gaily. She could feel herself being pulled out.

'I think I'm in trouble,' she called to Carl.

She looked at his face. He was stronger than her and he was in trouble, too.

Two things happened at that instant. A wave crashed on to her and she panicked. Her lungs filled with water. She felt the power-ful rip dragging her down and out. She surfaced. And went under again.

Suddenly she felt her head being lifted to the surface. Carl had got to her, somehow. She looked at the setting sun, the beach, the tourists. And suddenly, the banality of death in shallow water on a glorious evening struck her like a cheap deal.

'Turn on your back, I'm holding you,' he yelled. 'Relax. Try to breathe. When a wave comes, lift your head.'

Later, she marvelled that he had done it. Perhaps the same thought that made her angry had made him angry, too. But he got them both in.

They collapsed on the beach. Her lungs full of water and her head full of light. When he recovered his breath, he pumped her ribcage. Water spewed out. She coughed and then she was laughing.

'You saved my life,' she croaked.

He carried her up the beach to a cabana and laid her, like a wounded child, on the bed.

She put her arms around his neck. 'Thank you. Thank you. You saved my life back there. I don't know what to say…'

He silenced her with his mouth.

She kissed him back, deeply, passionately this time.

He moved down her body, kissing her neck, her breasts, her navel. When her reached her small, cropped vee of hair, he looked up.

'You smell terrible.'

She checked.

'You're right,' she said, sniffing. 'I wonder why? It must be a reaction with the seawater. Or panic, adrenalin.'

She went into the tiny bathroom to wash, lathering herself inside and out, until she smelled of nothing but fresh rose skin and soap.

'Try now,' she said.

She tasted like no woman he had ever been with. Exquisite. Like wild fruit in a faint salt-breeze.

They lay smoking and listening to the rhythmic ocean through the palms. Gentle, tamed, on its best behaviour. Every hour or so the small coast train clattered by with a blast from its whistle. 'Good day, good day, good day,' the wheels called as they approached. 'Goodbye, goodbye, goodbye,' they called back as they rattled south.

Twenty-three

When they returned, there was a stack of messages beside his telephone: small reproaches for being away. So much had happened, so much was happening, that Navahiru's disappearance risked being lost in the clamour. The war, which had re-opened like a wound refusing to heal, was becoming nasty. As nasty as the death in the south. Fifty Muslims had been hacked to death with machetes while praying; four fishing *valaams* had been blown up off the same coast in a fiery rain of fish and body parts; and thousands of refugees were fleeing to makeshift camps, trailing their smells of poverty and fear. That was just in the north-east. In one of those errors of judgement that can change fate, rebels in the south had threatened the army's families, inflaming the troops and causing a secondary war by poster: 'One of ours for twelve of yours' the army's read. Promotions were being offered for body-bags; body-bags were being used to settle neighbourhood scores; and at crossroads, the tell-tale inner rings of tyres snaked around the embers of the dead. It was like being caught up in a maelstrom, a foul wind from hell.

Carl's paper wanted him to go east to report on the Muslims' massacre.

'Why don't you come with me? It'll be good working together.'

But Eva wasn't sure. Navahiru's fate still spun on a thread and telephones in the east were cut. She didn't want to be out of reach. 'Next time. When all this is over, one way or another.'

He swivelled his chair, finger between his lips, thinking. 'What will you do? I'll be quick. Two or three days. But I think you should stay here. Mary'll look after you.'

Eva smiled. 'I'll be OK at home. I've been away a few days. They've probably lost interest.'

He leaned forward on the desk, chin in his hand, looking at her. She stood against the wall like a boy; careless, confident. His eyes shadowed. 'Eva, I don't think it's a good idea. Especially not with me out of town. I won't be long, I promise. But stay here. Please.'

She looked at him. His eyes had surprised her. 'You really care about me, don't you?'

He smiled, running his middle finger between his lips, gazing at her. 'Yes,' he said slowly, as if still considering it. 'Yes. I guess I do.'

She came around to his side of the desk and stood between his legs, running her fingers through his hair. Then she bent down and kissed him very softly.

'Don't worry about me. I'll be all right. Really.'

She watched him as he packed, grabbed a few notebooks and a camera bag, and yelled instructions to Mary. The black gates swung open and he drove out, watching her in his rear-view mirror. Tendrils of hair blew around her face, her skin glowed and there was a look in her eyes that he recognized. He smiled to himself, like a deep-sea fisherman at the tug of a big fish. Wondering how long she'd play him, how long it would take to reel her in.

She heard it ring out in the silence before dawn. It snapped her awake: the unmistakable rapport of a pistol, from the golf course. She sprang up, pulled on her jeans and was at the front door when she stopped. What was she doing? She tiptoed to the window and peeped through the *tats*. Mist shrouded the fairways. Only the tops of the flame and cotton trees and a few ghostly markers floated, disembodied. She hesitated, then quietly unbolted the front door and eased open the latch. There was an unmarked jeep in the road by the twelfth hole.

She pulled the door gently to, ran back into her room for the Leica and a 90 lens, and slipped out. She rarely used the camera, except when she needed to be very quiet. She slid down beside the doorway until she was hidden from the road by a jasmine bush and waited. A faint yellow appeared in the sky to the east. Slowly the clouds turned light pink and then deep rose. The dawn ballerinas coming on stage. She was shivering slightly.

At last four men in khaki appeared from the mist, carrying something heavy towards the jeep. It was a man. His head had fallen away from her, but even from a distance she knew, from the marionette limbs, that he was dead. Quickly, she shot off some film, trying to keep her hands from shaking.

One of the men turned to look back down the road. His gaze seeming to pause on her gateway. She held her breath. Wondering if he'd heard her. Insects rustled in the silence. Then he jumped into the jeep and the diesel engine coughed over, shattering the morning. She shot on, until they were out of sight. Then very slowly, she stood up, still wary, watching the grey tarmac snake into the mouth of the dawn.

There were only three other houses in her street, but it seemed no one else had heard the gunshot. The road was still and the houses slept, their nightcaps pulled down. She eased open the gate and walked to where the jeep had been, glanced quickly around and jumped the culvert on to the green.

The twelfth hole was a prayer mat of velvet turf, a few metres from the road, marked by a flag. But for a few patches of darker green where the dew had been disturbed, death had left no fingerprints; any blood had been swallowed by the wet earth. The course was empty at that hour and still as a cathedral. Above the silver fairways the great trees rose, as silent and indifferent as they had been since the day they were born. Eva took some more pictures but there was nothing to see. She wasn't sure what she had expected to find.

It was an execution. That much was obvious. Nothing else. Who it was and why it had been done here instead of at one of the killing grounds outside the city, she had no idea. She flipped through the images, pausing at the frame of the policeman looking at her door. Wondering if it was just chance, if she was reading too much into it.

The thought she had been avoiding fell into her like a stone. She told herself she would have recognized him. The shape of his body. The colour of his skin. A spark. Something. Or would she? She had seen enough dead bodies. They looked no more like the living than their clothes.

She glanced at her watch. It was five-thirty. Too early to start making calls. She walked into the kitchen, filled the *cafetière* and began peeling mangoes, busying herself with small things. She surprised herself again by wishing Carl had stayed.

Twenty-four

It was quarter to eight and the sun was hot as dragon's breath by the time Sergeant Piyadasa let himself back into his office. The heat toasted his eyeballs and fried his brain. It had been another all-nighter. Not for the first time he asked himself why they didn't recruit more men: it wasn't as if there weren't enough loafers picking their noses and scratching their balls. He sat down heavily on his chair and rested his elbows on the desk, feeling like a blazing building that had just collapsed.

He pulled out the .45 Magnum (his proudest possession, bought on expenses on a visit to the US of A) and the set of keys bulging his right and left trouser pockets, slapped them on the desk and pressed the small steel button bell bolted on to the desk top, wincing at its piercing *dring-dring*. A nice cup of *kiri thay* was what he needed now. Then he slumped back, head in his hands, letting his bruised-black eyelids sink mercifully over his eyeballs. He looked like a Giant Panda masquerading as a policeman taking a nap.

'Yessir!' The brisk bark of Constable Somapala startled him awake from Lalitha's sweaty embrace. Instead of her nylon nightie, his wife had, for some reason, squeezed herself into a white boob tube and tight white pants. His hands were clutching the sturdy love-handles around what used to be her waist.

'Wazzamazza?' he asked bleary-eyed. Then he remembered. *'Thay mata gennda. Ickmanta.* Sharpish!'

When Constable Somapala had saluted and left to order tea from the *peon*, Piyadasa glanced at the wall clock. He'd been asleep for two minutes. He stared down at his favourite *pilum* star, her lips eternally pouting up at him. He was too tired this morning to leer back, but he had to admit she looked a helluva lot better in that white outfit than his wife. Arranged marriages, he sighed to himself, wondering what had happened to the curvaceous nymphet of their wedding night. The memory aroused him slightly, reminding him that he should finish up and get home. He wondered if he could persuade her into a quickie later. After he'd had breakfast and a few hours' sleep.

Constable Somapala had personally supervised the production of tea, taking care to ensure that the *peon* mixed enough milk (half a cup) and sugar (four spoons) to form a sticky soup. He knew what his boss was like when he was tired. It wasn't worth taking any risks, he thought, watching the old man pour the steamy liquid back and forth between two tin jugs, making it froth like cappuccino.

Good fellow, thought Sergeant Piyadasa, as he sucked at the scalding brew before the bubbles settled into a nasty brown skin. With the smallest key, he unlocked his bottom drawer, took out the White Book and opened it. Now where was that name and when had he been brought in here? He flipped through the pages, trying to focus his tired eyes on the blurring calligraphy. A-ha. Here it was. A day ago. Brought from that Special Ops army camp they were all so tight-lipped about, he now remembered. Taking a red ballpoint pen from the holder on his desk, he carefully drew a line through it. Present and Absent. Registered and Erased. Job entered, Done, Finished. With the satisfaction of the born bureaucrat, he snapped the register shut.

If only it were that easy, he thought in an unfamiliar moment of introspection, wondering why real life had to be so messy. He shared with his sister a certain obsessive fastidiousness, inherited from their mother, in such matters as tea drinking and office paperwork.

He thought back to the events of the last twelve hours and grimaced. *Annay*, that one had been a struggle. What was it about these fellows that made them feel they had to give you some mumbo-jumbo lecture even after you'd ripped them a new arse-hole? I should be lecturing them, he thought. Still, he had to admire his guts. While they'd been shivering their balls off on that bloody golf course, he'd kept his dignity even if he couldn't walk. None of that whining and clinging to their feet. No. That one was fearless all right. Right till the end.

If he'd been more poetic, he might have said that he'd looked destiny straight in the eye. But Sergeant Piyadasa didn't think like that.

Tired out by the effort of so much thought that late in his working day, he reached down, opened his bottom drawer, chucked in the ledger and locked it shut.

'Somapala,' he yelled, knowing the fellow would be waiting outside his door for orders. (He must change that desk bell, it was getting on his nerves.) 'Somapala,' he repeated when a second later the constable was standing to attention at his desk, 'I'm off for the rest of the day. Don't call me unless it's urgent. I mean really urgent. No big shots under a cabinet minister, or the Chief. Understood?'

'Yessir!' The wiry little constable snapped back to attention. 'Understood.'

At that moment the two-way radio hanging from his belt crackled to life. Piyadasa winced at the static, fiddling with the volume. 'Yessir.' He groaned inwardly. Why did the Chief have to call him now? 'Yessir. I'm off now, though, sir.' He hoped the big boss wouldn't say it was urgent. 'No, sir, not long, sir. Yessir. I'll get round there with the boys tonight, if that's all right with you, sir. Sure, sir. Best time, sir. Yessir.' The crackling stopped. Bloody nuisance, he thought, firmly switching the radio off.

Outside the station a staff car was waiting to take him home, its engine throbbing. The white Honda Civic was on loan, today's baksheesh from the big-wigs higher up for a job well done. A promotion was in the offing, he was certain. As he passed the tyre shops, now open for business, Sergeant Piyadasa gave a tired smile.

Twenty-five

'Do you see that tower?' They were lying by the old hotel swim-ming pool, their chatter syncopating with the longer rhythm of the surf. She had driven here on impulse that morning, want-ing to escape her thoughts, to clear her head by swimming hard in salt water. She had running-dived into the pool as if saving her-self from drowning. A bronze streak slicing into the blue. When she emerged, dripping, into the sunlight, she saw Marianne, a friend from a Scandinavian mission, sunbathing. Her honey skin radiated with the glow of pregnancy. A madonna in a mauve bikini.

She turned to where Marianne was pointing. A stained, four-storey concrete structure rose beyond the high wall, separating the hotel from the city's shabby backside.

'Sure,' said Eva. It was part of the backdrop of the pool: the tower behind the army camp she and Carl had visited, visible only from the beach or the sea.

'Take a good look at it,' said Marianne.

It looked like any such structure in the city-centre. Pockmarked, stained with rust, built for some long-expired purpose. An ocean look-out perhaps, or a Port Authority building, abandoned to rats, tramps and drunks.

'I give up.'

'Look at the windows.'

Eva saw it now. She turned to her friend for confirmation. 'They're bricked up.'

'Recently,' said Marianne. She reached into her beach bag and took out a large manila envelope. 'Now take a look at this. I got it this morning.'

Eva pulled out a slab of white paper. On the title page in bold type were the words 'The Silent Scream: Torture in Custody', and beneath it the name of a human rights organization that had been banned from the island. She flipped through it quickly. The report consisted mainly of clandestine interviews with survivors.

'How did you get hold of this?'

'It doesn't matter. I got sent it,' said Marianne. 'Now look at the page I've marked.'

Eva turned to it, reading the passage that had been highlighted:

'...Many of the interviewees detained in the city reported hearing sounds of trains and surf breaking. Because they were blindfolded, they did not know where they were being held. But the location has now been identified as a tower behind an army camp bordering the Orient Hotel.'

She put the pages down and stared at the tower and the low incline behind it. Surf was pounding on the rocks and the break-waters. She looked in the other direction, the side that faced the city. There were railway tracks: the beginning of the coastal line going south.

'I'd heard about this. But just rumours...'

She turned back to the page, skipping down until she saw a second marked passage. It was part of an interview:

```
...At the site, Sumana says he was stripped naked and had
a shopping bag containing petrol and chilli powder pulled
over his head and tied to his neck. He was then beaten
with PVC pipes filled with concrete.
```

```
When he refused to confess, his hands were tied behind
his back and he was hung from a hook on the ceiling by a
nylon rope tied to his wrists. He was blindfolded again
and electricity was...
```

Her eyes recoiled from the page as if she had been struck. She glanced quickly down once more. Past the words 'Electric drill. Heels. Pliers. And penis.'

At the bottom of the page, Marianne had highlighted the last few words of a final sentence: 'Despite repeated representations by foreign embassies and human rights organizations, the tower, which is now known to be a security forces "safe house", is still in use.'

She looked at herself and Marianne: two women in bikinis surrounded by sunbathing clutter. At the far end of the blue-glass pool, a white-liveried waiter hovered, silent as a prayer. The pale down on her friend's flawless limbs glimmered in the sunlight. She smelled of motherhood, pine forests and fresh-water fjords. She looked back at the filthy tower and turned again to Marianne. Green eyes gazing into blue. The Swedish woman raised an eyebrow.

'Nice, isn't it?'

Eva looked down at the dossier in her hand. 'Can I copy this?'

'No, but you can make notes now, if you like.'

She fished in her bag for a pen and notebook and began speed-reading; scribbling down names, places, methods. Marianne's highlighted passages maked her task easier; but she read it all in case there were details she had missed. When she had finished, she lay back silent, staring at nothing.

She was unable, then, to imagine terror, shame, loss; to smell sweat, blood, fear and excrement. Or to think beyond it.

'There's stuff that isn't in there. I heard about it yesterday.'

'What's that?' asked Eva. Her curiosity had curled up and died. She wanted to run. From there, from the island.

'They shove barbed wire in a plastic tube up their anuses. They pull out the plastic. And then the wire.'

'Christ.'

'The other one is petrol enemas,' Marianne went on. 'They give them a petrol enema and then light a match in their mouths. They've been doing that in the police stations in the hills and down south.'

Eva sat up. Navahiru. Battered and bleeding, curled naked like a foetus in his own shit. She felt like vomiting. A gale was blowing through her head.

'Are you OK?'

'I'm sorry, Marianne. I've got to go.' She swung off the long chair, gathered her things and bent forward to kiss her friend. 'Thank you for letting me see that. I'm really grateful.'

She could barely remember leaving the hotel or getting into her car. When she finally came to, it was late afternoon. She had left the city's boundaries and was on the road leading into the southern hills. She thought of driving on into one of the villages to give faces to the faceless. To know that there were still human beings who wept, feared and loved. She refused to think of Navahiru. But suddenly she remembered the shooting that morning. She had forgotten to ask Marianne.

She stopped the car at a telephone kiosk and began dialling. On the third try she got through to a friend at a local news agency. She had tried him once, earlier in the day, but he had no news.

'It's on the wire,' he said.

'What is?'

'The thing you were asking me about this morning. It says it was an "encounter", though.'

'It wasn't,' said Eva. 'Unless it's another one. Just tell me who it is and where they're saying it happened.'

'I can't. Not over the telephone.'

'For heaven's sake, you've just said it's on the wire.' The islanders' paranoia about telephones was exasperating.

'Yes. But they go out abroad. If you come round I can show you, but I'm in a rush.' He hung up before she could say anything.

There was nothing for it. Wearily, she turned her car around and headed back into town, concentrating on the road, letting the wind still-birth her thoughts.

It was dark when she reached the agency's office on the third floor of a tower block in the city centre. She had been caught in traffic. Her head ached with exhaust fumes, blaring horns and grime. She pushed open the heavy glass door. A blast of arctic air-conditioning hit her, freezing the sweat on her body. The place smelled of new plastic and controlled industriousness. She felt like a tramp. Her friend was at a computer screen in a corner. He looked up when she came in.

'Here.' He handed her a sheet of wire copy. 'That's all there is, so far.'

She read the headline: 'Rebel Leader Shot Dead in Police Encounter.' Relief flooded over her, tinged faintly with foreboding:

```
Rukman Weerasinghe, fugitive leader of the Marxist group
waging a 'People's War' against the island's government,
was shot dead in a police 'encounter' in the capital this
morning.

   Weerasinghe, founder and leader of the Janatha Muksha
Peramuna (JMP), who has eluded government forces
for seven years, had been leading police to a rebel
safe-house in a residential neighbourhood of the capital,
when insurgents opened fire from the grounds.

   Describing yesterday's shooting as 'unfortunate', a
senior police officer said: 'Mr Weerasinghe was acciden-
tally caught in the crossfire. We deeply regret this
incident.'
```

Four days earlier, Special Operations forces, acting
on a tip-off, had surrounded the isolated tea estate
bungalow in the southern highlands, where Weerasinghe
was hiding with his family, and brought him to the
capital for interrogation.

Police sources close to the operation, code-named 'Red
Flag', said that the rebel leader 'surrendered without a
fight'. His wife and children are believed to be in police
custody pending their likely release.

Police say no government forces were injured in the
shoot-out. Rebel deaths and injuries are 'unknown'.

International human rights groups today questioned the
circumstances of Weerasinghe's death and called for an
end to 'encounter killings' and 'the continued existence
of secret interrogation and torture camps'.

But within the island, the rebel chief's capture
was hailed as a coup for the government. His earlier,
televised confession, which will be broadcast island-wide
tomorrow, was attended by the Defence Minister, the
Commander-in-Chief of the Army and...

The story ended with a few nondescript biographical details: studied at Moscow's Patrice Lumumba University; regarded by many as a popular and credible nationalist leader; led an aborted coup in 1972; revived the movement four years earlier; and so on.

For no particular reason, one small detail of the story struck Eva. It was two o'clock in the afternoon and he had been shaving when his house was surrounded. Odd time to shave, she thought. She wondered idly if he had just made love to his wife. She handed the sheet of paper back.

'I'd better go.' It was too late for pictures, but she would have to call her agency anyway. She wanted to do something about the torture tower as well. But on both stories, she would have to be careful.

'By the way, what was that you said about it not being an encounter?' Her friend was pretending to be casual.

'Oh, did I say that?' she lied. 'I'm sorry, I must have muddled it up with something else.'

At the door she turned back. 'Thanks for letting me see it. I'll call you for the latest, if that's all right?'

'Sure.'

On the drive home, she thought about the story; how she could photograph it beyond the standard pictures that the wires would already have sent out. And then she thought about him. The fear that had been lurking in a crevice of her heart all day rose up to greet her.

How much time did he – did they – have left? And would this new twist release him into her arms, or the grave?

Twenty-six

Sergeant Piyadasa awoke in a sweat with his sleeping sarong bunched into a sodden nappy. He glanced at his watch. It was three o'clock and a fat beam of sunlight was focusing all its energy on him: Lalitha had forgotten to close his curtains. He had slept for six hours but it might have been six minutes he felt so washed-up. On the window-sill, an overturned blue-bottle buzzed, chain-sawing through his nerves.

'Lalitha!' He listened to his own yell echo through the house. He could hear her, clattering away in the kitchen; or perhaps it was the boy. He yelled again. There was silence. Must be napping in their son's old bedroom, whence she had decamped after his last drunken bout. He thought of those opulent limbs glistening with sweat, the pillowy stomach and melon breasts ripening in the soft bed of her blouse. A small tremor of lust nudged at his groin. It had been six weeks now. If things went on like this, he would have to talk her into getting a maidservant. Some ripe young village mango. Fresh and juicy.

These musings woke him up a bit. He raised himself up on one arm: a sea lion rising to a mating call. He reached out a paw, swatted the bluebottle and tugged shut the blue Dralon curtains. 'Gunadasa!' The clattering in the kitchen stopped. 'GUNADASA!'

He heard feet padding down the corridor and a timid knock. 'Bring tea,' he grunted through the closed door. 'Fast!' The padding receded. He hauled himself off the bed and, with his sarong clutched loosely in one hand, lumbered into the bathroom and turned on the shower. It wasn't going to be easy, he told himself, thinking of tonight's operation, as the shower head above him spluttered and farted. It was a bloody messy business all round. Of course the boys would be up for it: nose-picking ball-scratchers. But he would have to get them tanked up, and if things went wrong, which they always did, he knew who would get the blame. He might even lose his promotion. Bloody Chief and his damn fool schemes. He wished he could think of some way of getting out of it. Wasn't there another station he could pass the buck to? He would have to get on the phones double-quick.

He dried himself, wrapped the towel around his waist and went back into the bedroom, where his tea was waiting. To his disgust, he saw that it had already grown a fine brown skin. With surprising delicacy, he plucked off the greasy film and flicked it into the wastepaper basket. Not for the first time, he wondered what his wife was doing sleeping and when she would stop sulking. At least she knew not to bring him tea before time.

'GUNADASA!' The roar resounded through the house. In the kitchen, the reedy young houseboy (who, despite having been with the Piyadasas since childhood and thus being considered one of the family, lived in mortal terror of Sergeant Piyadasa), almost dropped the rice platter that he had been absent-mindedly soaping. But in the spare room, Lalitha, whom the roar was really meant for, snored on happily, oblivious to her husband's bellowing. She had long ago trained herself to sleep through the disgusting noises emanating from the man she had married: his roars, snores, burps, bellows, grunts and farts.

'Bring me my clean uniform. Sharp!' he yelled at the trembling houseboy when he opened the door. 'And make sure the driver's ready and waiting.'

The brass clock on his office wall read ten to four when Sergeant Piyadasa strode into the station. Constable Somapala could tell, by the way he walked, that his boss was in a bad mood.

Piyadasa selected a small silver key from the bunch in his pocket and unlocked the steel cabinet in a corner of his office where the *arrack* supply was kept. He counted twelve bottles of brown-gold Old Faithful, closed the door and re-locked it. That would do the trick. Then he walked over to the large teak desk, sat himself down, pulled a small address book from his breast pocket and ran a pudgy finger down the pages. He was just pondering who to call when he remembered something. 'Somapala!' The small constable snapped into the room and stood smartly to attention. 'Somapala, get hold of that telephone linesman, will you? We've a job for him later on.'

It was almost midnight. Outside her house, the street was dark and empty; her early-rising neighbours had long gone to sleep. The lone lamp-post, which normally cast a pool of light and sanctuary over her end of the road, had failed. The blackness of the golf course stretched like a monstrous yawn, swallowing the house.

She had just got off the telephone to her agency and was undressing when she heard the low growl of an approaching diesel engine. It stopped outside her front door, panting like a jungle beast. She was reaching for a cotton kimono on the door, when something, a note in the beast's growl perhaps, changed her mind. She snatched her dirty jeans and shirt from the floor, and was struggling into them when the doorbell rang. A long, hard ring, splintering the night. Without even looking, she sensed, as jungle creatures sense a prowling tiger, who it was. She tiptoed into the little hallway and gently lifted the telephone. The line was dead.

She had been tired, but now her adrenalin-charged brain raced through the options. Useless to pretend there was no one at home: the house was ablaze with light and her car was outside. She could

171

barricade the front door or even her bedroom. But it would hold them off only momentarily and, if they were drunk, anger them more. There were the french windows on to the small back garden, but it was enclosed by a high concrete wall and the only exit led to the front of the house. If she could open the french windows and carry out a stool unseen however, there was a faint chance she could climb the wall.

The doorbell rang again, drilling through the night. In a minute they would begin hammering. She eased out the telephone table, hoping it would bear her weight, and padded towards the french windows. A metallic clicking noise stopped her. Someone had got there first and was trying the latch. She put the stool down. Her heart pounded against her chest, clamouring to be let out.

'Who is it?' She is by the front door. Listening. She speaks in English to tell them she is a foreigner in a country where foreigners are among the few to have rights. She can sense more than one presence, weighing heavily against the night. There is shuffling. And then a loud burp. But no reply. Instead, the doorbell rings again. Insistently, as if someone is leaning on it.

'Who is it?' She repeats her question, trying to sound commanding. 'What do you want?'

Silence. Then a low murmur and a short laugh, like a fart. The doorbell rings again. Accompanied by a pounding fist. For a minute, she hopes that if she can hold them off and if they pound long enough, the noise may wake her neighbours. But she knows as she thinks it that it is a reedy hope. She curses herself for sending her maid home. Now she is alone.

Something in her kicks in then. Obstinacy, courage, an oddly welcome sense of that aloneness and anger, driving away her fear.

'What do you want?'

There is silence and more shuffling.

She tries to remember other times this has happened. Other men, banging on doors, with guns. But every place, every motive is different; though, in the end, the same. Her mind races, wondering what to tell these men now.

'I've called the army chief,' she says at last, naming him. 'A detachment will be here in ten minutes.'

She speaks loudly and slowly, bluffing, hoping her dead telephone is a coincidence. Her voice echoes back, thin and feminine. It isn't the voice of someone in command.

She hears a drunken laugh and knows they are no more fooled than she is.

There is a thump and the pistol-sharp report of splintering wood. Her eyes dart to the heavy door bolts, willing them to hold, and then dart back across the room. Behind her glass is shattering to the tiles: someone has smashed the panes of the french windows. She does the sums: the door frames are fragile. They will last five minutes, at most.

Moving fast, with a strength that surprises her, she pulls out the heavy teak dining table and drags it to the windows. Pushing, pulling, cursing, but thankful for its weight. A man's face leers drunkenly at her through the windows. He is wearing jeans and a T-shirt. No uniform. That scares her. But she has no time to think who he might be.

Sweat pours down her face. She brushes back a loose tendril of hair and looks around for something to barricade the front door. Her sofa and chairs are rattan. Too fragile. She grabs a dining chair and jams it under the door handle. There is nothing else but the beds and they are too heavy. She looks up. The screws on the front door bolts are straining. From behind she hears the noise of firecrackers and spins around. The french windows have snapped.

Time seems to rearrange itself. Expanding and contracting against the moment. Moving very fast or very slow. There is a blur of motion; the room swirls around her like a whirlwind. And then the gale abates and everything is still. She is in the eye. She thinks of a car crash, when everything goes into slow motion. It is ridiculous

173

and frightening. Slow and fast. The world spinning on its head. She wonders if this is the nth degree of fear. Or if she has just gone mad.

Two sounds rip through the house at the same instant. Breaking wood as the front door splinters and a bolt clatters to the floor. And the purr of a car coming to rest. A flame licks up from her heart. Hope.

The police posse was too drunk to register more than the arrival of an unwelcome vehicle. But a policeman's gut instinct, working even under the influence, said something had gone wrong. The party was about to be spoiled. Only Sergeant Piyadasa, who had come along reluctantly, under orders, to supervise the operation, and who had consequently stayed mostly (but not completely) off the liquor, saw what was going on. And immediately tried to rewind the frame. The driver of the car was a *suda*, a white man. And across its windshield was blazoned the word 'Press'. A *porener* and a journalist. His stomach heaved on a choppy sea. He watched his promotion flutter over the waves and then sink. Thank God they were in mufti. For a millisecond he felt proud of himself for insisting on that, at least. His stomach crested on a wave. If they'd been in uniform? It sank into a trough.

'Stop, boys!' The men looked around them, confused at this contradictory order from the boss.

'Wazz 'appening?' one of them ventured, as his mates staggered back from the doorway, trampling each other's toes.

'That's enough, lads. Time to go.'

It was turning into one of those Marx Brothers *pilums*, thought Sergeant Piyadasa, as his men fell over each other. He plastered himself in a smile and turned to greet the white man advancing on the house. Curse himself for not thinking of it, the *sudu* had a boyfriend. Now he'd need some double-quick on-his-toes thinking. And as Lalitha kept reminding him, thought, fast or slow, was not his strong point. The *suda* was putting his hand in his pocket.

Not a gun, surely? No, he was extracting something from his wallet. A laminated card.

'Good evening, sir,' he mumbled, trying to arrest the snot-coloured smell on his breath as if it were an unruly drunk outside a bar.

'Press.' The man stuck out the card.

Sergeant Piyadasa cast an uninterested red eye at it. He knew what it said.

'So, who are you and what's happening? This is my colleague's house.'

A gluey green smile stuck itself to Sergeant Piyadasa's face. He still wasn't sure how to handle this. He glared at the boys capering drunkenly in the doorway, as if for inspiration. Monkeys, he thought dismally. Naughty monkeys. Caught stealing booze.

'Eva? Are you all right?'

Sergeant Piyadasa thought he detected a note of panic. Although, to tell the truth, he found the actions and reactions of white men as impenetrable as the mating habits of the three-ringed stoat.

A muffled voice floated out.

'Look!' The man shoved his card under the policeman's nose. 'Press!' He jabbed at the plastic. His face was red and angry. 'Press! We're both press. OK?' The man was screaming. 'Go away! Business finished. No trouble. OK?'

Sergeant Piyadasa stared at him, hypnotized. A red-faced demon had materialized from the shrubbery and was jabbering at him in pidgin English. He rubbed a clammy paw over a sweaty forehead, and wondered dimly if this was the effect of too much cheap *arrack*. He must switch to a better brand.

'Carl?' The voice rang out from inside again, clear over the static of crickets. 'I'm fine. But watch out. I don't know who they are.'

The Sergeant cocked his head. The realization that he had lost command of the situation perched fleetingly on his brain and then plummeted groundwards with his promotion. He felt impotent out of uniform. That was the trouble with these dirty undercover jobs. Over the shoulder of the white man, he spotted one of his men grinning inanely. The drunken constable had shaped a cocked pistol with his fingers and was pointing it at the *suda*'s back.

The gesture snapped Sergeant Piyadasa out of his inertia. He shook his head at the man, furiously. Fool! he thought. Drunken fool! '*Yammu*. Cummon boys,' he mouthed at them, cocking his head at the van. Drunk or sober, Sergeant Piyadasa had the finely-tuned radar of all career policemen. He knew when he was out-ranked, outmatched, bowled out.

The police posse weaved unsteadily towards the jeep: a truncated centipede with a numbing hangover, waiting like a burp, to come out. Carl watched until the unmarked van had turned the corner. Then he and Eva struggled to open the battered door of the house.

Twenty-seven

It was mid-morning when Eva went down to Carl's office. Panes of flat white light pressed against the blinds. She raised the bamboo slats and opened the windows, but the air outside was still and heavy; it flopped over lazily when she turned on the fan, sleepy as an afternoon courtesan.

She had come downstairs intending to sort through the boxes they had moved from her house – her computer, light table, cameras and equipment, a few clothes – before they could be looted from the house by junkie caddies from the golf course. But she already felt exhausted: either by the heat, or the strain of the previous night. She wiped the sweat off her forehead with her sleeve and dropped into his desk chair.

He had taped a note to the computer screen; a sheet of lined paper torn from a notebook. She pulled it off. In sloping, slightly unformed handwriting it read: 'If you only knew how many times I dreamed of taking you away. To a place where I could smell you and love you and tie you to me. If only I knew of such a place, we would fly there tomorrow.' A PS said that he would be back for lunch.

She leaned back smiling, the note in her fingers. The serpent coiled around her heart loosened its grip, releasing a drip of happiness that entered her veins like an uninvited but unexpectedly agreeable guest.

She looked around. The room was like the rest of his house, barren and unfamiliar. There was a shelf containing the only books she had seen, each promising to re-order life as a painting-by-numbers: a 'How To' manual on journalism; a religious tract called *Daily Thoughts*; and three classics: *How to Win Friends and Influence People*; *The Joy of Cooking* and *The Joy of Sex*.

Idly, she opened the top drawer of his computer table. It was empty but for a key chain with two keys on it and a miniature address book. In the next drawer was a small black book and, beneath it, a photograph. She pulled it out. It was a colour snapshot of a dark-haired woman in a red polka-dot dress. She had a good figure: small breasts, flat tummy, smooth legs. Attractive more than beautiful with a full mouth and high cheekbones. Because she wasn't facing the lens directly, it was hard to read her expression. But she looked loved. Happy.

She picked up the address book. It was a sad little thing, containing a few names from various countries, noted in the same unlettered hand. The small book contained the sayings of St Augustine. It was inscribed in a hand similar to his: 'May these words guide and protect you, son. Love Mom.'

'Please don't read that.'

He had come into the office without her noticing, but his face, which had lit up at the sight of her, had turned cloudy.

She looked up. 'Why not? It's beautiful.'

A coy smile slid across his face. He was like a nerdy schoolboy suddenly finding a friend who shares his interest in Pakman. She thought of the sad little address book, with so few names.

'Maybe I just don't want you going through my stuff.' He perched on the desk beside her and gently took the book out of her hands, as if he wasn't cross but sad.

'I'm sorry.'

'It's OK.'

'Is that your wife?' She took a chance, indicating with her eyes the photograph she had propped up on the computer table.

'Yes.' He reached over for the picture and slipped it back in the drawer with the small book.

'She's beautiful.' She wasn't really, but Eva wanted to say it.

He sighed. 'That was the trouble.'

'Do you still love her?'

He smiled. 'No. Or at least, I don't think so. Not any more.'

But he didn't seem sure. She thought that he probably hadn't found anyone he loved enough to replace her. His loneliness had seeped into the house like dregs from a used teabag. But then she thought of the previous night, of how he had saved her. It occurred to her then that he was a refuge. A buffer between herself and the island's demons. An emissary from a sanitized, more orderly place of wide blue skies, hot tubs and wholesome cheerleaders. A place where everything could be learned, quantified, classified, put in neat linguistic boxes, but where there was also justice. And rights.

'That's the second time you've saved my life,' she said. 'I owe you. Double.'

'I don't think I saved your life last night. But if I did, the benefit was all mine.' He leaned over and kissed her, lightly.

She looked again at the bare walls and pink terrazzo floor, the rented furniture, the tired macramé plant-holder, the cheap varnished wood. The characterless house seemed at that moment a haven, too. As welcome as a hospital room to a wounded man, with its soothing white sheets and blank white spaces, its promise of nothing more threatening than boredom.

She thought of her own house, the doors hanging off like skin from mangled wounds. At least those men hadn't penetrated it. Her maid had been hysterical when she saw the damage. She had wanted to call an exorcist to cut limes and burn herbs. Eva had refused, but perhaps she was wrong. Perhaps the gods slumbering in the island's rocks, rivers and trees needed propitiating, lest they emerge angry as spoiled children for want of attention.

She looked up at Carl. 'Thank you,' she said. 'Thank you so much all the same.'

He ran a finger down her cheek. 'I've got to run out. I just came back to get something.'

She jumped up. 'Are you going anywhere near the DHL office? I need to courier those pix I took of the house.'

'You're sending those? What for?'

'Evidence.' She smiled up at him. 'I just think it's best to get them out of the country.'

She rummaged in one of the boxes, extracting a large brown envelope addressed to her agency and gave it to him.

A framed photograph lay underneath the brown envelope and when he had left, she pulled it out, wanting to look at it alone. It was her favourite picture – less for its style than its atmosphere and content – and she had carried it through countries and wars. It had been taken in Hanoi in 1968 by Marc Riboud, in the garden of Bao Dai's former palace. Ho Chi Minh, *'l'homme pur comme Lucifer'*, sat at a wrought-iron garden table in front of a pergola, talking to Pham Van Dong. He was dressed in his familiar khaki drill, woollen socks flapping around his ankles, the wispy beard making him look like a sage in a Chinese scroll. But what she loved most about the photograph was its evocation of a certain time and place. The air of tropical decay, of elegance and austerity; the overgrown garden, the simplicity of the bentwood chairs, the table, the stone flags; the face of the man that Graham Greene had called a kindly Mr Chips: 'prepared to inflict punishment, but capable also of inspiring love'.

She gazed at it again, comparing it to the pictures she'd taken in the last few months, wondering if she would ever be able to achieve the purity of that image; and whether its purity came from age, or skill, or just the workman-like nature of the cameras used then. It was like Lorne, she realized: the simplicity amid lushness and decay. And he was, in some ways, like Caspar.

The asceticism, the ability to command respect and also love.

On impulse, she went into the sitting room, where the rest of her stuff was piled. The slides she had taken of Caspar at Lorne, that afternoon sometime before Navahiru was taken, were in there. She pulled them out, with her light table, and carried them upstairs to the spare bedroom, where she laid the pictures out. She separated the close-ups and began poring over them with a magnifying lens. She was searching for something, she was not sure what. A hint, a grain, lodged somewhere in the overlapping folds of the past. When she had finished, she leaned back in the chair and, before even calling for coffee, flipped out a Camel. And as she smoked, she thought.

'Stand still.'

She had been in his house for over a week, barely leaving his room. Now it was past midnight and they were upstairs. Mary had gone to bed and Toots was outside, dozing on his black plastic chair under the stars. The house was silent; as empty and hollow as a locked church. Eva, who was undressing in the upstairs bedroom, paused, her bra in one hand. The single ugly ceiling light flattened the contours of the room and her body, casting no shadows, making the bare room look seedy. She felt as if she were in a motel room. Or a low-budget porn film.

'Now turn around.'

He was sitting in a cane armchair, his middle finger between his lips, examining her. She couldn't read his expression. He looked like an entymologist scrutinizing a rare butterfly.

She turned slowly. Shy, embarrassed. She felt as peeled as an undressed mannequin in a shop window and as un-human. A sex toy. She turned again. Her back was to him now. She heard him get up behind her.

'Don't move,' he said.

She stood there, hypnotized. It was unexpectedly erotic. A childhood game of blind man's buff perverted into a deeper, darker fantasy. A tremor of apprehension tingled between her shoulder blades. From far away, the voice returned.

'Now lie down.'

She lay down on the bed, watching him curiously, half wary, half amused, her arms stretched above her and her feet dangling over the edge of the bed. He walked over to the wardrobe and rummaged in it. When he turned back towards her she saw that he held an assortment of objects in his hands. He put the scarf on her first, covering her eyes and then turned her on to her stomach.

'No,' she said. 'Take the socks off. I want to feel.'

She felt the coarse hairs of the twine bite into her skin as he pulled the knots tight. Then she felt him tie her wrists. She waited.

'You look nice,' he said. He was standing back from the bed, appraising her. Like a fisherman who has just caught a prize fish. She heard the faint jingle of a brass buckle and a dry sound, like a snake moving through grass. She tensed.

Downstairs in the driveway, Toots heard nothing. No screams. No snap of leather on skin.

'Did I hurt you?' he asked later as they lay on the bed together. He was still dressed, his face so close to hers on the pillow it was slightly out of focus. All she could see was a pair of soft, blurry brown eyes.

'No. Not enough.'

She felt his palm move along her breast, moulding the curve of her waist and hip. It felt tentative, uncertain, like a blind man learning braille. She leaned back to read his expression. He looked perplexed, like a diner presented with an outlandish dish.

'Is that the first time you've done that?' she asked. Her eyes were laughing.

He looked embarrassed. 'Yeah. I guess so.'

'And did you like it?'

'I guess I could get into it.' He paused. 'If you want me to.' He ran his large hand gently over her.

It was an interesting balance of power, she thought. Tipping between them like finely-calibrated jeweller's scales. She had little doubt who held the balance now, though. Perhaps it had always been hers to give or withhold.

Then something in her, a childhood genie corked in a bottle, made her push the advantage, raise the stakes. 'You know I'm going to make you fall in love with me,' she said. She stroked his cheek with the tips of her fingers.

She had uncorked the bottle. The genie was out. It was a threat and a promise. One that would return one day to devour her. But she couldn't help herself. She was taking revenge. Although for what, precisely, she couldn't have said. Perhaps it was for love. Or love lost.

Twenty-eight

'What's your greatest fear?'

They had begun playing this game in the hot bluebottle afternoons, when they lay lazily nuzzling on his bed and the air flopped over them like a wet dog. She had found it in a very old book: a dialogue between the king of the birds and a mythological crow that took the form of questions and answers about life and turned it into a sort of truth or dare.

'Go on,' she said, seeing his puzzled expression. 'I'll ask you a question and then you ask me.'

His fingers paused in the dell between her hip and stomach, strolled up on to her hipbone and began tapping, as if sending messages to his brain.

'This is serious?'

'Deadly. But we can improvise.' She lifted his fingers off her, interrupting their morse code.

He thought back to his days in the wild north Pacific, the waves as tall as apartment blocks.

'Drowning.' He paused and screwed up his eyes. 'No, not drowning. Failure.' But he sounded undecided. 'Perhaps I should say death, after all. That's everyone's greatest fear, isn't it?'

Blades of air-conditioned air mowed an icy swathe through the humid undergrowth of the room.

'Not necessarily. My greatest fear is fear itself.'

'What do you mean?'

She had a story. A myth, perhaps. One of those tales travellers tell. But in the thin mountain air where she had first heard it, with gods and demons dancing between the peaks, it had seemed believable. It involved an esoteric practice – a 'yoga of the left-hand path' her informant called it – that either sent its practitioners mad or gave them instantaneous liberation.

'The practice was very simple. But also very difficult. It involved meditating on one's greatest fear. The thing that fascinated me, though,' she went on, 'wasn't whether it worked or not. It was the concept. What *was* my greatest fear?' For several years, she told him, she had thought about it, keeping the notion in the back of her mind. 'Until one night, in a very old house, I met it.'

She scanned his face, but his eyes showed no signs of doubt.

'Go on,' he said. He had never heard anyone talk like this.

'I don't know if I can explain. I don't know if I want to. But at the end of several intense hours, when I was sometimes more terrified than I've ever been, I finally understood what my greatest fear was. It wasn't outside me and it wasn't any*thing*. It was in me and it was fear itself. Perhaps fear is the fundamental negative, the opposite of love. Useful, because it stops us walking off cliffs, but also potentially destructive. I suppose it was typical of that particular religion's esoteric practices, many of which involve meditations on fear, or frightening things. Another way of overcoming the ego, you could say. Something like that.'

'Boy, you've lost me,' he said, breaking the spell. He thought how different were their interior worlds and wondered if, for all her western-ness, she really was part-pagan.

'That's OK,' she laughed. 'It probably wasn't true anyway. Shall we go on?'

'Sure.'

'OK. This one's traditional. What's the greatest virtue?'

'Let me think.' He ran a finger between his lips. 'Generosity.'

That's what my dad always taught me, anyways. And you?'

'I don't know. It's an odd question, even though I asked it. Humility, because without it you can't learn anything.'

'That's a lot like generosity.'

'Yes. A cousin.'

She reached for a pack of untipped Camels, shook two out, lit them and handed him one.

'And now the corollary. What's the greatest vice?'

'Murder. Premeditated violence. An act that robs someone of their liberty. What would you say?'

'I suppose it depends what aspect of the human condition we're talking about. If it's an act, then yes, no question. But in intellectual terms, I'd say a closed mind.'

'Interesting. Why's that?'

'Because it robs life of possibility.'

'Hey, this is too much of a strain for a hot afternoon. Anything easy?'

'OK. Where do you feel happiest?' She smiled.

'Not counting here, now?' he asked. 'That's easy. In hotel rooms. I love them.'

'Me, too.' She laughed at the serendipity: in the ocean of differences, they'd found a raft with oars and water. 'But I'd add a bed with very good linen and a duvet to nest under.'

'What's a duvet?'

'A puffy quilt with feathers in. Cheap travel revolutionized the bedmaking habits of the British. Before that we slept under blankets, like you. Now we don't have to make beds. It's perfect for a nation that never got over losing its colonies.' She laughed. 'They arrived in England sometime after indoor loos.'

'You had johns *outside*. As in outdoors?'

'Well, I'm joking. But a long time ago, yes. In poorer areas of London and the country.'

'I knew British bathrooms were primitive, but not *that* primitive.'

'And you still use blankets.'

'Nothing wrong with that. Say, this is fun. What've you got next?'

She smiled. 'What's the most important thing in life?'

'To me?'

She nodded.

'Achievement. No question.'

'Really? The most important thing?'

'Sure, I'm an achievement junkie. Why d'you think I do this job?'

'But achieving what?'

'Come on, Eva, you know what I mean. Anything.' He shrugged. 'Could be big or small. Though the bigger the better, obviously. Depends what's going on. Junkies don't care much what drugs they do, as long as they're drugs. What's your answer?'

'Love. Real love. The rarer kind.'

'Why did I know you'd say that?'

She had meant something different, but she let it go. Instead she asked, 'If you could have one wish, only one, what would it be?'

'Success.'

'You're very sure about life, aren't you?'

'Not really. I just have the wish list down.' He smiled.

'How do you define success?'

'That's part of the quiz?'

'It's not a quiz, but no, I just want to know.'

'Cummon. You know what I mean. Succeeding at what you do. Being recognized. Making enough money, I guess. What's your wish?'

'You can't tell people your special wishes!'

'That's not fair. I told you mine.'

'World peace.' She burst out laughing.

'That's what the Miss World contestants say!'

'I know, I was joking. But something like that. No more wars. And for myself, joy, contentment.'

'That's the same as being successful – or the same result.'

'No! It's totally different. Contentment is a state of being. Success is like achievement.'

He shrugged again. 'Well, I'm not sure I believe in that. Let's stick with what we can see and touch. Absolute fulfillment, for me, would be a million dollars in the bank. No question.'

She was about to ask him if he really meant it, but stopped herself. Perhaps she decided she didn't really want to know.

'OK, my turn,' he said. 'What's the quality you most like in a man?'

'Retreating hair? OK, OK,' she held out her arms to stop him tickling her, 'I didn't mean it. Lots of things. Generosity of spirit, a sense of humour, being good in bed, brains.'

'I don't have a sense of humour.'

'But you have the others, right?' She laughed. 'You do have a sense of humour. It just takes a while to spot. So, what about you? What quality do you like most in a man? Or do I change it to a woman?'

'A woman.' He looked at her for a long time, running his forefinger over his lower lip.

Outside, the light softened from bone-white to gold, highlighting every leaf on the tall tamarind tree as if it were on stage. When he finally spoke it was very softly and she almost had to strain to hear.

'I like skin the colour of honey. Long legs, green eyes. A red dress. An old car on a hot night. The taste of seaspray and wild berries...' He reached out and pulled her to him. 'Yes. I like all those things and more.'

Twenty-nine

A large *betel* buzzed angrily against the green metal lampshade, frustrating its kamikaze attempts on the bulb. To Carl, who sat alone in the office at his computer, it sounded like his mind hurling itself at his tortured prose. It was useless. The image of her body, where words should have been, kept interrupting him, ruining his concentration. He struggled for a few minutes more and gave up. Swivelling away from the screen, he reached for a small black film canister, a pair of scissors and some papers, and rolled a joint. She had gone somewhere for the evening, 'to talk to someone'. She said she'd be back early but it was nearing midnight. The smoke coiled around his thoughts, stoking his emotions. The anger he seemed unable to control these days rose up in him and with it, a small flame of jealousy. Was she with someone else? Who was he? His mind was off, racing uncontrollably.

He thought back to that afternoon, trying to apply the brakes. Her body winding its way through the sheets. She looked like a sleepy brown jungle river. Mysterious, unfathomable, with hidden depths and currents. He thought of the intensity with which they made love. And knew that he was being swept away by those waters. Where to, he had no idea. But for the first time in his life, he realized with a slight shock, he didn't care. He felt as reckless and free as a bare-assed kid on a hot summer's day, enchanted by water and sunshine and magic. As if he were under a spell.

Her eyes came swimming up to meet him. Green rockpools glinting with tiny fish. Did they love him, those fish, or were they laughing at him? He had no idea. She made love with an abandon that took his breath away and yet she never lost control. Never gave herself completely.

Absentmindedly, he glanced at his watch. It was past midnight. For a second, a dart of paranoia pierced him. He tried to reject it, but already, in his mind, another river was flowing in, its darker waters mingling with hers. It wasn't true what she said, that she didn't play games. How boring, he'd first thought, when she first told him. Games were what made life and love fun. But now he wasn't so sure.

He heard a car hoot outside the gates. He relaxed. But then he heard the sound of heavy footfalls on gravel and cursed, remembering. It was the Captain. As usual, he'd come late. He wondered how to get him out of the house before she returned.

'So, my friend, how's life? Good, eh?' The young soldier had the disarming directness of all military men. The big-booted innocence of a life protected from commercial grubbiness. He strode into houses as if they were the officers' mess. Before Carl had really noticed, he was in his office, pulling up a chair. The Captain took a bottle of Jack Daniels out of a brown paper bag and plonked it on the desk. 'Bringing you something,' he grinned. 'Special stores. So, what we celebrating?'

Carl generally found the Captain's company easy-going. His bluff simplicity was a foil to his own tortured psychology; and his certainties about life (birth, childhood, education, job, marriage, children, grandchildren, death: identical, neatly wrapped packages, presented to everyone on the day they were born, like birthday presents in advance), were soothing. They helped him believe there might be some order in chaos; even if, as values, they were not for him. But tonight Carl wasn't in the mood. The man had begun to jar on him. And he wanted to be alone with Eva and his thoughts.

'Hey, what's up, man?' asked the Captain, after several attempts at bonhomie had flopped like dead flies to the floor. 'Want me to get you a girl?' He slapped his thigh. 'I knew it. Not enough *sax!*' He mispronounced the last word with a roar of glee. Like most islanders, the Captain was a sensitive man and thus extremely insensitive to anyone else.

Carl shook his head, wondering how to explain himself and his relationship with Eva. His thoughts were turbulent and his feelings for her were still so raw and, he realized, precious. Too precious, he now understood, to share with another man. But the Captain was his friend... When he had finished mumbling, the soldier was grinning.

'So man, this girl, does she *do* it... I mean, *everything?*'

Carl looked down and said nothing. He was embarrassed. Whether for Eva or for himself, he wasn't sure.

'Hey, *machan*, what's the trouble? Not like my sex guru to be so quiet.'

Carl suddenly felt angry and sullen. His face reddened. The colour travelled into his rising hairline and along the little pathways on his scalp, like iron-rich water seeping into a paddy field. The vein on his temple throbbed. 'Look. I just don't want to talk about her any more. I'm sorry. OK?'

The Captain grinned amiably and threw out his hands in a half-gesture of surrender. For a while they were both silent. Carl pulling on his joint, thinking; the Captain grinning to himself over his glass. Then Carl got up, went over to the other side of the desk and put his hand on his friend's shoulder.

'Another night, eh? She's going to be back soon and, no offence, but I'd like to be alone with her.'

The Captain went, holding the half-empty bottle of scotch, which Carl had guiltily insisted he take. He was hurt, that was obvious, Carl thought, but so what. He'd forget it and be back. The house was silent now, but for the electric trill of cicadas and a sudden wind, rustling the million leaves of the tamarind. The monsoon was overdue and it was as sodden and steamy as a Turkish bath. Perhaps this was it. He felt tired and on edge. It was almost one o'clock. He was wondering whom to call when he heard a car outside the gate.

Her smile disarmed him more than any words. That same smile he had seen on the night they met: childlike, radiant. She had never looked more beautiful, he thought, standing in the driveway, the wind loosening snags of hair, her skin and eyes alight. The sight of her sliced into him like a surgical incision. Clean, with a slight gasp. He took her in his arms and squeezed her tightly. 'I missed you. I was getting worried.'

She ran her fingers through his hair and along his neck, saying nothing. Without a word he took her hand and they walked back into the house.

Only one other person heard their double footfalls on the stairs. She waited until the bedroom door shut, then reached a hand inside her pillow, closed her eyes and went to sleep.

The next morning, while they were drinking coffee, Carl told her about the Captain's visit, glossing over some of his more sexist comments, making him sound as much like a hero as possible, a man anyone would be proud to have as a friend. He wasn't sure why, but he wanted Eva to like the Captain. As if his friends could supply the qualities he lacked.

Eva had once gone out with a poet. A difficult man, ruled by his rages, who wrote taut, clever poems that he would hound her to read. Carl was a bit like him.

She turned to him suddenly. 'Did you ask him about Navahiru?'

Carl looked down.

'Well, did you?'

She was in a strange mood. A sudden squall that seemed to have come from nowhere. Eva's mood changes would mostly arrive without warning, like a storm in the tropics – a swift, contrary burst of bedevilled weather – and then leave as quickly as they came. At those times, she would go to bed, or run into the sea, strip off and swim hard, or tumble in surf until the mood passed. But today something else was snagging at her. She could feel it, without knowing what.

'No, I didn't, Eva.' He suddenly felt miserable. 'I'm sorry, I should have. I just forgot.'

'But he's the obvious person. He's a paramilitary. He knows all these people.'

'Look, Eva, I've said I'm sorry. I feel bad enough about it. Just leave it, please. It's first thing in the morning. I'll call him later, if you like.'

'What do you mean, you feel bad enough about it?'

A wasp, trapped between the window blind and the frame, buzzed loudly, filling the room with an angry insect noise.

'I don't know. Look, can we leave it for now, please? I haven't even finished my coffee. I promise I'll call him later. Really.'

But Eva couldn't leave it. 'Don't you think it's odd I've never met any of your friends?'

'Do you want to meet him? The Captain?' Carl's tone was even. Hoping for a truce.

'No, I don't mean him. Any of them.'

He looked down. 'Perhaps it's because I don't have any.'

'Really?' She sounded scornful.

'Yes. Really.'

'Perhaps it's because you're ashamed of me.' She shot him a piercing look. 'Is it, Carl?'

'Maybe I'm ashamed of them.' He still didn't meet her eyes. 'My parents always used to ask me why I didn't bring home my girlfriends. They'd say: "Are you ashamed of them or us?"'

'And which was it?'

'Look, Eva, I don't know. Maybe I just want to keep you to myself.'

Armand had kept his two last wives caged up in a bedsitter,

carved from the old servants' quarters above his flat, like a modern Bluebeard. She called it 'the stepmothers' garret'. It was like a student's digs. There was a small white-painted bookcase, a cheap coffee table, a bed with an old-fashioned candlewick bedspread on it and a teddy bear. Her last stepmother was a middle-aged woman. Armand had come up there only to spend the night, as if he were visiting a mistress. The rest of his life bore not a trace of her. Not even a safety-pin, or a lipstick. He had isolated her like an infectious disease. Armand hadn't had any friends, either. Or none she could remember. Not since he and her mother had divorced.

'Maybe I don't want to be locked up,' she said.

She got up, wrapped a sheet around her like a toga and went into the spare bedroom, shutting the door. Reclaiming her body, re-staking her territory. He picked up the paper and tried to read it. But nothing made sense.

He was dressed, still reading the front page, over and over, when she emerged from the room next door, washed and smiling. She walked to him, bent over the newspaper, crumpling it, and kissed him on the lips. He kissed her back.

'Read this,' said Carl, handing a vertically folded newspaper to Eva.

Dear Sir,

I wish very much to complain about the dead bodies untidying your beaches. My clients are not used to this in our country when we go to the beach.

Your government should make effort to clear them away so our tourists do not have to see them.

Hoping you will seriously take this letter,

Helga Schmidt

Fischer Blau Travels

Eva burst out laughing. 'That is *so* unbelievable. Don't stop killing people, just clean up the bodies after you do!' She handed him back the paper. 'Oh, God help us.' Her eyes were watery with laughter.

He flung himself on to the bed, pulled her next to him and put a hand on one breast, as if to stop it laughing, too.

'Aren't you supposed to be working?' One eyebrow was raised but she was smiling.

'Aren't you?' he mumbled with a mouthful of nipple.

She slid down the bed and, with a look of concentration on her face like a child's, undid his belt buckle and, one by one, the buttons of his jeans, feeling him grow as her fingers released his flies. Suddenly he leaped up, remembering. He bounded over to the door and locked it.

He was hard and smooth and very clean. American clean. Wholesome, with no additives.

A little later, he looked down at her. Her pupils were as wide as a river and her lips were flushed like berries.

He lit a cigarette, passed it to her and glanced at the bedside clock. 'Jesus! We've been here all morning.' It was midday. He got up, wrapped a towel around himself and went out on to the landing. 'Mary!' he yelled down the stairs. 'Fix us coffee and a couple of toasted sandwiches.'

He came out of the shower. His swimmer's body was outlined against the light: lithe, strong, honey-coloured.

'You've got a beautiful body,' she said.

'Not as beautiful as yours.'

'Thank you.' She smiled. 'It was a present.'

'Yes, I know,' he said looking at her. He was chuckling. 'And just what I wanted, too.'

There was a timid knock. Mary, probably.

'Just a minute,' he called. He quickly put on his shirt and jeans and went to the door to take the tray from her.

'I think Mary's upset,' she said when he returned.

'Sure she's upset. A thirty-nine-year-old virgin from a country town? This place smells like Cupid's gym.'

It was true. They had spent days locked in his room. The atmosphere was unmistakable. A boudoir full of promises with secrets in its folds.

Thirty

Mary had indeed been put out by Eva's arrival. By the end of a month, she was not just upset but scandalized. Each time she saw Eva, her mouth pursed above the starched collar and she blushed. A pungent, purplish odour trailed her around the house like a big cat on heat.

When Eva's old car first drew up, Mary, who had been watching through the flowered curtains, noted with alarm that she carried two bags. When they were taken upstairs and deposited, not in the spare bedroom, but in the *mahataya*'s room, she was outraged. Then, when days at a stretch passed without either of them emerging from the bedroom, her brain went into a spin. Although she couldn't imagine what might actually be *going on* in there, the sight of the closed door was enough. Porener? *Tchick!* she thought. For all her madam-ing and chi-chi-ing, she was nothing but a *vesige*.

It was not just Mary's notions of propriety that had been turned upside-down, or even her heart. It was her sense of status. The same muddled arithmetic used to calculate her relationship with Burt had been used to inflate her role in Carl's household; so that, if she did not imagine herself as Carl's beloved and future wife, she certainly saw herself as mistress of the household.

Eva's presence in the house was therefore a direct threat and, as days passed, small affronts – the locked bedroom door, the peremptory orders yelled hastily down the stairs, the *mahataya*'s generally distant air – combined with the loss of previous small intimacies (the early-morning slap on the bottom, the occasional chat) to become full-scale bereavements.

Mary did not intend to leave this assault on her terrain undefended. When a fortnight had passed with still no sign of Eva's departure, she consulted her almanac and noted certain propitious times. Then she sat down with a new Basildon Bond writing pad and blue Bic, to compose a letter to the *nona*.

'Dear Madam,' she began. She sucked her pen. What to say next? She stared at the small photograph of Nancy smiling in the sunshine outside their old house, willing it, as one might will a miraculous image, to dispense inspiration.

'Dear Madam,' she began again. 'I am very well. I hope you are too. Everything is fine. Master is fine.' No, that wasn't right. Everything wasn't fine. Why else was she writing the letter?

'Dear Madam, I hope you are well. I am well but things are not so fine with the Master.' No, that might worry her. She might think he was ill, or had had an accident. She frowned hard at the paper and then at the *nona*'s face. It smiled back at her, its expression fixed, by time and the lens, as inscrutably as a Chinese Buddha.

The incongruity between the happy moment of the photograph and the information she was trying to convey hadn't struck Mary. As it was, she was having trouble trying to put anything into words; her emotions were far too turbulent. It never occurred to her that Nancy herself might not wish to know the intended contents of her letter. So far as she was concerned, Nancy *nona* was the *mahataya*'s wife. And it was to her she considered herself loyal.

It was in this guise that Mary would assign all her subsequent actions. She was doing it for the *nona*, whether she knew about it or not. She carried that idea like a banner. A noble motive that would nullify all lesser motives. Like jealousy and spite.

She put the pen and paper down. Perhaps tonight wasn't an auspicious time to write. She re-consulted her almanac. As she suspected: a bad conjunction between Venus and Saturn. The letter would have to wait. She sighed, muttered a prayer for herself and the *mahatayas*, past and present, and made an obeisance to her altar. Changing into a frilled cotton nightdress, she brushed her teeth and slid into bed.

Inside the pillow-case were Burt's socks. She reached in, as she did every night, to ensure that they hadn't mysteriously disappeared, and then, reassured, fell asleep. In her dream, she was hunting for some lost object. It lay tantalizingly out of sight, something she hadn't quite identified.

The first thing Toots smelled at the end of his shift, just before dawn, was the stink of crocodile's piss. By which, since he had never smelled it, though he had seen plenty of crocodiles sunning themselves on the river bank, he meant the worst smell he could think of. Something like crocodile's piss mixed with snake's blood, whatever that smelled like. The thought made him shudder. He sniffed. It was coming from the outside kitchen by the staff bathroom. He ambled over sleepily, to have a look.

The stink at the kitchen door was so overpowering that Toots retched and clamped a hand over his nose. In the smoke-blackened kitchen, Mary, her back to the door, was muttering incantations over a sooty rice *kati*, her hair hanging loose and tangled, enveloped in a haze of noxious steam. She looked like a *yakkha*. Without a second glance, he fled.

His knees were still trembling like jelly when he let himself out of the gate with his tea flask. It wasn't the sight of Mary casting spells that had so unnerved him, though that was unsettling enough, but how narrowly he had escaped being spotted. He was far too afraid of her temper even to contemplate what she was doing. All he could mutter on the way home to his lodging was a prayer, since he was a devout Catholic: 'Thank God, thank God,

Mary mother of God protect me.' In all the years Toots had been a night watchman, Mary making black magic potions in the kitchen was the most frightening thing he had ever faced.

Mary was far too busy trying to remember the right words, and the correct order and amount of each ingredient, to notice Toots. The ingredients consisted of various packages and measures of roots, dried rare plants and herbs, ground-up insects and reptile bones and salt. There was no crocodile urine or snake's blood. But it was true the whole thing smelled abominable and she had recoiled at some of the instructions. It was only after consulting a well-known *kattadiya*, who poured scorn on her squeamishness, that she was persuaded, albeit very reluctantly. She couldn't wait for the whole thing to be over, so she could read the signs.

An hour later, the mixture was cooling in a lidded clay pot in Mary's bedroom, and she was bathed and back to normal, her sins and omissions hidden beneath crisp blue cotton, hair oil and hairpins. Tonight, at a precise time already determined in her almanac, she would find out what to do next.

At eight o'clock sharp there was a knock. Before Carl could leap out of bed to open the bedroom door, Mary had deposited the tray on the upstairs hall table and was walking briskly downstairs, her white-heeled sandals clattering crossly on the cement stairtreads in a sympathetic bate.

Over the next few days Eva felt as if she were being watched by a crocodile submerged in a river. Each time she left a room she would run into Mary busily dusting, or fussing with some household knicknacks. She seemed to be everywhere, behind doors and in corners. A shadow in corridors. Once, coming downstairs, she caught her lurking in a recess: a flash of starched cotton, a pair of simmering eyes and a strong purple smell.

'Madam wanting something?' she asked. Eva felt like a deer at a waterhole, sensing but not seeing the menace beneath the brown waters. Finally she told Carl. Cautiously. She knew he was very attached to his servant.

He had formally introduced them when Eva arrived to stay. 'Eva, meet Mary, the best maid on five continents. Couldn't get along without her.' He had put his hand on her shoulder, showing her off, as if she were a prize pupil and he the headmaster; and she had smirked back at the praise. When Carl spoke, she looked demurely at her white sandals. But when Eva put her palms together in greeting she didn't return the salutation but instead, stared at her. Directly, challengingly. It was obvious how she felt.

'Yeah, what's up with her?' He was at his computer.

'I don't know. I just get the feeling she's watching me.'

He shrugged and smiled. 'Maybe you're going a bit stir-crazy in here. Maybe we both are.' He spun around from the screen. 'Let's go somewhere. Do a trip together.'

'Maybe.' But Eva wasn't so sure. She had seen something in Mary that Carl, too New World, too blue denim against a too-blue sky, could not. Something very old and dark. The oily black recesses of an ancient shrine.

Thirty-one

Two days later, they set out together. The road east took them into another country; a part of the island she hadn't been to since long before the war. The army had torched a wide strip of jungle between the johnny mines buried under the roadside and the wooded hills, burning the houses down to their walls. All that remained were a line of hollow-eyed skeletons pointing charred finger bones at the sky. Even the road surface was worse, its edges gnawed by neglect and military vehicles.

At the final checkpoint the soldiers were white-eyed and jittery. A large round mirror to scare off the evil eye hung above their hut and they fingered their guns nervously. Beyond, the road was empty even of dogs or cowpats. Not a crow cawed. The silence lay hot and dry; glinting under the afternoon heat like a dagger hidden beneath a veil.

'I don't like this.' He was driving.

They had been playing Guns 'n' Roses, their going-to-war music. But before the last checkpoint he had stopped the tape.

'Nor do I,' said Eva

He slowed and, at that moment, they both saw it. A chance beam of sunlight catching a fine silver gleam.

'STOP!' yelled Eva. But he was already braking. The car screamed to a halt three inches away from the trip wire.

'Shit!' They both turned to look at each other, hearts thumping.

'Fucking army,' said Carl when he had caught his breath. 'They could've said the road was booby-trapped.'

'What do we do now?' she asked.

They turned back through the wasted landscape, looking for another road.

There had been a massacre; the story had been on the wires that morning. But it was sketchy, giving only rough numbers and the general area: a place that had once been the ancient capital of Pulastya, forefather of the island's demon king, at a time of other killings, other wars. Eva had agreed to go, despite her misgivings. Partly to be with Carl, partly to get out of the house.

When they reached the Base Hospital beside the lake, it was almost midnight. It was a clutch of single-storey concrete buildings equipped to offer first aid and rudimentary natal care to the surrounding villages, not to handle a major disaster. The forecourt was like a battlefield foggy with cordite and shell-shocked survivors. Ambulances had been called from larger, better equipped hospitals and, under a neon porch light, bleeding villagers were being loaded into the vehicles by panicking orderlies in brown uniforms. People ran in every direction, screaming at each other in the seedy half-light.

Eva shot off a roll of pictures, wanting to capture the strange atmosphere of a Goya; the horror, the stark light and dark. But then an orderly saw her and screamed at her to get out.

The killers had been professional. They had used machetes, a villager's tool, but had aimed for the head, striking deep. The wounds were hidden under snowy white turbans, but deadly red blooms were already appearing in the snow. It was a patch-up and the orderlies and doctors knew it, though they carried on the fiction that all would survive the trip.

Carl and Eva slipped past the stretchers and wheelchairs into the main building. The place smelled of poverty and neglect. Urine, grime and stale blood mingled with the stench of disinfectant.

Dying men, too ill to send away by ambulance, lay next to the less gravely wounded on iron bedsteads with grubby sheets, their faces etched grey beneath a single low-watt bulb. The harsh laws determining who lived and who died, laid bare.

They hung back for a while, hoping to catch the attention of three starched-coat doctors bent over charts. But they were too harassed to cope with reporters and, when they saw Carl and Eva, they brushed them away.

At last, a Cuban volunteer surgeon emerged from the operating theatre, his coat spattered red. The door swung open, for a second, with him. Eva had seen battles fought at a distance, where war could appear clean and tidy, like a tableau in the war museum. But not here. The theatre was a bare concrete room with a single aluminium-topped table, standing in a pond of blood. But for the anaesthetist's paraphernalia, there was no equipment. It looked like a field hospital from the Crimean War. The doctor's features were crumpled with exhaustion. And the resignation of someone who knew he was fighting not just death but poverty too.

'Please, come back tomorrow,' he begged. 'I'll talk to you then.'

They took one look at him and left.

'Shall we try the army? See if they can tell us what happened?' asked Eva.

Carl shrugged his shoulders. 'Sure. Why not?'

The brigade was headquartered near the hospital in a set of similar buildings, except here there was new white and red paint and thousand-watt searchlights. Eva and Carl waited, listening to the scurry of small nocturnal creatures beneath the silence. At last, a sleepy soldier let them in through the metal barrier. The brigadier was awake and would see them in his 'den'.

'So,' he said, steepling his fingertips under his chin, once they were seated clasping glasses of arrack. 'What can I do for you gentleman and lady,' he gave a small bow in Eva's direction, 'of the press?' He smiled, but beneath the bruised hooded eyelids, his eyes were as impenetrable as a shark's.

Carl went through his questions: numbers, likely perpetrators, how and why? The brigadier drawled out statistics, scenarios. Laying his trail of falsehoods: the official version, given to the wire services that day. But when they said that they might travel to the village, a shadow crossed his face. He sat up, put down his glass and leaned across the coffee table.

'I'm sorry,' he said. 'Can't allow that. Too dangerous. Can't guarantee your safety.'

'But surely you've got men out there?' Eva asked.

'Of course, of course. Twenty-four hour protection.' He paused for a moment to mammograph Eva's breasts with his eyes. 'But I still can't allow it.' He paused. 'Sorry.'

'We'll take full responsibility for ourselves,' Carl cut in. He was angry; his eyes had chased the soldier's.

The brigadier smiled. 'Come back tomorrow. We'll have more news for you then.' He stood up and put out his hand. 'Always delighted to meet you press people,' he said.

They walked out into the night.

'Something's going on,' said Carl.

'I know,' said Eva. 'But what?'

'Hell knows. Let's find out.'

Outside, a cool wind blew off the lake. Eva stretched and looked up. The moon had not yet risen and the arid, eastern sky was bristling with stars. She stood marking the constellations. It was peaceful; the war an irrelevance, a tiny blip in the infinite grandeur of the universe. She listened, straining for the sound of mortars. There was nothing but the occasional plop of a fish and a faint change in the silence as a bird flew past. That night, they slept beside each other in the back of the car, too tired even to touch.

Thirty-two

The first rays of dawn were lighting a cornflower-blue sky when they drove out to the scene of the massacre. By the time they arrived, the few wisps of cotton wool cloud had burned off and the morning was already hot. Three dead cows lay bloated in the village square, legs pointed stiffly at the sky like inflatable toys. A cloud of blue-bottles buzzed over them in the hot, still air. Otherwise, the village seemed empty.

'Is anybody here?' yelled Carl. Silence.

'Halloh-oh.' His call was swallowed up by the shimmering air. The flies over the cows buzzed angrily, as if he had disturbed them.

Eva opened her camera bag, fitted a wide-angle lens and snapped. She changed lenses and moved in, bending down on one knee for a closer shot of the dead cattle, then she returned to where Carl was making notes.

'What shall we do now?' she asked.

'I guess look around. Maybe someone'll show up.'

'Do you really think all those people we saw at the hospital were injured here?' asked Eva. 'It looks too small.'

It was more of a hamlet than a village. Dirt-poor, with a makeshift look, as if its inhabitants were refugees or people who had recently been re-settled. The two dead cows seemed to be the villagers' only livestock – unless they had moved their animals elsewhere – and there was no cultivation. No shimmering fields of paddy, or vegetable patches, or fruit trees. Apart from the six or seven mud-walled houses, squatting in a wobbly U around the baked square, there was nothing. Just flat, baked earth.

'Who knows? It's hard to tell. These places can have lots of nooks and crannies. Let's take a look.'

They were walking towards the broken-down houses when they heard the growl of a diesel engine. A dark-green army jeep was careening over the rutted red track to the village. It pulled up beside them in a cloud of dust and fumes.

'Fuck!' said Carl. 'They followed us.'

The brigadier was in uniform this morning. Three brass pips gleamed on his epaulettes, he wore polished black jodhpur boots and carried a swagger stick. 'Good morning!' he said in a hearty voice. 'Just thought you fellows might need a little help.' He gave them the same reptilian smile, but the eyes above it were angry.

'We're fine,' said Carl, not bothering to be polite.

'I thought you might be interested in meeting one of the villagers.' A thin frightened man with grey hair was clambering from the back of the jeep. 'The village schoolmaster,' he said, like a conjurer plucking a rabbit from a hat. 'He was there. I'm sure he'll be happy to help you.' The brigadier grimaced like a hanging judge pronouncing sentence. Then he climbed back into his jeep and left in a belch of dust and diesel smoke.

There was nothing they could do; there was no one else around.

Once the brigadier had gone, the schoolmaster relaxed. Carl and Eva listened as he recited his story. The rebels had come just after midnight; first laying seige to the village with automatic weapons and mortars, then entering it with machetes and swords, hacking their way from house to house.

'Do you want to see where they came first?' he asked, pointing in the direction of the village's only concrete house. 'Fourteen people, dead. The whole family. Women, babies, children, everybody. We heard them crying. That's how we ran.'

Carl and Eva followed him across the scorched earth into the house he had indicated. Someone had returned to wash it down; the floor was still damp. But they had not been able to wash away the fear stained into the walls.

She took a few pictures but there was nothing much to photograph. The only furniture was a bare wooden cot. The real images, the pictures of what had happened that night, were hidden in the floors and walls. She stared at the sluiced concrete, trying to see them. The sleeping infants and their mothers, the sun-blackened farmers. The flashing steel, the feeble protecting arms, the screams, the blood. With an effort, it was possible to imagine the victims. But the killers eluded her, masked by a cloud of incomprehension and unanswered questions. How had they done this? Were they drunk or crazed or both? Why machetes? And finally, how much alcohol was required to butcher someone so intimately, with a blade and not a gun? She felt sick: the stench in the house was overpowering.

'I've got to get out,' she called to Carl who was making notes. She had clamped her handkerchief over her mouth. 'I'm going to throw up.'

The steel glare of mid-morning outside the darkened house slashed her like a sword. It was late for pictures, but she wanted to walk, to get away from that house with its blood-drenched ghosts. She wandered between the mud-walled huts, looking for images.

The schoolmaster had spoken of a seige with automatic rifles and mortars, so she searched for signs of the shelling. There was nothing. Just blank-featured walls, the three dead cows and a mangy pi dog, rooting in a pile of rotten vegetables. She called to the dog, but he barked, ran away cowering and then barked again from a safe distance. So she returned to the main square, where Carl and the schoolmaster were still talking, miming to Carl that she had something to say.

'Later,' he called. 'I haven't finished.' She moved over to listen. 'So, tell me again how you escaped?' she heard Carl ask.

'I'm telling you, I hear the crying, I wake up. Then I'm running. In the back, where they aren't looking.'

The schoolmaster seemed oddly calm. Too calm, Eva thought, for a man who had narrowly escaped being butchered to death only twenty-four hours earlier.

'But I thought you said they had been shooting for half an hour before they came into the village,' Carl asked in a quiet voice. 'Surely that woke you all up?'

There was a hole in the story. Either the brigadier or the schoolmaster had been careless. Carl waited for the man to reply.

A grey flicker crossed the schoolmaster's thin face. 'I'm sorry. I'm not remembering everything well. I think some people are waking with the gunfire, some people are sleeping. I wake when I'm hearing crying from that house.' He smiled like a pupil who hopes he has guessed the correct answer.

But Carl had decided to let him go. He knew the man was trapped. 'Yes, of course,' he said, flipping shut his notebook. 'You must still be very shocked.'

When they were in the car, Eva turned to Carl. 'Something's fishy,' she said. 'There are no bullet or mortar holes anywhere. That's what I wanted to tell you.'

'I know,' he said. He turned the engine. 'We'd better try those doctors again before we leave, but we need to be quick. I've gotta file.'

They bumped down the rutted track from the village in a cloud of hot air and dust, leaving the schoolmaster waving tentatively behind them, unsure whether he had passed his exam or not.

The chaos of the previous night had subsided when they returned, leaving behind the apathy that follows drama. Heat had intensified the smells of grime and poverty, and the patients slumbered uneasily in the airless wards. The doctors had left. They woke a dozing orderly who directed them to the mortuary, where he said they might find the Cuban surgeon.

It wasn't the cold store, with refrigerated filing cabinets of bodies, they had expected. It was a concrete charnel house in a field, where men in rubber waders worked thigh-deep in blood, sluicing down the dead. Next to it, a pile of bodies jumbled indecently on top of one another: barebreasted women, men, their brown skins charred down to white, babies bloating in the sun like ripening melons. A gaggle of little boys hung over a fence watching the corpses, eyes wide with excitement, handkerchiefs clutched to their faces.

She glanced at the corpses and reached for her camera. Through the viewfinder she saw a little boy in navy school shorts, a half-naked mother clutching her infant, an old woman, blouse hiked up to reveal spent old breasts, waiting for the dignity death had promised and then denied. She lowered her camera without taking a shot.

Carl had found the surgeon. He seemed less exhausted than the night before, but now anxiety creased his face.

'It's not so simple,' he was saying in response to something Carl had asked.

'What's not so simple?'

The surgeon sighed, raised his shoulders and spread his palms: the gesture of the ordinary man faced with injustices he was powerless to change. Carl saw the struggle in his features – between the good, honest man he was and the man his position forced him to be – and waited, giving him time.

He sighed again. 'The situation is very complicated. The authorities, they don't want to speak of what really happened...' He trailed off, still wrestling with his conscience.

'And what did really happen?' Carl's voice was soft, cajoling. 'I won't quote you, of course. I promise,' he added quickly.

'I'm sorry. I'd like to tell you. But I can't. My position here. You must understand, I am a foreign doctor, an exchange volunteer, on trust...' He trailed off again. He looked defeated. The honest man in him had lost.

As if in compensation he turned now to Eva, who had been listening. 'Please, let me take you round the wards. Perhaps,' he said, turning again to Carl, 'one or two will talk to you themselves.'

'You go,' said Carl. 'I'll look around on my own. If that's OK?'

The surgeon took Eva through the massacre wards, explaining injuries and conditions. The men's ward was cavernous, lit by an oblique, pearly light from a single high window. The men dozed, their pain momentarily traduced by beauty. She worked quickly to capture the light and shadow. When she had finished, he led her into a smaller room, where a dozen women and their grizzling children lay awake, scared-eyed, on metal cots. Eva asked to take their pictures but they refused, as she guessed they would.

They wandered into a smaller ward, which seemed empty. The laundry-worn sheets on the iron bedsteads were flat and waiting. Perhaps they were just passing through. Then she saw a tiny tumulus on the bed the doctor was approaching. A hump, no bigger than a child's grave.

'Would you like to see?'

'No. Please...'

He pulled down the sheet before she could stop him. She closed her eyes, not wanting to see another mutilated child, revolting against the horror. And yet, despite herself, she looked.

She was a pretty little girl with golden skin, soft brown curls and a face washed with innocence. An angel asleep in a bright pink skirt, a sticking plaster on the satin dome of her tummy. A brown cardboard label tied her toes, like a parcel. It read 'Wounding Calamity'. That was all. No name. Just an announcement. All there was to say that she had gone. Wherever dead children go.

Eva froze. Her thoughts in a blur. At last, she reached for her camera, took three clumsy shots and ran. From the child. From the hot little room. From the hospital. From the decomposing flesh, bad blood, faeces, urine and disinfectant. From the stink of deprivation and death.

She was sitting on a wall in the hot sun, sobbing, when he found her. Her damp shirt had fallen open and a gaggle of youths were sniggering. She didn't even notice when he buttoned her up. He led her gently to the car and steered them, in silence, out of town, on to the ragged east coast road.

It wasn't the dead bodies. They were corpses, hollow shells. It was the child, her *aliveness*, that brought home to Eva the finality of death. This child would never wake, or call to her mother, or play in the dirt, or laugh as she chased a bird in the sun. It had been the defining moment, she realized later. The point at which she understood that paradise had been betrayed, not by an external force but by its own denizens. She felt not just bereaved but robbed. And she was, once again, a child in the road by her father's car, begging him not to leave. It was then that she decided to escape that life sentence. To embrace love, not run from it: its dangers and its sweet, sad treasures.

It was dark when they arrived at the empty hotel by the sea. Eva walked straight to the beach and sat alone on the black titanium-streaked sand. The moon was rising, sending a silver runner across the ocean, eclipsing the necklace of lights from the fishing fleet. As she watched the storm clouds, the heaving ocean with its dark-water monsters, she thought of the fishermen alone in small open boats on a hostile sea. Most couldn't swim and, without radios, they had no way of communicating with each other or the shore. No wonder they drank or ate *afium*. But it was also calming. Ancient and peaceful. Perhaps because here it was clear that destiny lay in the hands of nature and of God.

He came out to join her, after finishing his story. The pictures weren't needed yet, he said. Not wanting to disturb her mood, he sat down silently beside her. She stretched out her hand to show that he was welcome and when he put an arm around her, she leaned into the crook of his shoulder like a nuzzling dog.

'It's beautiful, isn't it?'

'Yes,' he said. 'It is. It really is.'

Later, in the hotel's empty, cavernous dining room, they talked about the massacre and she told him about the little girl.

'It was the army, wasn't it?' she asked, finally.

'Yup, that's what I think,' said Carl. 'But I couldn't write it, we didn't have proof.'

'But why that village?'

'Who knows?' He shrugged. 'I heard they killed people from three villages. The neighbouring villagers came to the first one, when they heard the gunshots. Maybe they were supporting the rebels. Maybe there were rebels holed up here, in that house they first attacked. Could've been anything.'

Both of them knew, though, that finally it was just another senseless killing in a long chain of killings; a landmark in hell.

When the moon dipped past the horizon and the night was velvet, they stripped and walked into the ocean. It was cool from the sea-storm, just below the temperature of blood. He took her into the fortress of his arms and held her in the dark surf. Washing away the gulf between them, letting their bodies slide along each other like seals.

Thirty-three

Storm clouds of bats were gathering in the rain trees when they returned to the capital: another world, another century. They drove past the glitzy new casino ('Entry to VVIPs Only'), the Emperor City five-storey shopping mall, the glossy emporium of last season's western clothes, and into the lane. On the corner, the old *betel*-seller nodded in greeting. Next year, he'll be a porno-video rental store, thought Eva. The old slum was dolling itself up with tack.

The house was waiting, open but silent. Mary had spied the car from her window and retreated to the servants' bathroom. When Carl strode into the kitchen, she ignored his calls. He poured them both a strong, ice-cold gin and tonic and brought them out to the verandah steps where Eva was sitting, knees hunched up like a child.

He sat down beside her, feeling her warmth and her emptiness. 'To our first assignment together.' He raised his glass. She raised hers back, smiling weakly, both of them hearing the unsaid words. 'Great pictures, by the way,' he added, handing her the negatives they had processed in the first large town. 'The paper'll love them.'

He was trying to cheer her up, but she couldn't pretend. She felt numb. Later, she would feel many things: anger, pain and a deep, abiding sadness. But at that moment all she sensed was that they had entered a twilight world from which there would be no escape. Only more death and more sorrow.

'Why don't you go have a nap?' he said, although he knew that what she was suffering from wasn't tiredness but something else. 'I've a few calls to make and then I'll join you.'

He went into his office, closed the door and flopped down behind the desk, his head in his hands. Then he sighed, flipped through his address book and picked up the telephone.

It took him a while to make the operator understand him but eventually, after several bursts of static, he heard the Captain's voice on the line.

'Hey, *machan*. Great to hear from you. How's my old buddy?'

'Fine. I'm fine. And how are you? Still stuck in the office?'

'Yeah.' He sighed. 'Wish those buggers in the south'd stop killing our boys. Let us get on with some real man-to-man fighting.'

An early mosquito had flown in through the open window and was buzzing around Carl's head like a tiny gunship. He paused, resisting the impulse to follow through on the Captain's remark, reminding himself that he hadn't rung for an interview. He was wondering how to open the conversation, when the Captain did it for him.

'So *machan*, anything I can do for you?'

'Well, yes.' Carl paused. He hadn't thought about what to say next. He just knew that something had changed for him, too. In that God-forsaken village and on the beach beneath the moonrise. Something he had to act on. 'You remember that guy?'

The Captain laughed. '*Which* guy, *machan*? Please give your old buddy a clue.'

'You know...' Carl was hesitating. He felt ashamed, embarrassed and guilty. 'The guy who was hanging around my girlfriend.'

'Riiiiight?' The Captain was wracking his brains. 'A-ha. Got it. I remember. What about him?'

Carl hesitated again. The bald facts glared accusingly at him like the eyes of a murdered man. 'Well, he's disappeared. I was wondering if you could do anything to help.' He paused again. 'Eva's pretty upset about it,' he added quickly, as if to explain himself.

The Captain burst out laughing. Guffaws of locker-room noise barrelled down the line. 'You know one thing? I'll never understand you guys,' the soldier said, when he'd finished laughing. He was genuinely puzzled. 'No offence meant.' He paused for what seemed to Carl like a very long time. Then he laughed again. 'Sure, man, anything for you. I'll do what I can, though it's going to be damn difficult to trace him.'

Carl breathed a sigh of relief. He had done what he could. He and the Captain could talk easily. They chatted for a few minutes and then, pleading exhaustion, he hung up. Dusk had fallen like a piece of dirty washing over the day. A small squadron of mosquitoes whined around his head, echoing the thoughts inside it. He felt lost in a whirlpool of conflicting emotions, a rapid in which bobbed one small life-saver of hope. He closed the windows, considered checking his messages, decided not to and, at last, plodded up the stairs. In the kitchen he could hear Mary clattering. She seemed to have become both noisier and more absent these days. But he couldn't really dwell on it. He had other things to think about.

No one heard the slow hiss of a betrayal. Nor the deflation of his self-esteem soon after. It had, after all, been just a matter of two conversations. A few words lost in the infinity of the world's words.

Thirty-four

It was after breakfast by the time a bleary-eyed Sergeant Piyadasa drove home. Past the tyre shops, past the Kreme Kake bakery, past the New Delite Ladies Store, past the Mon Repos Travellodge, past the movie poster for *Fatal Beauty* – Adults Only (which lured in passers-by with blatantly false promises of slipped brassieres and stocking-tops), and on through the overgrown village. At the turning by the banyan tree he slammed his foot on the brakes, cursing. Chutti the Down's Syndrome five-year-old, was standing plumb in the centre of the road like a misplaced garden gnome. As usual, his shorts were around his ankles and he was waving his willy at the jeep, his face lit up by a smile of pure happiness. Sergeant Piyadasa was about to wind down the window and yell, when the child's mother rushed out and scooped him up into the folds of her sarong, scolding. Chutti, who was far away leading a presidential parade, carried on beaming and waving his penis until long after the vehicle had rounded a corner. He loved police cars and missed no opportunity of demonstrating his affection.

Too much hot and botheration, that's what it was, thought Sergeant Piyadasa. His mind was not on the child, who would probably get run over sooner or later, but on the previous night's business, which he viewed with an odd mixture of pride and disgust. The pride had come before, the disgust later. Like a hangover.

They had spent the night dumping bodies at crossroads in the neighbourhood: twenty-eight in all, in batches of seven. He had counted them out, making sure there were enough for every likely trouble spot, and enough tyres and kerosene to burn them, proud of his efficiency. But it was a messy business. The corpses, which had been delivered from outlying stations the previous afternoon on orders from the higher-ups, were already stiff and stinking to high heaven. And it was a hell of a job getting the fresher ones to burn on the rubber.

By 4 am, when exhaustion and self-doubt were settling in, Sergeant Piyadasa had begun to wonder if quite a few weren't recycled they smelled so rotten. It was one thing to dump fresh bodies, he thought, with warped policeman's logic. Scare off any village-boy trouble-makers, act as a deterrent. But old corpses? That smelled bad, and it wasn't just the bodies.

He had shuddered then, trying not to think of things like karmic consequences or what his sister with all her hocus-pocus and superstitions would say. But in the pre-dawn chill, with death in his nostrils and on his hands, it was hard to keep away the demons. What he needed, he had thought at that moment, was a good shot of *arrack*. Or better still, another job. Something better than gravediggers' work. It was bad enough needing booze to sleep, and now, when he slept, he had nightmares.

That thought had provoked another depressing moment of truth: he wasn't qualified for anything other than policework. Not even clerking, at half the pay and no perks. Bloody madman, he thought (referring not to himself but his boss), with his AK47s and automatic pistols and promotions on body bags. Everyone knew the fellow had gone *pissu* after his whole family got killed in front of his eyes. A wave of self-pity at his miserable lot in life swept over him.

Now, though, he was too exhausted even to feel sorry for himself. Sleep. That was all he needed. As he turned into the driveway of his house, his mind on a cool shower and Lalitha's clean terry cotton sheets, he saw an unfamiliar car, a battered white Fiat, parked in his space under the jambu tree.

'Gunada—!'

The houseboy's name was half out of his mouth when he remembered. His mother-in-law. He'd forgotten the date. The thought of her – a fatter, older, bossier version of his wife, with spectacles and a huge set of keys (even in a policeman's house she locked up *everything*) – snapped him awake. She was like that. A dose of bloody castor oil. He was just wondering how to get into his own house without being spotted when two things happened simultaneously. Gunadasa ran out: and a head-splitting burst of static screeched from his two-way radio.

'BLOODY HELL!' he roared, blowing his plan for an invisible entry. He seized the instrument.

'Yessir?' Gunadasa was trembling even more than usual.

'NOT YOU, FOOL!' he yelled, waving the radio at the boy. A barely incomprehensible voice was stuttering out through the static.

'Yessir!' Gunadasa gave his idea of a salute and fled – straight into Mrs Upasena who had heard the roar and stormed on to the narrow verandah, in her voluminous pink housecoat, accompanied by Banda, Lalitha's black-and-white pi dog, who had heard the shout, too, and was quivering for action.

'So?' she called out, shrugging off the hurtling houseboy with one arm and slapping away the dog with the other. 'You're calling this time to be coming home and making a fine hullabaloo for the neighbours?' Banda got in three full-throated barks before Mrs Upasena slapped him again. 'SHUT UP!' she yelled.

The dog yelped and fled to the safety of the kitchen, where he lay, snout grounded, tan ears back, gazing sulkily at the verandah. He disliked Mrs Upasena almost as much as her son-in-law did. In the corner of his brain a plot was hatching. He could smell it: the appetizing, leathery pong of New Delite Ladies Store slippers.

Sergeant Piyadasa gave a feeble wave and winced as the radio screeched into his left ear.

'Yessir! Right away sir!' he said.

It was the Chief on the other end of the static wanting him back at the station, double-quick.

But Mrs Upasena was only just working up a head of steam.

'So? Is this the way to greet your old *nandamma*, even? Just a dirty face?' She gave a snort. 'Fine fellow my daughter's been marrying, not respecting his elders and betters, even.'

Satisfied with her opening salvo, she flounced back into the house where Banda was waiting, teeth back in a fake jester's grin. 'OFF!' she yelled, batting the mongrel away before he could get in a quick nip. Damned woman was like an elephant in *must*, thought Sergeant Piyadasa. First destruction and then off, trumpeting. Suddenly he was glad of the radio. He turned the key and reversed, trying not to run over the crotons Lalitha had re-potted, or her dog, who was out again barking at the car. Ten minutes later he was unlocking the door of his office.

Constable Somapala was waiting to tip him off when he drove in. There had been a call from the Special Forces' switchboard. The caller hadn't left his name, but the constable had recognized the Paras' operator.

'Any clue? Rank? Where from exactly?' asked Sergeant Piyadasa. His brain was too sluggish to start connecting dots at that hour.

'Nossir. Just ringing back in an hour, sir.'

Sergeant Piyadasa waited until the constable had crisply saluted his way out and then sank his head on the desk. Forty winks before the call, then maybe he'd get the lads to rig up a cot. Better to sleep here and face the old she-elephant fresh, he thought. Cheered by this idea, he closed his eyes and sank instantly into a deep slumber.

He was dreaming of Lalitha and his mother-in-law. They were dancing to the latest *pilum* song. Their frilly housecoats, which had somehow become soaking wet, clung to their shuddering curves, making them look more like a pile of laundry in a washing machine than two screen sirens. Beside them danced a chorus line of svelte young *pilum*stars in tight white pants and white boob tubes. Mrs Upasena was demanding they change into something more respectable, when the girls transformed into a line of gyrating corpses. His mother-in-law continued scolding. But he was gratified to see that the corpses were laughing. Sergeant Piyadasa wanted to see what would happen next but a jangling noise was piercing his dream, spoiling his favourite song.

He opened one black-rimmed eyelid, revealing a blood-red eyeball. The black Bakelite telephone on his desk was ringing. He reached out to take it off the hook. Then he remembered.

'Hello-oh,' he said in the polite-but-on-the-ball voice he used for talking to superiors. He had raised his tone an octave, hoping not to sound sleepy.

'Captain here,' said a brisk voice on the other end. 'I haven't woken you up, have I?'

'Nossir,' he replied, raising his voice another octave and clearing his throat. He now sounded like a buffalo being strangled.

There was a guffaw at the other end. 'Hey, man, what's up with you? Pants too tight?'

Sergeant Piyadasa blushed. 'Nossir, just the line sir,' he lied.

'"Yessir nossir." You've forgotten your old *machan*? I'm just after a quiet chat. Casual like, OK?'

'Sure, sir.'

By the time the Captain had finished his 'chat', which lasted barely seconds, Sergeant Piyadasa's face had turned from livid black through brown to charcoal grey. A Giant Panda masquerading as a chameleon.

'I'll check it out, sir,' he had ended, stalling. But he knew already what had happened.

The Captain's tone might have been casual, but he knew the damage a Special Forces captain could inflict on a mere police sergeant. Casual? he thought. As casual as a bloody sleeping cobra. When he put down the receiver his hands were trembling.

'BUGGER!' he roared, thumping the desk with his fist. 'BLOODY FOOLS!'

He mashed at the steel bell on his desktop several times, as if it were a stubborn lump of potato. The piercing *dring-dring-dring-dring* catapulted Constable Somapala out of his chair, his salute present and correct before he even turned the doorhandle.

'Get me the register! Now!' yelled the sergeant.

'It's, it's in you... your your desk, sir.'

Sergeant Piyadasa swooped down and wrenched open his bottom drawer, spilling it and its contents on to the floor.

'FOOLS!' he roared.

The constable, who had catapulted across the room and was on his hands and knees picking up papers, shot his head up, banging it on the underside of the desk. 'Sssorry, ssir.'

'Not you, fool!' he yelled. 'Those coconut-heads down there! Now get out and let me think!'

Constable Somapala bolted out of the room as fast as he had entered.

'And bring me some tea. Fast!' Piyadasa screamed at the closing door.

The wiry little constable skeltered down the passage to shout at the tea *peon*, who in turn yelled for the store *peon* to bring more milk and sugar. Fast.

When the door had firmly shut, Sergeant Piyadasa sank his head in his hands and tried to think through the fog of fatigue. What he needed was a cover-up, something that would shift the blame somewhere else, if he was going to keep his promotion. He gave a bitter laugh. Promotion? What for promotion? He'd be lucky if he wasn't *de*moted to traffic. He knew what had happened to the boy, of course. That, in a way, was part of the problem: things were so much easier to fudge when you were ignorant. Not that he had been there himself, but the boys had told him before he left this morning. It had happened last night. An 'accident', of course.

He gave in to a rare moment of reflection on the follies of fate. If only the Captain had called yesterday. Curse those fools and their bloody over-enthusiasm. He rubbed his red-veined eyes with one weary paw, as if trying to kick-start his brain. Then he reached down below his desk for the White Book.

In the grey half-light just before sunrise the following morning, a green Bell 212 helicopter with army markings flew westwards over the ocean. No one noticed. At that hour, the fishermen were still strung far out along the continental shelf and the coastal villagers were snoring off their *toddy*. In any case, at high tide the clamour of the rotor blades would be drowned out by the surging surf.

On board the craft were four men: an airforce pilot, a captain, a flight engineer and an airman, who sat propped against the open doorway by the machine-gun mount, except today there was no gun. The wind had dropped, there was only a thin grey haze and the craft flew steadily towards the horizon. Beneath it, the ocean beyond the raucous shoreline was calm, its bosom swelling gently in long deep grey sighs. One breath in, one breath out.

The airman leaned his head out over the water. It was his first time, either in a helicopter or on one of these flights, and he felt panicked and queasy. 'Lower!' he yelled, fighting the airstream and the roar of the engine. 'Bring it lower!'

'What?' yelled the pilot, his head tilted back over the seat.

'Lowww…'

His words gusted out of the doorway and over the ocean. But now the helicopter had found its mark, an invisible radius beyond the reef in the blacker water, and was circling slowly downwards.

'OK!' bellowed the pilot.

The helicopter wobbled and settled on a column of air. The airman scrambled back into the belly of the craft and began tugging and then heaving at the heavy shapes on the steel floor. The thought of them and their smell made him retch.

'They're too heavy,' he yelled aft. 'Help me.'

This time the flight engineer caught his words and scrambled over his seat into the back. One lifting, one pulling, steadying themselves against the helicopter's rocking motion, they bumped and dragged a first sack and then a second, over the corrugated metal to the open door.

'Now!' the engineer screamed.

If the fishermen had looked up, they might have seen two small black shapes tumbling into the water, followed by a fine mist of vomit. But they were sleeping the sleep of the weary and the drunk, deep in dreams of *pilum*stars in swelling bodices and marble mansions that smelled of roses instead of fish, blood and the sea.

Thirty-five

Mary looked over, yet again, at her altar. Yes, it was still there, the blue envelope with the red and blue border and the Man with the Torch stamp – or was it a woman? – nestled beneath her prayer book. It was already worn slightly pale at the folds, although it had only arrived two days ago. She reached over – unable to resist reading it once again – although by now she almost knew its contents by heart, plucked out the single sheet of pale blue airmail paper. '"Von von nout seben Pranklin Abenew, Tchigaco, ILL"' Ill? Vhy so sick?', she read out loud, her forehead puckering slightly on the final word. But this evening she was content to let that niggling question be and instead lapsed into a happy fantasy provoked by the address itself.

Amerika. The super-abundance of street numbers confirmed all her notions of a land of plenty: a vast country with streets so long they stretched almost beyond her powers of imagination. To cope with this unmanageable idea, she had simply transported what she knew – Carl's rented house in the capital and others like it – enlarged it until it slightly resembled the White House, as per a grainy photo once seen in the local paper, added a few more balustrades, a flock of white plaster cranes, a pink plastic chandelier, as seen in Zap Electrics, Lunuwalla (motto: 'We Will Elektrify You') and, perhaps, a dash of mint-green housepaint. Then she had added other similar houses and a few larger versions of the shops that she frequented, which sold a logic-defying array of goods (electric kettles, dog biscuits, hairbands, T-shirts, greetings cards, music tapes and so on). The fantasy got updated from time to time, of course, as she received new titbits of information. But this was how things stood tonight, in the land of her dreams. She let it float for a moment and then continued with the letter.

'Dear Mary,' it began in a neat, sloping hand, which went on to ask how she was and a few other opening enquiries. After a paragraph or two of general news, which gave Mary either a glow of vicarious pride – 'I'm working for a Professor at the University now' – or provoked a *Tchik*: '…but the pay is lousy' – came the real news: 'I am thinking of visiting the island soon with a friend and hope I shall see you.'

At this point she put the letter down again, as she had a dozen times before, removed a black wriggly hairpin from her bun and absent-mindedly scratched her skull with its tiny round tip. She was thinking, or rather, daydreaming. Thinking and planning. There was, she noted, no mention of the *mahataya* in the letter, but she ignored that as easily explained: not nice, no, washing all personal things in public. All that mattered was that Nancy, the *mahataya*'s wife would be returning to take up her rightful place.

Already, Mary had mentally installed her in Carl's bedroom, reproduced a squalling baby and was now bossing around the *aiya*. As for that *vesige*! She gave one of her snorts. Well, she'd see to her. For the umpteenth time she reviewed the plan she had refined. All this letter meant was that she had better get moving, *ickmanta*. With that reviewed and decided, she put the letter back, re-installed her hairpin, after checking the ends for foreign objects, looked at her imitation gold ladies' wristwatch and switched on the small-screen television Carl had given her. Nine o'clock. Time for the news.

The screen flickered and then grew blue into the room, just as the state TV channel's logo appeared, accompanied by a pop version of the national anthem: an unfortunate 1950s calypso melody, which, in this rendering, sounded even more like something from *Blue Hawaii*. Mary's interest in television news wasn't current affairs, although she noted that the price of onions had risen, but education. She studied the newsreaders – their clothes, their hair, their make-up and, most of all, their BBC diction, with only an occasional relapse into island-speak – as seriously as an eager finishing-school girl.

'Good evening and welcome to the nine o'clock news from here in…'

'Good EBEning,' she mimicked in an unnaturally prissy falsetto. 'And velcum to the NINEohCLOCK nuooaz prom hair in…'

For the next ten minutes, her brow puckered in concentration, her hands folded neatly in her lap like the newsreader's, she parroted her way through the international news: 'Varships in the Fershan Gulp; Fresident Vush at the Vite House; Hurricann ob Plorida.' The domestic news: 'Vus crash in Lewalla, nun dead; Rise in onion frices; Fresident ofens pactory.' There was no mention of the rebels north or south; or the war. And the weather: 'High fressure, hebby rain and fossivle storms expected opp the coasts.'

The newsreader had been wearing peacock-blue this evening, and Mary noted that her hair seemed to be done in a new, very fetching and more natural style. Subconsciously her hand slipped up to her own severe Olive Oyl bun and loosened a few strands slightly, as she made a mental note to see if that colour blue suited her. She sat through the national anthem once again, and then switched off the television. Before undressing, she undid her bun and posed in front of the mirror, cheeks sucked in to achieve the required pout, hair held up in a messy approximation of the newsreader's French pleat. 'Sorry, no way,' said the mirror. Mary let her hair back down. '*Tchik!* All nonsense,' she muttered, in consolation for the mirror's verdict, and busied herself for bed.

If television had been more pervasive and Mary more impressionable, she might have been the kind of girl who watched

Baywatch and grew up wanting to be a silicone-enhanced lifesaver. But as it was, TV was too intermittent, and its satellite programmes too alien, for anyone in the island to confuse it with real life. Besides, Mary had an unshakeable sense of herself: newsreader-speak was the limit of her schoolgirlish fantasies. She slipped into her frilly nightdress and, with a reaffirming glance at her unmade-up self, got into bed. As her hand reached inside the pillow-case, she remembered: an old friend, neglected recently. What if that letter had been from Burt? A whisper of nostalgia blew over her heart and was quickly dismissed. *Paaf!* she thought. No use thinking of that now, she had work to do before the *nona* arrived. With that she smiled a secret smile, nuzzled into the pillow and fell asleep almost immediately. With unremembered dreams.

Eva sat cross-legged alone on Carl's bed, thinking. It had been how long now? She reached over and pulled out her diary from a leather satchel, counting back the time to when Mohan had first called her. Nine weeks and five days. It was a long time. Too long. She flipped through the files in her brain, looking for instances of people who had been released after disappearing, doing the arithmetic of hope. But the truth was: no one had been released. No one that she had heard of.

She flopped back on the bed, staring at the ceiling. A firefly had flown into the room and was hovering perilously close to a large spider's web. She watched it, half-consciously hoping for its survival, seizing on it as a symbol of something very fragile that might still escape death. She dared not admit that what she feared, almost as much as him dying, had happened: Navahiru was becoming a memory. The shadow of someone she had loved, but, as always, not enough. She fought now to envisage him – his smell that she never could unravel, his velvet skin, his smile – as if those memories were talismans that could bring back the living from the dead. The firefly still hovered in a corner of the ceiling, the bead of light in its tail flickering like a goblin's torch. She sat up, grabbed her address book from the bedside table and flicked through it. There was one chance left.

She ran downstairs to Carl's office and dialled a number. A flunkey answered the phone.

'The Minister is very busy.'

'I know, but we're very keen to photograph him,' Eva said, appealing to his well-known vanity. 'Please at least tell him who's calling.' She named an international news magazine. 'We want to feature him as Man of the Year.' It was an inspired lie.

'Madam, I am telling you. He is very busy. You must be knowing how important he is—'

'Please.'

There was a silence on the end of the phone. Eva breathed a small prayer.

'Just a minute,' said the flunkey.

She heard the receiver being laid down, footsteps on a hard floor and then voices. Five minutes later, the man was back.

'The Minister has kindly agreed to see you at ten o'clock tomorrow morning, in his office.' The flunkey's voice was newly oiled. 'I will notify the guards.'

Eva put down the phone. When Carl returned half an hour later, she told him.

'What do you think?' she asked. She had followed him into the kitchen.

'You mean, do I think he'll help you?' He reached into the fridge for a beer. He wanted to tell her about his call to the Captain, but he didn't want to raise her hopes and it was complicated. She might ask questions. He decided to say nothing, at least for now.

'Ye-es.' She was hesitant. She didn't really know what to do or how she felt any more.

Carl shrugged, pouring the beer. 'I guess he might. It's worth a try.' He took a deep gulp. Something niggled at the back of his brain. 'Say, isn't he the guy with the camp? The one who likes watching kids being tortured, puts them in acid baths?'

Eva winced. 'Well, that's the rumour. But he's still the Interior Minister. If anyone can get someone released it's him.'

'Good luck,' said Carl, raising his glass. 'Rather you than me.'

'Won't you come with me?'

'Look, Eva, it's better you go alone. More likely you'll be able to charm him into a corner. If I go I'll have to interview the bastard.'

She had been hoping for company. For moral support. But he was right. She had a better chance on her own.

A livid sun beat against the walls of the cramped old quarter, fortifying the odours of rotting fruit, cow dung, palm oil and sweaty grime, as if out of spite for being trapped. As Mary passed the open lavatory on the corner of the *penakaraya*'s lane, her nostrils clamped tightly shut, she was sweating. *Tchik*, no wonder this place stinks like a sewer, she thought. She picked her way across an open drain filled with oily sludge. Past a volley of ripe remarks from a line of rickshaw drivers that made her blush: '*Aiyo, madam ennewa*'; '*Annay*, check that arse'. And finally to the snake-paint door. She knocked. There was no reply. She put her ear to a crack. From behind it she could hear the unmistakable high-pitched monotone, sawing through the wood.

She pushed gently and the door creaked open, complaining. The shaman was in the early stages of a trance, head thrown back, scrawny neck exposed, irises vanishing into his forehead, as if looking for something mislaid in his brain. On the mat in front of him, with his back to the door, sat a tiny old man in a spotlessly cleaned and pressed white shirt and sarong. His face was twisted, like a pickled walnut. Mary recognized him as the *dhobi* from a neighbouring embassy. His Excellency's underpants had gone missing off the line and the *dhobi*, who, in fifty years of washing clothes, had not lost so much as a sock, was determined to catch the culprit. She filed the information for use, if necessary, at a later date.

Her mouth opened to say something unpleasant to him, when the atmosphere in the stifling little room rushed at her, shutting her up as surely as a frightened passenger on a runaway train. She tiptoed to a corner and sat down. The *penakaraya*'s upper torso was still revolving like a top, filling the rooom with his bat-like sonar. Suddenly, he jerked, swivelled right-face about and became still. What Mary saw then wasn't the *penakaraya* but something far more frightening. All thoughts of using him to further her own ends evaporated like water in the fire of his gaze. The *dhobi* sat rigid. Transfixed like a mouse in front of a cobra. The hex he had intended to put on His Excellency's chauffeur, whom he suspected was the underpant thief, instantly aborted. Suddenly, without warning, the *penakaraya* loosed a thunderstorm of blows and abuse over the old man. Horrible howls rent the hot, fractured air. Mary would have fled but her leg muscles had turned to jelly. She burrowed into the wall like a mouse, hoping to disappear.

As abruptly as a needle lifted from a record, the *penakaraya* stopped his assault; gestured to the *dhobi* to take off his shirt and launched his mouth at the old man's stomach, sucking noisily. Finally, he raised his head, spewed a stream of what looked like blood into a small brass bowl and with a final, almost school-teacherly pat on the old man's head, indicated the session was over. Mary's eyeballs strained in their sockets. She scrutinized the *dhobi*'s stomach as he put on his shirt. It was a smooth, brown rice-ball, with only a faint red mark where the *penakaraya*'s mouth had been. The old man was smiling, the wrinkles ironed from his face, the spite sucked out of him. He looked childlike. Purified. Mary's mind emptied like a dustbin into a cart.

The *penakaraya* gestured rapidly to her to come closer. Involuntarily she felt herself get up, move forward and sit down. Now that she was in front of him, she no longer felt frightened but worried. Part of her seemed to be hovering near the ceiling, look-ing down, curious, in a disembodied way, to see what would happen. For a long while, the Penakaraya stared at her. She could feel him uncomfortably roaming around her interior rooms, peer-ing under furnishings and inside long-locked doors. Although he wasn't speaking, he seemed to be saying something. She tuned her ears to hear.

'I can do nothing for you,' the voice was saying. 'Your heart is closed. Pride has made you and pride will kill you.'

From her perch near the ceiling, Mary tried to decide if the words were meant for her or someone else.

'You must go. But I cannot force you,' the voice went on calmly. 'I can do nothing for you until you are ready.'

Mary was certain he was addressing someone else.

The *penakaraya* now spoke out loud. 'You!' He bellowed, shooting a thin dagger of a forefinger towards her. 'You are knotted like bamboo. Twisted as creeper. You are like a dog, poking its nose in wrong places. And like dog, you will get bitten…'

Before Mary could decipher anything, she felt her eyes close. She was falling down from the ceiling into the depths of a limitless blackness. Far above her, as if on the surface, she could hear the voice thundering like storm waves, but she could no longer make out the words. It was cold and almost pitch-black, and she could feel fleshy things writhing against her. Beyond them, other creatures were coming steadily closer. She felt icy and afraid.

She heard howling like a deep ocean wind, filled with pain and sorrow. Then, she too felt a terrible pain, as if she were being eaten alive by a creature inside her. She could feel it, tearing first at her internal organs and finally her heart. But now, the creature seemed to be going for something else. At that moment, she screamed, with all the force left in her: a prayer to the Buddha and all the gods.

She opened her eyes. She was lying on her bed at home. The window was open, letting a cool night breeze into the room. She had no memory of how she had returned from the *penakaraya*'s room. But she could feel something in her hand. When she opened her fingers she saw a small sachet of herbal powders. She smelled it, trying to decipher the ingredients, but they were unknown to her. She re-wrapped it and placed it on her altar. Then she dozed off. It was almost midnight when she re-awoke. Outside, she could hear the white-noise of the crickets. They seemed to be cheering although she couldn't be sure.

The Minister had the trappings and mannerisms of the powerful. His office occupied most of the first floor of a dazzling white wedding-cake, which had once housed a governor's mistress, but now sat on a traffic island, blinding motorists and causing the occasional crash. He had a tennis-court-sized lawn of scarlet carpet; a monstrous desk, empty but for an unused gilt pen-set; a fleet of limousines; and a football team of frightened flunkeys. He also had the ability to convey anger without raising his voice, and multiple commands with a single wave of the hand. In public, a phalanx of courtiers trailed behind him, like exhaust fumes from a jet. And in private, the same people hovered invisibly, ready to spring into action at the press of a bell.

When Eva crossed the scarlet lawn, he was on the telephone.

'...well, why isn't it here?' His voice was as chilly as reptiles' blood.

There was a long pause, while whoever was on the other end of the line spoke. She got out the medium lens, took some establishing shots of him at the desk and then swapped it for the 105. Close up, he had the pasty skin and open pores of a sensualist and a drinker. But his eyes, beneath a set of sparse eyebrows, were passionless and flat, and his face was almost boyishly hairless. It was a corrupt face, Eva thought, reflecting on what she knew of him. But a corruption so complete and well-learned it came with its own façade, like a creature that evolves a protective camouflage. This was a man skilled in the habits of hypocrisy. He had never been innocent. Even in nappies he had had that face. She wondered why she had come.

'Yes. *Immediately*,' he said, emphasizing the imperative. He put down the receiver and looked up. His brow puckered, as if he had forgotten who she was and what she was doing in his office. Eva prompted him. She knew it was a pantomime, a throw-back to the days when he was less important than he was now.

'Of course, of course. What a pleasure. It's been so long. Please, please sit down.' He motioned to the chair. 'Surely we can chat before business? Now,' he continued, his hand poised above the receiver, 'what will you have? Tea? Coffee? Coca-Cola? Or something else? A scotch perhaps? You know I always keep my own supply.' He waved airily at a cabinet against a wall, proof of his status, his immunity to restrictions forbidding alcohol in government offices.

'Coffee would be lovely,' said Eva, as he simultaneously lifted the receiver, summoned the flunkey and despatched him. He seemed to have a gift, this man, of highly economical gestures. The fluency of power, she supposed.

'And now,' he said, brushing back a hair that was already in place. 'Tell me more about this Man of the Year business.'

Eva stumbled through the lie: brilliant career; economic miracle-worker; iron fist in velvet glove (that bit was true, at least, she thought); shining example to the region; local hero; etc.

As she spoke, she reflected on this career herself. The unofficial version. He had flunked his degree at an English technical college turned university, having spent his time and his father's money on fast cars and rent-boys; run up a £50,000 bill at a London bookmaker's and fled the country; entered his father's practice (probably under duress); won a safe seat in parliament, with his father's influence; rose quickly to power with the help of money and muscle; and amassed considerable wealth beyond his known means of income. He also ran a small private army. All that was normal for the island. What wasn't normal was that he tortured young men in his spare time. *That* wouldn't be going in the magazine. An icy ghost touched her. Once again, she wondered why she had come.

He had been nodding and smirking as she talked. Finally he put up his hand in a gesture of modesty.

'Please,' he said. 'Enough. You are too kind to me. Now, how would you like me to be?' He ran a foppish hand through his hair once more and sucked in his rice belly.

For the next twenty minutes, Eva acted through the fiction, while the Minister ran through various expressions and poses. Serene, commanding, amiable, forceful. Against the desk, on the telephone, by the window, by a plastic palm tree. Under the poster of Van Gogh's *Sunflowers*. When she had finished, she packed away her lenses, wondering what to say next.

'Minister?' she paused, uncertain of his reaction.

'Yes?'

'There's just one thing...' She summoned her courage. 'I wonder if you could help me with something.'

'Of course, of course. Anything.' He leaned back in his chair. His vanity had been flattered by the photo-shoot and he welcomed the chance to bestow a godly favour, to sprinkle a little of his power.

'Well...' How could she put this? 'I have a friend, a nice young man, a law student...'

'And he needs a job?' Job petitions crossed his secretary's desk daily. He leaned forward, poised to fulfill the easy request, like a greyhound scenting a hare.

'No,' said Eva bluntly. 'He's missing. We think he's been taken by the police or perhaps the paramilitaries. I've spent weeks trying to find him.'

The Minister leaned back again, his eyes wide. Then he leaned forward, rested his chin in his hands and stared penetratingly at Eva with his flat eyes. Like a cobra readying to strike. 'My dear miss...' he said searching for her name and not finding it. 'Are you really sure you should be getting involved in this kind of thing?'

But now it was out, her courage had returned. 'Yes,' she said. 'Yes, I do. I know him very well. He's innocent. He should never have been taken. Wherever he is, you have the power to have him released. It's your ministry. Besides,' she added in an inspired flash, 'he comes from a good family, a well-known family. His father was a senior lawyer. If anything happens to him, there'll be publicity. It's inevitable.'

She watched the changes in his face as she said this and took a final risk. 'I also imagine the President won't want that sort of press.'

It was more than sly, it was blackmail. But to her amazement, it worked. He was angry, but the arrow had struck. Like all bullies, he knew when he was outmuscled.

'OK,' he said gruffly. 'What's his name?'

She watched him as he wrote the details on a piece of paper. Then he picked up the receiver and made a call.

'Done,' he said, a minute later. He was beaming with pride. He was again the champion weight-lifter flexing his muscles. 'Anything else?'

No, there was nothing. Eva burbled out her thanks as effusively as possible and re-crossed the scarlet lawn.

At the door, he called to her as if remembering.

'And please, don't forget to send my secretary the photographs.'

She drove home, shivering despite the noon heat. Unable to escape the feeling that part of her had been robbed. She was sure now that his call meant nothing, or it had come too late.

'What did he say?' Carl asked her when she got back. He put his arms around her and kissed her forehead. 'I've been thinking about you all morning, wondering when to come get you outta jail.' He was laughing, stroking her head and shoulders.

Eva smiled. 'He made a call. I guess to the paramilitary commander. Said it was "done".'

'Well, that's great,' said Carl. 'I'm really pleased for you.' He held her out from him. 'Cummon,' he said seeing her face. 'Don't worry. It'll work out.' He lifted her off her feet with a hug. 'Now, let's go and finish what we started before you went out.'

Eva wanted to believe him. But something in her couldn't. A bell tolled deep in a well, close enough for her to hear.

Thirty-six

I f Mary's basic nature had not been so ingrained, her experience
at the *penakaraya*'s house might have been enough to halt her in
her tracks, or at least give her pause. As it was, she decided to dis-
miss the shaman's warning as the babblings of a mad old man.
(*Mona pissude*, she thought. Waste of money.) She would put her
own plan into action. That night, after the *mahataya* and the
woman had gone out and the house was empty, Mary crept
upstairs, as silently as a spectre. It was dark in the room but she
didn't want to switch on the light for fear Toots might notice. She
tiptoed to one of the fitted cupboards and quietly eased open the
door. Lighting a wax match, she grasped what she was looking for.
Then she padded softly over to the bedside cabinet, lit a second
match and extracted something else from the small shelf. She had
reached the bedroom door and was opening it, when a dreadful
crashing sounded above her. She jumped and dropped the match.
Tchik, stupid woman, she thought. It was only the polecats,
thumping like a furry cricket XI in the ceiling.

Quietly, she slipped back downstairs and into her room, put the
objects in her bag, took off her apron, smoothed her bun and put
on her black leather pumps. Switching off the light and locking
the door behind her, she walked briskly out to the gate, where
Toots was dozing. The crunch of feet on gravel woke him. He

stretched his eyes into two ketchup-drizzled saucers and raised his eyebrows.

'Going out? So late?' he asked, genuinely surprised.

Mary didn't bother to answer. She trotted out of the gate, heels clattering sharply in the night, and down the lane to the main road, where she hailed a passing rickshaw. Forty minutes later it dropped her on the edge of the old city. She got down, forgetting to argue the fare, and waited until the putt-putting had receded.

Above her a full moon sailed across the sky, filling the sky with cold, pale light and illuminating the sandy ground before an old stone shrine. Hugging the shadows of the rain trees, she made her way to a crumbling, waist-high colonnade, climbed a few steps and entered. It was damp inside and chilly as a tomb. A smell of bat guano mingled with rancid coconut oil and cheap incense. For a moment, she stood in the shadows waiting for her eyes to greet the dark. Then she felt her way forward, moving by instinct rather than sight, to a small sanctum, built at the back of the shrine, in which stood three formless stones. The shapeless trinity of a faceless god. A god so ancient he bore no name. *Deviyo*, they called him. The god. In which simplicity lay the root of all his power.

She sat down on the rough stone flags, opened her bag, produced the objects and laid them out in front of her. Then she waited for her ears to filter out all other sounds. For a long time there was silence. Faintly at first, then swelling louder and louder, the shrine began to echo. It was like being inside a giant bell. As she listened, she shivered. Alert and afraid; straining to understand. She could feel the power of the shrine expanding. Swirling around her, threatening to sweep her up, to dash her against the walls, like a branch in a hurricane. Fingers of fear crept towards her brain. But she sat, tense and cold, focusing her mind on the task, immobile as a corpse. The objects before her seemed to move. At first a little, then more, until they glowed and danced. This was the moment she had been waiting for. Around her the sounds raged and crashed, like a storm. Then slowly, as slowly as they had begun, the crescendo dropped, the notes sank one by one, until there was nothing but a faint hum, the gentle soughing of a wind in the trees. She fell to the floor in prostration before the stones. And for a long while she lay there, barely conscious.

When at last she emerged, the moon had dipped below the horizon and the night was dark, its blackness deepened by the massive bulk of the mara trees, looming beside her. She walked quickly, anxious now to escape the morbid atmosphere of the place. The dribble of houses thickened; then lit streets appeared, empty and ghoulish under fluorescent lights. She was hoping to spot a late-night rickshaw, but the city slept. Nobody had seen her come and nobody saw her go. She moved through light and shade, past shut-eyed windows and faceless glass, silently, like venom moving through a vein.

Next evening, when the house was again empty and Toots had not yet come, she crept out into the driveway, dug a hole and dropped in the objects. Then she re-sprinkled the gravel and returned to the house.

Part Three

Thirty-seven

They are on a little blue boat beneath a blue sky on a blue ocean. A dot of blue enclosed in a transparent blue sphere. A bubble in which they float. She is sitting, her bare legs straight out in front of her on the deck, trailing her fingers in the water. He is behind her, leaning lazily against the house, one knee up, one leg reached out to touch her. The sea is warm. And clear as liquid glass to the ocean floor. Electric-coloured fish swim in this paperweight bubble: damselfish, minstrel sweetlips, moorish idols. A tiny puff of sand from a tiger-striped crustacean floats up. And the girl in the bubble points and says: 'Look, a nautilus.' It's like a dream. Of a place far away from the clamouring world. His dream. And now hers, too.

'I think we're falling into a well with the sky at the bottom,' she says, feeling herself falling, falling: softly, warmly, a delicious blue glass fall.

'Eva. Wake up. Wake up.'

She opens her eyes. Someone is stroking her cheek. She looks up, sees a pair of brown eyes and puts her arms up like a child waiting to be kissed. He kisses her on the lips, but quickly. A kiss in a hurry with something else to do.

'Babe. Wake up.' He shakes her. 'There's a call for you.'

'Must I?' She blinks and smiles, three-quarters asleep. She wants to stay in the blue blue bubble and float with the rainbow-coloured fish. 'S'important?'

'Yes.' The brown eyes look worried. 'Please, Eva. You have to get up.'

'OhhhK.' She yawns and swings her legs out of bed. 'Where?'

'Downstairs.'

The blue bubble is fading too quickly into grey. Expressionless and cold, the day still in bed without its face on. Somebody is pounding rice. *Thump pah, thump pah, thump pah*, syncopated like a drumbeat. But there are no birds. And the cicadas have gone to sleep. It must be very early, she thinks. She picks up the receiver. She recognizes the voice. It seems far away already. She sits down very suddenly in the chair. The paperweight bubble falls to the floor. And shatters into a thousand fragments. One word is left. A glass splinter searing its way into her heart. She folds up in the chair and screams.

The beach at Ambuwa is a long, uninterrupted strip of crunchy golden sand hidden behind the cheap concrete housing and shabby shops that cling to the southern edge of the city like beggar children to their mothers' skirts. Because it is neither in the city nor out of it and there are no respectable access roads, it doesn't rate a mention in any guidebook. Nor is it marked with a jaunty blue-and-white striped umbrella (indicating a 'Popular Beach') on tourist maps. Only the fishermen who drag their outriggered *oruwas* up and down its slopes, and the dark and ragged children who hunt for mussels and play cricket on its sands, know it. It's beautiful, but it's a slum beauty. Undiscovered, uncelebrated by the world beyond.

His body had washed up there, the previous morning. Carried ashore by a freak storm far out to sea. The fishermen found it floating in an island of driftwood, a dark log amid the pale ones, scooped it up in a net and hauled it in to shore. When they stretched it out on the beach they saw that he was young and hand-some. Not bloated or sea damaged or gnawed by fish. He couldn't have been in the water very long. '*Pau naeda?* Sin, no?' they said, their leathery hearts cracking. But when they inspected the body and saw the pulpy mess in its crotch, the burn marks on its taut young skin, the bullet wound in its back, they looked at each other, snapped their hearts shut and said nothing. They were poor men who drank toddy to dull their terror of the sea. They knew when to talk and when to keep quiet. They covered him up with an old striped sarong and went to find the village elder. Then they returned to unravelling their nets, their thoughts locked up in their hearts.

In due course, according to the sleepy timing of all tropical para-dises, a policeman arrived with a notebook to record the event. It was a formality, naturally. He panted over the burning sand, sweat-ing from the weight of his responsibility and his rice belly. But he knew what had to be done. He glanced at the corpse, fired off two or three questions, noted a 'Death by Drowning', snapped his notebook shut, straddled his motorbike and left in an overheated roar. Later an ambulance arrived to take the body to the morgue. There, primed by the police station, someone tied its toes togeth-er with a brown cardboard ticket that read 'Drowning Calamity'. Its scars, its mutilated scrotum, the bullet wound in its back, were thus miraculously healed by bureaucracy. The rest would be taken care of by the crematorium's fires. Or so they thought.

He heard her scream and came running. A barely human howl, halfway between the strangled cry of a peacock and a wolf, rang through the house. One word had lodged in her throat like a splin-ter. The word she wouldn't accept and couldn't reject. When he reached her she was crouched against the wall, arms hugging her knees, rocking, her face as white and blank as a board.

'Babe, what's up? What is it?' He spoke softly as one would to a weeping child.

She buried her head further into the dark cavern of her body, rubbing her forehead against her knees, as if to erase the word that had branded itself on her brain. She was dimly aware that she was biting her arm.

'Please, babe.' He reached out a hand again to stroke her hair, but she shook him away. Her tears and her silence unmanned him.

'Please. Tell me. Talk to me.' He spoke softly, as one would to a frightened animal.

Finally she said it, in a whisper. The word she feared to say, because speech would give it life.

'They tortured him. They found his body yesterday morning. He's dead.' Her face was blotchy and twisted, a cubist painting by a bad artist or a child, filled with things she wished she hadn't heard.

He put an arm around her shoulders but her recoil pushed him away. 'Can I do anything?' he whispered.

'NO! NO! NO!' she screamed. She grabbed a marble ashtray from the desk and hurled it at the wall. It bounced off and on to Carl's computer, smashing the screen.

'Hey, Eva, stop it. Please.' He had grabbed her arms and was shaking her. 'Please. You've got to calm down.'

Before he could stop her she had leaped up and was out of the door, running. Through the sitting-room windows, across the gravel and out of the gate. Her feet were bare and she was wearing just a thin silk kimono. He waited, wondering whether to let her go. Whether he *wanted* her to stay. But then something greater than love or loathing grabbed him. He ran after her, to catch her before she reached the main road.

The lane was quiet and empty, the tarmac wet beneath her feet from the night's rain. She ran until she was breathless, until the noise in her head had stilled enough to hear birdsong and chanting, from the white temple by the road. She slowed, drawn by the ancient, sonorous rhythm. When he reached her, she was leaning against the arch of the gateway, cheek pressed against the stone.

He stood next to her in silence. Wishing that whatever had calmed her could calm him, too. When the sutras were over, she opened her eyes and saw him. She smiled, her eyes alight. 'I'm sorry. I'm so so sorry,' she said.

He put his arms around her and they walked back. In the east, pink and yellow delicately bruised a pale-blue sky. The birds sang discordantly, like schoolboy sopranos without a choirmaster. The crisp, hot smell of roasting rice pancakes and coconut *sambol* rose from the house next door.

Thirty-eight

The small house of mourning is packed and hot. Tight-muscled rugger players, wormy students, pretty girls in garment-trade dresses, with thin, hairy legs, relatives, close and distant, friends, colleagues of his father's, ladies from the frayed edges of society in polyester Kanchipurams, minor politicians with synthetic smiles, hoping to capitalize on the death, people no one has ever seen before; all spill out on to the verandah, drawn by the universal appeal of other people's misfortune. Funerals were great crowd-pullers. It was important to see and be seen. Nobody seems to be mourning. Everyone is chatting gaily and drinking cups of tea and glasses of passion crush.

The only person who is truly grieving is his mother, a small black-haired woman in white. As each new arrival comes up, she smiles weakly and mops her eyes with a lace-edged handkerchief. But mostly she stares at her lap, as women hold her hand and their husbands stand by. Embarrassed by the outbursts of emotion. She looks wracked with the effort of containing her grief in a white lace handkerchief, of not letting it spill all over her guests. Over the living room hovers a word. The one word everybody knows and nobody says. Not even in a whisper. It hangs around like an uninvited guest. A jilted suitor at a wedding party.

He lies in the middle of it all, in a bed of cheap purple satin.

Propped around him are stiffly-dressed anthurium and lily wreaths, which stick out like bridesmaids' dresses. Funeral flowers, as kitsch and waxy as the corpse. The morticians have magically removed his wounds so that he now looks like a normal dead person: wooden, grey, with grotesque make-up and blow-dried hair. Everybody but his mother ignores him.

When Eva walks in, the room falls silent and people look up. She is the only foreigner. She lays her flower by the coffin, a single white rose, and looks at him, wishing she could breathe life into death. She wanted to see him one more time. To hear his voice, to touch that velvet skin, to look again into those beloved eyes. But he is gone. Leaving behind a hollow made-up shell. An empty violin case. She is glad they have hidden his wounds. She didn't want to see that beautiful violin smashed, its strings and neck broken. She wants to remember him as he was: young and handsome. A flash of white teeth in a dark pool. A burst of early-morning sunlight.

She says a few words to his mother, introducing herself as a friend. The older woman responds automatically. Her eyes are puffy and red and her voice is like weak tea. She is welcoming, but Eva doesn't want to stay in that house, suffocating with grief, hypocrisy and the smells of hot flowers and sweat. She walks out into the starlight.

The western sky is ablaze when they finally light his pyre. His body lays out of sight, the silent centrepiece of a ritual he won't take part in. Hidden behind a white cloth pagoda that towers like a giant wedding cake above the crowd.

The rambling cemetery is packed with people dressed, like Eva, in white; a bride dressed for a funeral. They surge towards and are pushed back from the pyre: a roiling sea crashing around a rock. In the centre, clustering around the funeral pagoda like rock-crabs, are members of the family, friends, journalists, human rights activists. But beyond, in the sea of people, are ordinary citizens: the curious, professional funeral-goers, passers-by, small boys perching in the branches of mango trees, beggars in tattered sarongs with amputated limbs, lepers, junkies. Drawn by the crowd like a second line of shellfish, attaching itself to its edge.

Eva fights her way through all these people until she reaches a small parapet wall from where she can see. She has brought a camera with a motor-drive but she doesn't feel like using it. She wanted to be alone, to have a space to mourn in private, but there is nowhere. Hot, white-nylon hips and shoulders press around her like a shoal of fish. She closes her eyes, retracting into herself, and tries to remember him. But all she can think of is the irony of death and instant celebrity.

She sheds no tears. But as she watches the pyre alight and glow like a lantern, eclipsing for a moment the fire of the setting sun, she feels as if her heart has been ripped from her body and is flying up into the flames.

She forces herself to shoot a roll of film. For the record. Though she knows she will never look at the pictures.

It's true, she thinks: we love people most when they are gone. She wonders, then, in the half-mad way of the grieving and bereaved, if he died because she hadn't loved him enough. But this evening, as she watches him burn into the night, the thought is still a small wave in the ocean. Only later will it grow into a raging storm.

The sea and sky are welded together by molten sun when Eva arrives at Ambuwa beach. Yesterday's tragedy bled of colour by the midday sun, like an over-exposed photographic print.

She runs down to the water's edge and cools her feet on the damp, ribbed stretch of shore exposed by the tide. Then she wets her hands and face. For a long time she stands and stares at the sea, hands cupped over her eyes. Like a mariner scanning the horizon for a ship. Or a lover waiting for a loved one. But the ocean gives back nothing. It lies leaden and mercury in the glare like a giant thermometer, burst in the heat.

She turns and looks at the beach. The sands are empty. Only the beached fishing *oruwas* lie side by side like lobsters on a fishmonger's slab. The fishermen are asleep in their huts. She doesn't really know why she came or what she expected to find. She wants to cry but something has boiled away the tears. She gets in her car and slams the door so hard, the frame rattles. As she turns the engine, a child comes running towards her. A barefoot little girl in a faded pink cotton dress two sizes too big, which hangs off her sparrow shoulders.

'*Nona, enna.*' The child is gesturing towards a *cadjan* hut: a battered palm leaf shelter with a steep roof that grazes the sand like a tent. She can see a thin bare-chested man standing in the black rectangle of the entrance, beckoning. More children cluster in the skirtpleats of a plump, dark woman, who must be his wife. She climbs out of the car and follows the child, who is racing ahead, like a pebble skipping on water. Back across the burning sands.

After the glare of the beach, the inside of the hut is pitch-black and, for a moment she is blind to everything but the reek of fish, sweat and urine that grabs her throat. The blackness pulses with invisible curiosity. Someone pulls at her shirt to sit her down. She is handed a scalding glass. She sips. It is strong, very sweet black tea. Gradually seven pairs of eyes and seven rows of milky white teeth emerge; and then the bodies to go with them. The hut is crammed with children pressed together on shapeless bundles of faded cloth and coils of net, like puppies. Everyone is grinning and staring at her expectantly. She makes out the polished ebony torso and faded blue striped sarong of the fisherman. On his lined black face is written the poor man's suspicion of the unexpected, the unknown. The hot little hut feels like a trial in a mediaeval allegory; a halt in a strange descent into hell. She remembers now, through a daze of heat and mild sunstroke, why she has come.

She offers credentials and careful questions. Cautiously the fisherman spins out his story: the line on which dangles one small fish. He tells her about the helicopter, circling far out over the ocean that morning. Its military markings. And the two bodies (he knows now that they were bodies) tumbling into the sea. Then, skirting warily around the details, he recounts how they found the young man that morning. When she uses the word that has not been spoken all week, he nods and is silent. They both know that some things are better not said. Not now, in these days.

The image of the helicopter stirs something deep in her brain. A fragment of memory. No, less than that. A grain of intuition. She sniffs, as if it had a smell, an elusive perfume. The scent of betrayal. She thanks the fisherman and walks out into the white noon glare.

She doesn't know why but she doesn't want to go home. She turns her car away from the city, southwards. Along the winding coast road, across the paddy fields, through the invisible, looking-glass barrier to the tricky turn by the banyan tree. Into the gates of Lorne.

Thirty-nine

Night had fallen like a shutter and with it his spirits. Carl had spent hours doing next to nothing. Opening books and closing them. Picking up the telephone receiver and putting it back. Pouring a scotch and swigging it back in two gulps. Tapping half-heartedly at his laptop. A half-finished joint lay in the ashtray. And a half-finished story glared at him from the screen. He glared back at them both: daring either one to tempt or reproach him.

It was seven. He didn't know where Eva was. He hadn't gone to the funeral house or the funeral. Perhaps he should have. He had told himself that he didn't want to intrude on her grief. It was her thing, not his. But the truth was, he felt locked out. Excluded from a part of her he suspected he could never enter. It wasn't the guy. He was dead now. History. It was the intense almost obsessive relationship she had with the island. He suspected that she had gone now to Caspar's. To that other rival for his love.

All these were only half-truths, of course. His excuse for getting angry. With her, with the place, with the hand life had dealt him. The real truth, which he could not acknowledge, was that he felt guilty. Another chasm had opened between his real self and his ideal one; he was back on the crab boat. He slumped back in his chair and kicked the bottom drawer of the desk, as if slamming it shut on his thoughts. Then, for the twentieth time that day, he picked up the telephone. And this time he dialled.

'Captain, please.' His eyes were hard and the vein on his forehead stood out. Through a burst of static, he guessed more than heard the usual question.

'It doesn't matter. Just put me through!' he yelled. (He added a 'for fuck's sake' under his breath, knowing the operator would cut him off if she heard it.)

More static and then a waiting silence. Finally the familiar voice came on the line.

'Captain here. Who is it?' The voice had a brisk, parade-ground starch.

'It's me, I've—'

'Hey, *machan*, how—' said the Captain, slopping into civvies.

Carl stopped him. 'Cut the crap. Do you know what's happened?'

'No. What?' He sounded uncharacteristically worried.

Carl told him. In four words. The vein on his forehead was throbbing.

'Shit!'

There was a long pause. Carl waited until the Captain spoke. His fist clenched and unclenched.

'Listen man, I promise you—'

'No! You listen!' Carl shouted. 'You promised! I trusted you! Trusted! D'you understand what that word means?'

'Cool down man, I'm trying to tell you—'

'Don't you fucking tell me to cool down! My relationship with the woman I love is gonna be fucked! Fucked! Because of you. Your guys. D'you understand that? You were my friend. I trusted you.' He was on the verge of tears. 'For Christ's sake, man. What am I going to say to her?'

'She doesn't know, does she?'

'No, but...' Carl slumped back in his chair. 'Oh fuck, man.'

'I'll be there at twenty-two hundred.'

'No, don—'

But the line had gone dead. Carl kicked the bottom drawer so hard it broke. Spilling pens, paper, files, old notebooks, unwanted thoughts, the detritus of his life, on to the floor.

'Mary!'

The door opened almost immediately. 'Yessir?'

She stood in the doorway in her crisp cotton frock, hands clasped demurely in front of her like a schoolgirl. The faintly flirtatious look of her early-morning wake-up slaps had returned. But with a harder edge. If he had thought about it, he would have said she was defiant. But he thought no more of it than he did of her prompt appearance.

'Help me clean up this mess, will you?'

When they had finished she stood by the desk as if waiting for something. Carl looked up from the old notebook he had retrieved from the floor.

'That's OK, thanks, Mary. You can go now.'

He returned to what he was reading, distracted. But she didn't move.

'Yeah? What's up?' he asked. He wished the hell she'd get out and leave him in peace.

'Sir...' She seemed uncharacteristically excited. 'Sir. Please. Read.'

She had pulled out a worn blue airmail envelope from the pocket of her apron and was thrusting it at him. Even before seeing the writing on the envelope, he guessed who it was from. He brushed it back at her.

'Not now, Mary. I don't have time. Anyway, it's to you not me.'

But her face was bright and bursting. 'From *nona*, sir. She's coming back!'

'*What?*'

'Madam, sir. She's coming.'

'Shit!' He thumped the desk so hard the jar holding ballpoints and pencils leaped on to the floor, smashing. Mary jumped back as if she had been hit. 'Shit! Shit! Shit!' He thrust a fist out for the letter. 'I'd better read it.'

As she watched him read, a cloud crossed Mary's face. A small, uncomprehending rain cloud lost in the middle of a sunny day.

'It's good news, no, sir?' she asked more tentatively, when he had finished.

'No, Mary, it's not good news. It's a goddamn nuisance, that's what it is.' The vein on his forehead had started throbbing again. 'Just get out, for Christ's sake!' When she had gone, he sank his head in his hands.

In her bedroom, Mary re-read the letter. Slowly, the lonely rain cloud was joined by others. The blue-sky day turned stormy. 'It's all her fault,' she muttered. Well, this time, she thought, I've fixed her. She replaced the letter on her altar. Pleased with her own ability to build dams across life's unruly river. Paddy bunds on chaos.

Forty

She rang the old bronze bell and waited. Its hollow laughter echoed back at her. She rang again. Still silence. An orange wasp buzzed crossly, trying to get back into its mud nest in the door-jamb. Eventually, she let herself in through the small garden gate.

The late-afternoon sun stagelit the Italian garden, transforming it into the set for a tropical *Romeo and Juliet*. But still Eva was shocked by its appearance. Long weed beards grew from the cracks of the dried-up water garden, the lawns were hairy and unkempt, a tree lay collapsed like a drunk, and the statues wore skins of slimy moss. It had been little more than two months, but decrepitude had advanced on the garden with the monsoon rains, like the ravages of a wasting disease. She called out. But heard only the birds preparing for bed. She walked around to the pergola. The familiar planter's chair was empty.

She ran into the house and down the corridor, calling. Her heart catching. His bedroom door was shut; the white panels stared back at her emptily. She tapped and then knocked. Louder. Finally, she turned the old brass handle. The door creaked open, crack by crack, annoyed at being disturbed. At the far end was the high white bed. She closed her eyes and prayed.

She stood there for a moment, letting her heart quieten. Then she opened her eyes. The long body lay stretched out beneath the white sheet like a burial mound, its eyes closed. She tiptoed towards it. The rise and fall of life was barely perceptible. Like a whisper. A spider-thin thread.

'Caspar?' she murmured. There was no movement. She took his large bony hand in hers. It felt like the papery skeleton left behind by a leaf. 'Caspar?' she called, louder.

He opened his milky eyes and looked at her. Feeling the presence he could not see. With her free hand she stroked his high marble forehead.

'Vivien? Is it you?'

'No. It's me. Eva.'

She felt a moth-like pressure on her hand. 'I'm so happy,' he whispered. He shifted now and winced. He wanted to be moved. She slipped her arms beneath his shoulders but he was too heavy. 'No. Please,' he said. 'You can't. Call Shanta. He's somewhere here.'

When Shanta had come and they had propped him on a throne of pillows he turned to her. 'So ,as you see, my pharmacopia of ailments has expanded its range. I'm thinking of opening another branch soon.' An echo of the old bass laugh wheezed from his throat. She bit her lip. A wave of love and sorrow washed over her. She frowned, to stem the tears.

'Caspar, what's wrong? Have you been in bed long?' she asked when her voice had calmed.

He coughed.

'It's OK,' she said quickly. 'Please, don't talk if it's difficult.'

He wheezed again like an unused trumpet. Brushing away the irritation with a hand. 'No, no. I can talk. It's just...' He winced and gripped tight her hand. 'It's just, I'm so sick of it. I wish that quack of a doctor would euthanase me. It'd be a lot cheaper than his useless potions. But he won't, of course. I've asked him God knows how many times. Useless fool.' He closed his eyes and let his head fall, exhausted.

Eva was alarmed. Depression and poverty had crept in with illness, holding him hostage. No wonder the garden was so rundown. It was his pride and his art, and she knew that he would have spent any spare cash on it. She wondered how long he had left.

'And you, my dear?' His voice broke into her thoughts. 'What have you been up to?' He fidgeted, wanting to sit up. 'Please. Can you call Mahinda? I've just remembered. Something to tell you.' He sank back, eyes closed. She half ran from the room and down the corridor, reluctant to leave him for a minute, now that she was here.

'Tell her what those boys said,' Caspar asked Mahinda, when they returned. His cloud eyes floated towards her. 'We have some news about your young man.'

Mahinda smiled a brilliant white smile. Not knowing what had happened and what was to come.

'Well,' he said, running a hand through thick hair. 'We've found out where he is.'

For some time she let him talk. Interrupting only with questions. Navahiru had been picked up by policemen, not paramilitaries. They had been watching him after his first trip. He was on the verge of being freed, after calls from his father's old colleagues and various appeals. But then something happened – an order from somewhere, no one knew where – and he had been moved to one of the paramilitary police stations in a suburb of the city. Where he was now. The chief, who sat elsewhere, was a notorious paramilitary colonel. But the police sergeant running the station was a cop seconded to the paras. She wrote down some names. None meant anything to her.

When he finished, Eva spoke. She told them what had happened.

'But this is terrible,' exclaimed Caspar. He tried to raise himself and failed.

Mahinda shook his head. 'I am so sorry.' He looked at her, eyes saying what words could not.

'Why didn't you tell us?' Caspar stretched out his bony hand and pulled her to him. 'My poor girl.'

She crumpled into his embrace, releasing tears dammed all week. A reservoir of sobs collected in her heart flooded out, sweeping Navahiru, sweeping her, sweeping everything before it.

Caspar said nothing but squeezed her to him. When she was done, she pulled away, groping for a shirt-tail.

'I'm sorry,' she said. 'You are so ill and I didn't want—'

'Please.'

There was one more thing. Something still unresolved. She turned to Mahinda. 'Did they mention anything else? Anything about why the cops came to my house that night?'

Mahinda shook his head. 'No. But surely you can guess why. They came because you're a journalist and you were nosing around.' He was troubled by her grief. The women he knew cried in hiding. 'Do you know how many boys in our village go missing every week? How many bodies we find on tyres? None of those boys has done anything. But some bastard in our village or some other village doesn't like the colour of his face. Or their family has a score to settle.'

She nodded, miserable.

'This is what we have sunk to,' he continued. 'Some bastard has a grudge and the next morning your son is dead on a tyre. Or in a mass grave. And you ask why they came to your house? Thank God they didn't kill you, too.'

Eva felt shamed. But with his anger spent, Mahinda was embarrassed. He reached out to press her arm. 'Never mind. What's done is done. Nothing much we can do about it.'

He left the room and returned, seconds later, with a bottle of brown-gold liquid. 'I think we all need something a bit stronger.' He turned to Caspar. 'If you don't mind, sir?'

Caspar, who had drifted far away, opened his eyes and smiled.

But something remained. When the teapot had been emptied – she had refused the *arrack* – she kissed Caspar and signalled to

Mahinda with her eyes. By the Adonis at the head of the steps, she turned to him.

Caspar's funds, she discovered, had almost run out. Mahinda's face flamed again when he told her of his brother's meanness. She fumbled stupidly in her bag for whatever cash she had. He refused it as she guessed he would, but let her take down a bank account number. Then she turned down the stairs. In the doorway she had arrived at, so many months before, she hesitated, wondering if this was the last time she would see him, if she should stay. But the story Mahinda had told her was worrying at her. She needed to think, to get back to the city. So she stepped back through the looking-glass and on into the world.

At the point where the avenue of royal palms turned a corner, she looked back for the last time. But the doorway to the house that had never seemed like a house was blank-eyed and empty. As it had been on the first day she had come.

It was late when she turned into the lane that led to Carl's house. A jeep was hurtling towards her, headlights blaring. As she pulled over she saw that it was a military vehicle: green with army markings. A phrase Mahinda had used – 'the order came from somewhere' – drifted into her mind, trailing a question mark.

Forty-one

Carl was sitting at his desk. In the halo of lamplight she saw the vein on his temple throbbing. Beneath the tan his face was red, the colour of island dirt.

'Where've you been?' The question halted her as she walked towards him. The room stank of alcohol and cigarette smoke.

'Whose was that jeep?' she countered. She saw the two tumblers on the desk, the dregs of golden liquid; the other chair pushed back from the desk, still bearing the imprint of another body; the second ashtray filled with stubs.

He shrugged, avoiding her eyes. 'Look, Eva, it's late, I don't know where you've been—'

She interrupted him. 'Caspar's. If you really want to know.'

'I thought so!'

'Oh for heavens' sake! You haven't shown any interest *at all* in where I've been in the last few days and suddenly you *have* to know? We're not living in some TV mini-series!'

He winced. 'If you're talking about the funeral, you know why I didn't come.'

'No, I don't. We speak the same language but we might as well be on different planets. Caspar's dying, by the way.'

Before he could speak, she left, slamming his answer in the door. He heard her footsteps crunch away on the gravel. For a moment, he waited, watching the grey fog of misery roll towards them. He leaped up and ran out. She was getting into her car.

'Please,' he said, grabbing her shoulders, forcing her towards him. 'I'm really sorry, about Caspar. It's a bad time for you, I know. But please. Let's not fight.'

Her face was twisted. 'Just tell me who was here? Was it your SF friend?'

He released her, avoiding her gaze. 'Yes,' he said.

'Why? What did he want?' Her tone was sharp. She looked ugly. He forced himself to remember the woman he loved.

'He just dropped in.' He sighed. 'I didn't even know he was coming. You know what people are like here. They don't ring, they just come round…' He took her shoulders again, but she shook herself free.

'I want to know who he is. What he does. You've never intro-duced us. I don't know anything about him. He could be respon-sible for Navahiru's death, for all I know.'

'He's just a soldier.'

'He's not. He's a para. They're part of the police. Navahiru was taken to one of the stations they control.'

'How do you know that?' He was suddenly on guard.

'Mahinda told me. They found out what happened to him. Where he was taken. The only thing they didn't know was that he'd already been killed.'

'OK. But it's nothing to do with the Captain, Eva. I'd swear that on my life. You're chasing the wrong lead.'

'How do you know?'

Carl let out a deep sigh. 'Look, I know. I know him. He's my friend. He's clean.' He took her arm, trying to ignore the demons tugging at them. 'Please, babe. Let it go. Let's just go to bed.'

She was exhausted, it was very late and there was nowhere to go. 'OK,' she said, at last. But far out to sea an eddy had stirred, a vortex of misery and suspicion.

*

It was dusk and bats were circling the mara trees, their sonar piercing the gloom. He was ready to go out, in a grey summer suit and loafers. Waiting for her to finish getting dressed. She ran her hand along the shelf, under the piles of folded clothes, feeling the wood beneath her palm. A smooth, blank surface. Her forehead wrinkled into a question mark.

She had worn them a few nights earlier, remembered putting them on the shelf when she got home. Now they were missing. She went over to the bedside table. There was only the lamp, an ashtray and a few hairclips in a black oyster shell. She opened the small cupboard and looked inside. Some books, a hairbrush, odds and ends. She felt underneath them, running her hand around the inside. Nothing. Then she looked on Carl's side. That was empty, too.

'Come on, babe, we're gonna be late.' She was dressed in the same red dress in which he'd first seen her. He thought she looked wonderful. A gypsy princess with a rope of damp hair snaking down her back.

'I can't find my earrings and necklace.'

'You look great as you are. I love that dress. We'll look later. Mary's probably put them somewhere.'

'I can't understand it,' she said when they were in his car. She didn't care about the jewellery. It was pretty but valueless. There was something else. 'I know I left them there...' Her voice trailed off into an inventory of thought.

'Well, it's not Mary. I'd swear by her honesty,' he said firmly.

She told herself to believe him. The trinkets were worth nothing to a maidservant. They liked sparkling, Christmas-cracker jewels. But their disappearance nagged her. No one but Mary had access to the house.

Later, when they returned, she slipped some money into the pocket of a pair of trousers and threw them in the laundry basket. It was an old trick.

*

When their clothes returned, two days later, as neatly ironed rectangles of cloth, she searched the pockets. They were empty but for worms of lint in the seams. She waited a day or two for Mary to mention the money. Then, very casually, she asked her to buy a packet of cigarettes.

'I've run out of cash,' she lied. They regularly left small change around the house. 'Have you seen any?'

'No,' she said. 'There's no money.' Her face slammed shut. Before Eva could say anything, she had turned and marched out.

Carl and Eva were living a truce but not a peace. Both knew it, though he tried to bridge the gulf between them. He took her out to dinner, to the beach. But there was a shallowness, as if each were afraid to dive deeper, to uncover the many layers of hurt. Finally she decided to confront the issue she had been avoiding. But, like so many angry lovers, she picked on the small thing. The real thing remained unsaid.

'I think Mary's stealing,' she said.

He was kneeling on the floor of the living room sorting through tapes. He looked up.

'Are you sure?'

She told him about the money.

'I don't believe it. Not Mary. Look, again, it's probably some-where else and you forgot.' He continued sorting and stacking the plastic cases.

'I didn't forget. She's stealing. I know it. I'm also pretty sure she took that jewellery. I just don't know why. Yet.'

Carl sat back on his heels and stared at her. 'OK. Suppose you're right. What do you want me to do about it? Fire her? She's the best maid in the island. She's been with me for years. I'd trust her with my life. If you want, I'll talk to her but what's she gonna say? Just forget it, babe. It'll probably work itself out.'

'No!' she was angry. 'It's not just that.'

265

'So what is it?' He tried to control himself, to speak softly as if coaxing a child or a madwoman. 'Please, tell me. We've got to talk.'

She stared back at him.

'Please, babe. You've got to talk to me.' He could feel his temper rising. 'For fuck's sake. What do you want me to DO? I'll do *anything*. Anything to sort this out. But you've *gotta* tell me what's bugging you.'

She wanted to scream, to tell him how much she hated him for being alive while Caspar lay dying and Navahiru was dead. But she didn't have the words, not even for the small things. Something black and heavy had invaded her spirit. She knew that silence was bad, but talking would be worse. So she said nothing. Caught in the current dragging them apart.

It was impossible, he thought, staring at the lights of the container ships on the horizon. He was an ordinary guy from an ordinary home in an ordinary town. All he wanted was a woman to love, a job and a cold beer in the evening. It wasn't much. Sure, he'd known they were ill-matched when they met. She was from the other side of the tracks. He was a hard-working nobody. It was a challenge, that was for sure, and he'd fought to get her, like he fought to get everything else. He thought he could make it work, but Jeez, was it hard.

He took a gulp of beer, wiping the rim of foam from his top lip. For the first time since they'd met, he wondered why he always fell for complicated women. If only she wasn't so damn sexy. Sex. He laughed out loud thinking of the whores in the hotel. Why the hell couldn't it just be simple? But he knew as he thought it that simplicity wasn't what he wanted. Not out of love, nor out of life.

He had come here, to the terrace by the sea, to drink cold beer and think. But his thoughts spun in circles. He stared out at the velvet expanse of sea starred with phosphorus. A gull, grey in the dark, flew silently by. The air was soft, as soft as her skin, and the ocean heaved gently, like her breasts in sleep. She was part of this place, more part of it than him. He would always associate her with it: its earth, a curve of hip and breast and thigh; its wind, her caress. She was a goddess, hanging like the moon stretched out over the ocean: the current between her thighs, her salty skin, her seaweed hair, her pink seashell lips; a siren singing an old sea song.

But he'd had enough. Enough of the lies, the fake smiles, the killing. The place was fucked. He had to get out. Would she come with him? Did he want her to? Would it work any better somewhere else? Perhaps she belonged here. With Caspar and Navahiru, or another guy like him. No, not Navahiru. Of course, he should have remembered. A cold trickle of guilt leaked into his mind, but he quickly suppressed it. The trouble was, he still wanted her. As much as he had on that first night. The thought of her with *anyone* else was like a stab in the gut. He sighed and lit another cigarette. If only they'd quit fighting. It wasn't just Mary, of course. It was the death. He ran over once again his conversations with the Captain. For Chrissakes, he thought, he'd tried to save the guy. It wasn't his fault.

'Good evening.' The voice was only slightly accented. He looked up, surprised.

'Philip!' He was conscious as always, of spoiling the sybilant French name.

A tall, fine-boned man in a blue cambric shirt and khakis looked down at Carl, eyes twinkling above a world-weary smile. Philippe, the aristocratic French chief of a Swiss aid mission, who wrote love poetry and liked Lacan: hobbies that Carl admired for not understanding. The two men were as different as Haut-Brion and Kool Aid, but there was a bond.

'May I?' He nodded at the spare chair.

'Sure,' Carl extended his hand. 'Great to see you. So what's up with the war?'

Philippe had more information than anyone. His was the only mission on the ground with contacts on both sides. But he was cautious, unless he had a reason to talk.

'Ah. The war?' The coathanger shoulders lifted in a Gallic shrug that encompassed not just the war but the world and everything in it. 'I was mistaken. I thought you wanted to talk about life.' He gave Carl an amused look. 'Or perhaps love? An even better subject.'

His long-boned fingers flicked. A white-liveried waiter appeared like a rabbit out of a hat. Breeding, thought Carl, observing the waiter's low bow. It had taken him twenty minutes to get attention earlier. Waiters were the same the world over: as class-conscious as pi dogs.

Philippe ordered a vodka and tonic. 'And for you?' He turned to Carl.

'No... Or, yes, I'll have another beer.'

'So,' asked Philippe, nibbling a cashew nut from a small glass bowl, 'how is your beautiful woman?'

'Still beautiful.' He sighed. 'I guess that's the problem.'

The Frenchman raised his eyebrows. 'Of course. She is interesting. And if you love an interesting woman, you must not expect an easy life.'

'So, what's your secret?' Carl asked. Philippe had been happily married to a beautiful painter from an old Ticino family for most of his adult life.

'*Arrosez la rose.*' He raised his glass, which had just arrived.

'What does that mean?'

'Water the rose. No woman can resist attention, or to be flattered. And with beautiful women one must worship, adore. You know that.' He stared mournfully at his drink, as if every beautiful woman he had ever known lay curled unattainably at the bottom of it.

'Sure,' he said. Perhaps he was right: he was too anal, too American.

Philippe lit a Marlboro and crossed his long legs. 'I have a proposition for you, by the way. Something that might interest you. We're starting our first emergency boat service to the north.

It'll be taking medical supplies, mainly; the first time we've been permitted to. Perhaps you'd like to come. You could see our work at the hospital and look around a bit. It might be a good story for you.' He flicked his ash. 'After you've watered the rose, of course.'

'Great. I'd love to.' Carl leaned forward. It would be the first chance he'd had to cross the lines, to talk to the elusive northern rebel fighters. 'When do you leave?'

'The day after tomorrow night. From the east coast. Call my office tomorrow and my assistant will give you the details.' He threw his drink back, stood up and held out his hand. 'And now, if you will permit, my own rose is waiting.'

Carl watched the tall back, bent slightly like a comma, as he quietly tipped the waiter and flowed out of the hotel. He moved through life like a brief punctuation mark between elegant phrases, neither too heavy, nor too light. Carl wondered about the passion, contained so effortlessly beneath the world weariness, and envied him. Perhaps it was easier being European, he thought. He admired Eva, that was obvious, but then who wouldn't? He felt a proprietory glow. He was being hard on her, he realized: the boy's death had torn something out of her. And if she was angry, it was only to fill the void left by loss.

'I want to come.' Eva was standing in his bedroom in a crumpled linen shirt and jeans, smoking. A pile of books lay open on her side of the bed; riffled through and discarded In an ashtray were several half-smoked cigarettes.

'It's late, let's eat,' he said. He had bounded upstairs, fired with schoolboyish enthusiasm for the trip, too excited to see the traces of her restlessness.

'I'm not hungry. I want to come with you.'

The storm clouds gathering all week were ready to burst, but he ignored them. He needed time alone to think. 'Babe, you can't. He invited me.'

'Call them. Or I will. I know Philippe as well as you. You'll need pictures anyway.'

'*Don't* call them. Please.' Her insistence was annoying him. 'This is between him and me. A favour. If you start bugging them you'll fuck it up for us both. I can take my own pix if we need them. It'll be night-time, anyway.'

'I'm not going to bug them. But I can ask, can't I?' The prospect of escaping from the city was lifting her spirits. 'Come on, Carl. There'll be stuff to do the next day, you know that. It'll be an adventure. I need to get out as much as you do.'

He hesitated for a second, torn between himself and her. But his native stubbornness had kicked in. 'I'm sorry, Eva. I don't want you to come. It isn't safe and I want to do this trip alone. You'll get another chance later. I promise. And now I've gotta go eat.'

She called after him, but he could no longer hear her. She grabbed a glass of water from the bedside table and hurled it at the door. A starburst of light and water, brief and satisfying as a firework, splintered across the floor. She burst into tears.

It was Mary's day off and she was out. He opened the fridge and pulled out a plate of chicken she had left under clingfilm. Why was he being so stubborn? he wondered as he gnawed on a leg. It probably wouldn't hurt if she came; it might even do them good to get out of town for a few days. And yet... he wanted the story to himself. It was a male thing, a buddy thing. He smiled, wryly, remembering Philippe's words. Water the rose? It wasn't how the Frenchman would have handled it. He knew he was making things worse but felt powerless to stop himself. It was the same old story. These things had a hideous momentum of their own. He wondered where they were going and where it would end.

He tore at the remains of the roasted leg, ripping the flesh from the bone with his teeth. She wasn't a rose, she was a strange, rare bloom requiring specialized treatment. Yes, she could be poisonous and flesh-eating when treated wrong, but exquisite when well-tended. The trouble was, he was no longer sure how to treat her; what magic potions, what elixirs of life to use. He had lost his way. They both had. He tossed the cleaned bone into the dustbin and reached for a breast. Halfway to his lips, he put it down. He had lost his appetite.

He put the dish back in the fridge, reached for a tumbler and poured himself half a glass of neat scotch. Then he went into the living room and drank like a Russian sailor on payday.

It was after midnight by the time he went to bed. She was asleep, her eyes red and swollen like a child's, her cheeks streaked with tear stains. He fell into bed beside her, still in his clothes. She stirred once and stretched an arm across him. But he was too drunk to respond. 'I'm sorry,' she murmured. He couldn't tell whether she was awake. So he wrapped his arms around her and fell asleep, nuzzled between her shoulder blades.

Forty-two

The sea came as a surprise, as it always did. A miraculous jewel, shimmering in the afternoon sun. He looked at the jade water undulating in the inner harbour and beyond it, the darker sapphire of the great outer port, bounded by the same jungle headlands and bays that had once sheltered a fleet. Along the docks, a yellow crane yawned, still and bored, over the empty deck of a rusted container ship. A flotilla of faded blue and tan fishing boats drifted beside the pier, their outboard motors up, napping. Two crows squabbled in the hot air, but otherwise the place was asleep. It looked like a port from a forgotten century. He stopped the car to drink in the salt air, cleansing the dust and fumes of the road. The city seemed a long way away. It would be a good trip, he could smell it.

He turned away from the sea and down the narrow lanes that led to the docks and jetties. Port entrance number three, Philippe's assistant had said; the *Celine*, an old fishing trawler. It had sounded simple but now he was here, he quickly saw that it was not. A maze of potholed roads, rusted steel arches leading nowhere and disused runways wound around the back bays and inlets of the great harbour, all punctuated by a system of roadblocks that forced the lost visitor back on himself. It was hot. A heat haze shimmered over the empty pockmarked roads, and there was no one to ask for directions. Even the naval guards at the road blocks were napping, or more interested in scratching their blue-camouflaged balls.

In the end, he came on it purely by chance: faded yellow letters at the end of a lonely road: Nilapatram Port Authority Gate 3. He drove beneath the flapping metal sign, past an empty hangar and the rusted wreckage of a vintage Avro, across a wide apron of weed-cracked concrete and down to the dock. The *Celine* was there, heaving gently in the water. He recognized the agency's red and white flag flapping crisply from the stern.

The narrow rail-less gangplank was down and a chain of bare-bodied coolies, balancing fat nylon bales on their heads, was swaying up it like bow-legged models on a catwalk. He parked, got out his kit – some shaving gear, a change of clothes, a sleeping bag, a waterproof – and strolled over to watch the action: the loinclothed men swarming monkey-like over the deck; the captain and pilot bent over charts on the bridge, occasionally looking up at an extra-loud shout; the crewmen busying with rope, tackle and the thousand other mysteries of seamanship; the landlubbers in agency T-shirts trying not to get in the way and failing: all the satisfying commotion and hullabaloo of a ship leaving port. A young man with close-cropped fair hair and an open face, wearing the familiar red T-shirt, was ticking off bales on a clipboard, before sending them down to brown arms reaching up from the mysterious depths of the hold. He seemed to be in charge.

'Welcome. You are in good time,' a voice behind Carl said. 'How was your trip?'

He swung around. Philippe had a feline ability to appear from nowhere. At this moment, he was standing under the shade of the Avro, an elegant punctuation mark, looking as unruffled as he had while talking about love over a vodka and tonic.

'Are you coming with us?' Carl was pleasantly surprised. The Frenchman's conversation would be an unexpected bonus.

'*Hélas*, no. I am just here to bid you all *bon voyage*. Unhappily, I'm imprisoned by my office. But Alain,' he glanced at the younger man on deck, 'will take care of you. He is our delegate for the north-east. And perhaps, as an experienced mariner, you can also take care of him?'

Carl smiled at the compliment. 'I'd be glad to. But it's a shame you're not coming. I could do with some more lessons on rose-tending.'

Philippe laughed. 'Oh, I think you have green enough fingers; but what you may need tonight is *le pied marin*. What do you call it? Sea legs?'

'Nah. It'll be smooth sailing. Look at it. Not a cloud in the sky.'

The Frenchman shrugged. 'The forecasts are mixed, as always. Some say the monsoon is already on its way.' He paused. 'As you know, one never knows with the sea. She is a woman, she can be capricious. Now, if you will permit, I have to check some things.' He held out his hand and smiled his sad smile. '*Bon voyage*. I look forward to your story.'

The pictures from her Leica were spread out on her light table. They weren't good. A record, more than anything else, of a moment. But Mahinda's words had made her pull them out; an instinct that they contained a vital piece of a puzzle. She scrutinized the images through a glass: an unmarked jeep, rising from the mist by the twelfth hole; four cops, crumpling the marionette corpse into its rear; the empty green, with its swallowed secret. And then the picture she was looking for: that moment the policeman had looked back at her.

She examined him carefully. It was a coarse face – thick features, pockmarked nose, black-ringed eyes – and corrupt. Not the refined sadism of the Minister, but the brutishness of the cheap bribe, the casual act of violence, the crapulous carnality. He hadn't been born with this face. It had grown on him over the years, like a crust of filth. There was something familiar about him and yet she couldn't place him. She made a mental note to ask Carl if he recognized him. He had left for the east before daybreak and when she awoke the mattress beside her was cold. She had felt for a note, but there was nothing; just an indent in the pillow. For a moment, she was free of the past. But then it marched back like an advancing army digging in, priming guns.

She had buried her face in his pillow then, as if that could bring him back. Bring *them* back. But his smell had faded, too faint to comfort her. So she had distracted herself by sorting through negatives. Using pictures of other people to fill the hole where they as a couple should have been.

She scooped up the transparencies, filed them away and pulled out the slides of the Minister. There was some reason why he had lied to her; why the cop had looked at her door; why they had come to her house that night; why Navahiru had been murdered; a web of secrets, lies and motives. But who was the spider at the centre of it?

She jumped up, ran downstairs, ferreted on Carl's desk until she found her address book and dialled. Marianne answered on the third ring.

'Sure. Come round for coffee,' she said.

There was a knock on the door as she hung up. It was Mary. Who had probably been listening.

'I have to go out for the day, madam.' The courtesy sounded like an insult. 'Please tell the *mahataya* if he calls.'

'Fine, please go.' She was relieved. Without the maidservant the atmosphere in the house would lighten.

She grabbed her car keys and was running out when Toots knocked on the open door. It was past his working hours and she wondered why he had stayed. She hardly ever saw him. He was just a hesitant smile by the gate; a pause between arriving and leaving. Suddenly seeing him in daylight inside the house, his kind face blinking like a mole, made her realize how little she knew about him.

'Yes, Toots, what is it?'

He wrung his hands and hopped from foot to foot. 'Ah, madam, I... I...'

The words sputtered and died like her car on a bad day. She tried encouragement. At last a torrent of sound gushed out. She had no idea what language he was speaking.

'Toots, I can't understand. You'll have to speak more slowly.' She pulled out a chair and smiled at him. 'Here, sit down.'

He took two steps into the room and stopped. 'No, madam, please, it's OK...' His hands and face performed a dislocated dance.

Eva tried another tack. 'If it's important, Toots, you can wait till Carl returns. He'll be back in a couple of days.'

'No, no, madam. Please, excuse me but I must talk to you...' He petered out again in an incoherent stutter.

The story emerged like a difficult birth. It was about Mary. He told her how he had caught her brewing spells; how she went out, returning very late; how he suspected that she had buried charms in the house; and finally the things she had said, her plotting, her simmering hate. He had come to her, Eva, because it was his duty and because he knew how fond the master was of Mary. He didn't want to hurt the *mahataya*'s feelings, so he hoped she would tell him instead. At the thought of Carl, his eyes welled. He owed him everything, he said: his son's education, his job.

'Bad business, too dangerous,' he said at last, shaking his head. 'I know you are not believing. But I am telling you this business is too dangerous. Peoples have died. You must bring down a *katadiya* quietly to stop this bad thing.' He fell silent, overcome by his unexpected speech and the enormity of what he had said.

Eva was silent, too. Toots watched her, waiting to be dismissed. Then she remembered that it was long past his going-home time. She watched him leave, shaking and muttering. It was impossible to tell whether he felt better or worse for his outburst.

She had no trouble believing him. Magic ran through island life like veins through rock and disgruntled servants were well known for casting spells. As for the efficacy of those spells? She laughed. These things functioned on the power of belief. But was she an unbeliever? Toots's garbled story had awoken something. An atavistic knowledge, buried in her past, reached out its bony fingers and tapped her on the shoulder. Despite the mid-morning heat she shivered.

He stood on deck breathing in the sea air. The barrier of the outer harbour, curved like a long beckoning finger into the ocean, was a thin white line far behind them. They were approaching the edge of the continental shelf and, beyond that, the deep, sapphire sea. To the west, the setting sun was unrolling a canvas of rose, gold and violet, but ahead, dusk had already cloaked the horizon, sending up a sharp wind. He breathed in deeply again, rubbing his arms. It was time to get a jacket. For the first time in months he felt alive, free. It was great to be back at sea.

Steadying himself against the soft pitch and roll, he walked to the hatch. Below were six narrow berths, slotted between the galley and the miniature mess-room: the tiny world he and Alain would occupy for the next twelve hours or so. It was as cramped as he remembered from his fishing days. If it stayed clear and wasn't too cold, he might sleep on deck. He pulled a windcheater from his canvas bag and was swinging back up when Alain called to him from the galley.

'Like some coffee?' The Frenchman was grinning like a boy, as delighted as Carl to be at sea.

'Sure, coffee'd be great.'

The two men squeezed around the doll-sized table and, over thick mugs of coffee and cigarettes, they chatted. Alain hadn't Carl's sea experience although he sailed a little, back home in Honfleur. He had been based in the north for three months, organizing supplies to the only functioning hospital; a ragged building cratered by incendiary bombs. He was new and young enough to have kept his enthusiasm and was bubbling with tales. For an hour or two, they swapped stories – the titbits of each other's lives that strangers proffer; bragging a little, circling each other like bulls in a ring – until finally they returned to the subject of the trip.

Alain told him they were heading north, roughly following the contour of the island. They hoped to dock the next morning at a small landing stage on the north-western corner of the peninsula and, from there, travel by road. For more detail Carl would have to consult the captain. He himself was eager to discuss the implications of the trip: the large quantities of supplies and medicines they were able to transport in relative safety; the comparative speed and efficiency of the operation; and other such information.

For a while, Carl half listened to Alain's earnest statistics, his keen chatter about medicines and bandages and road routes. He rose to fetch a notebook from his pack. At that moment, the boat pitched violently, almost knocking him off balance. He grabbed a ledge to stop himself falling and then stumbled, drunken-legged, towards the berths. The narrow gangway was heaving like a roller-coaster. Whoa, he thought, things are getting rough. Balancing against the walls of the narrow corridor, he staggered forward to the stairs, grasped the rail and clambered up, tight-knuckled to avoid being thrown back. Up top was a different place to the one he'd left. It was thick black and raining heavily; water was pouring off the deck; the wind and sea were howling. Before he could clamber out, a left-hook of wet wind slammed him in the face. He ducked back down.

'It's getting nasty up there,' he said, stumbling into the galley, wiping his face.

Alain looked up, worried. 'Can't get this damn thing to work.' He was fiddling with the dials of the agency's radio.

'Don't worry,' said Carl. 'We'll be OK. I've been in worse than anything that's likely to happen out there.'

Forty-three

Several hundred kilometres away in the capital, Thamba, the night watchman at the department of meteorology, felt two drops of rain on his shoulder and looked up even though it was dark. It had been sweltering for the last three months and now he hoped these two small drops might signal release from the suffocating weather. He cocked his head and listened but the sounds he was waiting for were drowned out by the squeaking of bats in the mara trees. It was a long weekend and the other staff had gone away, leaving him alone in the empty campus grounds. Only a single lit window, upstairs in the new wing to the south, signalled the presence of the duty meteorologists, but otherwise the old buildings snored behind locked doors. He looked up again. A flock of starlings were gathering in the ficuses: he could hear the coming rain in their excited chatter. A cool breeze lifted, slicing the thick blanket of air.

Thamba got up from his chair, encouraged by the breeze, folded and re-folded his sarong around his ebony trunk, and slowly began his round: a thrice-nightly walk that began along the perimeter walls, continuing in ever-decreasing circles, like a reverse pebble in a pond, past the garden of meteorological instruments that whirred and scribbled and cocked their mouse ears to the wind, then back to the main buildings.

The campus had been built long ago and glimpses of its former grandeur still showed through the decay, as unmistakable as breeding in a dowager. Magnificent old trees, their great trunks veined and knotted like welders' arms, stood in the grounds: as much the keepers of memories as the thermometers, thermographs, hydrographs, anenometers, rain guages and barometers were the keepers of weather.

Thamba knew the trees as characters, each with a different face, figure and temperament. There was the fat lady: a ficus with an elephantine trunk that ended in plump little feet. The Africans, with their sinuous, rope-like muscles and serpentine roots. Or the giant Malayan, whose trunk soared upwards scraping the sky, until it ended far above, in a top-knot of leaves. In the old days there had been an orchid house, too: an emperor's harem where exquisite, vampiric concubines lived on adulation and air. But that had long gone. Thamba knew, though, in the way groundsmen know these things, that had it continued, it would have survived the fiercest storm. Orchids are like that. Steel-souled. Rare.

Both trees and instruments had been planted and installed by white men in long socks and solar topis, with ruddy necks and constitutions as stout as their morals, in the days when the department's purpose wasn't just to predict the weather, but to embody the achievements of colonial rule. There was always a bit of brass, a bit of crackle and polish then, even on the night shifts. Thamba's father and grandfather had worked at the department before him and he still retained genetic memories of those starched, shipshape days. Now? Well!

The old watchman spat out a gob of *betel* juice and shook his head at what he saw as the junglification of the country's moral standards, the inevitable conquest of civilization by weeds. He expelled another jet of juice, leaving a bloody trail in the sand.

If Thamba had known more about the workings of the instruments he was charged with protecting, he might have learned that those first drops of rain were the opening notes of Act II of an opera, begun six days earlier and a thousand miles away, off the western tip of another island. There, two time zones ahead, in a place so far from the island's consciousness that most of its inhabitants didn't even know it existed, an event had happened that would re-shape the landscape. An Act of God of the kind exempted in insurance policies.

A thermal blanket of hot air rising from a summer-baked ocean and a river of fresh, cold winter air had met and mated in the upper atmosphere and spawned a monstrous, uncontrollable child. For two days, this freak offspring had grown and raged off the distant island, whipped by the wind and its own towering bulk into a series of tempestuous tantrums. Then it had started to spin faster and faster out of control and, as it spun, it moved away from its birthplace, westwards.

That night, as Thamba made his rounds, this dysfunctional offspring of wind and water was heading straight for the longitude on which he walked. How close to him it would come was a question the department's assembled scientists, gathered around computer screens in the lit room above, were anxiously debating. But warnings were coming in from meteorological observatories all over the region and the airport was already in a state of alert.

Thamba paused in a patch of open ground between three ficus trees so old and huge they had grown secondary trunks, which now formed a grove. A few more fat drops landed on his shirt. Yes, it was definitely starting to rain. He quickened his step, heading back to the shed behind the main building, where he napped and kept his rain gear and odds and ends. A shaft of drizzle was now dancing in the beam of his torch and the wind had picked up, making the tree-tops whisper and sigh. Before the weekend was out, eight of these grand old patriarchs would be clean uprooted. Ripped from the earth as easily as cricket wickets; their immense, knotted roots exposed and waving helplessly. But tonight, all Thamba cared about was that the rains had come. He darted inside the shed, grumbling happily, lit a small kerosene stove, brewed himself a cup of tea, and settled in for the night. As he calmly sucked on a foul black cheroot he listened to the wind. It wasn't long before the old trees had soughed and moaned him to sleep.

Eva looked at her watch: it was nine o'clock. Mary hadn't returned and the house was in darkness. She put down the book she had been trying to read, switched on the upstairs hall lights and went down to the office. For the fifteenth time that day, she lifted the receiver and, for the fifteenth time, didn't know whether to be pleased or disappointed by the dial tone. She stretched, to shake off the inertia of a day spent doing nothing. She had been late for Marianne and her friend had gone when she arrived. So she had returned home, telling herself she had work; cleaning lenses; trying and failing to concentrate on editing pictures; pretending not to listen for the phone, while hoping to hear his voice, behaving like a lovesick teenager.

She hoped he might call from the port before setting sail. But now it was too late, he would be at sea. It would be twelve hours, at least, before she could expect to hear from him. No, more, she thought, trying to remember what Philippe's secretary had told her that morning. Twelve hours of sailing and then two more to reach the town, if there were no bombs nor too many roadblocks. She wondered if there would be a working telephone. And if he would call.

Yet again, she re-calculated, doing the algebra of rows. But everything was so inconstant. How badly had they parted? How angry had each been? How much did she regret losing her temper? Would time and distance heal or deepen the wound? No matter how she calculated there was still a bitter taste, the bile of an unresolved quarrel. For the hundredth time that day she forgave him. The question was: could she forgive herself?

It had become much cooler. She switched off the air-conditioning and went to open the glass doors. The force of the wind pushed her back into the room. The noise was terrifying. A howl

282

that swelled ever louder. It sounded like a squadron of fighter jets. A blast of icy wet air slapped her cheeks; she heard the explosive crack of a breaking tree and the crash of falling branches. She wrestled the door closed, ran back into Carl's office and switched on the television. It flickered like a hand opening and closing on a glow-worm. Then the lights went out.

She groped on the desk for a torch and radio, then twiddled through the Babel of stations: Chinese, Farsi, French, Turkish, Hebrew, German; Folk, Heavy Metal, Rock, Rap: unwanted snatches of the world. Finally she found an English station. There was nothing: a programme about water resource management in North Africa. She twirled again, searching for the weather. It was all right, she told herself. Tropical storms were violent, but swift and localized. She looked at her watch: nine-thirty. Turned the dial again until she found it. Fifteen thirty-five megahertz short-wave. The tune and the six short beeps. The twentieth century's version of the Army & Navy catalogue and a four-week-old copy of *The Times*:

'...Meteorologists warn that the cyclone which devastated parts of the island of Sumatra yesterday, leaving thousands homeless and hundreds feared dead, is likely to cause further destruction. They say that Cyclone Sita crossed an uninhabited part of the Nicobar Islands early this evening and is moving westwards towards the Southern Indian state of Tamil Nadu. Warnings have gone out to shipping, and villages in the path of the cyclone are being evacuated. Meanwhile, relief workers in Sumatra say that...'

She switched off. A cyclone. In the void left by sudden silence and darkness she could hear the glass-muffled moan of the wind in the trees. Her hands, cupped around her head, seemed to belong to someone else. Her mind was blank. Then she felt for her address book, fumbled for the torch and dialled. An answering machine. Of course, it was almost ten at night. She flipped through the address book, thumbed down a page and dialled again. A woman's voice answered.

'*Tchik*,' said Mary, scolding herself for not bringing an umbrella, as the same raindrops fell, in time to ruin her first-ever hairdo. She scurried along in the dark looking for a place to shelter. Above, the wind rustled the mara leaves like salt being shaken through a giant bag of crisps. A branch creaked, splintered and crashed into the road. She clattered on quickly, handbag clutched over her subsiding hair, looking for a doorway or an overhang. But this was an area of the city reserved for VVIPs – the Commander-in-Chief of the Army; the Treasury Secretary; the Prime Minister, and so on – and their grand, wedding-cake houses were set well off the road.

Contrary to expectations, Mary had not spent her day at the *penakaraya*'s; nor had she been invoking the gods or casting spells. Instead she had spent the afternoon under the helmet-shaped dryers of Ranee's Snip-Shape Beauty Salon (Hair, Nails & Wax: Bewtiful You Special Offer), being buffed, polished and tortured into what she hoped was a newsreader-like gloss.

'*Annay*, my, isn't that suiting you?' Shireen, the stylist, had lied as she removed the giant rollers from Mary's newly butchered locks.

'Luvly. So in mode, short, isn't it?' Delrine had quickly said, backing up her friend, as she caught Mary's doubtful look. 'Next, we'll be prettying you for marrying, no?'

And Mary, who had little idea what was in or what was out – only that a quarter of a month's pay ought to produce an improvement – turned her head this way and that, convincing herself that yes, she really did look… Well, what? For the moment, the exact word was not to hand. But she was sure it would come to her.

And what was this afternoon of self-improvement in aid of? During these painful, embarrassing hours in a bubble of acetone, body odour and bleach, she had seen her hair shortened by two feet, stretched on metal rollers, back-combed and lacquered into a helmet; refused a leg-wax, although God knows, thought Shireen and Delrine, noting the bearfur on her legs, she needed one;

accepted a nail clip, file and buff, but no polish; refused a facial with freckle remover and bleach; and wavered over the salon's special offer, a 'Twinkle-Toes' pedicure.

Mary told herself it was to get out of the house to avoid Eva and to look nice for Madam's visit. But the real reason, the one she hadn't even told herself, was that she was preparing herself for the time Eva would be gone. For her faith in spells was unshakeable.

So it was that, at one o'clock that afternoon, Mary had found herself seated in a black leatherette chair, thumbing through the pile of dog-eared German hair magazines, which the snooty teenage trainee, dressed in sprayed-on jeans, plastic mules, a purple lurex boob-tube with blonde streaks in her perm, had dumped in her lap.

'Liking?' the girl asked Mary, one plucked eyebrow raised in a question mark that wasn't a question. 'You can be choosing, we can be doing.' And with that, she wiggled her blue-denim bumcheeks behind a curtain; a retort in vernacular script.

Mary looked at the pictures dubiously. The point seemed to be colour and form. Kaleidoscopes of colour, fugues of form. Ash-blonde, strawberry-blonde, red-blonde, yellow-blonde, blonde streaks. Red-chestnut, dark-brown, even blue. All angled, razored, cut, permed, piled, twisted, tumbled and fluffed into afros, beehives, bobs, bouffants, braids, brushcuts, bubbles, buns, dread-locks, ducktails, feathers, flat-tops, flips, mohicans, pageboys, pig-tails and ponytails. There was nothing simple or sensible in plain brownish-black. Nothing she could remotely see herself in. In the end, she pointed to the only Asian model: an olive-skinned girl in a beehive. And that, more or less, is what she ended up with: a hel-met of hair modelled so closely on the salon's hairdryers, it might have been moulded, not dried, beneath one. It was this that was now subsiding like a failed soufflé, as the rain poured down, soak-ing the starch from her dress until you could see her underwear.

'Hallo, hallo, hallo-oho. Come in, sister, *come in.*'

The tiny tea *caday*, no more than a smoke-blackened hole by the side of the road, was crammed with labourers in drenched vests and cheap striped sarongs. Fifteen sets of white teeth leered out of the darkness at her. The place smelled like wet baboon. Mary clenched her nostrils tight and, remembering something someone had once told her on a long-ago visit to the zoo, avoided eye contact.

'Sit down, sit down,' said the same man, simultaneously clearing a space on a narrow wooden bench, wiping it with a greasy rag and eyeballing Mary's breasts. Mango, he thought, with the eye of an expert who could read form even through the armature of local corsetry. Or no. On second thoughts, perhaps, pawpaw.

'Come, sister, don't be shy. Plenty of room.' He nudged aside an earlier customer with a meaty elbow. '*Appah*. Make space, make space for a lady.' He flipped his rag ostentatiously at the bench. 'Please, madam.'

Mary had no choice but to perch down. She snapped her arms and legs shut and wedged herself against her heels in order to sully as little of herself as possible. She wished the *caday mudalali*, a brown bear in a greying vest stretched threadbare over his rice belly, would leave her alone. She was acutely conscious of the eyes still boring through her bra, the grime, the stink. *Tchik*, she thought, filthy dump, wrinkling her nose involuntarily. She hadn't been so embarrassed since the day a male pharmacist had sold her sanitary towels. But the *mudalali*, who had a poor man's radar for hypocrites, had spotted her discomfort and was enjoying it.

'Tea?' he asked, swirling at her a leaf-encrusted pan containing a brown soup. 'Vest. Vetter than up.' He raised his eyes in the direction of the VVIP houses. 'I should be knowing. Guards are coming here drinking and telling: "Vest is Vest".'

'Flease. No trouble. I am ferpectly pine,' said Mary in her best newsreader voice. She stared fixedly out of the door, where the weather had begun the first of Wagner's *Ring* cycles, and pulled at her frock, in an effort to stop the damp cotton from clinging to her bosom.

'Ferpectly pine,' said the man, mimicking her accent. Fifteen throats let out a hearty guffaw. 'And would madam fancy anything else instead?' he said, hamming it up now he had an audience. 'A Tango, perhaps. Or a *pfassshiona*.' He put as much emphasis as he could on the last word, winning himself another round of laughter.

In response Mary pursed her lips, shook her head and pretended to look for something in her bag. Don't make eye contact, she said to herself. Don't encourage them. They will get tired of this and go away. But there was nowhere for them to go and nothing to do but stare, nudge and wisecrack, since she was the entertainment.

'So, sister, ware prom and ware going?' the man continued. '*Eay*? So silent? Nothing speaking?'

It was too much. Mary got up, shook down her dress, ran a hand over the totally collapsed soufflé of her hair and clutched her handbag tightly to her breast. With a toss of her head, she gathered the shreds of her dignity about her, like a hen gathering her wayward chickens, and stepped out into the night. She had spotted one or two rickshaws passing, canvas flaps down against the rain, and hoped one might stop. An ocean of water was falling from the sky. It was dark. The sage old trees were swaying and rocking, in a frenzy of flailing limbs, falling branches and crashing leaves; a maelstrom of wood, leaf and water. Mary cowered, wondering whether to run or turn back to the humiliation of the *caday*, when she heard a crack, like the blast from a high-calibre gun, and a terrible rumble in the branches above her. Something was coming down. But in the dark she couldn't see what, or where to run to avoid it.

''Allo.' It was Gabriella, Philippe's wife.

'Hello, It's Eva. I'm sorry to bother you at this time of night, but is Philippe there?'

There was a pause as Gabriella glanced towards the drawing

room, where her husband lay unfurled, asleep on the sofa. He had been up all the previous night and had only just returned from the coast after an all-day drive.

'I'm sorry,' said Eva, 'but it's urgent.'

Gabriella hesitated for a moment longer. She hated waking him when he needed sleep. '*Aspetto*. One moment. Please.'

Eva could hear heels on terrazzo, a voice calling into another room and at last an extension being picked up.

'Eva, what a pleasure. How are you?'

She felt stupid now he was on the line. It was his voice: calm, reassuring, normal, as comforting as good Swiss chocolate. She had been to his house. It was the house of a tasteful traveller, furnished with Italian sofas, good tribal carpets, art and knick-knacks from his postings. His wife was a slim beauty in her early forties, who weaved around Philippe like the background notes of a sonata, and his three children were bright, Eloise schoolgirls. It was a perfect household run by well-trained servants who didn't cast spells. Imagining him there now, draped on a sofa, was like a reality check from another world; one where there were no demons, no bumps in the night.

'Umm, fine, I guess.' She wasn't entirely sure, any more, why she'd rung. 'Look, I'm so sorry to disturb you at home, it's just... I've just heard the nine-thirty news and—'

'You're worried.'

'Well, yes. Yes, a little. I was wondering if you—'

'Are in contact with the boat carrying the man you love?'

'Well, yes.'

'We're on the radio now.' He didn't want to tell her that they had been trying to get through and couldn't. That he was worried as well. So he kept his tone smooth, neutral, like Switzerland. 'I expect to have some news soon. But please don't worry, Eva,' he said quickly before she could interrupt. 'They'll be safe. I've just come from seeing them off. It's a good ship with a good captain, and Carl has a lot of experience of the sea, as you know. And now,' he laughed, 'why haven't we seen you for so long? Where have you been hiding yourself?'

'Have I? I don't know, Philippe. I've been a bit preoccupied. Life seems more complicated. More...' More what? She trailed off, not knowing what she was trying to say or how to say it.

'*Alors*, you are right. Which is why one has to simplify, *n'est-ce pas*, my dear? One does what one does and what one can and then lives with it, for better or worse, no? So please, no more worrying. Not yet. I'll call you the minute I hear something. And feel free to call me. No matter when. *Promis?*'

'Promise. And Philippe?'

'Yes?'

'Thank you.'

They hung up. With his voice still melting in her ear like warm oil, she felt comforted. But it wasn't enough. The storm was rattling the windows now and she felt exposed. As if nothing more than a few millimetres of glass separated her from tragedy. It wasn't only outside. It was in the house and in her head. Insistent, like endlessly repeating footsteps in a corridor. The sixth sense of lovers told her that nothing was right. The fates were spinning and weaving. But she had nothing to go on. No information, no tangible reason for feeling the way she did. And even if she had, would she have known what to do about it?

There was still no electricity. Half a kilometre away, a tree falling on an exposed line had blown up twenty transformers in a spectacular firework extravaganza. Without light, there was nothing to do but go to bed. Eva fumbled on the desk until she felt a box of matches. They were local: tiny splinters of wax dipped in sulphur, with the brand name Sunlight. She had once seen a documentary on the children who made these matches, or ones like them. *They* never saw the sunlight. Employed for their small fingers and smaller wages, they were cooped up like battery chickens and then sacked, without pay, when they grew to adolescence. Perhaps it was because the materials used were sub-standard, or perhaps it was a ploy by the manufacturers to ensure people consumed more boxes, but Sunlight matches didn't light. She cursed as she threw out match after match until one stayed aflame. It spluttered for a second, long enough for her to see the metallic blue of a Mini-Microlite on the desktop. She grabbed it, went into the kitchen and opened the fridge. Without electricity, it smelled of stale Frion and mould. Its old mustard, ketchup and sauce bottles, softening slab of butter, half-drunk bottle of wine, jam jars, sugar bowls and honey – the things people in the tropics keep in fridges – stared glumly at her like people in a dole queue. She slammed the door, found a pack of red-and-white Gold Flake, and lit up. She checked the window and door locks, before going upstairs, where she undressed, snapped a sleeping pill out of its packet, swigged it down and went to bed.

'Bloody buggers! What was *that*?'

Sergeant Piyadasa heaved himself up out of his favourite green flock armchair, bunched his sarong under his balls and peered out into the dark pool of the garden for the source of the resounding crash, which had interrupted a re-run of the Windies–South Africa match. Cupping his hands around his eyes, he could dimly make out what looked like a storm-tossed sea of vegetation. There seemed to be quite a gale going on.

'NOT THERE! Oh, foolish man I've married!' screamed Lalitha, from behind him, interrupting his inventory of the garden. 'HERE!'

At that moment, there was a second crash, which sounded ominously like collapsing masonry and glass. He turned to see his wife waving her arms, like an enraged Hindu goddess, in front of a margosa tree that had invaded the space where his kitchen had been, and was now encroaching with branches, twigs and leaves, on the hallway.

'GUNADASA!' he roared automatically.

'HE'S HERE! FOOL!' yelled Lalitha, gesticulating furiously downwards. 'DEAD, PROBABLY. OR INJURED.'

He followed her gesture. Sprawled at her feet on the kitchen floor, like the hapless man trampled by the goddess Kali, was the unfortunate houseboy. He appeared to be trapped beneath several very large branches. Around him were the remains of the kitchen cupboards: a baroque mess of broken cups, saucers, plates, pickle jars, powdered milk cans, coffee grounds and assorted foodstuffs, pasted over the floor like the remains of a rambunctious children's party.

'Bloody buggers,' he said again for want of anything better to say. 'Bloody buggers.'

He rubbed his head with a paw, hoping to clear his brain. He had spent the evening flopped in front of the new TV with the 33-inch screen, which his cousin Hema had brought back from Dubai, watching cricket replays and drinking Old Faithful, after a helluva day being hauled over the coals by the Captain about the death of that boy. (He had wriggled out of a demotion by the skin of his teeth.) And now this. Apocalypse in the kitchen.

'WHAT FOR JUST STANDING THERE, MAN?' yelled Lalitha. 'DO SOMETHING!'

He scratched his head again, wondering why it was she always seemed so much more belligerent after her mother's visits, and bent down to prod the houseboy through the tangle of branches.

'AIIEEEE!' screamed Gunadasa, who had opened his eyes to the terrifying vision of his boss's foliage-framed face inches away from his, concluded that he was dead and had arrived in a heaven populated by giant panda policemen, masquerading as wood nymphs. He quickly shut his eyes and screamed again.

'Well, at least he's alive,' snapped Sergeant Piyadasa. He stretched out a paw towards his wife. 'Phone?'

'Dead. As doornail,' retorted Lalitha triumphantly, glancing at the mangled remains of the hall telephone.

'THEN BRING ME THE RADIO!' he yelled.

'Phone, radio, scalpel, scissors. Whatall are you thinking I am? Nurse in the General Hospital?'

Before Piyadasa could reply he heard the unmistakable buzz and crackle of his radio coming from the direction of the bedroom, which now lay on the further shore of a sea of greenery. He hiked up his sarong, folded it into a mini-kilt and, lifting his legs as high as possible, began gingerly traversing the slopes of collapsed tree. Halfway across, his sarong snagged and caught on a branch, leaving him naked from the waist downwards.

'BUGGER!' he roared, clutching his balls and simultaneously bursting into the bedroom as the radio emitted another deafening burst of static. With his free hand he snatched it off the chair where he had thrown his trousers and shirt.

'YES! PIYADASA HERE!'

'Sir...' Constable Somapala's voice was drowned by another gust of white noise.

'SOMAPALA, CAN YOU HEAR ME?'

A voice returned faintly from what sounded like the bottom of the sea.

'GOOD. I need four of the lads here with a chainsaw, double-quick, do you hear me? We've a man trapped under a tree in my kitchen.'

There was another faint burst of voice, muffled by more static.

'What's that? WHAT!'

The connection was quite clear now. It was his brain that was buzzing.

It's not possible, he thought, wondering what the averages were of family members colliding with trees on the same day. It's. Just. Not. Possible.

But aloud, his policeman's pragmatism snapped into action. 'Dead or alive?' he asked briskly. As if enquiring after any routine, common-or-garden Incident, Irregularity or Disturbance of the Peace and not a possibly Fatal Accident involving his own sister.

There was a pause while the voice at the other end spoke.

'Well, send one of the more reliable lads down there. Odiris or Premadasa. I'll be down as soon as I can.'

Impossible, he thought again, shuffling through a drawer for a clean shirt and sarong. He shook his head as he considered the options. Well, it was in the hands of the gods now. As he pondered the possibility, there was a massive explosion from the corner of the lane and a scream, followed by a string of incantations from Lalitha outside the kitchen. Despite himself he clutched the blessed amulet around his neck (a tiny scroll rolled into a gold tube that she had brought him from the Murugan *devale*), and muttered a prayer. The lights had gone out and with them the television, entombing them in darkness and silence. He waited but nothing happened. It was as if they had fallen off the edge of the world.

Forty-four

'I can't get this bloody radio to work.' Alain was still at the mess table in the tiny galley, fiddling with the knobs and dials on the agency's big black radio, a packing-case-sized machine that looked like an old-fashioned telephone switchboard with switches and jackplugs. An ashtray of Carl's cigarette stubs festered on the table and the air smelled grey and stale. He gave the knobs another turn and plugged and unplugged a few switches. 'Bah!' he said. He threw off his headphones and thumped a fist on top of the machine. 'Why now? Eh?'

Carl shrugged. 'Murphy's law? SNAFU?'

'Mur fie? SNAFU?'

'You know. Sod's law.' He had learned the English expression from Eva. '"If there's a light at the end of the tunnel it's an oncoming train." "If something can go wrong at the time you most need it not to, it will." SNAFU's the same: Situation Normal All Fucked Up.'

Alain grimaced and nodded. In the last two hours, his youthful enthusiasm had been replaced by a stoicism inherited from a line of boules-playing Normandy farmers. 'So? What do we do, eh?'

'Have you checked the aerial?'

Alain gave him the withering look perfected by those same ancestors. 'Of course. It's fine.'

'And the batteries?'

'They're fine, too. There's a signal, it's just not clear. Too much interference out there.'

The boat gave another stomach-heaving lurch and both men clutched the table. Carl waited till it righted, grasped its ledge and stood up.

'Yeah, well, I don't know about you, but I need to get outta this heaving ashcan. I'm going up to talk to the captain. See how we're doing up there.'

'As you like. Let me know. I'll keep on trying to get through on this thing.'

Carl rummaged in his rucksack, pulled out a green L.L. Bean waterproof and re-stowed the rucksack under the shelf with his sleeping bag. Then he reached out, grabbed the ladder leading up on deck, waited for the boat to heave then level, and pulled himself up. Alain watched the open hatch gobble up his waterproof, his blue-jeans and finally his boots, like a python swallowing a rabbit. Then he clamped back his headphones and turned again to the sullen, uncommunicative radio.

Carl emerged above deck and ducked. A savage wet wind, blasting across the rubberized steel plates, almost knocked him off his feet. It was like opening a bar door and being knocked flat by a drunk, before even entering the room. What hit him hardest, though, was the noise: a low bass howl that clutched at his gut and shook it. He bent double and half crab-crawled, half lunged for the cockpit, grabbed the rickety steps and hauled himself up.

The captain was a Dane. A troll with the sea in his veins, wind in the crevices of his skin, drink in his nose and blue sky in his triangular eyes. When Carl surfaced into the cockpit the older man was hunched over the wheel. Even before he saw his face, he knew the Dane was having a hard time of it. They had introduced themselves earlier, so now, when he heard Carl's step, he just nodded with the back of his head as if to say: '*Velkommen*. But I'm busy.' Carl wedged himself tight.

'Need any help?' he yelled.

'Yah. The radio. I'm not getting anything. We need to listen in.' The captain's voice above the storm was harsh and ragged as a throatful of iron filings.

Carl had thought it would be better up in the narrow cockpit, above the storm, with its familiar touches of brass and wood, its gears and instruments and electronics, its bristle and seamanship. But it wasn't. The restless wind was chopping the foamy sea, like a dog driving sheep, and the night was black and impenetrable. He could barely see the waves until they were upon them, captured in the ship's light as sudden green mountains, rising from the watery fog, then vanishing, like poltergeists in a Kirilian photograph. But for the constant plunging and rearing of the ship – hauling up the long slope of a wave, then hurtling headlong into its trough – and the salt shark-toothed gale screaming through the rigging, they could have been anywhere: Antarctica, Alaska, the Dark Side of the Moon. It was like being on a roller-coaster to infinity's edge, beyond the light of the sun or the stars.

He clamped on the earphones. Channel Sixteen, the international SOS channel, was a gargle of noise. A stream of incoherent babble pierced the storm like the cries of drowning men. Could he hear the fear and the panic out there, or was it his imagination? Nothing was coming through. He took the headphones off.

'I'm not getting anything, either,' he yelled. 'It's just noise.'

'Well, let's get her battened down and keep listening. You wanna stay up or go down?'

'Up. If that's OK,' screamed Carl.

'Sure. But get a vest and a clip on and then let's dog her down.'

The older man jerked his head sideways and downwards, indicating a narrow cupboard beside the hatch. Carl pulled, but the wooden door was wedged tight and the bucking and lurching was making it hard to open. Finally he wedged himself against another corner and pulled. The door flew wide, disgorging orange vests, lengths of rope and clips, assorted tools and boat clutter, like children surprised at a game of hide and seek. He plucked out a vest and a rope and clip, snapped open the velcro fasteners, struggled into the stiff orange nylon and pressed it shut. Without the buoyancy of water, he felt as clumsy as a nesting turtle or a seal flubbering on rock. He knotted the rope around his waist, hesitated, then swung down the steps and back across the deck.

'Gotta dog down,' he screamed down the hatch. 'Captain's orders. It's getting bad.'

Below deck, Alain was locked in combat with the radio, twiddling dials, plugging and unplugging. He didn't look up.

Carl yelled again. 'I'm closing the hatch!'

The Frenchman glanced up, saw the cover closing, nodded and got up. Above him, Carl clipped on and set about the deck, battening down, checking, tightening. It was like the old days. The old routine kicking in and, with it, the first claw of fear. It was why he wanted to be up top. He knew, as sailors and soldiers know, that in times of danger it is crucial to be busy. When he'd finished, he lunged back through the wind to the cockpit, battened down that door and climbed up.

'All done,' he yelled, stowing back the clutter and picking up another life vest. 'Here's yours.'

'Thanks,' said the Dane, gesturing for him to drop it on the floor. Carl could sense the old sailor hunching to the wheel, riding the bronco, struggling with every sinew to keep her straight.

'You want me to take her while you put yours on,' he yelled.

'Not yet. Later,' the Dane shouted back.

The sea beneath them was big but not yet monstrous. But the swells were growing more mountainous by the hour and the surface of the water was chaotic, rushing furiously this way and that. He knew that if the gale got worse, the entire body of the ocean would begin to roll and the crests of the waves would crumble and fall. Already, the wind was unrelenting, sawing through his nerves like a dentist's drill. He wondered how big and how serious this thing was.

'What's the weather doing?' he yelled.

'Not sure, but I don't like this wind. It's moving round us and the pressure's dropping. We need to get some boogie-woogie, get someone talkin' to us. Check we're on the right frequency. And keep listening in.'

Carl busied with the radio, trying to listen for a voice through the static, another boat, the coastguard, the weather report. And as he did, he inventoried their options. She wasn't big. Wider than the crab boats and more stable. But still far too small for a heavy sea although she was made of steel. Her cockpit windows were tough and her hull, engines, pumps, mechanics and electrics had been recently overhauled. But there was no proper crew, just him and Alain; and if things went wrong...? He felt her tip beneath them and begin the slide down another wave. Down, down into the shadow of the valley of...

'Are you lonesome tonight,/ Do you miss me tonight?/ Are you sorry we drifted apart?'

It was the captain in full voice, interrupting his thoughts. Carl couldn't believe it. For a second he wondered if he'd been drinking but as quickly as the next crest, he knew he hadn't. It was an old seaman's way of keeping the merciless ocean at bay.

'Does your memory stray to a brighter sunny day/ When I kissed yoo and called you sweetheart?'

Carl joined in now, humming until they got to the last line: 'TELL ME, DEAR, ARE YOU LONESOME TONIGHT?'

The two men finished the verse together, bawling their lungs out, grinning like loons above the bucking water. Then they both shook with laughter.

'What do you think?' Carl shouted to the Dane when he'd got his breath back. 'Should we try and put in?'

'Sure,' he yelled back. 'But where?'

It was true. There was nowhere to land the entire length of the coastline. The first harbour or even inlet that would take their boat was around the northern tip of the peninsula, where they were bound. Carl tried to calculate how long they'd been out and where they were.

'How far are we? Any point turning back?' he screamed.

The Dane didn't hear him at first and he had to repeat himself. When he did, he yelled back the maritime co-ordinates. 'Just under halfway!' he shouted. 'But I must know first what's happening with the gale. We need to keep into this sea.'

The rest of his words were drowned out by a thunderous, shuddering roar, though Carl wasn't sure if he felt or heard it. Simultaneously, to his horror, he saw an immense wave reaching several storeys above them. For an eternal moment it hung, a green-black mountain, and then it came: driving them under with a mad fury, down into the black. He felt the boat shudder to its rivets and the agonized groan of a creature in pain. Then buoyancy took over, the boat rising and, with it, the fierce suction of a monstrous wave retracting its fingers, tugging them towards the torrents of water rushing over the bows and sides.

'Fuck, that was bad!' said Carl. He was shaking.

'Yah,' said the captain. 'If it gets any bigger I'm gonna have to turn her round. Can't see these freaks in the dark.'

Carl said nothing. Trying to ignore the lurching fear in his belly, the smell of disaster, a sailor's intuition that this voyage was rotten, that the albatross was flying overhead. He looked back at the retreating wave. A nest of half-empty oil drums, bolted on to the deck, had been squashed flat as dustbin lids, sending an oily rainbow across the deck.

'Are you lonesome tonight,

Do you miss me tonight?

Are you sorry we drifted apart?

Is your heart filled with pain, shall I come back again?

Tell me dear, are you lonesome tonight?....

'Come on, my friend, sing up!' bellowed the captain.

Carl wasn't a singer but the man's verve was irresistible.

'Dum, dum, dum, dum, dum...' They both shouted, neither of them remembering the words.

> Now the stage is bare and I'm standing there
> With emptiness all around
> ...
> Dum, dum, dum
> Is your heart filled with pain, shall I come back again?
> TELL ME DEAR, ARE YOU LONESOME TONIGHT?'

Pause...

'MOTHERFUCKERS!' they both screamed in unison and punched their fists in the air. 'M O T H E R F U C K E R S!'

It was corny as hell. It was out of tune. It was trench humour. It was the stuff brave, scared men and women do in the face of death. It lifted their hearts high above the ocean and Carl loved the Dane for it. If he lived – if they lived – he'd never forget this night or this man. But boy, could he do with something to ride him through the storm.

'Got any booze?' he yelled at the captain's back. He could feel the concentration coming off him. But he'd never known a Dane, or more to the point, a Danish sea captain, without a bottle of something to drink.

'One minute...'

There was a hiss and crackle from the radio. Then, faint as a message from a distant galaxy, a voice. Carl seized the headphones, clamped them on and turned up the volume. From the rhythmic cadence he knew, even before he heard it, that it was the weather report.

Forty-five

'What do you think? Will it hit?' asked Dr Muthalingam, the department's senior meteorologist, whose round mouse ears, protruding like anemometers, appeared to have uniquely qualified him for the job. He frowned at the message that had just appeared on the screen in front of him as if expecting the computer to reply. Which, in time, it probably would.

The other four meteorologists gathered in the operations room turned from the swirling black and white images on their screens, to look at his computer, which was linked by a dedicated line to the principal regional meteorological office, a thousand miles north. It read:

```
CYCLONE WARNING FOR WEST AND SOUTH BAY
Latest Satellite imagery indicates that Cyclone Sita, the
Severe Cyclonic Storm over the Carpenter Ridge, crossed
Lat. 8 N. and Longt. 90 E. around 18.00 and lay centred
at 2330 hours IST of 15 November over Lat. 9 N. Longt.
87 E.
   South Central Bay. System likely to move in a westerly
direction and gradually weaken.
   WARNING SIGNAL NO. II AND SECTIONAL SIGNAL NO. II
RAISED AT COOBY AND THIVANAPATRAM PORTS.
```

'So, what do you think?' he asked again.

'Hard to say, sir.' It was Mathews, the young communications director who, like many whose job is to communicate, rarely had an opinion about the messages he passed on. 'But we've issued the usual warnings to the media.'

'And the data from the coast, Sunda?' Dr Muthalingam said, referring to the three coastal observatories, whose instruments and computers returned more accurate local readings and would be expected to report hourly in an approaching storm. He turned to a dark-faced, thick-set man in a white shirt.

'Nothing so far, sir. The lines seem to be down and we haven't been able to get a radio signal through to them yet.'

'Well, keep trying. That information's crucial. Without it we're working with one eye shut.' Dr Muthalingam glanced now at a dark man in his thirties with a shock of porcupine quill hair and thick glasses. 'Ranil?'

'The pressure's fallen about five millibars, sir. As you'd expect. And wind speed is up to about a hundred knots locally, although we expect it to go higher, of course.'

Dr Muthalingam pushed up his brown plastic-rimmed glasses and rubbed his bright, mousy eyes. 'That's serious.' He turned to the communications director. 'Mathews, better get another warning out to all the usual people: civil aviation, the airport, the airforce, army and all the relevant ministries: Fishing, Agriculture and so on. Make sure we update them every hour from now on.' He stretched, got up and walked over to one of the computers next to him. 'Now, what's she looking like over here?'

From the point of view of the satellite currently beaming the image Dr Muthalingam was looking at, or to those ignorant of the technicalities of weather, the image staring at them from the third computer on the right looked like any satellite image of a cyclone.

Innocuous. Pretty, even. A Mr Whippy swirl of vanilla cloud. Dr Muthalingam and his team knew, though, that the hazy white spiral on their screens represented a granite mountain of cloud. An immense power engine ripped with lightning, rain and thunder, rotating anti-clockwise at three hundred kilometres an hour. Its wall was fifteen kilometres high but its eye, which in cyclones reduces with size, like a fat man's, was small and mean: a ten-kilometre respite; a brief, false glimpse of heaven. To be in the path of this monster would be to be present at the Apocalypse. Giant trees would snap like matchsticks. Villages would melt like mud in water. Iron pylons would corkscrew like indiarubber. Who knew how many would die?

At sea, wind speeds would reach two hundred kilometres an hour; waves would rise to twenty-five metres or so. Boats smaller than an ocean liner or a container vessel might be driven to the bottom of the ocean, or so badly crippled – their windows blown out, their hulls twisted – that they would be lucky to survive. Container ships would lose their loads. And thousands of fishermen's wives would be widowed, as the body of the ocean would begin the dance that ends the world.

'She looks like a big one,' said Dr Muthalingam with a practised eye. 'What are they calling her? Sita? Looks more like Kali to me.'

Sunda smiled wryly. He was the only other Hindu in the department and thus the only one to wholly appreciate the analogy to the goddess of destruction, consort of Shiva whose dance destroys the world.

'Well, as I said,' the director swung back to his own desk, reaching for the mouse and clicking, 'we'd better watch her closely. See where she goes in the next two hours. My hunch is that if she hits it'll be the early hours of tomorrow, or she'll peter out first.'

In his hut beneath them, Thamba turned, opened his eyes and sat up. A terrifying roar had woken him, as if the demons of the underworld were emerging from the earth. He jumped out of bed, grabbed a torch and poked his head out of the doorway. One of the grand old bodhi trees that had stood there since the time when there was no department and no city, only jungle, leopards and bears, staggered and keeled. There was a roll, like the thunder of a big gun battery, and the ground shook. Very slowly, the great patriarch collapsed to the ground, taking with it a smaller mango and a flamboyan. When a monarch falls, he takes his courtiers with him, he thought. But out loud he said: '*Amma suru,*' and then for protection: '*Siva, Sivaya.*'

He shook his head, contemplating the ruin of the tree. There'd be enough time for the funeral honours tomorrow: it was far too dangerous to be out tonight. Five minutes later he was snoring on his cot. But above him the necklace of satellites stayed awake, beaming their warnings. A string of tigers' eyes, glittering in the jungle of the night.

'Attention all shipping. Attention all shipping. Cyclone Sita currently in south-east bay earlier moving N. N. E. Now moving due west but forecast gale force winds seas 30 to 40 feet. All ships advised…'

The rest of the report was lost in white noise, but it was enough. For a minute or more, Carl and the captain were silent. Both knew winds of that speed would churn the ocean like milk in a giant pail, sending it foaming and spinning. As it did when the gods used Mount Meru as a paddle and, from the primordial ocean, churned the earth. The *Celine* would be helpless, tossed like a cork in a white vortex of wind, air and water. For unless things changed, they were set on a collision course with a cyclone. A one-way ticket to hell.

Carl turned white beneath his tan. He was more frightened than he'd ever been. Even in arctic seas. Shit! he said to himself. Out loud he tried to still his voice, to iron out the fear. 'How come we didn't know about this?' he asked. He sounded as quakey as a broken-voiced schoolboy.

'We did,' replied the old man. Carl could tell the grim set of his face, even from the back of his neck. 'Yesterday's weather report said she was moving north and falling apart.'

'Whadya gonna do? Find a hurricane hole?' He spoke very slowly, hoping to even out his tone.

'A what?'

'A hurricane hole. A bolt hole, in the mangroves.'

'Yah? Good idea. Better get out the chart.' He nodded curtly towards a large map drawer.

Carl went over, opened it and thumbed through until he found what he wanted: a detailed sea map of the north-east coast, rippled with the contours of the ocean, its vital statistics. He spread out the chart, took a reading on the GPS and then thumbed over it inch by inch, exploring the sea as one might explore an unknown continent, noting its safe havens, its windows of hope.

'I think I've got the place,' he said at last. 'It's our best bet.'

'Know how to plot a course?'

'No. 'Fraid not.'

'Know how to steer?'

'Yup.'

'Good. Take her for a minute while I punch in a new course.'

From the wheel, the rise and fall of the boat was majestic and almost hypnotic: the narrow prow rising and dipping over the heavy green mountains, lit like giant aquamarines by the boat's arc lamp. But the chaotic sea, which daylight would show to be streaked, like cheap meat, meant that he had to strain to keep her from veering broadside and stay head-on into the waves. After five minutes his shoulders ached and he could feel the tension crippling his neck. But at least the work, the concentration, was quelling his fear.

'Boy, she's hard work,' he said when the Dane finally took the wheel back from him.

'Yah. Like all women,' grunted the old man. 'Now, let's get her back home to bed...'

305

His sentence was killed by the sudden gunning of the throttles. Carl knew immediately what the other man was going to do and didn't like it. It was every sailor's nightmare. He was going to turn her in a heavy sea. For half a minute, a minute – long enough to push her over – she would be broadside to the waves. She, they, would be in mortal peril. He felt terror rush back into his guts like a pack of hounds, grab them and rip them out.

Beneath him, the screws were turning; he could feel them straining every joint and rivet in the hull. Slowly, painfully slowly, the boat tilted, her starboard rising, her port dipping almost to the water, her deck angling steeply, up, up, to an angle he barely believed possible. He looked up. Beyond the steeply tilted broadside, he could see black water swelling and rising. He closed his eyes and prayed.

Eva had seemed a million miles away. On another planet, far from this black and frightening world, this monstrous roiling sea. But the captain's words had brought her back, conjured her from the ocean floor like a sea-creature, or a mighty genie released from a bottle. For an eternity, he felt her hanging, vast, dark, powerful, a thin foam cap like a tiara cresting her hair, as high above them as a moonlit cloud. And then he heard her. A roar like a wounded tiger close by, a mother separated from her cubs. At that moment, he heard his own voice calling: 'Eva.'

And then all went black.

Forty-six

Caspar lay motionless in the high white bed, hearing but not seeing the terrors of that night. He had no sense of time now, but it must have been a few hours – or perhaps it was only a few minutes – since he had felt Shanta's hand on his forehead and heard his unasked questions. The boy had been nursing him for so long that they had melded together, like form and shadow. But now he could tell, from the shape of the air in the room and its smell, that he was alone.

He listened. His ears, sharpened by years of blindness, could pick out the direction of the wind. It was coming off the sea, howling across the shore and inland over the paddies, flattening the electric green shoots, like a giant hand brushing a green pile carpet, turning the field into a mosque courtyard of Muslims at prayer. For a second, he even thought he could smell it: the salt, the power, the anger of the waves, mingled with crisp-crunched sand and wet leaves.

He listened harder. The trees were complaining bitterly. Poor trees, his friends. He could hear their cries for help: the great oak, the mara, the andaman redwood, the jak, the massive banyan, the showy flamboyan – all of them in agony. Suddenly he heard a crack like a rifle shot, a rending and then an almighty crash of branches and leaves, ending in a long shuddering sigh: the death rattle of a mighty tamarind.

It had been planted as a sapling at his birth, its myriad tiny leaves symbolizing the infinity of creation. Now it had been felled by the wind. The order and justice of that struck him, although he had loved that tree. He was not a religious man. He had no time for the *bikkhus* and their hypocrisies, nor the fraudulent holy men, the *fakirs*, nor the imams or the priests. He agreed with Karl Marx. But he knew then, that his fingers were being prised away, one by one, from their grip on worldly attachments; from the garden riddle he had created, loved and nurtured; from the men and women he had loved. The iron bonds that bind men to their fates were loosening. Faster, now the time was growing near. He knew then, as that same night Carl would know, that life and death were in his hands. Or rather, that the cards were equal. He would choose death not because he had to, but because he'd grown too weary of the struggle. He longed for death and he would choose it, as much as death would choose him. It was a lover's pact. A leap, hand in hand, from a cliff into the sea.

As he thought this, there was another hideous crash. Something else felled by the wind. The sacred bodhi tree, which would take with it fourteen lesser trees and shrubs, was falling. A bad omen. He listened. First, creaking and groaning, the sounds of a tree fighting against the storm. Then a series of bullet-retorts and crashes; a movement of earth, the trembling of its smaller neighbours. One by one, he heard the branches fall: a finger, a hand, an arm, a limb. The tree was fighting valiantly. Old elephants take time to die. Old warriors take time to kill. And as he listened, he remembered an afternoon long ago when both of them were young and smooth-skinned.

Vivien and he were sitting beneath that tree on a mossy, white stone bench with lions' paw feet. She had led him there, to the most secluded part of the garden, where they would be undisturbed. He was wearing white trousers and an open-necked shirt, in the days when he still wore white men's clothes: uncomfortable things that clung to the legs and trapped the balls. And she? She was as lovely as ever in flowered voile and a picture hat, fragile as a butterfly wing. Or was he remembering a photograph? But it was her face and her eyes that had stayed with him, that afternoon. She was serious, with the single-minded look of someone who has something very important to say. Serious and scared. He had never seen her like that. She was brave as a young buck and as nerveless. A fearless rider, equal to the best in his regiment. He had watched as she broke in Mickey's ponies; and again, in the old man's colours, taking hurdles that would scare him. She had wanted to be the first woman to do everything. To fly a seaplane, to give a speech in parliament, to cross the high mountains and learn from the yellow-hatted monks, to traverse the old silk route by camel. But she had done none of it in the end. Probably because of what she had told him that afternoon. Yes, he thought, it was the only time he had seen her frightened. What was she so scared of? Something so small it could have fitted on to a button; so innocent it could hurt no one. Something that would soon tug at her heart and lay claim on her life, with all the irresistible ferocity of the defenceless. He knew even then, stupid and green as he was, that it was that which scared her most.

He had offered then to marry her and meant it. He loved her and would always love her in his way. But she had turned him down. It wasn't right, she said. It wouldn't work: he would always prefer men and boys. Armand had appeared and fallen in love with her. The wedding was fixed. So she had married him and sailed away. Towards the setting sun. Out of their lives. He had seen Eva once as a baby. Vivien had wrapped her up like a present, in white muslin. She was the loveliest thing he'd ever seen, with a mouth like a tea-rose and eyes like peppermint kisses. How sad it had been to leave her in that cold country. Vivien had brought her out to see him later, a curious little girl full of questions and the lateral conundrums bright children pose. ('How do priests know you'll go to heaven, if no one's come back to tell them?' 'Why don't brown people who live in cold countries go white?' 'Why can't all the rich people give a bit of their money to the poor people?' And: 'Who made God?') They were alone without Armand – it must have been the school holidays – but still he'd had to hide his pride in her.

He had seen her only once again, in Europe, on the pretext of going to stay with his cousin in France. That time, he had squeezed himself back into trousers, sweaters and a tweed jacket: clothes that probably still mouldered in some wardrobe. She was a puppy-fat schoolgirl then. But bright as she'd been as a child. They had gone to a well-known museum of art, since art was one of her subjects (he liked to think she had inherited that from him) and together they had gone on a voyage of exploration through the ship of modern art: the bowels of its engine, its rigging, its great canvases. It had been especially painful to leave her then. She was on the cusp of adulthood and he wanted to be there. To take her mind and help shape it. To show her the things and people and places he loved, that she might love them, too. To watch her grow into the swan she was now. To see that first bloom.

Now, at last, she had come here. He thought back to the last few months they had spent together. She had grown into the woman Vivien had wanted her to be, after all; the vehicle for all those adventurous dreams she had been unable to realize herself. And Eva had proved, with her simple trust and causeless affection, to be a true child of his. He was proud of her and had wanted, so many times, to tell her. But it was clear Vivien never had and he believed that it was her secret to keep or share. And now it was too late.

Was it always a hurried departure? Things left undone, plans still to complete? But no, on second thoughts, he wasn't leaving hurriedly, there had been time. And he would tell her in his own way. She would learn from what he left to her: his legacy, his continuing love.

As for the rest, it didn't matter any more. The daily struggle, the quarrels, the hopes, the ambition, the greed, the jealousies, the ego. How small and insignificant it all seemed. His quarrel with George. Over what? A box of jewellery. Some furniture. A few possessions. Pointless sibling jealousy. Was this what he had wasted a lifetime over?

And his own pride. How much he had enjoyed the praise and, later, the notoriety. How proud he had been of his ADC's uniform and what it meant, his reputation as a bohemian, an artist, a bon viveur. How stupid even the words sounded now. How little it all meant.

What was important? He saw it so clearly now. It was love. Love and wisdom. Love he had given and taken, freely. But wisdom? Not worldly wisdom. But real wisdom.

A memory came back to him from long, long ago and with it the scents of moss and gentian and a faint resinous breeze. He had met an old monk in a *bothy*, a hermitage above the tree-line, where they had stopped for the night while hunting mountain deer and wild geese. He had spoken quietly, almost off-handedly, as they said farewell in the doorway of his hut. A truth as old as the fierce, beautiful mountains and the gods whose names they bore. It wasn't the words so much – something like: 'the most profound thing in life is your breath', or was it: 'Know thyself' – but the understanding he had transmitted.

But he hadn't listened. And now it was too late. Was that how everyone left the world: with a sense of lost opportunity? He smiled to himself, remembering an old story. Who was it whose last words had been: 'Too bad, too bad. It's too late'? Was it Rabelais, Beethoven, or Harry of his old regiment? What would his last words be? 'I love you.' Or something more prosaic: 'I need to pee.' Would there be any words left? We talk too much, anyway, while saying very little. He hoped there would not.

His thoughts stopped; he was drifting, floating over those same high mountains like one of the Canada geese that had soared far above the range of their guns. Below, he could see the old monk's hermitage and, above it, a crystal blue lake, glittering like a sapphire in the snow and rock. As he peered down, the waters seemed to part and from them emerged a beautiful golden child holding in his outstretched palm a crystal orb that he also knew was a key. The child was smiling at him. The smile of a seducer, but without guile, only love. He felt himself yearning for that key, reaching down to touch it and yet, being pulled back. It was almost there, in his grasp. He could feel its warmth, its promise. Ah yes, now he had it. And here it came, flooding over him and into him like a balm, filling him with golden light.

At that moment, a terrible noise – the howl of a sacred tree in its death throes – sounded from the dark, storm-tossed garden. There was a great shudder, then the sound of a huge tree trunk, its thousand leaves and branches, falling. The earth shook as if there had been an earthquake. And then, as though in lament, the trees, the plants, the grass, the flowers; the reptiles, the insects, the creatures, the birds, the whole garden, the magical kingdom of Lorne and all that was in it, gave a great collective sigh. But Caspar no longer heard it. For he had gone.

Forty-seven

Next to a desert of white sheet, Eva, alone, lay in bed. The tombstone wife of a marble crusader whose husband hadn't returned from the Holy Land. Sometimes, she drifted beneath the skin of sleep. But most of the time she lay awake, thoughts buzzing, the storm outside ringing in her ears, the house swirling with spectres and shades. The sixth sense of lovers and mothers whispered to her that something was wrong, though she dare not wonder what that might be.

At last just before dawn, in a moment of exhausted clarity, she saw the images of her life spread out, like overlapping negatives on a light table. It was clear, in the harsh light that cast mistakes into sharp relief, where she had gone wrong. Which images were clear and which were out of focus; which were light and which dark. She saw then that in refusing to love, to seize whatever gifts were offered, she had denied herself the only thing in life worth having. And once again she asked herself why she always loved too much, too late.

Words he had said one evening returned to her. They were standing in his bare bedroom beneath the harsh, overhead light. She was in a hurry, coming or going somewhere. He had stopped her, caught her by the shoulders and looked hard at her.

'Eva, we waste a lot of time not saying what's in our hearts for fear of seeming weak or being rejected, so I'll tell you now what I feel.' And she had flicked her eyes away, as he told her he loved her, pretending to be engrossed by a gecko eating another gecko near the ceiling. He had offered her his heart on an open palm, and she had brushed it aside, embarrassed. Real love and real feelings were like sweets from a stranger – things she had learned in childhood not to accept.

She turned to the bedside clock. Four-thirty. Too early to call Philippe or anyone else, to pull in the net she had cast the night before. She closed her eyes. She was exhausted. Her eyeballs were inflamed by tears and her mind ached. But it was no good, sleep had picked up his coat and left. She paused a moment longer, then threw off the sheet. Twenty minutes later she was on the road east, heading into a wan, grey sky.

The rain had stopped and the clouds had curdled themselves into grubby lumps of bad milk. But the wind was still wailing and the road was torn by tree trunks and foliage. Several times, Eva had to stop and wait while ant-runs of slim-hipped, sun-blackened men cleared the way. The birds chorused mutedly, as if water had got into their systems. And when the sun finally emerged from the haze, it simply heated the sodden air like a Turkish bath. It felt like the morning after the end of the world party, hungover and bad.

Eva had set out with one idea: to reach the harbour from where he had sailed. It was her only point of reference, that final point of land before the sea. Although she knew there was no logical reason why he should return there, if he returned at all, she still went. She had no idea what she would do when she arrived. She drove because she had to; because she was tired of the island – of life – doing things to her. It was time for her to act herself. She also believed that, however late, she could change the course of fate. That she could will him to live, as a mother wills her child to live. That in the battle between love and fate, love could win. And so, hour by hour, through that gloomy day, she followed the torn ribbon of road to the sea. And because she had things on her mind, the miles and the time went by swiftly, as if in a dream.

It was dusk and the light was seeping away when she finally arrived. The day was ending as it had begun, grimly. There was no sunset. The weather had clamped down like a steel shutter. Beyond the harbour's outer wall, the sea was sullen and angry, spuming white caps like foam at the mouths of rabid dogs. A gale was still blowing in strongly enough to raise large waves in the harbour itself, but its edge was gone. All that was left were its ravages.

What looked like the remains of a vast, dysfunctional children's party – bottles, broken glass, a bicycle wheel, driftwood, sandals, a headless rubber doll, odd items of discoloured clothing, shapeless pieces of discoloured plastic, sodden biscuit packets, and variegated odds and ends – lay strewn over the sand of the inner bay. A jagged frill of torn and decapitated coconut palms swayed at its edge. Trunks and branches lay scattered like giant spilled matches. And boats blown inland by the storm wallowed, lopsided and drunken, in places no boat should be. Eva, exhausted after the long drive and sleepless night, barely took all this in. She felt drained and lifeless, beyond even depression. Like a sleepwalker she turned her car away from the shore and up the narrow winding road that led to the promontory above the bay.

The old resthouse, set on a hill with a spectacular view of the town and harbour, had been built originally for colonial civil servants and their retainers, in the days when such buildings were solidly constructed. Before contractors skimped and finagled and mixed too much sand into the cement and houses could be blown down like leaves in a gale. So although the building had long lost its brass and polish, the linen was grubby and the posters faded and it was now patronized by threadbare officials and budget travellers, it had remained untouched by the storm.

Eva was too tired to notice the view or the tattered decor. She followed the 'boy', a bandy-legged old retainer in a stained white sarong and jacket, along the red-waxed verandah, past a row of empty planters' chairs and frosted glass doors, to the farthest room (although the rest were empty). His hands shook as he fumbled the long brass key into the door and he called her 'missy'. It was like his own sobriquet: a hang-over from the days when drunken men in khaki socks and shorts had yelled 'boy!' from the depths of the planters' chairs and he had come running. Barefoot, bow-legged, bowing. She shooed away his feeble attempt to undo the mosquito net, and slumped into a chair.

She snapped awake, disoriented by her sleepless night and the long journey. The room smelled of *arrack* drunks, cheap cigarettes and solitary meals. Her watch and the quality of light seeping through the limp curtains told her it was dusk. She felt the sadness of something ending: a departure, a theatre when the last stage-hand has left.

She went into the bathroom. The loo had a long, old-fashioned chain. When she pulled it, the cistern cranked loudly and emitted a fine mist of rust, but no water. A plate-sized spider, with legs as sturdy as a space-landing craft, abseiled down towards her on a fine silk thread and hovered near her wrist. It was like the bathroom in the resthouse she had stayed in when she first arrived. The same spider even seemed to have taken up residence. She remembered back to those first days in the island. A time when it had seemed like paradise. She knew now that it was not.

She pressed the room bell. Nothing happened. She stepped out into the corridor and called. Silence. Below, the town, the harbour and the ocean beyond were fading to grey. A drawing on a child's magi-board slowly disappearing, until the board was black. The disaster had swallowed the town's electricity like a python, and with it all activity. She called again. But even the auto-rickshaws with 'Amma' or 'Tata' written on them in curly script; even the lorries named after wives or daughters – Gyathri, Renuka, Malini; even the bicycles with no names but tringing bells were silent. Eva sat in a planter's chair and watched the blackness spread beneath her. Dark ships passing in a dark night on a gun-metal sea.

She sat for a long time, too worried to go to bed, uncertain what to do. In the end, just to do *anything*, she returned to her room, fumbled in her case for a torch, shoved some notes in a pocket and re-locked the door. The long key with its heavy brass tag fell into her other pocket, weighing it down lopsidedly. She set off down the steep path to the harbour, spurred by the same instinct that had driven her east.

It took Eva much less time than it had taken Carl to find her way around the tentacles of the old port. Darkness had simplified everything into form and space: open stretches of concrete or roads on which the hulks of abandoned buildings and hangars rose like rusty dinosaurs against a moonless sky. The place was empty at night except for the packs of dogs, which accompanied Eva with their howls and barks, as she sensed her way towards the open cool of the sea.

Gate number three. She walked under the sign, across the tarmac and along the pier. At the end that jutted out into the harbour, she sat down. Letting her feet hang over the black water, straining to see the faint smudge of the outer harbour wall and, beyond that, the subtle change in the darkness, where the horizon met the sea. She was listening for a sound within the sea sounds, watching for a change in the layers of darkness. She tried imagining him as they set sail, recreating the bustle of a ship leaving harbour. Seeing him on deck, an old fisherman back at sea. And she, a fisherman's wife, watching the hourglass sands of hope and despair.

She stayed at the pier that night, and the next day and the next night. Feeling mad, feeling foolish. Feeling she was in the wrong place; then the right place. In the distance she could see lines of ebony-chested men strung across the sands of the inner bay and the town's sea road, salvaging. Small piles of lumber and roof tiles were stacking up near a row of decapitated houses, and nets were being checked on the sand. Late in the afternoon of the second day, a team of labourers tried to move a boat that had run half up a coconut palm; she could hear their shouts, faintly on the salt breeze. But although she had brought her cameras, she didn't have a picture in her.

Instead, she seized on the small things: the miniature world in a seam of moss between two slabs; a hard-eyed seagull, the bird that screams not sings, perched on a rusted capstan for an afternoon; a colony of shiny black mussels, opening and closing along the high water mark. In a clear moment, the second night, she asked herself why she was so disturbed. They had known each other for barely a year. But at once she knew it was because she dreaded losing love – at the very moment she had reached for it.

Early on, in the flotsam and jetsam by the pier, she found a piece of pig glass worn smooth by the sea, and its twin, a sharp fragment of green bottle. She put the pig glass in her pocket as a talisman. And with the other she traced a line across her wrist, over and over, until the blood ran and startled her out of her trance. She licked the wound and tasted warm metal. But she felt no pain then or later. It was as if she had been anaesthetized, or a greater pain had swallowed the smaller pain, like a shark eating little fish.

The servants in the resthouse treated her like an invalid or a madwoman, in the brief intervals she returned to sleep, and made her soup and cups of sweet milky tea. Then, in the twenty-fifth hour, as the sky was lightening to grey and the ocean was still as glass, she heard something faint but mechanical within the larger sounds of the sea.

She watched the small speck on the horizon as it grew larger and closer. Shutting her eyes, she let the faint, pre-dawn breeze brush her cheeks and smooth her brow. Listening to the engines thud nearer; wanting to be surprised; imagining him on the deck; and his surprise to see her standing there.

She heard the engines slow and the sound of voices and opened her eyes. But it was only a navy patrol boat.

It was five in the morning and she was exhausted. She trudged away from the water, up to the room on the cliff, the hospice for dying dreams.

Forty-eight

Light danced a stately waltz across the room. Time dripped drop by drop into the saline tube of the day. There was a grimy smell in the room, of stale fear, salt-stiffened hair and graveyard exhaustion. She opened her eyes and quickly shut them against the light and shadow that passed over her, not believing what she saw, fearing more illusions. Beneath their lids, her eyes slid away as they had done so many times before. Feeling the braille of his skin on her fingertips. The smells of warm blood and the sea. Like a trick of the mind or a dream.

The first time, she stayed out of reach. Unmoved, smiling over his hard brown body, the sound of the sea carrying her far away. 'You didn't come,' he said, insulted by her eyes. He chased her until he found the crack in her shell, the way in.

She knew that he loved her the first time he hurt her, trembling as he did. 'You really care about me, don't you?' she said, amazed that anyone would. She thought of him, sometimes, as a butterfly collector. A man who caught beautiful flying things and pinned them on a board. And sometimes, as a symbol. A man in blue denim leaning against an Arizona blue sky. They were both solitary. She, because she had been an only child. He, because he was insecure. He thinks she will leave him. All men think that of her.

But she knows that love like that is impermanent. And it will be him who leaves her.

At a party he watches her across the room and she, feeling his eyes on her, hungry as a dog, feels everything in her swell and contract, like a sea anenome. He listens for her laugh and the smell of her scent in strange places. Turns when he catches it and then, finding someone else, quickly turns away. She never looks for him. She knows he will come to her, until the day he won't.

He had seen her before she saw him. An acute accent in the grammar of the jetty. But he knew, with the telepathy of lovers, that it was her. As they drew closer, he watched the small oval of her face form into features and felt the old clutch at his heart. So he turned away and clenched his hand against the rail white-knuckled. Ashamed to face himself in love's mirror. And when he turned back, moments later, she was gone.

So he'd found her at last in the room on the hill. And for a long time he watched her, shy to wake her, scared to face the task at hand. So he sank into the chair by the window, his chin in his hand, a finger on his lips. Watching her as he had watched her so many times. And watching, he too fell asleep.

A curve of hip, breast and thigh. Golden, undulating sand dunes. A caress. The feel of her lodged in the tiny ridges of his fingertips. Her skin a kaleidoscope of colours. A goddess hanging like the moon in his sky. Its silver path stretched out over the ocean. The waves her gently heaving bosom. A current running between her thighs. Her skin tasting of salt. Her seaweed hair. Her pink seashell lips. The wind gently rustling her hair.

He thinks: 'You've got the prettiest arrangement I've ever seen.'

'Really?' she says wordlessly. She raises her head as he strokes her and then sinks back. A small flame flickers and pulses.

'Yes. Of course.' He is concentrating on her now like a watchmaker. Setting the tiny wheels and cogs in motion. Making her tick. His fingers run along the inside of her thighs, exploring her crevices, leaving the touch of her in his fingertip ridges. He kisses her lightly and quickly.

'Do that again.' Her voice cracks, caramelized crust on cream. He bends his head again and buries into her. Taste of buttermilk and wild fruit. He sinks down into the deep dark sea.

She woke at one, the time of no colour and hard white light, and saw him: a fragment of ancient wreck dredged from the sea bottom. Laid out on the hot, flat sand next to a bone-bleached sea. His beard was rimed with salt and his face canyoned with grime. He looked as old as the Ancient Mariner. And for many minutes she thought of him as that. A figment of her imagination. A myth. An old rhyme. A sea creature from the depths of his dream.

'Carl? Carl.' She was beside him now. Shaking him. Gently at first and then more roughly.

His jacket was stiff with salt like his beard, but his blood was warm and his body was solid.

'Carl, wake up. Carl. Oh Carl.'

He opened one eye in her direction, bleary with salt and blood. And then he opened both eyes and saw her. Without thinking, he opened his arms and she fell into them. And for a long time they stayed like that. Blood to blood, heart to heart, pulse to pulse, warm body to warm body. Melded together in a single form beyond thought, in the slipstream where life beats.

They stayed there, barely moving, until the laser beam of light boring through the curtains softened. And when they disentwined it was only to stroke eyebrows and lips and cheeks; to kiss a salty forehead; to run a finger along the hollow of a throat; to read the runes of skin and bones and blood; to marvel at the miracle of life.

At last when she spoke the light outside was golden. 'I can't believe it,' she said softly. 'I thought you were dead.'

His voice was hoarse and she had to lean against his mouth to hear it but she heard him whisper, 'And I thought I'd lost you.'

'Come to bed,' she said. She pulled him up, straining against his weight. He staggered, the sea still in his legs, and righted himself like a boat coming to. With her help, he pulled off the salt-stiffened clothes until he stood naked: lithe legs, strong shoulders, a swimmer's body, painted coffee and vanilla by the sun. She led him into the bathroom, stripped off and held him beneath the lukewarm water, a mother and a son, a swimmer and a seacreature, until the storm and its scars had been washed away and he was once again what he had been: a man met on a rainy night who saved her from rape and drowning; a fellow swimmer; the holder of the key to love's possibility; in a lifetime of love lost, the lover who could be found.

'What happened? How did you get back? Tell me everything, the whole story.'

The day had long since folded into night, tucking the little room in with it. Lamplight had swept the ghosts of lonely *arrack* drunks beneath the curtains. A tray of half-finished omelette and chips, a smeary ketchup bottle, two thick-rimmed, government-issue white tea cups and a half-drunk bottle of beer lay between them on the sheet. And when he smiled, the bedside light shone topazes off his eyes, though they were still red and puffy from saltwater.

'The whole story?' He laughed. 'Not now. I'm still beat, out of it.'

'Well, just the end of it.'

'Philippe. Alain finally raised him on the radio. He got the navy out and they got to us. We'd almost bought it, we'd taken on so much water. The captain wanted to stay with the ship, but they talked him out of it. They lifted us off.'

'That man's a magician.'

'I know. We owe him. And I owe you. For being here. God, babe, am I happy to see you. I was never so scared in my life. I thought we were gonna die.'

He leaned forward and took her in his arms. Blood to blood, skin to skin. His hardness melting against her warmth and softness. She felt his shoulders shake. The release of tears. Fear and exhaustion flowing out of him. And if, in that moment, there were unsaid things still to be said, she didn't notice and nor, really, did he. For at that moment he was alive. And that was all that mattered.

Forty-nine

Por heez a jollygood pelloh
Por heez a jollygood pelloh
Por heez a jollygood peh elloh
Anzo zay arlove uz
Anzo zay arlove uz
Por heez…

'What the hell's that bloody racket?' Sergeant Piyadasa scowled and turned to the window.

Outside on the sandy forecourt, two neat khaki lines of bawling men stood to attention in the boiling sun, knees locked, shoulders back, chests out.

'It's the boys, sir. They're waiting for you, sir. It's their serenade, sir.'

'Well, tell them to bloody well shut up. It's hot enough out there to fry an egg and this isn't *Romeo and Juliet* performed by a bunch of bloody monkeys.'

The younger policeman looked hurt. 'But, sir, it's their send-off sir. We'll all be missing you, sir.'

'Yes, and I'll miss you,' replied former Sergeant Piyadasa a little testily. The memory of his lost promotion and resignation was still sour enough to singe his stomach.

He pulled a damp handkerchief out of his pocket, mopped his brow and sighed. How did Humphrey Bogart, or was it Cary Grant, play this scene in the *poren* detective *pilums*? For the last time, he realized, watching himself in slow motion, he unclipped his pistol holster, laid the gun and his sergeant's badge on the desk and gave another heavily dramatized sigh.

He extended a meaty paw. 'And let's not forget the congratulations to you, *Sergeant* Somapala. Best man. Right stuff. No?'

'Yes, sir. I mean, not really, sir.' From sheer force of habit the wiry former constable remained standing sharply to attention.

'Relax, man, relax, I'm not your boss now,' he guffawed. 'Back to civvies. More pay less work.'

He smiled and patted his top shirt pocket where a sheet of headed A4 paper, notifying him of his acceptance as Head of Security for a firm of arms dealers, dampened against his chest. Lalitha had been pleased and that could only be good. With any luck, it wouldn't take much coaxing to get her back in the marital bed. At this happy thought he broke out into a little hum. A throttled version of his favourite *pilum* song.

'And sir, forgive the liberty, sir, but may I be asking after your sister and your houseboy, sir?'

Former Sergeant Piyadasa stopped humming abruptly. 'She's still in hospital and he's on crutches. Bloody tree broke half the bones in her body. Damn nuisance for everyone, as usual.'

'I'm sorry, sir.'

'So am I.' He snorted. Sergeant Somapala's question had reminded him that *Akkhi* would be coming to live with them (Lalitha had kicked up the predictable fuss but they couldn't expect the old man to look after her) and destroyed his brief good mood. 'So. Am. I.'

For the last time, he opened and closed the warped old desk drawers. They were empty but for the White Book. That would be Sergeant Somapala's responsibility now, though he somehow doubted the little former constable would want to keep it. Too soft, he thought.

He tried to stiffen his jaw and straighten his back, which had the effect of making him look like a Giant Panda with indigestion. 'Well, goodbye, Sergeant,' he said between gritted teeth. (This bit was from the war *pilums*.) He extended his paw for the second and final time. 'And good luck.'

'Thank you, sir,' said newly-appointed Officer-in-Charge Somapala. Without thinking, his hand shot to his forehead in a crisp salute. 'Goodbye, sir,' he said. 'And,' his eyes filled with tears, 'good luck to *you*, sir.'

Sentimental fool, thought ex-Sergeant Piyadasa as, for the last time, he drove past the tyre shops, on his way home.

She heard the telephone ring in his office and knew after the second ring that something was wrong. Some telephone calls come with their own weather. Her internal barometer plummeted. A storm was gathering.

'What is it?' she asked when he finally emerged from the office.

'Nothing. Just the desk.' He was trying to squash the inflating balloon of his excitement.

'What do they want?'

'Nothing. Really, nothing.'

But she read his face clearly. As clearly as a fisherman reads the sea.

'I'm losing you, aren't I?' The words were out before she could stop herself.

He smiled at her absently and kissed her brow.

'Am I?' she insisted, worrying at it like a dog with a bone.

'I don't think so. Let's talk later, Eva.' He never called her Eva. 'I've gotta go see Mary now in hospital.'

'Are you going to sack her?'

He sighed and leaned back against the doorjamb: the man in blue denim leaning against an Arizona blue sky. The sight of him hurt, but she had to hold back the tears. He hated tears and would hate a scene now.

'Sure. If you want. But it doesn't look like she'll be working again. I think she's going to live with her ex-cop brother.'

'Her brother was a *policeman*?'

'Yeah. I thought you knew that.'

'No, of course not. No wonder she's such a bitch; it must run in the family. What did he...' For the second time in the last fortnight, she thought of that moment by the green. But again let the thought go. 'Oh, never mind.'

The room filled with silence. Unheard thoughts, bat-sonar, beyond the range of human hearing.

'You know I love you,' she said after a while. She meant it, but now the words were out, they sounded like pleading.

He looked at her and she read nothing in his eyes but the sun.

'Yes.' He spoke slowly as if weighing each word. 'Yes, I think I do.'

It was dusk when the wind came up across the valley. He heard it before he felt it: the pages of a giant book being ruffled by a giant finger, creeping towards him until at last it was there, caressing his brow and ruffling his hair. In this moment of brief twilight, the island's garish colours and florid, overblown landscape softened. Pale mountains rose out of the mist in the valley like phantoms in a Chinese watercolour.

It was only two years ago, yet it seemed like half a lifetime since he'd come here, full of excitement at covering his first war. He remembered those first images: surf rolling on to golden sand like cream on pumpkin pie; big-breasted women with almond eyes and hair they could sit on; aquamarine water, clear to twenty metres; a litre of beer for twenty cents; no parking tickets; no taxes; no cops you couldn't pay off. He laughed and silently offered a toast to bribery and corruption. ('Makes the world go round...', 'Can't get along without you...').

For two years the island had woven around him a spell. Drugging him with its silky winds and soft seas. Its starlit nights and cup-shaped moons. Its insidious, gliding nectar. Seducing him as adroitly as a beautiful woman. Now he couldn't wait to leave.

He looked into the dusk, unseeing, staring down galleries of memories, until a cloud of bats flying out of a jak tree startled him. A sliver of crescent moon had risen above the mountain and, hanging above it, a star: a jewel and pin in a woman's hair. He remembered the fisherman who had begged them to hire his boat. His desperation was a disease he hadn't wanted to catch; it had shorn him of the customary charm, or even servility. Carl had looked in his eyes and known his story: the terror, the shame and the pain; the stinking refugee camps; the hooded informers in a stadium; the boats grounded like dying fish; a living starved from the sea. This man had nothing but his boat left to give. So they'd taken it. He hadn't thanked them, either then or when they paid him. Carl didn't think he would.

Who can say sorry? Despair is its own solitary confinement. It had entombed a whole country. The fruit of the tree of good and evil had been eaten and its price was the death of innocence; the knowledge of the pain they shared; the sadness of war.

Snapshots taken over a year flickered through his head. A woman in red, a gold back sliced by a skein of black hair, like strings on a violin. A gash of blood on a white wall. Murder in a crypt. Air heavy with lust and queen of the night, weighed down by an orange moon. A tear-streaked face in a hospital yard. The smell of bad blood and bloated flesh. Rain on a windscreen, a crumpled child. A bronze body and a brown one: the sweet sharp pain of her other men. A trail of poetry on scraps of paper: clues in a treasure hunt. He wondered if he would ever find that treasure or if it would lie for ever at the bottom of the ocean. Had he found it and lost it or was it still waiting for him. On a white sheet in a white sea room. Beneath the palm of his hand.

They'd offered him another posting. But he would have left

anyway. The reek of that long-ago conversation with the Captain floated beneath his nostrils. A whiff of marsh gas from his subconscious, where lay that other betrayal: an incident on a boat, the outline of a skeleton in a closet. He asked himself if that was why he was leaving, and why he'd leave her. How much of history is written with the ink of guilt? How many of our actions are determined by small and grubby shames?

He quickly damped down the thought and lit a cigarette. Night had fallen fast, cloaking the valley. A skein of orange lights necklaced the mountain: villagers burning brush. There were no stars yet, only Venus; but here and there lights glowed faintly in the black. They were low-watt bulbs, or maybe gas lamps in poor village houses. He could see the woman squatting over a smoky clay hearth, stirring pots for the evening meal; her husband smoking a cheap *bidi*, perhaps already a little drunk on village-brewed *kassipu*; bare-assed, scarecrow kids scrabbling in dirt; a damp infant bawling. He wondered if their lives were any easier for being simple, or if they were just as hard in other ways. Are sufferings comparable, or do we suffer according to alien standards, in alien worlds? Is mental anguish harder or easier to bear than pain and poverty? He suspected that in the end it was probably much the same. Though, God knows, these people had enough of both.

He looked up. The stars were out now. A fathomless tracery linking him to other worlds. He got up and slowly drove back to the capital, his head filled with thoughts, decisions to be made.

Fifty

She ran up the wide curve of shallow stone steps as if she might still find him. His long frame settled in the planter's chair, his milky eyes focused on hers, his bony hand outstretched. 'So Squeeza, you've come,' he'd say, making the same small joke. And they'd both laugh. But the spot under the pergola was empty, his chair gone. She stopped in her tracks, realizing she had expected him to be there. Staring at the place where they had spent so many hours. Shocked by the vacant finality of death. Then she burst into tears.

'When? How? Why didn't you tell me?' She heard herself saying the pointless words.

'We tried. You weren't there,' said Mahinda. He spoke softly. There were black circles under his eyes.

'I was in the east,' she said miserably. 'There were no phones.'

'He died in his sleep. We laid him out in the hallway,' Mahinda said. 'He looked beautiful, like a saint.' He put a hand on her shoulder, gently steering her. 'Come. Let me show you where he is. The place he chose.'

They stepped from the shadows of the pergola on to the bright grass, towards the watercourse that sloped down towards a lily pond. It was still hot. Fish nibbled at jewels of sunlight strewn across the pond, like starlets shopping for baubles. Dragonflies darted over the water and a green lizard basked on a stone ledge, surveying them imperiously. It was pretty but she couldn't remember why he had found this spot, halfway down a slope, so special. She wondered if there were other places in the garden he had loved more. But Mahinda had said it was the place he wanted to be buried. She could see the house becoming a sort of shrine.

'Come.' Mahinda was ahead, weaving through the tall hedge that bordered the watercourse until he came to an open space. A plain clay water pot squatted in the bushes. 'He's here.'

What did she expect? It was just a pot standing in a hedge; it might as well have been empty. She wished she could talk to him one more time. But it was too late. His body had been destroyed, burned to carbon molecules by the heat from an old jak tree he had loved; both twinned in an embrace denied even to lovers, beyond the reach of death.

The embers from his pyre were still smouldering in the lower garden. She started, momentarily mistaking a charred log for his corpse. But that had gone. She understood that, now that she could see the pyre. All of him – his long frame, his deep laugh, his blind, focusing eyes, his tender jokes, his 'pharmacopia of ailments', his love – tipped into a clay pot. She could have balanced him on a hip. Or on her head. Hysteria surged up in her. She almost laughed.

'I'll leave you here.' Mahinda's voice breaking in. 'Come and talk to me later.'

What would Caspar have to say about death? she wondered. She knew whatever it was would tell her what she wanted to know. Her thoughts drifted to an evening spent together. The electricity had gone, as it often did at Lorne, ending their reading, so they had talked in the dark. That was the night she had asked him what it was like to be blind and he had told her of his visions.

She forgot now if he had said those visions were in colour: in her memory's eye they were like silent films, in black and white. But she had been fascinated by the sense of a hidden light, glowing inside a blind man.

She had asked him to describe it and his answer had stayed with her. 'It's soft and warm,' he said. 'Not hot like sunlight or electricity. But beautiful and full of love. I can't say more.'

She understood then what it was about him. The final piece in the jigsaw. And she remembered something he had said about his brother.

'George has always fallen in love with objects,' he had told her. 'But I've only ever been able to fall in love with people.'

It summed them up: one rich and acquisitive; one poor and full of love. She had no doubt who had gained in the end, though: Caspar had died surrounded by love.

The sun was sinking over the paddies. She could see now the beauty of the spot he had chosen. It lay straight in the path of the setting sun; the only point from where all of the garden could be seen. A garden made for secrets, and for love.

'I'm sorry…'

She looked up, startled. Was he speaking to her from inside the clay pot? One last joke?

'I'm sorry to disturb you. Can I talk to you, please?' It was Shanta. His eyes were knotted into a tangle.

'Of course. I'm so sorry…' She stopped, not trusting herself to speak without tears.

For some time, they looked out over the fields, saying nothing. The itchy silence of semi-strangers with things on their hearts.

'You know I was there the night he was dying,' he said at last.

'The night of the storm?'

'Yes.' There was another long pause.

She looked at his face. His eyes and mouth wrestled together. She touched his shoulder. 'It's all right, Shanta. You don't have to tell me anything.'

'No. I want to.' His eyes still struggled. 'He was in a lot of pain, you know that. Very bad pain. He begged me so many times to help him finish it. You know that, too?'

'Yes, I did know. He said it often.'

'He asked for these pills. He couldn't bear it. So that time I...' Sobs broke out of him. 'I gave him the pills that killed him. What to do? He can't bear it, I can't bear it...' His words drained into a moraine of grief.

Eva waited until his crying stilled. 'You did the right thing,' she said, at last. 'It wasn't wrong. It was right and brave. Forget it, please. It's what he wanted. Don't ever think anything else.'

The young man's face brightened, with the sunny ease of a child. But he hadn't finished.

'There's something else. We found it in a box in his cupboard. Mahinda is holding it, he wants to show you. I think it's maybe something important you must know. Come.'

For the last time, she looked out at the spell he had woven. The mysterious garden of pathways, bowers and sudden vistas. The riddle of a place larger than the space it inhabited. Secrets in a secret garden; mysteries in an illusionist's paradise; talismans in a jak-wood cupboard. His hand had reached out across the infinite gap between living and dying, no bigger than a breath no smaller than the universe, with a benediction. And she felt blessed by something she could no more have grasped than the wind.

Alone in the capital, he dreams he is making love to her in a room hung with heavy tapestries, deep inside the fortress of an ancient city long, long ago. Is it Hastinapura? Persepolis? Ur of the Chaldees? In the dark desert beyond the walls, a sandstorm is raging, blinding the moon and the stars. But inside the room it is silent save for their sounds. What is the name of the palace? The Palace of Sands? No, the Palace of Sighs. He turns in his sleep, hugging the pillow to him in place of her body. And falls into a dreamless world beyond the seven oceans, beyond the three worlds, beyond the light of the sun, the moon or the stars.

It is silent but for the sound of love letters falling from a yellowed folder. Wedding confetti found in an old suit pocket after the divorce. One says: 'Because of the place we met, because of the places we've loved, because of the time in my life, because of the time in yours, because none of these things will ever be exactly like this again. I love you.'

In her sleep, she hears him say it. In a whisper softer than a moth's wing, a dying promise, a faded hope.

Fifty-one

A little blue boat beneath a blue sky on a blue ocean dotted with white sand islands. A dot of blue enclosed in a transparent blue sphere. Clear as glass to the ocean floor. The islands are sighing in the sea breeze, because they are sinking back into the ocean, the beautiful warm womb that they came from.

She sits on the deck, trailing her fingers in the water, a sun-striped mermaid. He leans lazily against the house, one knee up, one leg reached out to touch her. They are sailing to a coral island where the houses are made of coral. Sea castles, hard as rock. It's like a dream far away from the clamouring world, which is why he has brought them there: to give life to a dream and to tell her something. But now his heart is tossing like a buoy in rough waters and he doesn't dare speak. She looks like a goddess, a seacreature.

> Full fathom five thy father lies
> Of his bones are coral made
> Those are pearls that were his eyes.
> Nothing of him that doth fade
> But doth suffer a sea change
> Into something rich and strange.
> Hourly sea nymphs ring his knell,
> Ding dong, ding dong bell…

'You know Caspar's dead?'

'Yes. I read it.' He bends down and kisses her on the lips. His eyes are large and brown. 'I'm sorry. I'm so, so sorry.'

'It's OK. He was old and in terrible pain. He wanted to die. I just wish I had seen him once more. And that I hadn't missed the funeral. But of course, you know that, too.'

She reaches into her pocket and pulls out a letter, smiling. 'But you don't know this.'

The yellow paper is fragile and stained with age spots like an old person's skin. As fragile as a cobweb, or a train of thought from long ago, penned by a girl in a sloping italic hand. A girl on a cold, northern island, with grey skies in her eyes and the sun in her soul. A girl touched by madness and magic and homesick for the enchanted island she still calls 'home':

My darling C,

At last I have news that I hope will make you as happy as it has made me. Eva, for that is what I have named her, was born last Sunday at four on a bitterly cold wintry morning. (Why do babies always arrive at such inconvenient times? The poor nurses were kept awake all night.) But she brought with her all the warmth and joy in the world. I have named her after the first woman – and hope you approve – as a reminder of another paradise, as well as in the fervent wish that she learns wisdom and discrimination from the fruit of the Tree of Knowledge.

How does she look? She is simply the most beautiful creature I have ever seen and I expect, like all doting mamas, that you will think so, too. Ivory skin covered in fine black fur like a little monkey (the nurses tell me this disappears; one hopes so). Huge marmoset eyes, still grey from the birth and not yet focused. Fine-boned and tall, of course. Though, naturally, one hopes she won't be as tall as you, being a girl. She is a gift from the

gods. A tiny angel from paradise. We are so blessed. I
will bring her to you, or you must come to her, as soon
as ever you can without trouble.

Your ever loving V

PS: A knows nothing and is happy as Larry, but I can
scarcely bear to look him in the eye. Pray for me.

He puts the letter down very carefully and looks at Eva. 'Oh. My.
God,' he says very slowly. 'So this means...'

'Yes.'

'Are you OK, babe?' He stretches out an arm to her. 'God, what
a shock. How do you feel?'

She was silent for a long time, not knowing what to say, unable
yet to re-arrange the puzzle of her life, to find words for the tide of
happiness and sadness, the sense of excitement tainted by missed
opportunity, love lost. So much history had to be re-written. A new
inventory of life had to be made. Yet again she wondered why
Vivien had never told her and felt angry with her for cheating her
of Caspar's care. But perhaps she hadn't cheated her. Perhaps
Caspar had given her what he could.

'I don't know. I just wish I'd known. At least before he died. I
wish one of them had told me.'

'Perhaps they didn't want you to know. Especially if your mom
never told you.'

'No,' she says. 'There were hints. But no, perhaps not.'

All day they watch the sun move around the room. The light running through its tonal scale, combing sea-strands across the whitewashed walls, making the room seem deep beneath the ocean.
Apart from a round table, a cane-bottomed chair and a low bed,
there is no furniture and no colour. Beside the white bed hangs a
full-length mirror, capturing passion, indolence and dreams.
Outside, the sea is dancing a quadrille with the shore, stupefying

them with its rhythm. He wants to stop time there in that room, to hold them in its embrace and never move. Time, enemy of lovers, friend of the bereaved.

When finally he finds the courage to speak it is dark. They haven't lit the lamp yet so their voices are disembodied like ghosts in a mist, lending an unreality to their conversation.

'You know I brought us here to tell you something?'

She is silent for a while. Hardly daring to breathe.

'Is it because you're ex-wife's coming?' she asks at last.

'No, it's not that. She's changed her plans, it seems.'

'What is it, then?'

'They've called me back. They're offering me another posting.'

'And?'

It is so quiet in the room. Even the waves seem to have hushed. The earth turns a revolution around the sun. The moon spins twice. The stars dance very slowly, with the stately grace of ancient suns. The balance of the universe shifts ever so slightly. And still he says nothing.

She extends her hand, feeling the sheet rough beneath her crawling fingertips, but, sensing no response, retracts it like a tortoise retreating into its shell. She holds its pair in her lap, as if some boundary might soon have to be established. As if she doesn't want to find a hand on the wrong side of a wall.

When at last he speaks it is velvet-black outside and their night vision is as good as cats and owls.

'I guess you know I was going to leave without you?'

Her world stands still.

'But I can't.' He pauses for a long time more. 'Eva, please, come with me.' His voice cracks slightly.

She hears a feather fly in the silence of the night.

For as long or longer, she says nothing. Feeling her breath. Trying to make sense of a universe that has been re-ordered but is not yet complete. She can't think. There are too many questions, too many caveats.

'Are you sure you want me to come?'

'Yes. I'm sure.'

She tries to listen to her heart. Torn between fear and longing. Fighting the habit of lifetimes. But then, like an old ghost locked in the vault of remembrance, a picture returns from long ago.

A small girl is kneeling in the road, wearing a grey school uniform. Tears are streaming down her face and beside her is an open car. The roof is down although it is cold and windy. Inside the car is her father. But his face is turned away from the child towards the open road. The engine of the car is running.

She says the words she will never dare say again, until now. The words she will retract, as she has retracted her fingers tonight, for fear they will be crushed beneath the wheels of his car.

'Please. Don't. Leave me.'

He reaches out his arms across the snow of sheet and folds her into them.

'No I won't. I promise,' he says without speaking or needing to.

'Promise,' she replies out loud.

The cup-shaped moon is high in the sky when they walk across the coral sand. Hand in hand. Skin to skin. Silver and black in the moonlight. The sea is as warm as amniotic fluid. Starry with phosphorus and the night. They twine their limbs in the water, sliding along each other, sending out comet tails of fire. Seaweed hair brushes his face. Fisherman's hands follow the curves of her shell. Together they swim down the river of light. Until he wakes with the taste of sea-spray and she with the smell of the sun. Hearts beating to the endless rhythm of the sea.

Acknowledgements

M, the source of all my inspiration, for loving me, for saving
    my life

Toby Mundy, for having faith in me and the book and for being
    a friend

Louisa Joyner, Clare Pierotti and all at Atlantic Books for their
    patience and support

Cathy Scott-Clark and Adrian Levy for their unfailing generosity

Simon Trewin for loving the manuscript's shambolic first draft

Gillon Aitken for still smoking Senior Service

Dominic Lawson, Con Coughlin and Robin Gedye for letting me
    flee the coup

Bevis Bawa for leaving me his memories

Asoka Ratwatte, Liam and Digby Hill and Natalie Rogers for a
    view to dream on

Lila Bibile for giving me the right words

Carmen Perera, Manik Sandrasagara, Lucy Adams, Giles Scott,
    Viren Perera, Robert Drummond, David and April Gladstone,
    Piero Crida, Dominic and Nazreen Sansoni, Dooland de Silva
    and Nayantara Fonseka for giving me friendship and a bed

Yogesh Kumar for making me laugh and keeping my limbs from
    seizing up

MJ Akbar for his constant encouragement and wit

Kalyan Mukherjee for his passion for literature and his sound
advice

Jacquetta St Germans, India Jane Birley, Francis Pike, William
Ogden, Missy Mixon, Anne Spencer, Jon Swain, David
Jenkins, Meryl Dowman, Jago Eliot, Julian Zinovieff, Justine
Hardy, Diana Dantes, Deepak Raj Bhandari, Akash
Dharmaraj, Nila Mehta, Mala Shukla, Sophie Coats, Olivia
Richli, Susannah Baker Smith, Karen Davies, Sandra Roberts,
Jane Robinson and so many other friends I have not named, for
helping me through

And finally, Mark, for his encouragement, support and love, in
happier times